THE END GAME

A NOVEL

KATE MCCARTHY

© Copyright, Kate McCarthy 2015

THE END GAME

Copyright © Kate McCarthy 2015
ISBN-10: 0987526197
ISBN-13: 978-0-9875261-9-9

Editing by Maxann Dobson, The Polished Pen
http://www.polished-pen.com

Cover art courtesy of Mae I Design and Photography
http://www.maeidesign.com/

Interior Design by Allusion Book Formatting and Publishing
http://www.allusiongraphics.com/

Cover models are Maximilian Gust and Hannah Peltier

NOTE FROM THE AUTHOR

There are two main characters in this story. Jordan, an Australian, and Brody, an American, which begged the question, which spelling should I use for the dual point of view? I've decided to go with American for the entire story to reduce confusion. My reason being the majority of the story is based in America, however I *am* an author based in Australia, therefore you will find Australian slang and Australian terminology in this book from Jordan's perspective.

Due to the subject matter contained in this story, some Universities, sporting teams, and processes, have been fabricated for legal reasons.

Thank you for purchasing a copy of *The End Game*. I hope you enjoy Brody and Jordan's journey as much as I have writing it.

DEDICATION

To my mother with so much love.
You taught me the value of having dreams,
and how important it is to reach for them before it's too late.
I miss you.

PROLOGUE

JORDAN

I walk off the soccer field at North Sydney Oval. Dried sweat coats every inch of my skin from a bout of training I'd rather forget. I'm the best damn player this team has, better than all of them, and they know it. Yet I'm not wanted here.

Distrust glares back at me from my teammates' eyes as they make their way toward the waiting bus. Their open hostility should hurt, but I can't feel it. It's an odd feeling, I think. Numbness. Like being injected with anesthetic. I wonder how long it will last.

My brother is propped in front of the bleachers, leaning against the fence behind him. He looks like he always does. Honey-colored curls peek out from a gray beanie, skin tanned no matter what the season, and cheeks tinged pink from the cool air. His clear blue eyes stare back at me, solemn and resigned, beautiful, yet always so damn sad.

He's here to watch me train. I've been contracted to play for the Australian women's soccer team in the upcoming FIFA World Cup. It's a huge honor, and one I don't take lightly, but I'm tired. My mind is elsewhere right now, which means my focus is shot.

Forcing a smile, I wave and make my way toward him. It's a cool night and my cleats crunch loudly in the crisp grass, the rich scent of dirt rising up and teasing my senses. I breathe it in deep, feeling it lodge inside my lungs. It gives me no satisfaction. No sense of achievement. Tonight it gives me nothing.

He waves back. Nicolas, or Nicky as I call him, is my safety net. Being older by three minutes has given him a sense of responsibility, and he wields it like a weapon. Perhaps I'm selfish because I let him. How can I not? My brother's given up his own future so I can have mine. I owe him everything.

"You call that soccer?" he shouts as I get closer.

"What do you call it?"

He shakes his head. "A fuckin' train wreck."

My breath huffs out sharply, fogging the air in front of me. "Don't sugarcoat it or anything."

Nicky tucks his hands inside his pockets and shrugs. "Sugar is for girls and spice and all things nice."

I laugh, but the sound isn't a happy one. I'm not any lighter for it. It only weighs me down further because Brody's gone and I'll never laugh again. Not on the inside.

"And I'm none of those?"

"Nope," he says simply, his voice firm and matter-of-fact.

Reaching his side, I take a seat on the bench with a deep, exhausted sigh. Bending over, I begin untying my laces. "What am I then?"

"A fighter. Fearless. A fuckin' thing of raw beauty out there on the field. No one can catch you," he says, and I pause to look at him. Pride shines from his eyes, lighting him up from the inside, but when they begin to harden, my stomach sinks like lead. "Some of those girls out there play with heart, and some play just because they're good at it, but you? You bleed the game." He looks away, fixing his gaze on the field in front of us. "You play with a fire so bright it hurts my eyes. This game is a part of you. It's a part of you that no one should be able to take away, and out there you were letting them do just that."

"Nicky—"

"Don't." His voice is sharp and cuts right through me. Shaking my head, I return to my laces, unable to look at him anymore. "Don't let them."

One of the ties tangles in my fingers. I give up and rest my elbows on my knees, letting my head hang low. "They'll get over it and tomorrow it will just be yesterday's news."

"Bullshit, Jordan." Nicky jerks to his feet. Facing me, he crouches so I can't avoid looking him in the eye. "This kind of crap doesn't wash off after a hot shower. It sticks like fuckin' tar."

I force a chuckle. "Don't be such a drama queen, Nicky."

A strangled, angry sound rises from his throat. I know he's only five seconds from losing his shit, but I can't help it. I know what he's asking me to do, and the very thought squeezes all the air from my lungs. I won't do it.

"I love him."

"You *loved* him," he corrects me. "And now you have to let him go. He wants you to, honey. What happened out on the field tonight, teammates shunning you, hating on you, do you think he wanted that for you?"

No. He didn't.

My jaw locks tight in a desperate battle to hold back the tidal wave of pain. I lose and it crashes over me, ripping away my blanket of numbness. My body begins to shake, and I tense every muscle hard so Nicky doesn't see.

"Jordan?"

He says my name but I don't hear him. My eyes close and the world drops away from me. All I see is Brody in its place. He's wrapped around me, his naked skin pressed against mine, our bodies tangled in bed sheets. It's suffocating, but I love it. I'm warm and safe, and his lips kissing along my brow are heartbreakingly tender. He speaks to me, but my breathing is deep and even. He thinks I'm asleep.

"Don't go," he whispers, and his voice cracks with so much pain it squeezes my chest. *"You made me want you and need you, and now I can't live without you anymore. Not for a single second."*

I draw a deep, scratchy breath and open my eyes. My brother is standing now, rubbing a hand over his face like he has no clue what to do or say. I rise to my feet with purpose. What happened is my fault. I know it is. Brody needed me and I wasn't there. *I was never there.* And now it's too late.

"What, Nicky?"

His eyes turn hard. "Let him go."

"I can't." There's no letting go. Not ever. Even with him gone, Brody's hold on me will last a lifetime.

"You have to."

My chin juts out, stubborn to the core. "I don't have to do anything except what's right for me."

"Goddammit!" Nicky growls his frustration. Ripping the beanie from his head, he tugs fingers through his hair. "What are you going to tell them at the press conference in the morning?"

"The truth."

I begin the walk toward the locker room to collect my training bag. The majority of the team is already on the bus. They'll be waiting for me if I don't get a move on. Nicky doesn't follow.

"Which is what exactly?" he calls out.

I turn, walking backwards. "I'll figure it out."

But I already have. I'm just not prepared to argue about it with my brother any longer.

Head bowed, I make my way inside the locker room, water bottle dangling from my hand. Finding my locker, I pull out my bag and shove the bottle inside. After taking out my team jacket, I shrug it on, all while holding myself together when I feel ready to fall apart.

Changing out my cleats for a pair of slip-on shoes, I zip up the bag and carry it out toward the bus, my head held high.

My brother wants the truth? It's that I once believed being the best was all you had. So did Brody.

But we were both wrong.

JORDAN

Two years earlier...

The automatic doors at Austin International Airport whoosh open, ejecting me into a bright, sunny afternoon. I fill my lungs, taking in my very first breath of United States' air. It's thick and warm, and after spending seventeen hours stuck inside an airplane sucking down funky, recycled oxygen, it smells delicious.

It also smells like great expectations. My entire future is riding on my year in this country. Rather then crumble under the weight of the pressure, I've been telling myself I've got this. I'm going to be focused and determined, and I'm going to kick ass. The positive mantras worked well these past six months, which was how long it took for the college dean and my international scholarship agency to get the paperwork in place. Now that I'm actually standing here on American soil, my lungs have seized. I'm not nervous. I'm bloody *terrified*. I haven't *got this* at all. I've left behind my entire life in Australia to complete my senior year in college in a foreign country where I don't know anyone.

My next deep breath of United States' air starts to taste a little less like excitement, and a little more like an anxiety attack. I start to turn. My only plan: barrel through the elated hordes of reuniting travelers and demand a ticket from the departures counter for the next flight home.

"Jordan Elliott!"

A loud, Texas twang shrieks my name and halts my escape. I turn back, keeping a tight grip on the handles of my luggage as I scan the direction of the shout.

A long, waving arm catches my eye. It's attached to a slender, athletic female with tousled dark hair and impish brown eyes. She's looking directly at me, an excited grin plastered across her face.

"Elliott!" she shouts again and starts pushing her way toward me. She's wearing a Colton Bulls tank top, cute denim shorts, and cowboy boots that look like alligators have attached themselves to her feet.

A smile begins to form and recognition clears the panic from my eyes. "Leah?"

My inspection is interrupted when she envelops me in a hug and dances up and down. I'm squeezed and jostled, and when I'm eventually released, Leah spreads her arms out wide.

"Welcome to Texas!"

Leah's my new roommate in an athletes' apartment block right off campus. She's also a defender in one of the best women's college soccer teams in the world. After three months of pre-season training, I'll be starting striker for that very same team.

My lungs seize again. *Breathe, Elliott,* I chastise internally. *Enjoy the moment. The world is your oyster. Glory will soon be yours, blah blah blah.*

"Is that all you've got?" Leah's gaze takes in the two hefty suitcases resting behind me with disbelief.

"Yep, that's it," I reply.

"But..." she looks at me, doubt furrowing her brow "...you're here for fifteen months. You do know that right?"

"Of course I know! One suitcase alone is full of soccer gear. What more could I possibly need?"

Leah grabs the handle of the bag sitting on my right. "Screw the soccer gear. You know, if I had to leave my boyfriend and travel halfway around the world, one suitcase alone would be dedicated to shoes and vibrators."

I take hold of the other and walk alongside her as we make our way out to the parking lot. A sly grin forms on her face. "Did you pack any?"

"Pack any what?"

"Vibrators!" she says in almost a shout. The word garners the attention of several people around us and a flush heats my cheeks.

"No! Of course I didn't. I mean, those things show up on X-ray scans, right? How embarrassing. With my luck, the TSA would think I'm smuggling drugs inside them and take them out for a closer inspection."

Leah's laugh is loud. "It doesn't matter anyway. There'll be plenty of male bodies for you to choose from. The guys on campus love female jocks."

I snort. "I'm not here for sex."

"Of course you are. It's college."

After my luggage is stowed, we're in the car and zooming directly toward my new home. It only takes half an hour, but with Leah talking non-stop the entire trip feels like minutes.

I barely have time to take in the scenery, but it's enough to realize that Austin, Texas, isn't all brown dirt and tumbleweeds, cow dung on the sides of the road, and dusty cowboys riding horses into town. I knew it wouldn't be. Wikipedia explained in great detail that Austin is a beautiful, thriving city, with clean air and condos, yet I still feel slightly robbed.

"Have you lived here long?" I ask.

"Yep. I'm a born and bred Austinite," Leah replies as she accelerates through a yellow light. "What about you?"

"Born and bred Sydneysider."

"What about your family?" she asks.

The familiar pull of loss tugs at me. I try to get a handle on it and force a smile for my new friend. "I have a twin brother, Nicolas, or Nicky as I usually call him."

"Oh my gosh, that is so cool. Are you guys like, identical?"

I shake my head. "Fraternal, but we look a lot alike. Unfortunately, he's way bigger than me and the eldest by three minutes, so he likes to boss me around."

"What about your parents?" she asks.

"It's just the two of us." There's a brief silence, which I feel the desperate urge to fill before she starts asking more questions. "What about you?"

Her eyes light up and she starts telling me about her three older sisters, all of which are scattered across the country.

"You all sound close," I say. "Do you miss them?"

13

"Are you kidding? We fought like a pack of wild cats. My parents are enjoying their empty nest far too much." She grins at me quickly before returning her attention to the road. "I do miss borrowing their clothes, though."

Leah pulls into a parking spot in front of a majestic, red-brick block of apartments. The windows are trimmed with white timber and matching decorative grids. The surrounding gardens are lush and green, and well kept.

"This is us?"

She nods and grins. "This is Colton Park University, Elliott. Home to the best student athletes in all of Texas."

"Wow," I breathe as I take it all in, finding it hard to believe I'm finally here. "I wasn't expecting it to be so pretty."

Leah shakes her head as she gets out of the car. "What were you expecting? The Wild West?"

"At the very least."

The building is five floors and our apartment is halfway up on the third. We make our way up the stairwell. My suitcases make a loud clunk as we roll them up the wide, tiled steps. After moving down the long corridor, we stop at a dark timber door. Nervous anticipation fills me. This is going to be my home away from home for more than a year. It might not seem like much, but right this minute it feels like a big deal.

Leah hands me a key. "You do the honors," she says, bumping my shoulder with hers.

"You're not going to carry me over the threshold?" I ask as I take it.

With a laugh, she snatches the key back, unlocks the door, and makes a grab for me. "What are you doing?" I screech, leaping backwards with a giggle.

Leah crouches and locks her arms around me, just under my backside, and lifts me up. We're shrieking with laughter as she carries me through the doorway, but when she trips over my bag near her feet, we take a header and spill across the floor like a figure skating trick gone wrong.

"Oh my god," she gasps and rolls over, moaning loudly. "I think you dented my ass with your knee."

"Better that than your face," I reply weakly, getting up on all fours.

"That was," drawls a deep, amused male voice from somewhere in the room, "the single best thing I've seen all day."

I lift my head and my eyes climb upwards, slowly taking in the Viking warrior standing before me. Worn jeans encase brawny legs, and a Colton Bulls muscle tee shirt covers a chest so powerful and wide it deserves its own postal code. Further up I catch brown hair pulled back off his face with a tie, a scruffy jaw, and eyes the color of dark blue denim—one of which winks at me.

I close my mouth.

"Elliott, this is my boyfriend, Hayden. Honey bunches of love, meet my new roommate, Jordan Elliott."

I can't imagine this guy being a honey bunches of anything, but the endearment doesn't faze him in the least. He stalks toward me, powerful thigh's rippling with each step, and holds out his hand. A little dazed, I scramble to my feet and take it in mine. His handshake is firm and warm, and I like him instantly.

"G'day, mate," he says with an excited grin.

I burst out laughing. Hayden's attempt at an Australian accent is horrendous. His grin morphs into a pout. It should be ludicrous on such a colossal specimen of man, but on Hayden it's charming. "Too much?" he asks. "Not enough? I've been practicing for weeks."

"He really has," Leah corroborates as she picks herself up off the floor with a groan. "He's never met an Australian before so I'm warning you now, he's going to swamp you with questions, crack jokes about dingoes, and make lewd references about your vagina being the land down under."

"It sounds perfect," I reply with a grin, letting go of Hayden's hand. "Keep doing that for the next year or so, will you? My course load is going to kick my ass, so I could use a good laugh now and then."

"I like her," he says to Leah without taking his eyes from mine. "She can stay."

"Yeah? Good," she replies, already wheeling one of my suitcases inside the apartment. "Because I've already decided I'm keeping her."

After I bring the other suitcase inside, Leah gives me the grand tour, starting with the living area. A flat screen television rests on a small cabinet in front of a three-seated sofa. A PlayStation sits on the floor between both. The screen is paused in the middle of a game of Major League Baseball. It reminds me that Leah mentioned along the drive from the airport that her boyfriend plays college baseball.

"Nice," I say, waving my hand at his score. "You've got version fourteen, right? We have twelve back home on the PC and the glitches do my head in."

Hayden's eyes go wide and his nostrils quiver with ill-concealed excitement. "You play?"

"I have a brother. Of course I play."

"You want to play now?"

Leah shakes her head at me. "You haven't done yourself any favors, Elliott. My man is not going to leave you alone until he kicks your ass on that stupid baseball game."

"You only call it stupid because you're a sore loser, babe," he says.

A smirk plays on her lips. "I'll show you who the loser is later tonight. In bed."

Hayden jabs a finger in her direction as he sinks down on the sofa. "You better put your money where your mouth is."

"How about I just tell you where to put *your* mouth, and we can go from there?"

Leah's boyfriend groans as he picks up the controller and returns to his game, muttering something under his breath that sounds a lot like, "I'm going to eat you alive."

"How long have you two been together?" I ask when she leads me into the kitchen that sits off to the left of the living space.

"Three years."

"I don't believe you." I fan myself with my hand from the heat sparking between the two of them.

"Believe it." Her grin is smug. "He's a man madly in love."

Hayden's snort from the living room is loud, indicating he heard us talking. Ignoring him, Leah opens and closes a few cupboards, showing me where everything is kept before she leads me to the opposite end of the apartment. There are three rooms: two bedrooms with a bathroom situated in the middle.

My room has a double bed pushed against the far wall and a nice, wide window. Beneath it rests a study desk and chair, and beside that a single dresser with five drawers. It's tucked neatly next to a built-in wardrobe. The furnishings are basic, but it's clean and it doesn't stink like sweaty gym socks, which is always a huge plus when you're rooming with athletes.

The bed is already made with fresh sheets. "You can change them if you brought your own," Leah says, "but I figured jetlag would be making you its bitch and you'd want to crash for a couple of days before you settle in properly."

I face her, pressing my lips together to hold in the sudden well of emotion. I'm an outsider here, in senior year no less—where strong bonds and deep friendships have long since formed. I was prepared for it to take months to feel welcome and accepted as a team member, but Leah and Hayden have managed to do just that in one afternoon.

"Thanks," I choke out, my eyes burning.

"Don't cry over sheets, Elliott." She pulls me into a hug, one hand rubbing my back soothingly. "Why don't you go have a shower? Afterwards we can have dinner and something to drink."

I do just that, washing the stink of the airplane from my hair and pores. Not bothering to unpack just yet, I pull a tank top and sweatpants from my suitcase and get dressed.

When I pad quietly out of my room, Leah's on the PlayStation, and Hayden has his head buried inside the fridge. He holds out a dark bottle of something cold over his shoulder when I make my way into the kitchen.

"That's not some kind of American piss-weak beer is it?" I ask teasingly as I take it from him.

"You don't drink piss-weak beer?" After getting out another two bottles, he goes to snatch mine back. "All the more for me."

I jerk it out of reach. "Are you kidding? I'm Australian. We drink anything with alcohol in it," I joke, though in truth I rarely drink at all, but tonight is my first night in a strange, new country. If there ever was a time for alcohol, it's now. Before I take a sip, I clink Hayden's glass with mine. "Cheers."

He echoes the sentiment, and after bringing the bottle to my lips, I almost spray a mouthful everywhere when he asks me if I have a boyfriend back home. "I know a lot guys who are gonna want to meet you," he adds.

Hell no. Receiving this international sports scholarship is the equivalent of winning the lottery. I beat out thousands of foreign students for this chance. It's going to be the most influential year of my life, and I simply can't risk it for anything, or anyone.

"Thanks, but no thanks," is all I say.

With my head down, I immerse myself in the next three months of pre-season training. It involves getting acquainted with my new teammates, head coach, assistant coaches, team manager, nutritionist, sports therapists, the team doctor, and everyone else on board that makes our Colton Bulls soccer team the team to beat.

It's a whirlwind of activity: weight training, watching plays, endless drills, fitness tests, drug tests, and everything in between. I fall into bed exhausted every night with no time to wallow in my homesickness, or traipse around the countryside playing tourist. I haven't even had time to decorate my walls with my motivational prints and my treasured signed poster of Lionel "Leo" Messi, a forward for FC Barcelona. I could sit here all day listing out his achievements, but to put it simply, the man is a soccer-playing god. I also have a signed poster of Cristiano Ronaldo waiting to be hung on my wall, but that one's for more nefarious purposes. The Portuguese player is not only hotter than hell itself, he is, of course, my future husband.

The stadium we train in, and will play in, is bigger than I'm used to and seats a maximum of thirty thousand people. It sounds impressive, but it sits alongside the college football stadium, which seats over a hundred thousand, so our arena is nicknamed David, and our bigger counterpart, Goliath.

I haven't met any of the football players, despite sharing the same parking lot. We hear them train though, so I know they're there. Their grunts are loud and roaring shouts echo across into our field. It sounds more like an epic war rather than an ordinary afternoon of football training. Leah tells me they're all big, hairy deals on campus, with egos that match the size of their stadium, so I vow to avoid them where possible.

Two weeks before our senior year of college starts, our team has its first exhibition contest. I would call it a sell-out because the bleachers are full, but admission for the match is free. My nerves are shot, knowing it's going to be televised live on the Colton Bulls network. Through some miracle I manage to keep my head, and it's an easy win—six nil. It sets us up with confidence and before I know it, I'm back in an airplane, flying to Hawaii for the Outrigger Resorts Shootout. We play two matches against Arizona State and Hawaii and walk away with one win and a draw.

We touch back down in Texas on Monday night and start classes the next day. I have my schedule tacked to a corkboard on the wall of my bedroom and my campus map studied.

When Leah taps on my door at ass o'clock on Tuesday morning, I roll over with a tired groan and seized muscles.

"Say it ain't so," I whine, the sound muffled because my face is mashed into the pillow. *Her appearance is merely a hallucination from lack of sleep,* I tell myself.

"On your feet, sistah," Leah drawls, dashing my hopes.

I drag my exhausted body toward the edge, wondering if my legs will hold if I try standing. Probably not. They're going to buckle beneath me and I'll fall and hit my head, pass out, and maybe earn myself an extra hour in bed. My sleep-fogged brain decides that sounds marvelous, so I plant my feet on the floor and push up gingerly.

When I remain standing, I simply glare at Leah through bloodshot eyes. "I hate you."

Leah is a morning person, so she simply blows me a kiss and sings, "Hi ho, hi ho, it's off to the gym we go," as she leaves my room.

I acknowledge the voices in my head that tell me to throw my bedside lamp at her head and let them go. For now.

After weight training and five miles on the treadmill, Leah and I shower, make a protein shake for breakfast, and hit campus. It's the biggest college in the state, and reviewing it on my map is completely different than seeing it in person. Our apartment is right near the soccer fields, but campus is in the other direction. I haven't had time to familiarize myself with the buildings. Parting ways with Leah, I make my way toward where I hope my first lecture is held. Ten minutes later, I'm hopelessly lost. I have to ask three separate people for directions. When I finally arrive at my destination, I'm late. It sets the tone for my entire week. I'm late for every single class, and worst of all is my Business Law and Ethics lecture on the Thursday morning. I don't know how it happened, but I read my schedule wrong, so when I arrive two-thirds of the way through, books piled in one arm, my protein shake in the other, I'm flustered and out of breath.

When I race through the doorway, Professor Patrick Draper pauses mid-sentence and turns in my direction. He looks in his mid-forties, but he's ridiculously handsome and wearing a suit that looks as expensive as a brand new car. He makes an exaggerated motion of checking his watch before he looks at me again, his brows raised high.

Every student in the room follows his line of sight as though my interruption is the most interesting part of their entire morning.

"Sorry I'm late," I say.

I start scanning the room for a free desk. *Please God, point me to one right now,* I pray silently.

"Late?" my professor echoes, his tone aggravated and sharp, and I realize he's not going to let this go as easily as I'd hoped. "Late is ten minutes. You've almost missed my entire class."

Several chuckles dot the room, and I want to close my eyes and sink well below the crusty layers of the earth. Before I can form an excuse, he says, "I hope this doesn't set the tone for the entire semester."

I want to reply with "me too," but humor or flippant remarks aren't going to save me right now. "Of course not."

"Good." He jerks his chin toward an empty seat near the back of the room. "Take a seat so I can continue what you so rudely interrupted."

"Ouch," I hear a student mutter as I make my way toward the vacant desk. I don't look his way. I can't. My face is on fire and I just need to get to my seat so I can die in peace.

CHAPTER 2

BRODY

The first hour and a half of the lecture I'm in is about as fun as getting sacked repeatedly on the football field. I spend most of it wondering how I'm going to get through the course without failing. My professor, who also happens to be my mother's brother, may as well be speaking Spanish. My books are spread out in front of me and a pen rests expectantly in my hand, but my notes are non-existent because none of his words sink in.

Patrick pauses to take a breath, and I want to fist pump the air at the small reprieve, even if it is because someone made the heinous error of showing up with just a half hour to go. If it were me, I wouldn't have bothered turning up at all. Better to claim a sudden, debilitating illness than face the hardass that is my uncle.

Arriving five minutes late to class with my cousin and roommate, Jaxon, cost more than a glare. I was ordered to see him after class. That earned me a smirk from the teacher aide, Kyle Davis. I had to restrain the urge to walk over and punch the superiority off his face. Instead, I bared my teeth in a grin and gave him the finger as I took my seat, settling in for a nice, mind-numbing session on the need for ethics in the world of corporate law.

Davis has a beef with me. He was gunning for the wide receiver position in high school senior year and didn't make the team. I did. Now he never misses an opportunity to rub my shitty grades in my face. Being Patrick's TA this semester affords him the perfect opportunity to do so.

Giving up all pretense of taking notes, I lift my head. My gaze hits the berated student, not catching her reply as air leaves my lungs in a loud rush. She's making her way toward the last available seat beside me. Her stride is loose-limbed, her long, slender legs toned. They weave around desks and bags on the floor with a fluidity that's mesmerizing. My eyes rise further, watching her hips roll in a way that makes me want to hold on and take her for a ride.

My gaze reaches her face. It's a tomato, flushed bright and red. She doesn't catch my blatant stare. Her eyes are focused on her destination like she's adrift in a wild storm and the empty desk beside me is her life raft.

She slumps in the seat on my right and the appealing scent of vanilla hits me hard. It's sweet and tempting, and reminds me of eating ice cream on a warm summer night. Leaning over, she pulls books from her bag. Long tousled waves of honey-colored hair fall in her face. She straightens, tucking them behind her ears with an annoyed huff.

The sound brings me back to Earth. What in the *everloving* fuck? Vanilla? Honey? I write my response off as hunger. Fueling a body my size is a constant effort. I'm always eating, and when I'm not eating, I'm training. Between that, I should be studying because I'm on the fast track to failing my senior year of college.

Not a surprise. I scraped by the past three years—professors rounding up my grades by more than a single mark to see me pass their course. It's to be expected. I'm starting wide receiver for the Colton Bulls. I'm also a top draft prospect. Suspending me from play for poor grades would be an extremely unpopular move.

In the long run it won't do me any favors and I should care, but I don't. The game is more important to me than breathing. Whatever it takes to play, I'll do it.

It's been that way since I caught the quarterback pass in peewee league and ran fifteen yards for my first touchdown. The exhilaration, the slaps on the back, and the acceptance bore down on me like a tsunami. It filled a void I didn't understand was missing in my life. Sweeping me up, it took me along for a ride I never forgot.

So I kept at it. In training I worked harder, running until I thought my lungs would explode and my legs give out beneath me. I got better, and with it came more: more time on the field, more touchdowns, and more games. The back slaps got harder, the acceptance spread wider, and my love of the game grew hotter and brighter.

Now I'm facing the most important year of my life, the very cusp of an NFL career. I'm on the radar of several large sponsors, agents are taking notice, and the pros are calling. College football isn't just something I do between classes for fun. It's a full-time job. And this year I have a set of professors who aren't like the ones of my past. There will be no favors and no bumping grades. The safety net has been pulled out from beneath me, and I'm worried.

If I tell them I have dyslexia it will help smooth my path, but the shame runs too deep to shake. All these years I've managed to make do, thinking it better for my teachers to make allowances based on my football ability rather than bringing the real issue to light.

My father is a high-profile politician, my mother a society wife, and both refuse to acknowledge I was born anything less than perfect. All my life they've put my failing grades down to simple laziness. If only I *bothered* to apply myself rather than waste time on the field, I would be an intellectual success, blazing political trails like my father wants. Instead, I'm an unwanted inconvenience. All I have is football, a game they don't understand or support. Needless to say, my success in the sport remains unacknowledged in our house.

I was barely seven years old. We were seated at the table, finishing dinner, when my father first acknowledged my learning disability. "Your teachers seem to think you need some kind of additional tutelage."

I didn't know back then why I struggled to read and write. Other kids made it look easy, so when I met his gaze, the weight of his disappointment pushed me further down in my chair, and my feelings of confusion and shame intensified beyond repair.

Our housekeeper, Hattie, came in at that point, bringing with her my parents' after dinner coffee and a glass of milk for me. I thanked her quietly and stared at it, feeling it curdle in my stomach before I'd taken a single sip.

"Is that what you think, Son?" my father prompted, not acknowledging Hattie or the coffee she placed before him. "That you should get special treatment because you can't be bothered to read or write properly?"

There was no point telling him I wasn't lazy. My father was stubborn and an egomaniac, even before my failings came to light, so I bit my tongue, preferring to draw blood rather than show emotion at his ruthless spiel.

"No, sir," I replied quietly.

He gave a heavy sigh, not even happy when I gave agreement. "I'd tell you to try harder, but I don't think you know how. God knows I want to wash my hands of this whole mess, but then imagine how I'd look if you ended up hauling trash for a living. You're too damn stupid to do anything else, so you better make football count."

Despite his shitty delivery, I can't deny the ring of truth from his words. So I'm making football count.

As though she can hear my thoughts, the girl beside me lets out a deep sigh. I tilt my head and study her profile. There's something wholesome and appealing about her that makes it hard to look away. Her skin has a tanned glow and her cheeks are flushed a deep shade of pink, making her the perfect advertisement for clean living.

Pausing her mad scribbling, she lifts her head to the whiteboard, and I see her eyes. The color is a clear, arctic blue at odds with the warmth her skin radiates.

If she feels my gaze, she doesn't acknowledge it. She spends her half hour taking down the notes she missed earlier. When the lecture ends, she disappears into the herd of students and out the door.

With the room empty, I shoulder my backpack and make my way toward my uncle. All my classes are set in the mornings so I don't have to rush anywhere like everyone else.

At noon I usually grab lunch from the dining hall, followed by an hour of watching film with the team. Around two in the afternoon we hit the field until six. Coach kicks us out after that, enforcing the NCAA rules that say we can't officially train more than twenty hours a week. What we choose to do after that—hit some extra bags, lift weights, run a few more laps—is on us.

Reaching the front, Patrick looks me in the eye and gets straight to the point. "You're going to fail senior year, Brody."

Having my own fear verbalized makes the blood rush in my ears. My first instinct is *deny, deny, deny.* "I'm not going to—"

He interrupts me, his brow pinched. "You are. I was watching you today. You might have followed what I was saying, but you didn't take notes and you didn't do your assigned reading. I know because when I went over the case assignments your eyes glazed over."

"I—"

"Don't give me excuses. This has gone on far too long. God knows I've waited for your father to step in and do something, but I don't think that's ever going to happen." My uncle folds his arms. "I'm organizing you a tutor. Someone qualified to help you."

His words sink in and shame rises to the surface. "You can't," I hiss furiously, keeping my voice low in consideration of students passing the open doorway. "I don't need help. I've made it this far on my own. I have it handled."

"I'm not giving you a choice," my uncle replies coolly. Unfolding his arms, he opens his briefcase and begins sliding papers inside. "If you don't undertake the extra tutelage I arrange for you, I'm speaking to your coach."

My hands curl into fists by my side, furious he would so easily jeopardize my playing season. "You wouldn't," I grind out, knowing full well he would.

"I can and I will." He pauses for a moment to lock eyes with mine, letting me see the hard determination on his face. After a moment his eyes soften a fraction. "I don't want to see you fail, Brody."

After snapping his briefcase shut, he prepares to leave and panic climbs my throat. When he starts for the door, I know I'm screwed, but I make one last ditch attempt to get out of it.

"I won't fail," I shout after him. "But it's possible I might if you force me to do this. I don't have the time to go traipsing across the city every week to have a fancy tutor teach me something I know I'll never learn!"

My uncle turns to face me, his brow arching. "I figured you'd say that, and I do happen to understand the demands football places on you, Brody. I have a student tutor in mind. It means you can study on campus after practice."

He's out the door before I can argue further. It's probably for the best.

I'm already clutching at straws. There's nothing more I can say that will convince him to back down.

My thought process takes a turn for the worse. What if he lumps me with Kyle Davis? So help me God, if he does I'll be forced to shoot something. Preferably Davis. In the junk. Assholes like that shouldn't be allowed to procreate.

Jaxon materializes when I leave the room. "What was all that about?"

"Nothing," I mutter. A quick glance at my watch shows I have a half hour left to eat something before training.

We head for the dining hall. Eyes follow as we stride down the walkway. Flustered packs of girls giggle and stumble in my path, and guys try drawing me into conversation about the upcoming game this weekend. It usually doesn't bother me. I'm used to the lack of anonymity now so I don't notice, but today I do, and I'm too raw right now to deal with it. I slide on a pair of sunglasses and tug my baseball cap low. It's a half-assed attempt to keep people at bay, but it's better than nothing.

We're halfway across the quad when a commanding shout gets my attention. Ryan Carter is spinning the ever-present football in his hands as he makes his way toward us.

"'Sup, Madden," he calls out with a grin and throws a perfect spiral my way. I stretch up and the ball lands in my arms with ease. The star quarterback whoops loudly as he jogs over. A small entourage trails behind him, struggling to keep up with his long-legged stride.

Reaching the two of us, Carter points to my forehead. "Man, what the hell is that?"

"What's what?" I give him a blank stare and he jams his thumb in the spot between my brows.

"It's a fuck furrow, bro," he replies when I swat his hand away. "It means you need to get laid. Can't be stressed for the season opener."

My mind immediately goes to the blonde in class and my skin prickles with heat. Those legs wrapped around me right now would go a long way to easing this abrasive worry weighting my shoulders, but she had me distracted the entire last half hour. That's exactly what I need to avoid this year.

JORDAN

Saturday afternoon rolls around and my body is wiped from running around campus all week like a headless chicken. Leah is at Hayden's for the night, so my intention is to crawl my way onto the sofa, spread myself out like a starfish, and watch Thor pound his big hammer on the television.

I just finish popping a packet of buttery popcorn in the microwave when Leah sends me a message.

Leah: *Hayden has football tickets. Come pick us up in your new car!*

Jordan: *Can't. My feet fell off and I can't find them.*

Leah: *LOL! Look under the bed. And be quick about it or we'll miss kick off.*

I sigh wistfully, thinking of Chris Hemsworth waiting for me with his deep, sexy voice that reminds me of home.

Soon, I promise him silently and head to my room to find something to wear. Settling for comfort, I tug on a sleeveless orange hoodie with Colton Bulls printed on the front in navy. After teaming it with a leg-baring pair of white denim shorts, I leave my tousled hair hanging loose. With any luck, people will think the messy style is exactly what I'm aiming for.

Pocketing my keys and phone, I lock up and head for my car with an excited grin. As of this morning I have *wheels*. Granted they're shitty ones, but who cares? I have relative independence, and the chance to explore the Wild West like I've been desperate to do since the moment I arrived.

When the crapfest Nissan Pulsar I purchased that very morning coasts into a spot at an apartment complex within walking distance from ours, I breathe a happy sigh of relief. The car made the short trip on a wing and a prayer—and a few strategically placed strips of duct tape. I always keep some on hand because the tape is a crafty fix-all for most of life's problems: ankle sprains, tightening shin guards, emergency hem repair, and strapping guys to chairs if they get too handsy. Not that I've ever done the latter, but at least I have the option if needed.

Unbuckling my seatbelt, I step out into the late afternoon humidity and stretch hard. Every over-worked muscle in my body quivers with delight, and I even moan a little. It's not quite orgasmic, but it's damn close.

I hear a long, low whistle and my eyes fly open. Straight across from me idles a big black SUV. The tint looks dark enough to be illegal, but one of the rear windows is down, revealing a carload of guys. The back door opens and one of them spills out. His unruly blond curls are stuck to his temples with sweat, and a pair of black Ray-Bans cover his eyes.

"Yo, Damien!" he yells at the driver as he walks backwards to the block of apartments. A snug white tee shirt with red sleeves stretches across his broad, athletic shoulders as he moves. "You want anything?"

The front window comes down on the SUV, revealing the driver. He's wearing a baseball cap pulled low. It hides most of his face but dark hair peeks out beneath as he leans out the window.

I catch a glimpse of tanned skin and white, even teeth as he yells back at his friend, "Yeah, grab some condoms! I'm all out!"

As though feeling my gaze, he turns his head in my direction. Ugh. Busted! The guy in the passenger seat beside him looks my way too. Thankfully my phone beeps a text message. Reaching through the passenger window to grab it off the seat hides my flush.

Leah: *Hurry up, asshat!*

I tap out a quick reply to Leah and hit send.

Jordan: *Check your damage! I'm already here.*

I toss my phone back on the seat just as a small box comes flying out a third floor window and lands right at my feet. Shading my eyes, I glance up and see the guy from the SUV waving down at me.

"Sorry!" he yells. "My aim was off!"

My eyes fall back to the box. It's a packet of Durex flavored condoms. I reach down and pick it up. The front features a banana, apple, sliced orange, and a strawberry, with a tagline that reads *fruity flavors for extra fun.* I give an audible snort because nothing spells out sexy times better than fruit salad.

I glance up again when the guy comes bursting out of the apartment block, his sunglasses perched on his head. He jogs over, his tanned skin covered with a light sheen of sweat from the heat.

I hold out the box. "Wow. Fruity fun. Sounds healthy."

He gives me a quick once over before a cocky grin breaks across his face, showcasing deep dimples. He takes the box from my hand. "You look like you're into sports and nutrition. Wanna taste my banana?"

Did he really just say that? "What an offer. Unfortunately I have to wash my hair."

"Burn," says one of the guys in the back of the SUV and makes a hissing noise. The sound of laughter trails from the car.

His hazel eyes crinkle, and he cocks his head curiously. "You're Australian?"

"I am," I reply, surprised at him picking up the accent. "From Sydney. I'm here on a sports scholarship."

He leans up against my shitty car and folds his arms. It makes his biceps bulge temptingly, and I wonder if it's for my benefit. "What do you play?"

I shrug, deciding to humor him while I wait for my friends. "Soccer."

"A hot female jock that loves playing with balls? Sign me up!" He clutches a hand to his heart, and I can't help but laugh at the dramatic gesture *and* at being called hot. "I'm Jaxon Draper, by the way," he adds, holding out his hand. "But my friends call me Jax."

His palm is rough and warm, and I like the feel of it in mine far too much so I let go quickly. "Jordan Elliott."

"Wow, Jaxon and Jordan," he replies. "We sound good together."

"Really?" My brows rise dubiously. "I think we sound more like a nineteen-sixties singing duo."

He laughs and sidles a little closer, looking up at me from beneath thick lashes. "But I can't sing, so how about we skip the singing part and go straight to the duo?"

"Or we could just skip the duo part and go straight to the break-up?"

Jaxon's hazel eyes light up. "Make-up sex!"

I take a much-needed step back. "I won't win with you, will I?"

"Not if I can help it," he replies and peers inside my car. "What's with all the stuff?" he asks, looking at my bag of laundry. It sits next to a sports bag full of soccer gear: boots, shin guards, sweaty uniforms. I wince at the mess. I meant to get that stuff out the car, but I was too lazy to climb back up the stairs before driving over here. "You're not moving are you? What happened? Boyfriend dump you? Because his loss is my gain. I have an apartment right here," he says with a wave at the building in front of us. "I share it with two assholes, but I can kick them out."

The horn of the SUV blasts and the guy driving calls out, "Hurry up, Jax!"

Jaxon waves off his friends without taking his eyes from mine. "Shut up, Damien!" he yells back, not seeming bothered by it. "Can't you see I'm busy here?"

"Busy being a loser," comes another voice, making me wonder how many guys are squeezed in there. I risk another glance at the car, finding them all watching us with interest.

"You should go," I tell him, shifting uncomfortably beneath their stares.

"I should." He pushes off from his lean on my car. "When's your next game? I'll come watch."

"You already missed it. We played last night."

"Damn. Next time then?"

We can always do with more bums on seats so I shrug an agreement, careful to keep it casual.

"So did you kick ass last night? What am I saying?" he says before I can reply. "Of course you did. Look at those long legs and cute little biceps." Jaxon starts walking backwards, his eyes roving over me admiringly. Heat floods my cheeks from the aggressive flirting. "I bet you kill it on the field."

"I do," I assure him, the car keys jingling as I pocket them to head inside and chase up Leah. "I kill it off the field too, so consider yourself warned."

"Don't hurt me." Jaxon holds his hands up in mock fear, but underneath I can see his pleasure at my teasing response. He points the box of condoms at me. "I'm sure I'll being seeing you around, Killer."

30

Turning for the SUV, he holds the box crudely against his groin and crows to his friends, "Behold! The fruit of my loins!"

I ignore them after that, making it halfway to the building entrance before Leah comes jogging out the front door. Stripes are painted across her cheeks like war paint in our college team colors of orange, blue, and white. Matching ribbons flutter cheerily in her waves of dark brown hair.

"Ellioootttt!" she shouts loud enough for an entire mile radius to hear. Her shorts are similar to mine, but she's wearing a short-sleeved tee shirt that fits snug across her torso. Reaching my side, she makes a kissy face. "How do I look?"

I give her an exaggerated once-over as Hayden makes his way toward us. "Like an orange tabby cat out on the prowl."

"Perfect," she says, rolling her eyes. "That's just the look I was aiming for."

Hearing a squeal of tires, I glance over at the SUV leaving the parking lot. I catch a flash of red taillights, a black and white number plate that reads *MADDEN2*, and a sticker on the back window of a football above the words: *The person that said winning isn't everything, never won anything.*

Hayden and Leah are oblivious to the departing carload of guys. They're both too busy staring at my car, their expressions dubious. I spread my arms wide and grin. "What do you think?"

Leah opens her mouth to reply. A garbled sound comes out.

"I think it's great," Hayden says quickly, but we all know it's a lie. There's nothing great about my car. At least he tried.

Fifteen minutes later I squeeze into a spot at the stadium between a red Dodge Ram and a shiny black Escalade. Leah sinks low in the backseat with a humiliated moan, her brown eyes peering out the window to make sure she hasn't been seen.

"I'm not embarrassed at all, just so you know."

"No one can see you anyway. They're all inside." I yank the handbrake on and it protests with a loud, teeth-grinding screech. I flinch at the horrendous sound.

Hayden is more vocal. "Motherfuck!"

I glare at both of them in turn. "At least I have a car," I say, because the car Leah collected me from the airport with is Hayden's, and right now it's sitting at the mechanic's with a busted whozeewhatsit.

"Only because you have a brother who sent you money to buy it," Leah points out as Hayden makes his escape. She snaps her gum and reaches for her bag while I roll up the window. The air-conditioner is busted, so it's either warm air blasting from the open window or slow suffocation. "I think I'd rather have no car than one that has a front bumper held on with a bunch of tape."

"Just pretend they're silver racing stripes. Ta da! Instant street cred."

"People are gonna egg your car," I hear her mumble as she shoves open the creaky door and hops out. The central locking is also stuffed, so I jam the key in the door to lock it.

"Don't be ridiculous," I chide as the three of us walk around the front and examine the front bumper. Six vertical pieces of tape stretch from the bonnet to somewhere beneath the car. Nicky will shit a brick if he sees it. "You can barely notice it."

A hopeful expression lights up her pretty face. "Maybe someone will steal it while we're inside."

Hayden looks at my car, dubious. "Steal that?"

"You're right." Leah laughs and karma blasts a wave of humid air in her face, whipping strands of brown hair in her open mouth. She tugs them out. "Though stranger things have happened."

"Okay, enough dissing on my new wheels," I say and turn for the stadium entrance. "You promised me men in tight football pants, pounding each other into the ground with fiery enthusiasm. I'm here to collect."

After purchasing drinks from the concession stand, we clutch our plastic cups of coke and make our way inside where I promptly stutter to a stop, my mouth falling open. The brightly lit stadium is a screaming sea of Bulls fans wearing shirts in team colors. Energy radiates through the swarming crowd like electricity. It crackles in the air, raising goose bumps on my skin. Flags wave riotously, kids squeal, and grandmothers wear team caps with pride.

Leah grins at my stunned expression. "Ready to pop your American football cherry?"

"This isn't college football," I tell her as the charged atmosphere seeps through my skin and fizzes my blood. "This is mass hysteria."

I know football is a big hairy deal in the States, but hearing it and seeing it are two different things. I find myself getting swept away in the excitement as we make for the student section. When the crowds push in, Hayden shifts to the front, his weighty bulk leading the charge to our seats. I fall back a little as I squeeze my way through rabid supporters.

"Keep up, Elliott!" Leah calls over her shoulder.

"I'm right behind you," I shout over the noise.

Seconds later I'm shoved and stumble sideways, my drink tilting precariously. Holding it high to prevent further jostling, I turn, intending to apologize to the person I accidently elbowed by default.

"Watch it, sister," the girl snaps before I can speak. Her heavily made up eyes narrow threateningly, and she folds her arms over a blue tee shirt that boasts *MADDEN IS MINE!* in big orange letters across her ample chest.

I raise my brows coolly at her bitchy tone, feeling the petty urge to douse her stupid shirt with my coke. Leah grabs my hand before I can take action.

"Get over yourself," Leah retorts to the girl and yanks me forward before the situation escalates. "Don't mess with a female Madden fan," she warns me. "They don't just have claws in these parts, they have guns."

"Yeah, that's not scary," I mutter. I have no clue who Madden is, but if he belongs to that girl, she can have him.

We reach some kind of blockage ahead, which means maneuvering through the alumni section to reach our row in the student section. With my eyes caught on the on-field entertainment, I miss seeing the outstretched foot and stumble over it.

"Shit," I gasp when I manage to tread on it as I try righting myself. A firm hand comes out to grip my bicep, steadying me before I do any more damage.

"I'm so sorry," I say, lifting my head and the words trail off when I realize who I've just stomped all over.

Fuck my life.

Professor Draper is going to have my scholarship revoked and send me back to Australia.

"Are you okay?" he asks, perhaps mistaking my wide-eyed look of horror for something more concerning, like a mild stroke maybe.

I clear my throat. "I'm fine, just surprised to ..." *To see you here, considering the big stick up your ass.* I shut my mouth.

"To see me at football?" He arches a brow. "Even stuffy old professors like to get out and watch a game now and then."

This is so very awkward, and I suddenly feel like laying the blame at Leah's door for dragging me out tonight. I shoot her a quick glare and find her gasping with laughter. Hayden is seated on her right, pretending he doesn't know either of us.

"Patrick," comes the exasperated tone from the lady beside him. My professor's lips twitch visibly. "Leave the girl alone."

I give her my attention, curious to see the woman who almost made him smile. Her hair is blond. Sweeping bangs frame intelligent brown eyes that study me with a friendly expression. "You must be Patrick's new student transfer from Australia. Jordan, right?" He mentioned me? It can't have been good. "I'm Olivia," she continues with a kind smile, "but you can call me Livvy."

"It's nice to meet you, Livvy," I say and shift my drink to my other hand when she holds hers out. I shake it, finding the gesture oddly formal inside a football stadium, but Livvy's easy nature makes it less awkward.

Leah begins waving madly, and I think it's her sad attempt at a rescue. Either way, I'm taking it. "I should get to my seat before—"

"Actually, Jordan, I have an extracurricular task for you," Professor Draper interrupts. "Come see me early next week. Do you know where my office is?"

"Yes, sir," I say, which is a lie, because even if his office is marked on the campus map with a giant bullseye, my sense of direction will ensure I never find it.

"Good." He waves me off dismissively. "We'll talk next week."

I make my escape, and I know it's overly dramatic of me, but it suddenly feels like the weight of the world is on my shoulders. I have a huge course load and soccer commitments that tie up every spare minute. Now I'm supposed to fit menial tasks like photocopying or fetching dry cleaning in around it? I know I missed a class, but I have a horrible feeling the punishment is going to far exceed the crime.

"Oh my gosh," I burst out with, flopping down on my seat beside Leah. "Where are those rabid female Madden fans when you need them? I need someone to shoot me right now."

Leah clucks sympathetically while I take a big, soothing gulp of my coke. "Did you get chewed out some more?"

"Are you kidding? After missing his class, I go and stomp all over his feet as an added insult. I'm totally screwed."

Leah's lips slam together with excessive force, and a noise that sounds like the low-pitched whine of a dog rises from the back of her throat.

"What?" I snap, irritated beyond all belief.

A snort breaks free from her nose. "It's really not funny," she gasps and begins to laugh again. "I guess you won't be late for his class again."

"Not with Professor Hardass on the case," I mutter and train my eyes on the field because the announcer is introducing the team. His loud, booming voice echoes around the stadium dramatically, setting off loud squeals of excitement from around us. Four girls seated two rows from ours are the most ear splitting of all. They're each wearing matching orange tee shirts, featuring daring cleavage and the words *Madden Fever*.

Everyone stands up, Leah and Hayden too, and I'm dragged to my feet with them. The crowd begins to chant, "Colton Bulls! Colton Bulls!"

"Who the hell *is* this Madden anyway?" I ask, my voice a shout to be heard over the thunderous crowd. "Some kind of rock star?"

"Close enough!" Leah shouts back. "Brody Madden is a starting wide receiver this season for the Colton Bulls and a top draft prospect. He's also a six foot three, two hundred and twenty pound football god!"

"Amen!" preaches a female voice behind us.

The chants morph into a bevy of female squeals when the team trots out, right near our seats. Their proximity affords us a good look at their assets. I can't help but notice how amply they're displayed in those snug orange and blue football jerseys and tight white football pants.

Leah's cheeks are flushed with groupie fever and she points. "There! That's Madden! Number twenty-two!"

I squint for his number. It's dark out now, but the stadium lights are brighter than daylight. I find him easily. His back is facing us as he jogs out onto the rich green field. Madden is printed in white block letters across the broad width of his shoulders and beneath it his jersey number. My eyes fall lower and my pulse kicks into gear. His backside is round and firm, and his impressive glutes hug his football pants like he was born to wear them.

Brody makes a sudden turn and faces the crowd behind him. His helmet is already on and hides his face, but his intensity is palpable and raises goose bumps across my forearms. He lifts a sinewy arm high, biceps rippling as he acknowledges the crowd. It's a brief gesture, but they lap it up, roaring their approval while he's already turning back around, swallowed up with the rest of his team.

They disappear further down the side of the field, becoming harder to see, but cameramen stalk the sidelines, ensuring they capture every moment for ESPN and the enormous jumbotron sitting up high at the far end of the stadium.

Kick-off comes and goes as I try to make sense of the game. There's enough stopping and starting to give me whiplash, and when they score they call it a touchdown, but after passing the goal line, they don't actually have to touch the ball down. Halfway through the second quarter, I give up pretending I have a clue and choose to watch Brody Madden instead. Leah's right. He's golden. Untouchable. And I know it's cliché, but it's guys like this that make the term 'poetry in motion' ring true. Trying to follow the play doesn't seem to matter when you can watch him run down the field with the ball instead, his powerful thighs eating up the yards like he's flying.

Midway through the third quarter, Hayden's gone to get more drinks, and I'm slumped low in my seat, trying to stretch out my legs when a shout reverberates across rows and rows of seats.

"Killer!"

The crowd's settled down from earlier, and they're all intent on the game, so the sound rings clear across the student section. Dozens of heads turn, looking up in our direction.

"Killer!"

"Oh god," I moan, spying Jaxon down in the very front row. He's facing the crowd. One knee rests on his seat and both hands are cupped around his mouth to help direct his shout. He's looking right at me. When he sees he has my attention, his grin spreads wide, and he waves at me to come down.

Leah's brows shoot up so fast I wouldn't have been surprised to see them fly right off her face. "Is he shouting at *you*?" she asks, her tone incredulous.

"Of course not," I mumble, holding my giant coke up so I can hide behind it. The drink is empty but it's still proving useful.

"Jordan! It's Jax!" he shouts again. I peek around my cup and catch his eyes light up with mischief. "You know, the condom guy!"

This time a lot more than just a dozen heads turn my way. Hayden returns at that opportune moment and lets out a shout of laughter as he snatches the empty cup from my grasp. I protest at losing my cover, but he quickly replaces it with a full one before retaking his seat.

"The *condom* guy?" Leah hisses, leaning in close, and the tone in her voice says *we need to talk, girlfriend*. "You know that's Jax Draper, right?"

My brows pull together as I look down at him, trying to see if there's anything about the guy that jogs my memory. I get nothing apart from the brief moment where we met in the parking lot. "You say that like I should know who he is."

Leah's lips press together, and she shakes her head. I don't know whether she's about to burst into laughter or pass out from distress. Either way, uneasiness makes my hands begin to sweat.

"I don't know if I should tell you now."

"You can't do that! Is he Texan mafia? Do Texan's even have mafia?"

"Jax Draper is Brody Madden's cousin."

I shrug and the uneasy feeling disappears. "Okay, so he's related to football royalty. So what?"

"He's also Professor Draper's son!"

"Oh …" I look back down at Jaxon. He's still facing our way but the guy I recognize as Damien, the driver of the SUV, has his attention while he says something to him. "Shit," I mumble weakly and lower my head, covering my eyes with my hand.

Leah jerks in her seat beside me. "Don't look now," she says, and of course I spread my fingers and take a peek, "but he's coming this way."

There's no hiding so I drop my hand. Jaxon's striding up the stadium steps toward us, holding his drink in one hand and using the other to wave at his father as he pushes his way through our row.

"Quick, get up," he says urgently when he reaches me.

I look up at him, confused. "What?"

"Stand up, Jordan. Quick."

The people around us are watching so I stand quickly, wondering what on Earth is going on.

"Thanks," he replies and swoops in, sitting down with a deep, exaggerated sigh.

"Hey! You can't—" I'm yanked onto his lap before I can finish. My cheeks flush, and I squirm as I try to push up off him. "What are you doing? Let me up!"

"Shush." His arms slide around me like a steel band, pulling me back against his chest. "You're causing a scene, and I'm missing the game."

"Shush?" I twist in his lap to glare at him, pretending not to enjoy the feeling of being held against a male body, even though I secretly do. He's warm and firm and smells faintly of fresh sweat and deodorant. "Did you just tell me to *shush*?"

"I did. Wow, Killer. It's lucky you kick ass on the soccer field because your hearing sucks." Jaxon turns his grin on my friend but doesn't let go of me to extend a hand. "Hi," he says to Leah. "I'm Jaxon."

"So very nice to meet you," she replies.

Jaxon then gives Hayden one of those male chin lifts, and Hayden responds in kind, saying, "Come to sit up here with the commoners?"

Jaxon winks at me. "No, just Jordan."

"And now you can go," I tell him. Peeling his arms from around my waist, I manage to stand.

"But I like it here."

"That's unfortunate." I risk a glance in Professor Draper's direction and find both he and Livvy are watching us. "I really can't be seen with you."

Jaxon leans back in my seat like he's not going anywhere and takes a lazy slurp from the straw of his drink. "You can't?"

"Your dad and I don't get along," I explain. "I missed most of his lecture on Thursday, and now I've earned a place in his bad book."

"You didn't!" Jaxon holds a hand to his mouth, gasping in mock horror. Then he cocks head at me for moment. "Oh hey, yeah. I knew I'd seen you from somewhere before. We're in the same class. Your face turned such a brilliant shade of red I thought it was going to catch fire."

"Well, thanks for that. I don't remember you."

"Ouch," he says with a wince, rubbing his chest as if he has indigestion.

Leah and Hayden watch us avidly. Apparently our conversation is a lot more interesting than the football game playing out in front of them. I clear my throat. "Can I have my seat back now?"

Jaxon shrugs and stands up. He leans in close, his chest rubbing lightly against mine and his lips brushing my ear. "Later, Killer," he says, and I feel him slide something into the pocket of my shorts.

Drawing back, he grins and jogs back down to the front row and his friends. Leah turns to me, a smirk playing on her lips. "Explain everything. Right now."

CHAPTER 4

JORDAN

It's not until we return to Hayden's apartment after the game that I check my pocket. Leah and I are seated in the living room along with our soccer captain, Paige, who lives two floors above Hayden in the same building. Paige has silky jet-black hair, which is enviably straight. Cut in a bob, it rests neatly just beneath her jawline. She also has two vodka Red Bulls under her belt and brought the half-full bottle along to our impromptu gathering.

With drinks dispensed and Hayden and his roommate, Becker, safely tucked away in the kitchen putting snacks together, I dig my hand in my pocket and come out with a banana-flavored condom. Wrapped around it is a scrawled note with Jaxon's number and the comment, *If you change your mind about washing your hair, Jax xo*

With a speed almost invisible to the naked eye, Leah sets her vodka on the coffee table and snatches both the note and condom from my hand. Handing off the foil packet to Paige, she reads the note with a gleam so bright I fear it'll take out an eye. Leah's been making noises for weeks about me meeting someone and double-dating with her and Hayden. This note has given her the perfect opportunity to ramp up her efforts.

She looks at me, frustration evident in her eyes. "You told him you were *washing your hair?*"

"Told who?" Paige asks, stretching her legs out on the coffee table and crossing them at the ankle. She turns the wrapper over in her fingers before bringing it to her nose for a sniff.

Having heard the full story already, Leah can't contain her grin when she answers. "Jax Draper." Her voice pitches low when she adds, "He asked her if she wanted to taste his banana."

Paige's blue eyes pop wide and her feet fall away from the table when she sits upright with excitement. "He did not!" She faces me where I'm sitting cross-legged on the floor opposite the both of them. "And you told him you were *washing your hair?*"

"Newsflash, ladies. It's not an invitation to go on a date. It's an invitation to … to …"

"To get acquainted with his banana?" Paige prompts.

I jab a finger at Paige. "Exactly. So get your head out of the clouds, Leah."

"I don't know." Leah sits back on the sofa, pursing her lips. "Jax isn't the kind of guy that chases girls. He doesn't need to. They chase him."

"So?"

"So it looked like he was doing a bit of heavy duty chasing for you."

I snort. "Rubbish. I barely know the guy."

"His name is Jaxon Draper. He's twenty-one, and he's not only gorgeous, he's pre-med and smart. He shares an apartment on the floor above Paige with Brody Madden and Damien Reiner, and he's got a thing for female soccer jocks with blondish-colored hair and blue eyes."

I snort again, and Paige's head lolls back against the sofa as she gives a dreamy sigh. "I'd totally taste his banana if he asked me."

"You'll get your chance," I assure her, swirling the last of the vodka and soda in my glass before downing it quickly. "I'm sure he flirts with all the girls like he did with me."

"Uh huh." Leah shakes her head. "Not all the girls have your Australian accent. It's husky and deep and sounds like sex. Guys go mad for that. Isn't that right, baby?" she yells in the direction of the kitchen.

"It's how you sound after deep-throating my dick, so yeah, it's hot," Hayden yells back.

While I'm flushing deep red from the visual of Hayden naked with an impressive erection, Paige deepens her voice and tries to affect an Australian accent. "How does this sound?"

Leah snorts with laughter. "Try it with a little less Russell Brand and a little more Russell Crowe."

Paige tries again and whines because she can't get it right. Meanwhile Leah is rummaging inside my bag that's set by the foot of the sofa. Plucking out my phone, she glances from the note to the screen and commences tapping. Sensing subterfuge, my pulse kicks up in mild panic. "What are you doing?"

Intent on my phone, she doesn't look at me. "I'm adding Jaxon's number into your phone so you don't lose it."

"I'm not calling him."

"Okay," she says soothingly, and because it's a tone I recognize well, I know she isn't going to let this go so easily.

"Baby, catch!" Hayden shouts as he leaves the kitchen and fastballs a packet of Doritos at Leah.

With lightening reflexes, she holds up an arm and catches the bag single-handedly. Hayden swoops in and scoops her up off the sofa with ease, spinning her around with a grin. "That's my girl."

Becker dodges the twirling pair as he walks into the living room carrying a tray of carrot and celery sticks, cottage cheese, and water crackers. Hayden might have scoffed when Leah told me he's a man madly in love, but when you stock up on healthy snacks for your girl when she stays over, it means you're completely sunk.

Paige slings her arms around Becker's neck when he leans over to place the tray on the table. "Can I marry you, Becker? You'd make an awesome wife!"

Becker rolls a set of bright green eyes. He plays on the baseball team with Hayden, but he's not quite as big as his roommate. His body is leaner, and his dark hair short and always styled carefully in a mini Mohawk. Paige rubs her hand over it roughly, mussing it, and he ducks out of her way. "Suck my dick, Paige."

"Not tonight," she replies, and amusement lights up her eyes. "I'm washing my hair!"

Leah and Paige both scream with laughter and I flop back on the floor

42

with a loud groan. I fear I'm never going to hear the end of that particular joke.

The following Friday rolls around and despite Leah's daily insistence, I haven't called Jaxon. He's not the kind of guy who sits around pining for a girl to ring him, so I'm sure it's safe to say I haven't doomed him to a lifetime of disappointment.

My cleats crunch on the bright green turf as I head for the locker room. It brings with it the fresh scent of grass and dirt, and I relish it because no matter where I am—Austin, Texas or Sydney, Australia—it's the smell of the field. It's where I belong and will always be home to me.

Leah catches up to me. I hook an arm around her shoulders and yank her close. The final whistle blew just minutes earlier, and despite the heat and exhaustion oozing from my every pore, it's nothing on the elation I feel at scoring two of the four goals that left our team undefeated for another week. "Drink's are on me tonight," I declare rashly.

Leah shoves me away with an eye roll and a laugh because she knows the impoverished balance of my bank account. "What are you shouting? Shots of water?"

"Har, har," I retort. "I'm sure we've got lemons and mint sitting somewhere in the bottom of the fridge, so I can at least make them classy."

"Sounds delicious, but I'm in need of a real drink," she grumbles and then grabs my arm. "Speaking of needing a drink, you never mentioned what happened with Professor Hardass the other day?"

I groan and shake my head. I'd caught up with the professor three days ago and the outcome had been so much worse than I'd anticipated.

Rapping smartly on his office door, he invited me inside with what I likened to an evil smile. Positive he could smell fear, I straightened my shoulders and walked in, reminded of the one and only time I'd been in trouble at school. It was back in high school, and I'd caught Alex Thompson leaning over beside his desk in front of me during class, not even pretending he wasn't peering up my skirt. Anger and shame rose swiftly—my uniform was secondhand and seriously short because I'd outgrown it two years earlier—so I aimed a hard jab at the leg of his chair. My mouth fell open when it collapsed beneath him and skittered sideways.

Alex went down hard, his head smacking his desk and bouncing off it. After visiting the school nurse, she diagnosed him with a concussion. The episode cost me a three-day suspension and two weeks of detention.

It's hardly the same situation, but I felt the same sense of impending anxiety as I stood in front of my professor's desk.

"Take a seat," he said, eyes focused on the screen of his laptop.

Resting my armload of books on the edge of his desk, I sank into the seat behind me. "You mentioned an extracurricular task, Professor?"

"I did." With a furrow in his brow, he tapped a few more strokes on his keyboard and then gave me his full attention. I offered him a strained smile, which he didn't return. "I have a student who needs a tutor and I want you to do it."

My insides unclenched with relief. "I'm not a registered tutor, Professor. I can't—"

Cocking his head, he interrupted me. "Can't ... or won't?"

I paused and sat back in my seat. Five seconds in and he was going for my jugular? "I'm not sure what you're implying, but I'm here under an international sports scholarship. Not only do I have soccer commitments and a full course load, I have a GPA to maintain in order to keep my place in this country. Even if I wanted to, I simply don't have the time to tutor anyone."

"I figured you'd say something like that." Professor Draper leaned forward and handed me a sheet of a paper. I took it from him, glancing down at a detailed outline of my weekly timetable. "So I took the liberty of reviewing your schedule, Jordan. As you can see, there are three highlighted sections where I feel you can allow an hour of time toward tutoring."

How presumptuous! I wanted to scrunch the page into a ball and peg it at his head. Those three blocks of time were *mine*. My spare time to do laundry, scrub soccer cleats, Skype my brother back home, or just blob on the couch and numb my mind with television. Either way, it didn't matter what I chose to do with it, just that it was mine. Having no free time at all wasn't healthy, and surely a well-respected professor of this college would know that.

I looked up, ready to plead for my sanity. "Professor, I—" My eyes welled up. Taking a deep breath, I focused on a point somewhere over his shoulder. "I don't understand. I'm sorry for missing class. I'm not trying to make excuses, but I'm still learning my way around campus so it wasn't intentional. Is there something else I can do besides tutoring that won't take up so much time?" His brows rose slowly, and I realized how my question sounded. "Like photocopying or … or …"

"Miss Elliott. Jordan. Can I call you Jordan?"

No, I wanted to snap in a fit of angered pettiness, but when I met his eyes I saw a faint apology in them. "Yes, of course."

"Jordan, I'm not asking you to do this because you missed the majority of my lecture. While I didn't appreciate your untimely interruption, I'm really not that much of an ass." Professor Draper smiled at me but it was so faint I almost missed it. "I'm asking you this as a personal favor. Students don't fail my course because I simply don't let them, and this particular student will fail if I don't provide some form of additional tutelage outside the classroom."

I sighed internally. How was I supposed to respond to that? *Your student can go suck eggs because I need time to blob on the couch?* He continued on with his explanation, delivering a blow that saw my free time scatter to the wind like confetti.

"My student has dyslexia. He's managed to get this far under his own steam, but his grades have been slipping over the past two years, and as they're already low to begin with. He has no room for them to drop further." Professor Draper spread his hands wide, revealing his helplessness with the situation. "I don't know how else to help him, and I figured you might have some clue."

I stared at my hands where they rested in my lap. "You're asking me because you know about my brother?"

"Your student transfer information mentioned your experience with tutoring your dyslexic brother."

And it hadn't been easy. My brother had been difficult to live with, even after he was diagnosed. Nicky went through it all: sullen attitude, low grades, instigating fights, back chatting teachers. What no one ever saw was just how frustrating and debilitating it was for him. He endured bullying at school, coming home with grazed knuckles, black eyes, and regular detention. I was the only one he'd talk to about it. In one of his classes, his teacher would regularly make him read aloud in class, as if it would help him improve. All it did was make the problem worse, and rile my fury at his teacher's idiocy.

It was no wonder Nicky didn't give his tutors the time of day. I spent hours researching dyslexia and instead we studied together.

"I still don't understand why you're asking me. I'm not in any way professionally qualified to help. Whatever I did for my brother was done through sheer desperation because he wouldn't accept help from anyone else."

"That's the exact same issue I'm having, but I think this student will be able to relate to you. You're both athletes and study under the same schedule with the same pressure to perform." Professor Draper sat back in his seat and studied me carefully. "I'm not expecting miracles, Jordan, not this late in the game. I just need someone he can trust to provide him with some study mechanisms that will get him through his final year."

I raised my brows. "And you think he's going to trust me?"

"Yes, I do, because you're going to give him every reason to."

I am? Well, okay then.

"I'll do my best," I promised, and after running through the details of the general tutelage he wanted me to provide, he gave me a sheet of paper with the student's contact information.

Swiping my armload of books off the desk, I placed the note on top and stood. And because I hadn't embarrassed myself enough in front of my professor yet, I tripped over the leg of my chair. Unbelievable. I never stumbled. This added stress had turned me inside out.

"Are you okay?" Professor Draper asked, making his way around his desk, his lips pressed together like he was trying not to laugh.

My reply was muffled because I was crouched on the floor, collecting my books along with some of his papers that were knocked to the ground with them.

"I'm totally fine," I lied, grabbing at folders randomly, rushing to leave before I did something worse, like accidently setting his desk on fire.

With an awkward wave, I turned to leave. He called out my name and I paused in the doorway.

"Please keep this arrangement confidential. My student is extremely high profile and doesn't want it known he's receiving external tutelage for a learning disability."

"But ..."

"Coping with dyslexia is hard enough without having it spread across campus, don't you think?"

"Of course," I replied, because I got it. I really did. Bullying was shit, and my brother suffered through all of it, but I had no idea how I was supposed to keep it private.

"Good," my professor said, giving a short nod. "I've arranged your first session for Friday, 4:00 p.m. at your apartment. If you wish to arrange a different location moving forward, you can work that out between yourselves."

I gave him a nod. "Okay."

"Oh and, Jordan?" he called out again when I tried leaving once more.

I paused, surreptitiously checking my watch. I was going to be late for my next class. Again.

"Good luck."

The words sounded ominous, like I was actually going to need it. Rushing from his office, I glanced quickly at the page sitting on top of my armload of books. My brows pulled together. Kyle Davis. It wasn't a name I readily recognized but then I *was* new and knowledge of the campus social hierarchy hadn't been high on my priority list.

"Jordan!" Coach Kerr's shout snaps me from my recollection. She's standing on the sidelines beside our assistant coach, waving me over.

Leah jostles my shoulder as we pause from our walk toward the locker room. "So what does your professor have you doing?" she prompts. "Photocopying mammoth volumes of tax law?"

I make a face at Leah. "Something like that," I reply and quickly change the subject, calling out as I start jogging backwards toward our coach. "Hey, you're still going straight to Hayden's from here?"

Leah pauses midstride, cocking her head at me as though I have a screw loose. "Well yeah, that hasn't changed since you asked me five minutes ago."

I clear my throat. "Right." I wave her away and she peels off toward the locker room, shaking her head.

"Coach," I acknowledge when I reach her side. Our coach's tenure with the Colton Bulls began three years ago and her touch is golden. The team reached two consecutive NCAA tournaments, and I'm hoping for number three this year.

"Jordan. I just wanted to remind you of your appointment with the nutritionist on Monday afternoon." She doesn't look at me as she speaks. She's tugging a sheet of paper from her clipboard which she hands over. "Also, I know we've discussed putting you with a sports management firm at the end of the year. I put together a list of names. I want you to take the time to research them carefully. Talk to your team about recommendations."

"Thanks, Coach." I scan my eye down the list. I know I'll eventually need to sign with an agent, but here in the States I'm a fish out of water. I don't have any insider information on who's good and who to avoid. Those who've talked to me in the past have been quick to advise the best way to get recognition in female sports is to strip down, oil up, and pose for men's magazines. I'm not sure that's the way I want to go in order to be recognized.

"I can help you narrow down your choices, Jordan, but you'll need one by the end of your senior year. Seattle Reign is looking for someone young and fresh. Someone like you."

I look up at my coach, seeing her excitement and sincerity. Seattle Reign is the best team in the National Women's Soccer League. It would make my entire career.

"Don't look so surprised," she says. "You're a huge addition to our squad. We were lucky to get you. Eyes have been on you ever since you made your professional debut at seventeen. Australia's W-League Young Player of the Year, and runner-up to Riley for Australian Female Football Player of the Year. You'd be in the NWSL right now if you weren't so adamant about finishing college."

Wrapping up the conversation, I jog back to the locker room, my grin wide. It's quiet. *Too* quiet. I can hear water dripping from the showers and birds chirping from the trees that surround the back of the building, but inside is eerily deserted.

"Hello?" I call out.

Seconds later I hear shouts and squeals from behind me, and suddenly I'm doused in dark brown sludge. It pours down over my head like lava—sticky, warm, and oozing.

"Oh my god!" I shriek, making the mistake of opening my mouth. It dribbles inside and I start choking and spluttering, tasting chocolate syrup.

Gasps of laughter ring out. I wipe the goo from my eyes, flicking the excess off onto the floor. Paige stands in front of me and my teammates surround me, some of them holding the offending buckets. "Welcome to the Colton Bulls, Jordan!" she says with a perky grin I want to slap from her face.

I spit a brown glob on the floor and glare at her balefully. "Am I being hazed?"

"Yep," I hear Leah choke out between laughs from somewhere on my left. Another bucket comes at me, shooting a white cloud of shredded coconut over my head. It settles over the sauce and sticks everywhere. "And what better way to make you feel at home then by turning you into a human lamington," she adds, referring to the Australian dessert of cake, covered in chocolate sauce and coconut.

Glancing down, I see my soccer uniform is completely doused. The syrup has oozed over my shorts, down my legs, over and inside my shin guards, where I can now feel it pooling inside my cleats. In the grand scheme of things, it could've been much worse. Hazing can be horrific and all I've copped is a covering of chocolate sauce and coconut.

It's when I'm dragged outside the locker room, flecks of brown coating the ground in my wake, that I realize it's not over yet. Paige locks the door behind us all and plops the set of keys in her shoulder bag.

"What are you doing?" I cry out, and laughter follows the team as they head toward the parking lot carrying their sports bags.

Both Paige and Leah turn. "We're all heading out to celebrate our victory. Don't be too long. If you're late for the party, there'll be nothing left for you to drink but warm beer!"

My teammates leave in a group of giggles and sports bags, leaving me gob smacked. Am I supposed to drive home like this? The sauce has mixed in with my sweat, and standing here in the hot afternoon sun, I can feel myself baking like a week-old sundae from McDonalds.

I grab for Leah's arm and she stutters to a halt, grimacing at the chocolate fingerprints I leave behind on her shirtsleeve. I take some satisfaction from that minor victory. "Leah, my keys are inside my bag which is inside the locker room."

"No it's not. Hayden drove your car home. All your stuff's inside it." Shrugging off my arm, Leah smirks and begins jogging backwards, out of my reach. "Enjoy your walk home. I hear the insects love this time of day and you smell sweeter than spring right now."

"What?" I shout because she's already running, catching up fast to the other girls like the coward she is. "You can't do this!"

"Too late, Elliott!" she shouts back. "We already did!"

"Just for the record, you all suck!" Holding my arms up high, I flip them the bird with both hands. Leah's response is to take a photo with her phone. With a final laugh, she disappears with the team, abandoning me to the humiliating fate of walking home in view of the entire Friday afternoon swarm of students.

Trudging my way outside the stadium, I garner laughs and a wide berth, and begin the walk home. It's not fun, and it's not pretty. The syrup begins drying on my skin, making me itch and chafe in uncomfortable places. Students yell slurs from their cars as they drive by, and I catch the attention of several bees, causing me to squeal and run while slapping them away. The only positive is that the lengthy walk allows me time to plot Leah's murder.

I'm up to the part where she's strapped to a Segway and I'm rolling her off a cliff when I arrive back at the apartment complex. Students stare at me, but I focus on my parked car, pretending indifference as I aim for it purposefully. I walk around the side of it and catch sight of my reflection in my window. I don't recognize myself. After hearing one student comment that I look like the filling in a shit sandwich, I realize that maybe it was polite on his part because the reality is much worse.

Squaring my shoulders, I crouch down and peel away the small square of duct tape from the undercarriage. The spare key to the apartment is stuck to the back of it. I rip it away and make my way inside, dropping the mask of indifference. All I can bring myself to care about right now is a pounding hot shower, food, and having a really good crying jag.

But it's not meant to be.

After squelching up the stairwell with aching legs, I emerge into the third floor hallway. Greeting me is a Greek god. He's leaning casually against the doorframe of my apartment, and my pulse kicks up a notch as I take a moment to admire him.

His skin is golden, like warm sunshine that you could bask in and never get cold. Big, broad shoulders crowd the small hallway, and biceps thick with corded muscle peek out from beneath snug shirtsleeves. He looks strong and capable. The sort of person who could weather any storm and come out fighting.

His hair is the color of rich caramel and cropped short, but there's a slight curl on the ends that won't conform to any particular style. I catch a glimpse of white, even teeth as he bites down on his full bottom lip, dragging it inside his mouth while he taps away at his phone like he's bored and waiting for someone.

I swallow a groan. *The tutoring session.*

He's waiting for me.

Ignoring my out-of-control pulse, I clomp forward on syrup-coated cleats. I know the instant he notices me because he looks up and does a double take. With his coloring I'm expecting blue eyes, or a brilliant green, because they're the eye colors of the gods, aren't they? But his are neither. They're brown, and they're intense, and I watch them widen when he realizes I'm headed right for him like a badly guided missile.

He drops the hand that holds his phone and shifts sideways to let me past. It's a hopeful move, and I almost keep going, not having the heart to disappoint him.

Instead I reach his side, coming to a complete stop with an audible sigh of exhaustion that I just can't contain.

"Hi," I say and try for a smile. I feel my face crack a little and flecks of dried chocolate flutter to the ground between us.

He shifts back, brows rising as he stares. "Help you?"

I nod at the door we're both standing in front of. "I live here."

"You do?"

His tone implores me to say no, and for the second time in as many minutes I'm going to disappoint him.

"Yes," I reply and extend a hand, trying to be polite. "I'm Jordan Elliott. You're here for the tute?"

"Tute?"

"Tutorial," I clarify.

"I am," he replies and ignores my gesture of greeting. Instead, he leans back against the doorframe and folds his arms. Muscles bunch and flex, highlighting the powerful build beneath his tee shirt. It absorbs my focus, and I force my eyes to ignore the display. "And you're late."

His voice is a deep rumble, one I want to listen to on repeat until I'm lulled into sleep, but I find I don't care much for it when it comes out loaded with irritation. I drop my hand, embarrassed at his snub and disappointed in his attitude. I *am* late, but he's obviously the type of person who doesn't understand that sometimes shit just happens.

"Well, as you can see," I bite out as I give him my back to unlock the door, "my afternoon took a small turn for the worse."

CHAPTER 5

BRODY

Scooping my backpack off the floor, I sling it over my shoulder and follow Jordan inside her apartment, seething on the inside. Yeah it was rude not to shake her hand, but she looks like someone rolled her in a giant pile of shit, not to mention I don't want to be here.

Maybe I'm barely scraping by on my own, but I don't need anyone trying to make me better because it's an exercise in futility. I am never going to be intelligent, or sharp, or hold a meaningful conversation that doesn't include the subject of football. I am never going to be normal. I am who I am, and I have to accept that it's all I'm going to be without someone trying to give me false hope. No doubt Jordan plans to do just that.

What a waste of fucking time.

After I shut the apartment door behind me, Jordan turns to face me, lifting her chin like she's doing her best to hold her shit together. "Look," she says in an accent I'm pegging as Australian. Is she an international student? My uncle gave me minimal information. "I know I'm late and I'm sorry, but I really need to take a shower before we get started."

Started on what? Operation Grow Brody A Brain? Despite the shame prickling along my skin like a heat rash, I chuckle at the absurdity.

Jordan cocks her head. "What?"

I shrug and give her a quick once over. Her hair and features are mostly obscured with caked brown smears and flecks of white, but I can see she's geared up in a soccer uniform, shin guards and cleats still in place.

"What *is* that all over you?" Leaning in, I give an audible sniff. Rather than the stench of manure, she smells sickly sweet, like chocolate cream pie. "Hmmm, syrup? You're covered in chocolate sauce? What happened?" I ask, even though there's no doubt the girl just got hazed. I've seen the chocolate syrup trick a time or two and the opportunity to tease is too good to ignore. "Was it a kinky sex game gone wrong?"

There's something familiar in the clear blue eyes that narrow at my insult, but I don't know what it is. I cock my head, bringing a smirk to my lips. I'm being an asshole, but better her anger than pity. "You know you're supposed to take your clothes off before you let some guy lick syrup off your tits."

Jordan studies me for a moment. "Thanks for the advice. I'll be sure to remember that for next time."

I want to roll my shoulders, defuse the annoyance because I haven't managed to rile her. In fact, I just want to leave. "Look, Jordan, I don't know what they're paying you to tutor me, but whatever it is, I'll double it so you don't."

Her eyebrows shoot up underneath the chocolate coating her face. "You'll pay me *not* to tutor you?"

"That's what I said, didn't I?"

Jordan shakes her head. "I guess I wasn't sure I heard you right."

"Well you did, so what are they paying you? Twenty bucks an hour?"

After laughing outright, she says, "Seven-fifty."

"Is that all?"

I don't believe it. No one in their right mind would agree to that. Jordan has a secret agenda and it could only be one thing. Fury begins to build in my chest. Dumping my backpack on the floor, my eyes narrow as I stalk toward her, my steps slow and deliberate. She shifts backwards, eyes widening. I press my advantage by standing over her, the broad width of my shoulders intimidating and hostile.

"What do you want from me, Jordan Elliott? Money? The inside scoop on my life so you can sell it to the press?" I grab her chin in my hand, forcing her face upwards so she can see the contempt blazing from my eyes. "Or are you just after a fuck? You want everyone to know you had the honor of sucking my dick?"

Jordan jerks her chin free of my grip, and finally I have her anger. "You jerk!" She shoves me in the chest, and she may have strength, but it's not enough to push me off my feet. I don't even budge. "You may be a pretty package, Kyle Davis, but inside you're an ugly, conceited donkey," she hisses angrily, "and I have no time for people like you!"

A grin forces its way to my lips. "You think I'm pretty?"

Jordan jabs a finger in the direction of the apartment door. "Get out!"

It's a hollow victory, but I'm taking it anyway. Slinging my backpack over my shoulder, I'm halfway out the door when I realize she called me Kyle Davis. "Wait." I pause and turn back around. "What did you just call me?"

"A jackass!" she yells, and I duck when a soccer ball comes flying at my face. Jordan has exceptional aim, but I have better reflexes. It sails past, hitting the hallway wall behind me before bouncing back and whacking her doorframe with a loud thump. The makeshift weapon drops to the ground, and I put a foot on it, steadying it before I reach down and pick it up. I step back inside her apartment, the ball tucked under my arm. "Did you just call me Kyle Davis?"

"Sorry, Your Highness." Jordan bows theatrically, and it looks ridiculous considering she's a human éclair in soccer cleats. "Will I spontaneously combust if I say your name out loud? Will it jinx me? Or do you prefer something more formal, like Mr. Davis?" Jordan sneers at me. "If you ask me, I think asshat has a better ring to it."

My lips twitch and I have to bite back the urge to laugh out loud. Jordan has no idea who I am. For some reason, she seems to think I'm my uncle's douchebag TA. That means I must be wrong. How can Jordan have a secret agenda if she has no idea who I am?

Reaching behind me, I pull the door shut, closing us both back inside the apartment again.

Her brows pinch tight. "What are you doing?"

"You want to know what to call me?" Dropping my bag and the soccer ball on the floor, I lean against the back of the door, fold my arms, and smile lazily. "How about Lord and Master?"

Jordan makes a sound that comes out something like a high-pitched growl and reaches for a phone that's resting on the kitchen counter beside her. "How about you leave? I'm sure Professor Draper can arrange another tutor for you."

I shrug as if I don't care, but I know my uncle will only assign another tutor in Jordan's place. As much as I don't want to be here, I'd prefer Jordan over someone else. I might not know her reason for signing up for this, but at least I know it isn't because she's looking at me with dollar signs in her eyes the way most other girls do.

"If you can't handle being my tutor, then by all means, give him a call."

Jordan huffs, her fingers pausing over the screen of her phone, and I know I've got her. No one would ever tell my uncle they can't handle whatever he's dishing out and she knows it.

"You're a real piece of work, you know that?"

I grin, for real this time, and walk toward the living area. "You think it's easy being this much of an asshole?" Sinking down on the sofa, I reach for the remote and kick my legs up on the coffee table, crossing them at the ankle. "Getting soccer balls thrown at my head and being called a conceited donkey is not as fun as it looks."

"I can't imagine," she mutters and slaps her phone back down on the counter.

Pointing the remote at the television, I find ESPN and settle in for whatever sport is playing. "Go have your shower, Jordan," I command, my eyes fixed on the screen, "and when you come out, you can make me something to eat because I'm hungry, and then you can pretend to teach me something."

"Making you something to eat is not part of my job, unless you want to end up wearing it," she gripes as she stalks past me.

"Feisty," I murmur, but she's too far away to hear, already walking into the bathroom and slamming the door behind her.

The second I hear the shower start running, I toss the remote back on the tiny dark timber coffee table and stand. I want to know just who Jordan Elliot is, so I make my way toward her room.

The bathroom is sitting between two bedrooms so I take a guess and pick the one on the right. I have to blink when I walk inside because it looks like no girl's room I ever saw, and I've seen more than my fair share. There are no knick-knacks lining every available surface, or mementos from past events that mean something, no pictures on the wall, just … no personality at all. I wonder if Jordan even has one underneath that jockish exterior of hers.

There's a corkboard pinned to the wall so I study her schedule, grudgingly impressed. The list details an unbearable course load and subjects that only someone bright and gifted could possibly handle. It makes me feel like more of a dumb shit, if that's even possible. Resting up beside a bookshelf sits two rolled up posters. I make the mistake of unraveling one. Cristiano Ronaldo stares back at me with smoldering eyes. I shudder because it's almost enough to leave me feeling violated. The poster unravels further, revealing him in the buff, and I'm relieved to see him holding a soccer ball in front of his junk. I drop the poster like it's a rattlesnake and toss it back in the corner. Well. At least I know she's not a lesbian.

With a sigh, I spread out on my back on Jordan's bed, tucking my hands behind my head and closing my eyes. After taking a deep breath, the sweet smell of vanilla tickles my senses and my brows draw together. I know that distinct scent, don't I?

"Are you quite comfortable there?"

My lips curve instinctively, not caring that Jordan's found me in her room lying on her bed. "Not quite. Perhaps if you dimmed the lighting a little and sang me a lullaby?"

A wet towel slaps me in the face.

My eyes fly open and I drag the towel away with a chuckle. It dies quickly when I sit up on one elbow and let my gaze travel upwards. Only one word springs to mind. *Delicious.* Jordan's wearing black Lycra gym shorts. They're tiny, hugging her hips and ass in a way that makes me jealous. I want to be those gym shorts. My gaze climbs higher to the fitted tank top. It's white and thin, satisfyingly thin, and she's not wearing a bra. The outline of her nipples is clear and my pulse begins to thump hard. They aren't erect. Instead, they look soft and warm beneath the snug cotton. I lick my lips. I want to run the flat of my tongue over each one in turn, and suck them inside my mouth until they harden like the sweetest candy.

"What are you doing in my room?" Her arms cross quickly over her chest when she realizes I'm staring unapologetically at her tits.

"Huh?" I mumble.

My eyes finally reach her face, and I suck in a ragged breath. I'm not sure I even let it out. It's *her*. The blond jock from Business Law and Ethics who got chewed out for being late to class. Fuck me. How in the everloving hell didn't I realize?

"What are you doing in my room?" she enunciates clearly.

I shake my head to clear it and will the hot throbbing in my cock to calm down so I can take a breath. "I was looking for evidence of a personality," I retort and wave my hand casually, taking in the barren and boring room. "Clearly I failed."

Laughter bubbles out and she quickly presses her lips together.

"Ha!" I shout, and the sound comes out a little hoarse. "I made you laugh."

Though suddenly I wish I didn't. The sound is warm and throaty and resonates deep inside me, doing nothing to cool me off. I sit up and let the damp towel fall to my lap, hiding the thickening erection in my shorts.

"Congratulations." Jordan rolls her eyes and picks up a hoodie that's hanging off the back of the chair by her desk. She shrugs it on quickly and pushes back the hood, mussing her long, damp hair.

"Thanks." I scan the bare walls of her bedroom again. Textbooks are the only decoration on her shelves. Their spines add color to the stark white furniture. "So what's with the room, Jordan? It's like a prison cell in here."

Jordan sinks into the chair and faces me, folding her arms. "Seen the inside of one of those, have you?"

"Nope. My record is as clean as a choirboy's. So?" I prompt.

She shrugs. "I'm here on an international sports scholarship from Australia. There was only so much I could fit in my suitcase."

Once again, I'm impressed. Those kinds of scholarships are hard to come by. You have to pretty much be an athletic phenomenon to get one. Now I'm feeling the compulsion to go watch Jordan play. I want to know if she lives and breathes the game as hard as I do. I want to see her in action. I want to see her out of breath and sweaty.

"Mmmm."

"What?"

I flop back down on her bed, tucking my hands back behind my head. My eyes fix on the ceiling. I want to know about the life she left behind to come here, but I save it for another time. Instead, I ask the one that's weighing on me the most. "Why are you tutoring me?"

"Professor Draper asked me to," is her simple reply.

"And you agreed."

"Well ... yes."

"Why?" I open my eyes and tilt my head on the pillow, staring hard into her eyes. "Why you?"

"My brother is dyslexic. I helped tutor him through high school."

I grind my teeth, irritated. "So what? That somehow makes you an expert?"

Jordan's sigh is long and deep. "Not at all. I told the professor I wasn't professionally qualified to do something like this, but all he said was that I'm to provide you with some study mechanisms to help you through your final year."

Fuck senior year, I want to say, but I keep that to myself. I could've gone pro in junior year. I shouldn't even be here. The reason why I didn't is nobody's business, yet it weighs on me like a concrete block. The media was told I'd chosen to gain more experience and improve my game rather than declare for the draft. It made enough sense not to question it, but now I'm stuck, and there's every chance I'm going to fail spectacularly.

"You think you can help me?" I ask, breaking the silence.

"I don't know."

"At least you're honest," I mutter, and my eyes return to the ceiling. She isn't filling me with empty platitudes of false hope like I'd anticipated. I respect her for that.

"Can I ask a question now?"

I turn on my side, resting my head on my elbow, and look at her. It's hard not to. There's something about her that makes it difficult to drag my eyes away. Not because she's wildly beautiful, but more like she's authentic, I guess. A deep-seated knowing that Jordan is someone I can trust. With anything. "Okay."

"You wanted to know why me, well ... I want to know, why now? Why wait to get tutored so late in the game?"

I shrug. "I've never been officially diagnosed. It's not something we acknowledge in my house." Instead, my parents have chosen to sweep the embarrassment under the carpet. "And I've never been tutored." Her eyes widen, and I know she's wondering how I got this far on my own. Sheer force of will, maybe? "What's the point? My brain is wired all wrong. You can't just rewire it to make it work like everyone else's does." I pause for a moment, my jaw tensing, and I tell her what I've been told for as long as I can remember. "You can't fix stupid."

Jordan's brows draw together and her lips part, and I know she's ready to protest my statement. She has to. She's my *tutor*. But I don't want to hear it. I just don't. For a moment I hate myself. I hate the way I am. That I can't meet someone like her and feel like an equal. My hands curl into fists. I'm the cliché dumb jock that everyone likes to joke about and it frustrates me beyond all belief.

Thankfully her phone starts blaring a song I'm unfamiliar with and diverts her attention. She lets it ring out.

"Kyle …" she starts and I wince, because I'd actually forgotten she thought I was someone else.

Her phone starts up again and she exhales with an annoyed huff.

I raise my brows. "You gonna get that?"

"Wait here," she orders and leaves the room.

Not likely. That's my cue to call it a night. To go home to my apartment and tuck those angry little demons into bed. God knows they need their rest. I check my watch. Our session was supposed to finish half an hour ago.

I roll out of Jordan's bed and meet her in the kitchen where she's arguing with someone on the phone. After slinging my backpack over my shoulder, I get her attention.

"I'm not wearing the purple dress," she gripes into the phone and meets my eyes. "It's too loud."

"I have to go," I mouth silently.

Jordan shakes her head at me, holding up a palm for me to wait. "What's it saying?" she says into the phone. "Here I am. Fuck me. That's what it's saying."

I wave and she frowns. "I have to go," she says. "I'll pick you up."

That comment seems to cause a lot of loud protesting from the other end.

"Fine. Pick me up then. See you in a bit."

I'm already at the door when she hangs up.

"Party?" I ask.

"My first frat party."

Jordan says it with a grimace, and while she isn't broadcasting naïve innocence, she doesn't really have a *party animal* vibe about her either, meaning it's likely she's a bit clueless as to how wild they can get. I have to stop myself from offering to take her because that would be a lunatic move on my part. I'm on a girl hiatus. That means no dick near, on, or in, any girl's pussy. It's supposed to stop me from being distracted and keep me focused on football, but I'm a healthy, horny, twenty-one-year-old male. That pretty much means I'm a walking boner. So in actual fact, this break is going to kill me instead. Or blister my right hand.

Color floods Jordan's cheeks, and I realize I've been standing there holding her eyes for longer than necessary. Her tongue darts out to lick along her lower lip and my gaze drops to her mouth. It's lush and pink, like cotton candy, and my sweet tooth is craving a taste something fierce.

"Well, enjoy," I tell her and wrench open the front door before I do something rash, like pin her to the wall and feast on her mouth like a starving man. I pause before I step outside her apartment. "Can I offer a word of advice from a guy who's been going to frat parties since forever?"

"Sure," she replies, and the solitary word comes out a little breathy, like she wants me feasting on her mouth too.

I bite back a groan. "Don't accept a drink from anyone you don't trust with your life. Okay?"

I leave then, already halfway down the hall when she sticks her head out and yells, "Wait! What about our next—"

Turning, I walk backwards for a second. "My uncle gave me your number. I'll call you."

After jogging down the stairwell, I open the zipper on my bag and take out my baseball cap and sunglasses, putting them both on. It's early evening as I thread my way around the parking lot, but there's still a tinge of light in the sky and the air is fresh. It's just what I need to cool the lust punching through my body as if there's an animal under my skin waiting to be unleashed.

The hand that tugs the keys from my pocket is a little shaky, and shit I need to get home and have a cold shower. Ice cold.

Students are coming and going everywhere, the area dense with partygoers in various stages of getting where they need to be. My car stands out amongst the others. A brand-new tricked-out Chevrolet Suburban in black. Pretty much everyone on campus knows it's mine, as do most off campus.

"'Sup, Madden!" someone calls out.

I wave but move quickly to my car, pausing to take two slips of paper from beneath the windshield wiper. Wild squeals come from nearby when I pocket them. I don't read the notes but I know they're phone numbers with sexually suggestive words attached. A quick glance around shows a group of blushing girls staring my way. I wonder how long they've been standing near my car. Jordan is the sole focus on my mind right now, so all I can do is flash them an absentminded grin as I beep the locks on my SUV.

"Yo, Brody!" A couple of junior fraternity brothers jog over, and I pause. "You coming to the party tonight?"

"Can't. Leaving for the away game tomorrow."

They nod their heads in tandem. "Cool."

My phone vibrates in my shorts, so I tug it out, glancing at the screen. My father. If I don't answer, he'll just keep ringing until I do. Self-absorbed prick. He can't seem to understand that the world doesn't revolve around people kissing his ass. "I gotta get this, guys. See you later, yeah?"

They jog off in the direction they came, and I slide inside my car as I answer the phone. "Dad."

"Your mother says you haven't been by in two weeks. Dinner at the house, Sunday at six."

My jaw ticks. *Hello, Son, how are you? I saw you kick ass at the game this weekend. I'm so fucking proud.* "We have an away game. I'm not sure I'll be home by then."

I will be, but I'm going to be too exhausted to deal with family drama.

"Monday then. Make sure you win," is his parting comment before hanging up. I toss it angrily in the center cup holder and start the car, backing out quickly. When I arrive back at my apartment, Jaxon is spread out on the navy leather couch, scrolling on his phone, and Eddie's there yelling at a game of baseball playing out on ESPN. He's one of our outside linebackers and the biggest guy on the entire team. His elbows are resting on his knees, and he's leaning close as though they can actually hear his screaming insults.

Eddie tears his eyes from the screen to glance at me. "Where the fuck you been?"

Jaxon looks up from his phone, the same question in his eyes.

"Sorry, Mom. Is it past curfew?"

"Not yet, Son," he replies, smirking, and returns his eyes to the television as he speaks, "because Damien bought beer and we're all going to the house tonight for the party."

"I'm not going," I tell them and veer off, dumping my bag in my room. It's a toss-up between a cold shower or jacking off, when my stomach growls. I head for the kitchen to make a sandwich instead.

Damien's in there. He's got a girl pressed up against the counter, his hands up her tiny skirt and his lips attached to her neck. Her head's thrown back, one leg around his waist as he grinds himself against her.

I reach around them and grab a loaf of bread. My head is stuck in the fridge when the girl lets out a deep moan. I turn, my arms loaded with cheese, tomato, and thick slices of ham. Damien has his fingers shoved deep inside her, and it's all on display.

I shake my head with disgust. I'm not a prude, but unless you're participating in some kind of wild orgy, sex is best kept private, and it's one of the reasons why I wanted this apartment off campus.

"Dude, that's not sanitary," I tell him, dumping everything on the counter as far from their sexual exhibition as possible. "I'm trying to make something to eat here."

Damien's lips detach from the girl's neck, but he makes no effort to move. His conquest barely acknowledges my presence. Her pupils are heavily dilated and her body languid. She's wasted and Damien looks no better off. "You want her after?"

I pause halfway through slicing a tomato to raise my brows at him. "Do I want your seconds? No thanks, I'd rather …" My mind immediately goes to Jordan and how I want to— I cut that thought off at the knees.

The girl squeals as Damien keeps up his ministrations. "You'd rather what?"

"I'd rather concede defeat to Oklahoma."

"Dude!" Eddie yells from the living room as I slap ham and cheese on my sandwich. "I hear that from your mouth again, I'll wash it out with soap."

"Yes, Mom!" I shout back.

Leaving my mess on the counter, I maneuver around the sexed-up couple and make for my room, taking a giant bite as I go.

"Oh hey, I forgot tell you." Jaxon looks up from his phone, and the smugness on his face halts me in my tracks.

"What?" I mumble around a mouthful of ham and cheese.

"I ran into that blond chick in our law class."

My body snaps to immediate attention, each muscle tightening. Going by the gleam in Jaxon's eyes, I know exactly who he's referring to. Perching myself on the arm of the couch, I pretend interest in the television as I eat my sandwich. "What blond chick?"

"The one dad chewed out. She sat next to you, remember?" Jaxon's grin is self-assured as he tosses his phone on the coffee table, prepared to give the conversation his focus. Talking about girls—who he wants to do, who he's done, who he won't do—is his favorite subject. I will never understand how he can party so hard, and sleep with so many girls, while managing to maintain a perfect GPA. "I think she likes me."

Eddie snorts. "You think anything with a pulse likes you."

Jaxon ignores Eddie's verbal jab. "She's going to the frat party tonight. I'm going to make my big move," he announces, grabbing hold of his dick over his shorts and giving it a lewd squeeze.

I swallow down the last bite of sandwich like its sawdust, and with it goes the territorial growl that was rising in my throat. When I speak, my voice comes out like sandpaper. "Yeah? What's her name?"

"Jordan. Cool, huh? We match. Jaxon and Jordan."

The thought of my cousin's hands all over Jordan makes me want to snap something in two. Namely him. And it's odd, because Jordan's nobody special. At least not to me. She's just my tutor.

"Oh that's so adorable," Eddie interjects with sarcasm and an eye roll. "Next you'll have cutesy matching his and hers outfits."

Eddie's in a mood, and when he puts his right leg up on the table to elevate it, I know his old football injury pains him.

Standing up, I brush crumbs from my hands and jerk my chin at his knee. "You should put a pressure band on that."

"Yeah," Eddie mumbles. "I worked it too hard at the gym this morning."

"Where are you going?" Jaxon calls out when I start for the bathroom.

"To have a shower," I say over my shoulder. A cold one. "Looks like we've got a party to get to tonight."

CHAPTER 6

JORDAN

I can hear muffled sounds of student laughter, shouts in the hallway, and parties in progress, all while I sit at my desk trying to study. A heavy textbook lies open in front of me, the macroeconomics model mocking me with its complexity. Paragraphs of text are smothered in blinding yellow. I know I made the highlights because the colored marker rests in my hand, but I don't remember doing it.

Kyle Davis is like malware. He's infiltrated my brain in a sneak virus attack. Every time I try and focus, he pops in my head the same way internet windows pop up faster than you can shut them down. You know when that happens you've opened something you shouldn't have.

I slam my text closed and toss down my marker with disgust. It skitters off the edge of the desk and flies under the bed behind me. When I spin in my chair to retrieve it, my eyes fall to the rumpled sheets where he made himself comfortable earlier.

My pulse gives a little leap at the reminder of him lying there with hooded eyes after my shower. If only I can pretend he's the asshole he wants me to think he is, but I know he's not. The professor has obviously forced him into this, and don't we all lash out when backed into a corner?

When someone knows our weaknesses and can so easily betray us with them? Maybe it wouldn't be so obvious to anyone else, but it is to me. My brother used to lash out the same way.

Turning back around, I open my laptop and go to the tab where Facebook sits open. Clicking on the search box, I type in 'Kyle Davis.' It's not stalking. It's called research, and something we're actively encouraged to do in college. I'm sure he doesn't look as good as I remember him. If I can just look him up and see a few inopportune drunk photos, it will clear the distraction right up, and I can get back to my textbook.

I go to click on enter when Skype dings at me. The repetitious bell chime is loud and demanding, and why wouldn't it be when it's Nicky on the other line.

I answer the call and my brother's face floods my screen, the gray beanie on his head reminding me it's winter in Australia, and cold.

My immediate smile is warm. "Hey, Nicky."

He returns it. "How's my favorite sister?"

My smile evolves into an eye roll. "You mean your only sister?"

"And thank God for that."

"Har, har."

He leans back in his chair and stretches. Halfway through a yawn, he asks, "How was soccer?"

I do the math in my head. Sydney is fifteen hours ahead so it's Saturday morning back home. *Home.* A wave of homesickness rolls over me, and I have to force it back. "Good," I manage to get out.

"Good? Is that all I get?"

"We won," I offer.

"And?" he prompts.

"I scored two goals. One was a header in the final five minutes that clinched the game."

Nicky shakes his head, like he can't believe it but can, all at the same time. He's proud, but he always struggles to put his feelings into words. "You're fuckin' incredible," he eventually says and looks away for a minute.

I don't miss the flicker of sadness in his eyes that he tries to hide, or the way he swallows hard. It doesn't matter how much he wants this success for me, or that he wants it even more than I do, it's because every victory takes me closer to my dream and one step further from him. We're all the other has. It's been the two of us against the world, right from the very beginning. And now it's not even that.

A pang flares white-hot in my chest. "Nicky," I whisper and raise my hand to the screen, placing my palm flat against its buzzing warmth. He raises his own, and for a brief moment we're joined despite being half a world away. "You are too."

"Aww shucks," he says teasingly and drops his hand. The moment passes.

I tell him about getting hazed. It makes him laugh and hearing it warms my insides. In turn he tells me about his night out at an elitist party he went to with his best mate, Ben, and how they got kicked out when his wasted friend was caught peeing in the potted plant inside the house.

"Oh my god, that's disgusting," I screech. "And the guy works for a commercial landscaping business. Doesn't peeing on plants go against every ethical code he works for?"

Nicky laughs. "I know, right?"

Before I know it, half an hour passes by and a sharp rap at my open bedroom door interrupts our chat.

"Why aren't you ready to go?" Leah demands to know, and I half turn in my chair. Her dark brown hair is loose and curled, and she's wearing a pair of black hot pants with a floaty top the color of ripe strawberries. It sets off her gorgeous mocha toned skin and lightly muscled shoulders.

When she see's my brother on the screen she waves. "Hey, Nicky."

"Leah," he says. "How's it going?"

"Could be better."

"Yeah?"

"We've got a party to get to and a win to celebrate, but I have to wrestle your sister into a dress and get her out the door."

"Good luck with that," he says and yawns again. "I'll leave you to it. Catch up with you later, Jords." Nicky leans in, a finger hovering over the keyboard to end the Skype call. He looks up briefly, eyes the same clear blue as mine stare at me hard. "Be safe, okay?"

After his parting words, the screen goes black.

"Well ... that was intense." Leah shudders dramatically.

"What was?" I ask and shut my laptop with all haste because Facebook is now sitting wide open, Kyle's name blinking brightly in the search box.

"How Nicky went all fierce before he hung up. It was kinda hot actually."

"Gross, Leah." I stand up and make a grab for the purple dress she's scrunching in her hands. "That's my brother."

"What? I can't think your brother's hot?"

"No. It's a rule," I inform her as I toss the dress on the bed and peel off my hoodie. I drop it on the floor. "Thou shalt not covet thy best friend's brother or thy best friend shalt barf."

Off goes my white tank top, and I peel the gym shorts down my legs without inhibition. After years of locker rooms, stripping in front of my friend and teammate isn't much of a big deal.

"Thou friend has eyes in her head, and he's hot as hell so shut your mouth."

I snort in reply as I slide the purple dress up my legs and twitch it into place. It's stretchy and strapless, and far too bright. My mother always taught me never to hate, so I'm going to say that I really, really dislike purple. It stems from my childhood fear of Barney the Dinosaur. He was my favorite plush toy, and I took him everywhere to the annoyance of my brother, most especially because Barney was afforded certain privileges, like his own candy treats after dinner, which would go to me, naturally, because poor Barney couldn't swallow them. One day Nicky showed me a picture of Barney on the internet, complete with red eyes and wielding a bloodstained axe. I still live with the trauma *and* the fear of the color purple. Purple means Barney, and Barney is bad.

I cast my gaze down to take in the dress with a shudder. I don't wear a strapless bra beneath the stretchy fabric simply because I don't need it. My curves are less than remarkable. My lifelong membership in the itty-bitty-titty committee is firmly, and unfortunately, entrenched.

"Turn around," Leah commands.

I turn around and she tugs at the back hem until it sits in its proper place, which is alarmingly close to my butt cheeks.

"Some guy is gonna eat you up tonight, Elliott. You look delicious." She says it with glee, and only because she has Hayden, who's like the asshole antithesis, so she doesn't know any better. Even still, my thoughts turn immediately to the male who recently inhabited my room and I repress a shiver.

"I do?" Turning to face her, I fold my arms and arch a brow. "Better than I look doused in chocolate syrup?"

"We should go," she says quickly and spins to leave.

"Not so fast," I growl ominously and make a grab for her strawberry shirt. It's my luck that it's floaty and fans out behind her. I seize a fistful and she halts in her tracks, wary of it tearing right off her body.

"It was awesome!" Hayden shouts from somewhere inside the apartment. By the echo I'm guessing it's the fridge and he's got his head stuck in it. Leah's boyfriend has a colossal frame that comes with a matching appetite. The dude needs constant fueling just to breathe. "Leah showed me photos!"

I gasp loudly and let go of her shirt, my eyes rounding in horror at her betrayal. "You posted the photos?"

"I only showed them to Hayden. Honest. I wouldn't post them online. Come on, Jordan," she needles and starts petting my shoulder. "Everyone gets hazed. It's a rite of passage. And it was only a little bit of syrup."

"A little bit?" Hayden shouts again, and the sound is muffled because his mouth is no doubt full of food. The fridge door slams shut, and the tinkling sound of jars and bottles reaches my ears. "Where did you even find that much? And can you get more? I want to lick—"

"Okay, Hayden!" I yell back, cutting him off because I don't need to hear about him licking Leah's body parts. Not ever, but especially not right now, not while my skin feels too tight for my body and my mind is entertaining wild fantasies about a guy I'm supposed to be *tutoring*.

After sliding on a pair of gold-colored sandals, I get Leah to help me with my makeup. I know where my talents lie, and facial enhancement is not one of them. My attempt at sex kitten eyes usually makes my face look like a cat attacked it with a black marker. At least Leah knows what she's doing.

When she's finished, she picks up a plastic bag off my bed that's full of something suspiciously flamboyant.

"What's that?" I ask warily, because the bag appeared atop my sheets as if Leah conjured it with evil magic. She reaches in and plucks out a pink lei, slinging it around my neck before I can protest. I'm then handed a pair of sunglasses, the plastic frames a matching fuchsia with dark lenses. "Um … What the hell?"

Leah puts on her own lei in eye-gouging yellow, slides on sunglasses in the same color, and grins brightly. "It's a beach-themed party."

"Seriously?" I groan and jam the pink glasses on my face, because at least then I can barely see her.

"Yes, really. Be thankful we're not in bikinis. Hayden vetoed that idea," she mutters.

We arrive at the party and a shirtless Hayden, wearing only board shorts and flip flops, slings a heavy bicep over both mine and Leah's shoulders.

"Look at me with two dates," he says with a leering grin, maneuvering us toward the house. "It's like I'm on the set of *The Bachelor*."

"Just remember who gets the rose at the end of the night, He-Man," she says with a mock growl and elbows him in the side. With a fortifying shot of vodka already under our belts, it causes the three of us to stumble slightly.

Hayden's arm slips from my shoulder and he wraps Leah up, lifting her off the ground with ease. She squeals and tugs awkwardly at the hem of her shirt where it rides up her torso.

"Always you, beautiful," I hear him murmur in her ear.

His expression is soft, the way it always is when he looks at her, and while I don't begrudge their loved-up relationship, it's so very intense it sometimes makes me feel like a lonely, solitary island.

"Save the humping each other for when you get home," I suggest as we make our way up the front path.

Pulse-thumping music blares through the open doorway where two young, burly guys stand sentry. Bouncers for a frat party? That's either really smart, or they're really elitist. I'm hoping for smart. If it's one thing I cannot stand, it's snobs and bullies.

"Don't worry. We'll find you someone to hump too, Elliott," Leah replies, her voice brimming with encouragement.

As if on cue, a guy dressed in a French maid outfit complete with frilly knickers bursts from the front door, whooping. Two guys race out giving chase, both of them engulfed in thick white foam from head to toe. With their eyes barely visible I'm surprised they can see, and I realize they actually can't when one of them stumbles and goes down, face planting in the grass. He doesn't get back up.

I turn raised brows on my friends. "Maybe him, you think?"

A bikini-clad girl comes trotting out to bring up the rear, drink in hand. She teeters on her heels, waving her arms to get balance when she comes to a stop by the prone foam-covered form on the lawn. She crouches and leans into his ear, yelling, "Are you okaaayyyy?"

He doesn't move.

Bypassing the pair, Hayden leads us inside, through hordes of partygoers, until we arrive in the backyard where a keg stand is set up in the corner. Strings of green-colored lights adorn the fence line like a parsley garnish, and plastic blow-up palm trees decorate the lawn. An inflatable slide takes pride of place in the center. I watch a guy barrel down it face first, smacking into a pile of shrieking girls huddled in the little pool at the bottom.

Leah hands me a Solo cup of beer, and I take it, knowing I'll be sitting on it all night. I don't doubt it's cheap, nasty stuff that will leave me disgustingly bloated. I take a small sip, grimace, and a mechanical surfboard set up opposite the inflatable slide catches my attention. It's nestled in a bed of sand and being ridden by a beefy, shirtless guy dressed in a Baywatch lifeguard outfit. In one hand he holds a cup of beer, his arm outstretched so it doesn't spill.

The crowd surrounding him chants, "Hassel-hoff! Hassel-hoff!"

He's doing really well until he gets shoved off by a guy wearing a yellow grass skirt and a coconut bra. Everyone cheers when Hasselhoff staggers and falls over, his beer tipping over his face and chest.

"Really?" I rip the sunglasses from my face so Leah can get the full brunt of my glare. "This is your idea of good night out?"

Leah waves a hand at both the surfboard and the wasted Hasselhoff, who has apparently decided stripping is preferable to wearing beer-soaked shorts. The crowd chants anew at his antics.

"What? You don't want a turn?"

"Does it make me a killjoy if I say *hell no*? Because I'll happily wear that tag."

Leah laughs and after jamming the sunglasses back on my face, she grabs hold of my arm. "Come on. There's dancing in the basement."

We abandon Hayden to his circle of friends, and I'm led back inside the house and down a narrow set of stairs. It's hard to see, even more so with the dark lenses, so I traverse them carefully, one hand on the railing and the other holding my drink.

We reach the basement and it's overflowing with bodies, dark corners, and flashing multi-colored lights. "Happy Little Pill" by Troye Sivan plays, and hips thrust to the deep, sensual beat, hands sliding over exposed skin, tongues entwined as people make out on the dance floor.

"Chug your beer so we can dance," Leah orders from beside me where we stand on the fringes.

"No, I'm good. I can hold it and dance at the same time."

"Just do it. I don't want you sloshing it all over my new shirt while you crack out your Sprinkler move."

"I'm a professional athlete," I snap, highly offended because I did it one time. *One time!* And only because Hayden pretended he'd never heard of it. Jerk. "I know how to bust a move without losing control."

"Of course you do," Leah says, her tone soothing as if I'm an enraged beast.

I chug the damn beer.

Her grin is smug.

We're on the dance floor for mere moments when two hands plant themselves on my hips from behind. I tense and spin around, my eyes landing on a flirty grin and deep dimples.

"We meet again," Jaxon says.

He's like a bad, sexy penny, popping up all over campus. "So it seems."

"Cool outfit, Jordan. Very original."

"Are you teasing me?"

Jaxon's hazel eyes light up and his fingers dig in, pulling me close until there's no space between us. "That depends. Do you like being teased?"

"Only if it's done right."

Those pretty eyes of his slide down to my mouth. I shouldn't do it, but I bite down on my bottom lip, running my teeth over it until it's a little red and swollen. His gaze heats and a tinge of color hits his cheeks. He groans and I'm genuinely surprised I've managed to get to him.

"And you're a master."

I laugh because surely he's joking.

Jaxon spins me around, making me move with him to the music. I look over his shoulder for Leah. The crowd of dancing bodies have swallowed her, but I spy Hayden with his back to me. He's now wearing her yellow lei and sunglasses. His arms are wrapped tight around a body wearing a strawberry shirt, so I know she's okay.

"I didn't see you at the soccer match," I say, my eyes returning to Jaxon.

His lips curve with pleasure. "You looked for me?"

I shrug. "Maybe."

"How can you *maybe* look for someone?"

"I just happened to notice you weren't there."

The song ends but Jaxon doesn't stop dancing. He keeps hold of me until another one starts. "Did you win?" he asks.

"Of course."

Two girls try cutting in on our dance over the next two songs, the last one moving off with a glare aimed my way. "You should've danced with her," I tell him, my eyes following the girl as she stalks away.

"Why?"

"Because I don't know what you want, Jaxon," I say in all seriousness and lift the sunglasses from my eyes to rest them on my head, "but I'm not looking for anything with anyone, so you shouldn't waste your time with me."

Jaxon stops dancing and I still along with him when he stares down at me, a gleam hitting his hazel eyes. "Is that a challenge?"

"No!" I choke out, overwhelmed by his persistence.

"I'm going to the little girls' room," Leah yells in my ear from behind.

I turn my head. Hayden has hold of her hand, his jaw tight and his eyes on fire. Oh seriously? They're going to do the nasty here? She glances between Jaxon and I uncertainly.

"You uh … okay?"

"I'll look after her," Jaxon replies without taking his eyes from mine.

"See that you do," she says before they disappear up the stairs.

Jaxon slides his hands down and over the curve of my ass.

"Hey!" My reaction is reflexive. I give him a little shove and take a step back. As if waiting for just such a moment, another girl is on him, determination her expression of choice. Jaxon lets out an audible growl when she steps between us.

"What do you want, Lindsay?" he asks.

With Jaxon distracted, I make my escape, my intent to find another drink and see if Paige and Becker are here. Turning, I smack into a hard chest. It's attached to two brawny arms holding shot glasses of clear liquid. They rise quickly to avoid spillage.

"Sorry, I—" My apology dies quickly when I look up into the face of Kyle Davis. My pulse skyrockets.

His gaze rakes me over slow and deliberate, his eyes peeling away my dress, leaving me exposed and breathless.

Just when I'm starting to turn blue from the oxygen he's sucked from the room, he leans in close, lips brushing my ear, and says, "You wore the *fuck me* dress."

My toes curl in my pretty gold sandals. "The fuck me dress?" I repeat dumbly, my voice low and embarrassingly breathy. He was paying attention to my phone conversation with Leah.

"The very one." He pulls back, his height and wide shoulders overpowering the entire basement. I tip my head back to meet his eyes. They're impish, but they're also hungry, and it sets off an ache between my legs that throbs to the beat of the music. "You wear it well."

I don't know what to say. I'm unsettled and suddenly parched, so I steal one of the shot glasses that rests in his hand. I tip it down my throat, the burn of tequila making my eyes tear up.

His nostrils flare. "What did I say about taking drinks from people you don't trust?"

The dark tone of his voice has me reaching for the second shot. He sounds like my brother, but I definitely don't think of him that way. I down it too, trying not to choke.

"What are you saying? I can't trust you, Mr. Kyle Davis?"

He cringes and rakes fingers through his tousled hair. "Jordan ... can we talk?" His eyes glance about the room before they return to mine. "Somewhere private?"

The blessed warmth of alcohol has loosened me up—enough that I agree to his request against my better judgment. "Okay."

Removing the plastic shot glasses from my possession, he tosses them away. Then he takes my hand, enclosing it in his large, calloused palm. Zings shoot through me. "Where are we—"

I break off when I realize those nearest us are staring. The music still pounds, and dancers still grind, but they're doing it while watching us, Jaxon and Lindsay included. Jaxon's eyes are on our joined hands before they slide up, confusion clouding his eyes. The girl he's with doesn't look confused. She looks ready to maim.

Unnerved by the focus, I shift backwards and the grip on my hand tightens.

"You two know each other?" Jaxon asks, and there's hurt in his tone that I don't understand.

"Yes," I blurt out, for a moment forgetting the confidentiality of our tutoring agreement in my haste to explain. "He's—"

"We're dating," Kyle interrupts quickly.

"What?" Lindsay screeches from her narrow-eyed stance beside Jaxon. She looks at me. "*You're* dating Brody Madden?"

"What?" A hush falls over the room. Even the music is kind enough to hit an instrumental so everyone can eavesdrop with ease. "No! I— Wait ... Brody Madden? I don't—"

"Let's go," Kyle growls. I'm pulled roughly from the basement. People sweep to the side like he's parting the Red Sea. I'm oddly breathless, and confused, and somehow still managing to enjoy the heat of our joined hands.

"Stop," I gasp when we leave the basement.

He ignores me and I'm dragged toward another set of stairs. We pass by Leah coming out of a side hallway, fluffing her hair and readjusting her top. She stops dead and her eyes are dinner plates. She tries to say something but her mouth resembles a fish, opening and closing without speech.

"What ..."

Kyle doesn't pause his determined stride. I find myself jogging up the second set of stairs behind him or risk getting dragged along the ground. "I'll be down in a minute," I call out to Leah over my shoulder. "We're just going for a quick chat."

"A quick *chat*?" she bleats weakly.

Leah disappears from view as we walk along a dim, narrow hallway. He shoves open a door, and I'm pulled inside behind him.

"Hey!" shrieks a girl in her bra and panties. She's wrapped around a shirtless guy in a pair of jeans.

"Out," Kyle commands.

"Dude! What the f—"

The guy spins toward us, eyes livid. His anger drains quickly when he looks at us. "Oh sh-shit. Brody. Sorry." He ducks, grabbing at clothing and dragging his half-naked girl out behind him. The door shuts swiftly behind them, closing us in together.

It's suddenly quiet, the basement music a muted thump from below. We stand facing each other in the darkened room, and it's like I've been thrown in the lion's cage at the zoo. Pale moonlight shines through the window, and I see his chest moving up and down, his pulse throbbing in his neck.

I clear my throat. "Why is everyone calling you Brody?"

He pauses for a beat. When he speaks, his voice is hoarse, and I know I'm not the only one affected. There's attraction between us, hot and intense, but I ignore it because I feel like I've been played. "That's my name. Brody Madden."

"I see," I reply, when I don't really see at all. I sink to the edge of the bed behind me because my legs are jelly. "Brody Madden," I repeat, more to myself than anything.

I look up. He's shifted closer—too close. His deep brown eyes are wary, his shoulders and chest powerful, like glory and golden fire as they flex beneath the muscle tee shirt he wears. His calves are honed, hips slender, and his stance tense. He's number twenty-two. Wide receiver. Football royalty. And Jaxon's cousin, which makes Professor Draper his uncle. "You play football," I say in the silence.

Kyle ... no, Brody, folds his arms. "Yes."

"Oh my god!" I bite out at the confirmation. "You said we were dating! Why would you do that?"

"Because you were about to tell the whole world you're my tutor!" he replies hotly. "I had to say something. I was holding your hand dammit. It was the first thing that came to mind."

"I was not about to tell the world!" I yell defensively, shooting to my feet. "I was about to ... Oh shit, I was." I sink back to the edge of the bed, blaming the chugged beer and tequila shots for my unsteady legs. I place a hand on my forehead. It's hot and clammy. "I don't understand. Professor Draper said I was tutoring Kyle Davis."

"That doesn't make sense. Kyle Davis is his TA."

"Well why would he …" My mind flashes back to my meeting with the professor and there's a light-bulb moment. "Oh."

"Oh?"

"He didn't actually give me your name," I admit. "He handed me your information but it got caught up with other papers from his desk. I must have picked up the wrong sheet."

Brody begins pacing in front of me, and it makes the room spin. He shoots me a hooded glower, his tongue snaking out to lick along his lush bottom lip. My eyes follow its path.

"This whole tutoring thing is a bad idea."

"I agree completely," I reply, my heart beating hard and fast. I drag my gaze from his mouth and the effort leaves me dizzy. "But you know what's worse?"

He halts his pacing and pins me with his eyes. "What?"

"Failing."

His jaw ticks as he stands there staring down at me, tension thick in the air. "I'm not going to fail."

"Of course not. What would your professor know?" I snap, standing with a sudden surge of irritation. "If football's everything to you, you can't afford to fail."

Done with this conversation, I make for the door. Twisting the knob, I shove it open and blinding light streams in. I turn back. "But I guess you already know that."

It was meant to be a parting shot, but I don't make it out the door.

Brody's hand grips my shoulder, and I'm pulled back inside the room. He closes the door behind us and nudges my back up against it. He pins me in place with his hips, both hands planting flat on the door above my shoulders. His movements aren't rough, but they're forceful, and air leaves my lungs in a rush.

"You can't go out there."

"Newsflash, Brody. That's the *exit*. You expect me to go out the window?"

"Everyone thinks we're in here together."

"We *are* in here together."

He clears the matter up. "Having sex."

"Well that's just bloody awesome, isn't it?" I push back against him, and it brings us flush together, our bodies aligning seamlessly. "We're not *having sex*, and we're not *dating*."

"Stop it," he groans and grinds his hips into me.

I freeze. "Are you … *humping* me?"

"Of course not," Brody says and turns his head into my neck. I hear him exhale, long and ragged, his breath ghosting along my bare shoulder. My hands shake and I fist them so he doesn't see how affected I am. "Just … wait a minute."

"For what?" I whip out, anxious to leave. "The Tardis to magically appear and deliver me home?"

His lips twitch, but when I wriggle against him a guttural sound escapes his throat. His hips jerk forward, the bulge in his pants now a hard, throbbing pulse against my belly.

My body stills, the feel of him against me forcing an internal battle of need. "So help me, Brody, if you don't get off me right this instant I'm going to … to …" Dammit, I can't think. I can't deliver threats when he's pressed so close, his skin damp from the heat of the room and smelling of soap.

Brody's chuckle is low and breathy. "What are you going to do?"

"I'm your *tutor*," I hiss.

After a pause, his hands slip from the door behind me and he steps back, the moonlight leaving shadows on his face. "You're right," he says, and I breathe through the disappointment because I rather wish I wasn't.

"And you need to go back downstairs and clear up the whole farce about us dating," I tell him.

Brody cocks his head, dragging his bottom lip inside his mouth. He's contemplating me like I'm an algebra problem he needs to solve. "Is it so bad to have everyone think we're dating?"

I raise my brows.

"Tutor me like the professor wants. He's right, Jordan. You both are. I can't afford to fail, and it's possible I might," he says, looking away, and I know the admission is difficult. "I'm lucky I made it this far to be honest. I don't know if there's anything you can do that will help, but I guess I'm willing to try. And us dating will be a good cover for the study time we spend together."

"Seriously? No. The very idea is ridiculous. I'm not—"

His eyes narrow as he cuts me off. "Unless you're already dating someone?"

"I'm not dating anyone, but I don't plan to either."

"Good, then it's settled."

"It's not settled." I shake my head, but inside I'm wavering. My brother had been the same way. Frustrating, stubborn … vulnerable. It's hard to admit when you need help, and Brody doesn't have the luxury of time on his side. This is senior year. Do or die. No second chances.

"Football is everything to me, Jordan." He breathes in deep through his nose, letting it out as he meets my gaze. His expression is somber, fear lurking in his eyes. "I can't risk losing it."

"Fine!" I heave a frustrated sigh, knowing I'll regret this decision when the haze of alcohol wears off. "I'll do it your way."

Brody's lips curve.

"On one condition," I add.

The smile falls and resignation weights his voice. "What do you want?"

Your shirt, I think reflexively. *I want it off. I want to tutor you without your shirt.*

What am I thinking?

God, but whatever I'm getting myself into is not going to be good. I close my eyes and drag in a lungful of air. When I open them Brody is watching me, his expression now unreadable. "I want you to stop calling yourself stupid. Being dyslexic doesn't affect how smart you are, it affects your ability to learn. You just need more time."

Brody huffs sharply, frustrated. "I don't have time."

"I know," I reply simply. "That's why you have me."

CHAPTER 7

BRODY

"Do I?"

Do I have you?

Because damn, there's want inside me, crowding out every other emotion, like sense and self-preservation.

My heart bangs in my chest and it won't slow down. I tell myself it's because it's been too long. Celibacy isn't natural. My dick is craving hot, wet friction, not this abnormal prison I've sentenced it to. But deep down inside, something is different. Jordan is smart. Determined and talented. Real. With the same drive to succeed that I have. I'm responding to all that on some fundamental level that I can't begin to acknowledge.

"Yes. As your tutor." Jordan licks her lips. She's read the innuendo in my tone and it's unnerved her.

I take a deep breath, inhaling her vanilla scent. It must be her shampoo because I can smell it in her hair. God, it's good.

"As my tutor," I reiterate.

"Okay then." She gives a nod and reaches behind her back. "I need to get back to my friends." Twisting the handle, the door opens and she's through it before I can explain she can't just leave like that. She's throwing herself to the wolves. I don't date. I never have. My relationship-free status is common knowledge. There's going to be gossip and bitchy speculation, and she needs to know how to handle it.

"Jordan, wait!" I call out.

But it's too late. She's already reached the bottom of the stairs where her friends are waiting. I've met Hayden a few times. He's one of the good guys, and I know he and Leah have been tight since high school. We've always acknowledged each other on campus and had a mutual beer once or twice at parties, but now his eyes are tracking me down the stairs, his brow furrowed in a suspicious glower.

It deepens when I come up behind Jordan. She gives a quiet little squeak when I take hold of her hips, tugging her close so her back aligns with my chest. It's a proprietary gesture and speaks volumes.

I give him a nod. "Hayden Crosby."

"Brody Madden." His voice is cooler than I've ever heard it. "You remember Leah?"

My gaze shifts to his girlfriend. I register her same suspicious glower and offer a guileless grin. "You play soccer like Jordan, right?"

Some of the tension leaves her shoulders. "I play fullback, but Jordan," Leah replies with a nod at her friend, "is our superstar forward."

Of course she is. I'm getting the impression that Jordan Elliott is fast becoming Colton Park University's shiny new diamond, complete with an all-around good girl reputation to back it up. How far will I have to dig to reach the wicked layers that lie beneath? I've seen glimpses so I know they're there.

"And new to the team," I say to Leah, interrupting a conversation between her and Jordan that appears to involve nothing but facial expressions. "You always haze your teammates with chocolate syrup?"

The silent communication stops and Jordan groans. It vibrates through my chest and makes me want to rub against her. Before I embarrass myself by doing just that, I drop my hold and move to her side, yet I still find myself taking hold of her hand like a ship needing an anchor point. Her palm is small and damp, betraying her discomfort. Is it the situation that unnerves her, or me?

"I'm sure it's nothing on what you do to your new teammates, Brody," Leah retorts, and even though she's holding a cup of beer, her eyes are sharp on mine and Jordan's physical connection.

"We don't haze our teammates. It's a completely demoralizing and uncivilized activity." I manage to say that with a straight face until Hayden snorts loudly and we both laugh.

A quick glance at my watch shows it's getting late. We have an away game tomorrow, and I need to be up early, sharp and fresh. I give Jordan's hand a squeeze to get her attention. Our eyes meet and I'm struck anew at their clarity. "Ready to leave?"

"Leave?"

"I've got an early start tomorrow. I'd like to see you home first."

Jordan jolts with surprise. Has she forgotten our dating arrangement entirely? There are girls who would jump at a chance like this, even if it's just a pretense, so her reluctance is a blow to my ego.

"Yes, Jordan. You should let Brody *see you* home," Leah adds.

Jordan's eyes narrow at her friend's interference. "Actually, I think I'm just going to walk home in a little bit. It's nice out and it's not far." She smiles at me, polite and a little frosty. Jordan doesn't like being pushed. "Don't let me keep you from leaving."

I lean in until my lips brush her ear, pushing through the distance she's trying to create. She shivers and it takes considerable restraint not to tongue her lobe and take it in my mouth.

"Is this how you treat the guys you date? Because you need to work on that or no one's going to believe you're hot for me at all."

"And what am I supposed to do," she hisses back. "Stick my tongue down your throat in front of everyone?"

Hell yes. I want to sit up and beg for those luscious lips. Instead, I shrug like it's neither here nor there. "If you think it will help."

"We need some rules," she mutters.

Jordan is talking about drawing lines in the sand that I'm not allowed to cross. It sounds smart in theory, but I don't like idea. "Let me drive you home and we can talk about it."

I manage to extract her from her friends, but we don't get five steps before I'm bailed up by my teammate. Jordan comes to a stop beside me, her shoulder brushing mine because the room is a crush of people.

"What happened to my tequila shots, bro?" Carter looks at me, his expression wounded and legs unsteady. It's not like our star quarterback to drink the night before a game, but his on again/off again relationship is on a slippery slope and it's fucking with his head.

"I had them in my hands but there was a pretty girl in desperate need," I say, reminded of how Jordan had slammed them back with impressive speed. "What was I to do?"

Carter's eyes fall on Jordan and that quickly, I want to gouge them from his head. They leer and then widen when they trail over her legs. Slim, toned, endless. He's taking it all in like he needs to ace a test on it later. *They're my fucking legs*, I itch to tell him. *Go find your own*. But this isn't the schoolyard and last I checked, I wasn't ten years old and guarding a shiny new toy.

"I can see your dilemma," he says and drags his eyes away and back to mine. "Early night for you then, huh, bro?"

"You know it," I say before thinking the words through.

Jordan tenses beside me.

"Dude." Carter fist bumps me. "Score."

When we finally make it outside, she rips off her lei and tosses it angrily away. It floats carelessly in the air before fluttering to the ground without a sound. All the while she's stalking along the front path ahead of me, her long-legged stride eating up the distance quickly. I jog to catch up and she halts, spinning back around to glare at me. I almost duck from the sparks shooting from her eyes.

"Score?" she says. Then shouts it a second time. "Score?"

"Jordan—"

"Just what does dating mean to you? A regular girl on your arm to fuck? I didn't sign on for this to earn the reputation of a whore, Brody! That's not who I am. I'm a—"

"A good girl," I snap. "I get it."

Jordan flinches and takes a step back.

"Jordan," I say, my tone a little more appeasing this time.

She shakes her head and turns back around, muttering something as she continues her way down the front path.

I tug the car keys from my pocket and start after her.

"Madden!"

Damn it all!

I've made a mess of things and need to clean it up, but Jordan's making a rapid escape, and Jax is now jogging toward me, resentment clear in his expression. I'm not in the mood for it.

"What now?" I growl at him, stopping.

"What the hell, man? You're dating Jordan Elliott?"

"Yes. And I don't have time right now to soothe your ruffled feathers."

Deciding it will be quicker to get the car first and catch up to Jordan, I head toward it quickly, beeping the locks. When I get inside, revving the engine, the passenger door flies open. Jaxon climbs up inside, slamming it shut a second before I spin the wheels in a quick U-turn on the street.

"Why didn't you say anything?"

"Christ," I bite out, jabbing at the clutch with my foot as I shift gears. "Why does everyone care so much?"

"I'm not everyone. I'm your cousin, and I told you I planned on hooking up with her."

Jordan's already at the end of the street when I catch sight of her. "Well you're too late," I mutter because that's all I've got right now.

"You're such an asshole, Brody. King of fucking campus. You just swoop in and take what you want and damn everyone else."

I glance across at Jaxon, surprised at the tirade that's come from nowhere. He's not just irritated, he's *hurt*. No girl has ever meant more to my cousin then just a casual roll in the sheets.

"You really liked her."

"No. I really *like* her. So watch your back, *cousin*. A couple of weeks with you and she might just decide you're not worth it."

Jaxon's words wrench at me like a bad stomach cramp. Like he intended them to. But I don't think he knows just how close, or how hard, they hit home.

I shove it down and jam my foot on the brakes. The SUV screeches to a halt beside Jordan. She's reached the end of the sidewalk on the corner and about to cross the street. My cousin is out of the car before I even open the door.

I jog around the side in time to hear him say, "Not looking for anything with anyone, huh? I thought you were different, but you're just like every other girl on campus," he says with a sneer. "Holding out for a piece of Brody big fucking deal Madden."

My hands curl into fists. He has no right to be angry with Jordan. And does he really think of me that way? That I think myself better than everyone else? Because he has it all twisted around the wrong way.

"It's not like that, Jax," Jordan says to him, her cheeks flushed and sandals dangling from her hands. I know she wants to tell him about the mix-up, that she thought I was someone else and we're not really dating at all, but she holds it in. She's doing this for me when I've done nothing to deserve her loyalty.

"That's Jaxon to you. We're not friends after all."

"Jax," I snap. He's being a dick because he's had too much to drink, and I'm over it. "Get lost."

He holds up his hands in mock surrender. "I'm already gone."

"Get in the car, Jordan," I command as my cousin walks away, disappearing back toward the party. "It's not safe to walk home by yourself."

Jordan blows out a shaky breath, and I look her way. She quickly presses her lips together, but I don't miss the quiver in them. If I give her a hug to soothe away the hurt, would she punch me for getting too close?

Willing to risk it, I forge ahead bravely and take hold of her shoulders. Her lips press tighter, but she isn't scratching my eyes out. It's encouraging. With a slight tug, I bring her flush against me and fold her in my arms. She doesn't resist, but her body is stiff and unyielding. I breathe deep and press a soft kiss down on her head. I don't want to stop there, but I do.

"I'm sorry," I say, rubbing my palm in comforting circles on her lower back. "My cousin can be a real dick when he's been drinking. And I'm a selfish prick for putting you up to this."

"I agreed to it," she tells me, the sound muffled and resigned. "But I had tequila shots and forgot to read the fine print. I mean, I don't know you at all. I'm not sure I want to."

"Ouch." My hands pause. "You know, I'm pretty sure there's a cooling-off period somewhere in there. You can change your mind."

"It's fine." Jordan sniffs and makes a little huffing sound. I resume rubbing her back. Firmer this time. "*I'm* fine," she adds, her voice throaty. "Really."

My hand lowers and I keep rubbing. Bigger, warmer circles. If she gives me a moan, just one, I can't be held accountable for my actions.

"I'm just allergic to assholes," she adds. "Which means I'm not sure how this thing with us is going to work out but … you know, you can stop feeling me up anytime now."

"Are you sure?" I ask.

Jordan hesitates and it almost kills me. "I'm sure."

"I'll stop on one condition."

"Really? Because I'm pretty sure I can just knee you in the balls and that will work just as well."

I tut tut with mock despair. And I keep rubbing. "Violence is not the answer."

"Oh pray tell what is, Obe-wan?"

"Love of course, young Skywalker," I say with a grin. "Make love, not war, right?"

Jordan shakes her head, but there's no fight inside her to break free of my hold. Unfortunately we can't stay here all night, clinched together on the sidewalk like we're the last two people in the world. My car is parked on a wild angle and blocking the road, headlights blinding and the driver's door wide open. My sigh is long and heavy.

"Let me take you home, okay?"

She pulls back, staring up at me. "That's your condition?"

"Yep."

"Huh," she mutters as if I've confused her.

Jordan spends the drive home looking everywhere but at me, and when I pull to a stop in the parking lot, she's thanking me for the ride and out the door before I can stop her.

"Wait up!" Getting out, I beep the locks and jog after her. "I'll walk you up." Snatching the card from her hand, I swipe us into the building and hold open the door. "Ladies first."

My eyes are on her ass the entire trek up the stairwell. I'm not religious but hers is an ass deserving of prayerful thanks. It's high and round, and biteable like juicy apples. I watch it undulate hypnotically until we emerge onto the third floor.

By the time we reach her door, my dick is straining against my shorts. Jordan uses her key to unlock it, stepping inside as I reach down to adjust it. Turning around, she catches me and arches a brow. I shrug without shame.

"Goodnight, Brody."

This is the part where I'm supposed to leave, but my feet are super-glued to the hallway floor. It seems I can't move until I get some solid reassurance of when I'm seeing her again.

"So, Monday night?" I ask casually.

"I'll check my schedule."

"Really? You're telling me you don't have it memorized back to front?"

"Fine. Monday night."

"Great. See you then. I've got dinner with my parents, so I'll swing by after that." She gives me a nod, and I force myself to leave. "Night, Jordan."

Halfway to the stairs I glance back. Jordan is standing in the doorway, a flush high on her cheeks and honey-colored hair spilling over her bare shoulders. I turn and walk backwards, giving her a wink. "Sweet dreams."

It's a smooth move, and a total fail when her eyes widen on something behind me. "Brody, look…" I smack into a pile of bodies behind me "… out."

"Sorry, ladies," I say, extracting myself from two sets of amorous limbs while trying to steady the drunk pair at the same time. The two girls manage to right themselves and continue around me in a giggling stumble on their high heels.

"Did you hear that?" one of them whispers loudly while the other squeals. "He said *sweet dreams!*"

CHAPTER 8

BRODY

Last night's sleep was fitful, and I'm awake before the alarm goes off. My body is sluggish and my mind is on Jordan. Each time I try and focus on the upcoming game, it veers toward her like a car going off course. This is the exact distraction I don't need, and I have no explanation for why I can't seem to care. I'm anxious for Monday night when I can see her again.

Getting on the team bus, I pick a seat up front. Tired and irritable and in a weird headspace, I want to avoid my teammates and zone out instead. Slumping right down, I lift my legs up, resting my knees against the back of the seat in front of me. With my phone on my lap, I plug in my Beats headphones and set them over my head, fixing my current playlist to shuffle. The song kicks in just as the bus pulls out, and the way it begins to rock gently along the road soothes my irritation.

My gaze shifts out the window. The sun is just a mere glimpse of pink and orange over the horizon. I know it's early, but I like the idea of Jordan waking up to a message from me. Picking up my phone from my lap, I type one out. I don't usually like messaging because my words and spelling get messed up, but autocorrect fixes what I can't, and Jordan knows I'm dyslexic so I figure there's no need to hide.

Brody: *I don't like chocolate.*

It's a small fact about myself that's neither here nor there, but last night she said she didn't know me. If she responds in kind, then I know it's possible she might want to.

After tapping the send button, I drop the phone to my lap and stare out the window. A rush of pleasure zings through me when it beeps an immediate response, highlighting the name I added her in as a contact.

SweetVanillaGirl: *Who is this? And are you crazy?*

I chuckle softly and type out another message.

Brody: *Shame on u. This is no way to treat the guy ur dating.*

I follow it up with another.

Brody: *Ur up early?*

Carter slams into the seat beside me, the force making my own seat shudder in response. To his credit he looks fresh and firing on all cylinders. Whatever's going on in his life, he always manages to lock it down for the game. It's the kind of player he is: dependable, enthusiastic, and oozing energy from every pore. Ryan Carter is a bottomless can of Red Bull.

I pause my song and pull back my headphones, leaving them to rest around my neck.

"How was that chick last night?" he greets me, along with a waggle of his eyebrows. Did I mention he's also straight to the point? Carter doesn't like to waste time on the smaller details. "Trust you to be the one bagging the hot Australian jock. She didn't have much of a rack but those legs …" He trails off as though he's picturing them in his mind. "Any good?"

My stomach knots in anger. I don't like the way it sounds like he wants a turn, or that he checked out her rack. And so what if it's small. I'm not greedy, just goddamn fucking horny. "Jordan's not like that, so watch your mouth."

Carter's eyes round like saucers, and I know I've blindsided him with my response. I've never jumped down his throat over a girl before. For a moment he can't compute. His mouth opens and closes before he speaks.

"You didn't tap that sweet ass?"

I shift uncomfortably in my seat, unwilling to spill any more details then absolutely necessary. "Jordan and I are dating."

Carter laughs and I glare. He shuts up quickly, and after a moment cocks his head. "Holy shit, you're serious. I heard last night you were supposedly dating some chick, but I thought it was just gossip." Turning around in the seat beside me, my teammate gets up on his knees. Facing the back of the bus, he shouts, "Madden's got himself a girl!"

All kinds of responses are called back alongside catcalls, but it's the collective consensus of "bullshit!" that has me gritting my teeth.

"I shit you not!" he hollers. "Her name's Jordan!"

The team breaks out into chants of "Jordan! Jordan! Jordan!" because they obviously have nothing better to do than act like a giant bunch of dicks.

Pinching the bridge of my nose, I sink lower in my seat with a muttered curse. If Jordan wants out of this, well … it's too late now.

I tug my shiny dark blue headphones back on. They have epic noise cancellation. It's just what I need right now. After hitting play and cranking the volume, I close my eyes against the blurring scenery.

A minute later, my phone vibrates from where it's resting on my leg.

SweetVanillaGirl: *I'm out jogging.*

I can't fight the tug at the corners of my lips as I type out a lengthy reply.

Brody: *Don't u no it's dangerous to text and jog? You might run someone over or fall in a ditch.*

A quick sideways glance tells me Carter's decided to let it go. For now. He gets up and returns to his seat down back, leaving me alone. I return to my phone with a smile on my face when another message pops up. I flick it open.

SweetVanillaGirl: *Well stop texting me!*

Jordan's message is a red flag waving at a bull.

Brody: *Where's the fun in that?*

SweetVanillaGirl: *You remind me of your cousin.*

My brows draw together. After the events of last night, that comment is open to interpretation, and I want to know what she means.

Brody: *In what way?*

Jaxon and I might be similar on the surface, but underneath? Not so much. He's the son my father always wanted. The benchmark. I'm constantly reminded that if only I applied myself like Jaxon does, I would have a respectable future—politics, medicine, law. Frankly, he'd just be happy with a son who could read, he tells me. But I know that's not true. My father is the type of person who is never satisfied, and I know he expects me to fail at football too.

SweetVanillaGirl: *You're both very persistent. Can I finish my run now?*

It's true. We both are, so perhaps it's a family trait. Regardless, I choose to take it as a compliment. Ambition without persistence gets you nowhere.

Brody: *By all means… finish ur run.*

I close my eyes and spend time thinking about the upcoming game. We're well prepared. We watched a lot of additional play this week, and my extra training sessions are paying off. I'm working harder than I ever have. There's no reason why we should lose.

Before I know it, the gentle rocking of the bus lulls me into a light doze. Eddie nudging my shoulder wakes me. He says something, so I pull the headphone away from my right ear. "What?"

He holds out a water bottle. "Hydrate, dude."

"Thanks."

He disappears and I crack the lid, tipping half the contents down my throat in one hit. When I pull the bottle from my lips, my eyes fall back to my phone. Restraint and self-discipline are traits every professional athlete should possess, and I like to think I have both in spades, but with Jordan … Perhaps she's my kryptonite because I can't stop myself from sending another message.

Brody: *How was ur run?*

SweetVanillaGirl: *Don't ask.*

Brody: *U fell in a ditch, didn't u?*

No response. The message was meant teasingly, but Jordan is a tough nut to crack. Perhaps she's not a morning person. That leads to thoughts of Jordan in bed: naked, mussed hair, tangled sheets, and sweet, warm skin. My whole body begins to vibrate like it just received an electrical charge. I exhale in a deep huff and flick to a hardcore Eminem song on my playlist. There's nothing sexy about *his* music.

SweetVanillaGirl: *I don't like mushrooms.*

Her message comes in and I want to fist pump the air. I don't though, because that would be lame and this is not some cheesy eighties' movie. Hmmm … what next?

Brody: *My middle name is Abraham.*

I down the rest of my water. When I tuck the empty bottle beside me, her reply comes in.

SweetVanillaGirl: *As in Lincoln?*

Jordan knows some American history.

Brody: *Yes. My dad is a politician. He was hoping I wud follow in his footsteps.*

SweetVanillaGirl: *Was?*

How perceptive of Jordan to pick on that.

Brody: *His dream. Not mine.*

SweetVanillaGirl: *And your dream is football?*

Brody: *Yes.*

From the moment I came alive with that leather ball in my hands.

SweetVanillaGirl: *My middle name is Matilda.*

Jordan Matilda Elliott. Why am I smiling when I say that in my head? My phone vibrates again before I can reply.

SweetVanillaGirl: *I have to go. Leah and I are going out for breakfast. Talk to you later?*

I swallow the disappointment.

Brody: *L8r*

It's a nice casual response, but my insides curl with pleasure because I'm looking forward to it.

I manage to draw Jordan into messaging me on and off during the day. And when I'm sitting in the locker room adjusting the lace on my cleats before the game, the alert on my phone goes again.

So close to kick off I should leave it for later, but the anticipation is too much. If it's Jordan and I don't read it right this moment, I'll be thinking about it all game. *Preoccupation could cost us a win,* I tell myself as I reach for it. My brow furrows when I check the screen. The message is from Lindsay, one of the cheerleader's always hanging off Jax. I know she does it to get close to me. She's not the only one. And after my cousin's display last night, I get the impression he's over it.

Lindsay: *I don't know why you lied about dating that stupid jock. I set her straight. You can thank me later xo*

"Fuck!" I shout and kick the locker door in.

"Christ, Madden!" Eddie glares at me from where he sits, readjusting his glove. He has a soft, gooey center when it comes to girls. I know my dating Jordan will have his full approval. "What crawled up your ass and died?"

"Not what, but who."

I begin stabbing at buttons on the screen, intent on calling Lindsay to find out what she said. When it starts dialing, I put the phone to my ear at the same time Coach Carson storms inside the locker room.

"Now is not the time to be calling your goddamn mother and thanking her for giving birth to your sorry ass!" His bellow echoes through the mostly empty area Brows, drawn together, form one long, fuzzy caterpillar. It's his grouch face, and I'm not eager to be its focus. "Get out on the field, Madden!"

"Yes, Coach," I say quickly.

"Now!" he roars.

I hit the end call button before it answers and toss the phone in my locker before double-timing it out onto the field.

We end up losing the game. No matter how small the margin, it still burns like a motherfucker. When tied at fourteen apiece, we were forced into taking some crazy risks that didn't pay off. Carter threw me a long bomb and I reached up, but the ball tipped off my fingers and right into the hands of the opposing team. With Eddie winded, I was left open for a split second and took a huge hit. After getting slammed into the ground, it was a long while before I could peel myself off the grass. With a throbbing shoulder and three minutes left in the game, UCLA scored a field goal, and nothing short of a miracle would've saved us after that.

I jog off the field, grimy, sweaty, and devastated at the loss, knowing we let down the entire state of Texas tonight. I force a smile for the reporter waiting for an on-field interview. It doesn't reach my eyes, but no one who really knows me would ever notice. No matter what, you never show the media the truth. They don't want to see the self-recrimination and the self-doubt, *or* hear about it. They want sportsmanship. They want you to accept defeat with a rueful smile. They want to hear you felt honored to play a great game against a great team, and that you're coming back bigger and stronger for the next one.

"You play Iowa State next week and then you have a bye." I tuck my helmet under my armpit and brush the damp hair from my forehead while she speaks into the microphone, her perfect face angled professionally toward the camera. "After that you have Oklahoma. How are you going to come back from tonight's loss in preparation for what's touted as one of the biggest upcoming matches of the season?"

"That's a good question. Oklahoma is a grudge match for sure. They're going to come at us hard, but we'll be ready." I flash her a cocky grin alongside the diplomatic response. NFL scouts watch how you speak in front of the media. They want you seen as the all-round nice guy, bred tough. "We'll watch a lot of film and we'll work as hard as time allows. Despite the loss tonight, we're playing better than we ever have. I'm confident we're going to win, and not just for the team or CPU, but for the state of Texas."

She gives me a professional pat on the arm, no doubt hiding the grimace at the transfer of sweat to her perfectly manicured fingers. "Their hopes are riding on you, Brody Madden."

No fucking pressure, I reply silently. I give her a nod and the camera a cheeky grin and wave before I jog away, leaving her to sign off.

When we get back to our hotel room, Carter hands over a bottle of whiskey stashed in his suitcase. Tonight I don't hesitate and grab it swiftly. Tipping back my head, I pour it down my throat, relishing the burn because oblivion can't come fast enough. There are no bars tonight. No one wants to celebrate a loss. A small group of us gather in the twin room Carter and I share, and we drink in a show of solidarity.

It's not until we finish a long, drunken dissection of the match, and argue about our game plan for next week, that I remember Lindsay's message. The room spins when I stagger to my bag and rummage for my phone.

"Fuck," I shout several minutes later, straightening from my crouch.

"What?" Eddie leans back in his seat, looking my way. His chair tips precariously, and when Carter reaches over and nudges the leg, he spills onto the floor with a shout. Everyone laughs, including me.

"I can't find my phone," I say to the room while Eddie picks himself up and flops on one of the twin beds. "I need to ring my girl."

"Pussy-whipped after dating for two days," Carter says with mock sadness.

"Fuck off, Carter," I mumble.

"Yeah, Carter." Eddie reaches over with a long gorilla arm and punches Carter in the bicep. "This is young love in its blossoming, fragile stages. You can't mess with that."

Carter rolls his eyes and one of the guys tosses an empty plastic coke bottle at Eddie's head. It bounces off and skitters somewhere under the bed. When Eddie grabs for it, he comes back up with my phone. "Found it!"

He tosses it at me, going high and long. I leap up and catch it with an outstretched hand. A resounding cheer fills the room. "If only you managed that with Carter's pass on the field tonight."

I let the comment roll off my back and swipe the whiskey bottle off the table. I take it with me and sit on the edge of the bed. After dialing Jordan, I take a swig of whiskey and put the phone to my ear.

"Hello?"

Damn. Her voice. How could I have forgotten its allure? "You sound sooo good," I slur. Tucking the phone between my chin and shoulder, I reach down and grab my dick in my pants.

"Fuck, dude." Eddie shoves my shoulder because the bed I chose happens to be the one he's splayed all over. "I'm all for phone sex, but you need to take that shit somewhere private."

There *is* nowhere private. I stumble out onto the empty balcony, away from the guys. The breeze is warm and the city lights bright. They blur dizzily, and I steady myself against the railing as the sound of sheets rustling comes through the phone. I groan from the simple, torturous sound.

"Are you drunk?"

"Christ, Jordan," I snap in reaction to her censure. "I fucking lost the game. Of course I'm drunk."

Her voice softens. "And this is how you deal with losing?"

"Yes!" Frustration burns my eyes and chest, and the sound of my father's voice reverberates in my head.

You think you can make it in football? Forget it. It's not a career. It's a barbaric sport that's going to knock the last remaining brain cells from your head.

I hang my head, my chest tight from the effort of not screaming in rage. Not because of what he said, but the possibility he could be right. One loss can easily turn into two, and then three, and before you know it, you're on a downhill slide to nowhere. Fear makes my hands shake, and I almost drop the whiskey bottle.

"It's either drink or fuck someone. You're supposed to be my girl, Jordan, but you're not here for me to fuck, so getting drunk it is."

"This pretend dating thing does *not* come with those kinds of benefits," she hisses.

"Say it ain't so, baby," I slur before laughter erupts from inside me.

"You're drunk, Brody, and not yourself. I'm hanging up now."

"Wait! What did Lindsay say to you?"

There's nothing but recriminating silence from Jordan's end, which is followed by a heavy sigh. Intent on planting my ass on the seat behind me, I shift backwards and miss, landing on the ground with a hard thud. "Shit!" Laughter peals out of me in waves as the whiskey bottle rolls from my hand and onto the floor. "I fucking fell off my seat," I gasp.

Jordan's response is to hang up on me.

Huh. That's something new.

I hold my phone up high from my prone position on the ground. "My girl just hung up on me!" I yell.

"Trouble in paradise already," Carter yells back. "Better have another drink."

"Roger that," I reply, rolling to my side as I try to get my bearings. Only it's too hard, so I lie there quietly and close my eyes, and I think about how nice it would be some days to just not wake up at all.

By Monday evening it's clear Jordan's avoiding me. I don't see either her *or* Lindsay between classes, and my calls to Jordan are going straight to voicemail. It's left me in a bad mood, mainly from the guilt sitting like bad Chinese food in my gut. My phone call to Jordan on Saturday night was a disgrace. I still plan on showing up to our arranged tutor session tonight after dinner with my parents. I'll probably get the door slammed in my face, but I'm willing to risk it.

My feet drag as I walk up the path to my childhood home. It's a grand house. All white. Impressive pillars. Lush lawns. In terms of competition, it outclasses every other house in the street—just how my father likes it.

My jaw locks tight as I jab the doorbell. I hate coming here. There's only one person that makes it all worthwhile, and I wouldn't give up seeing her for anything.

The faint peal echoes through the hallway. I don't have a key. My father doesn't like anyone walking in unannounced, not even his own son. I try not to let it bother me, but it does.

"Brody's here!" my little sister shrieks and my heart lifts just that quickly. It follows the sound of feet stomping rapidly toward the front door. I wince, waiting for the reprimand. It doesn't take long.

"Annabelle Madden show some decorum or you'll be sent to your room." A scuffling sound is heard from inside, and my father's voice is now close to the front door. "Go sit down at the dinner table and wait like a lady."

After a moment the door swings open, revealing my father. He's still immaculate in the suit he's no doubt worn all day. His brown hair has a slight curl like mine does, but it's smoothed into submission.

I step inside the front entryway. Our family home is decorated in white and black. Checkered tiles gleam, furniture decorates strategically, and pretentious portraits adorn the walls—promoting the family values my father publicly advocates. It's about as warm and inviting as a dip in the arctic with a pod of killer whales.

"For fuck's sake, Dad," I growl quietly as I brush passed him. "She's eight years old. Let her be a kid."

My sister is an unexpected addition to the family, her arrival messing with dad's life plan the same way me having a learning disability did. Initially, I liked my sister because her presence shifted the negative attention off me, but it was when our dad reprimanded her for playing football with me in the yard and she flatly told him to "fuck off" that I came to adore her. I got a clip across the face for laughing so hard, but it was worth it just to see the look on his face.

"I don't *want* to eat roast chicken," comes her whine as I walk down the glossy flooring toward the dining room at the back of the house. "Have you *seen* chickens? They spend all day pecking at the ground and eating their own shit."

"Annabelle! Enough!" my mother admonishes and my lips twitch. I press them together quickly.

Dinner is already laid out on the table when I appear, and my sister sits fidgeting at her place setting. Her blonde curls have loosened from the tight bun on top her of head, reminding me she went to ballet this afternoon.

"Hey, Moo Moo," I coo, grinning at my sister as I take my seat.

"Enough with that infernal nickname," my father mutters as he takes his seat at the head of the table.

"She likes it," I retort. "Don't you, Moo Moo?"

Annabelle purses her lips as if annoyed, but her eyes dance with delight. "I'm not a cow, Brody."

I pretend to look puzzled. "But all cows are named Annabelle, and Mom said that when you came out you mooed just like a dairy cow that needed milking."

Mom gives me a sharp look from across the table. It makes me wonder when I last saw a smile on her face. Not one of those fake ones for the media that doesn't reach her eyes, but a real honest-to-god smile.

"I said no such thing. Now everyone eat before dinner gets cold."

We begin filling our plates when Hattie walks into the dining room, a gravy boat in her hand. I give our housekeeper a wink. "Hey, Hattie. Thanks for dinner."

Hattie's lips twitch as she sets the gravy in the center of the table, but otherwise she doesn't acknowledge me—not after seeing my father's nostrils flare. She's staff. I'm not supposed to thank her for something she gets paid to do.

"How was dance class?" I ask my sister as we eat.

Her bottom lip pokes out, and I know a complaint is imminent. Annabelle barely tolerates ballet. Our parents insist on it because they're hoping it will instill some grace in her tiny, clumsy frame, but I suspect she'd rather take up weightlifting than endure another season of én pointe.

"It sucked. Emily Simpkins did a ballonné and kicked me right in the ass. I think I have a bruise."

"So help me, Annabelle, if I hear another curse word pass your lips, you'll be going straight to bed," my father snaps, his face red.

The light in her eyes dims, and she hangs her head. My sister needs to stop cussing so much, but I know she does it for the attention. They don't pay her any otherwise. It makes my chest ache because I know how she feels.

I kick Annabelle under the table and when she looks up I wink. She doesn't giggle out loud, but I can see laughter in her eyes and that's enough for me.

Our parents talk between themselves during dinner, at least until the inevitable question is sent my way. "How's your school work going, Brody?"

My stomach drops instantly, and my knuckles whiten on the knife and fork in my hands. My mother's query appears innocent, but the innuendo beneath her words is not. God. Can't they just leave it alone? I know I'm a crushing disappointment. Do they really need me reminding them of it every time I come to dinner?

I glare at her. *Don't do it. Just let it go. Lie.*

I draw in a deep breath and let it out. "Fine."

Her brows rise and her expression is not only skeptical, it's cold. "Fine?"

"Is that all we get from you, Brody?" My father joins in, and now I have the both of them double teaming me. Awesome. "We're the ones sinking our hard-earned money into your education and all you can give us is *fine*?"

I might be attending CPU on a full sports scholarship but my father pays for the apartment, my car, and everything else. He wants to control what I drive, where I live, what I damn well *wear*, because the Maddens have a public image to maintain. God forbid I embarrass the family.

Annabelle sits quietly, not eating, her eyes focused on the table. My expression stony, I lift my chin, eyes shifting to my father. "What would you rather hear?"

"The truth," he bites out.

"Come on, Dad, really?" I force a chuckle. "You're a politician. You deal in lies, right? I'm just learning from the best."

His face reddens. I've riled his temper and that's never good. I should keep my mouth shut, but I can't seem to help myself.

"You want to know how it's going?" I put down my knife and fork with a clatter. What little I've eaten sits heavy in my gut. I won't be eating anymore tonight. "Two weeks in and I'm already flunking out. I'm going to take a stab in the dark and guess you both had that figured out already." With hardened eyes, I turn a glare on my father, unable to restrain the sarcasm from my voice. "But there are no expectations, right, Dad? So you could hardly be disappointed. On the plus side, Uncle Patrick arranged a tutor because he's willing to acknowledge just how low the levels of my stupidity go, so at least he gives a shit."

My gaze slides back to my mother. A glass of chilled white wine sits poised in her hand, and her jaw is tight. She doesn't like the reminder of my failures, so why she asked the question in the first place is beyond me. Every time a teacher suggested outside assistance during my formative years, my father always vetoed the idea. Knowing her place, my mother agreed. I hate that she's so weak. I hate that she doesn't care. I swallow hard, not allowing the hot prick of tears to reach my eyes.

"So yeah, it's going *great*, Mom."

Before I can draw breath, my dad reaches across and cracks his open palm across my face. My jaw snaps sideways, and I blink back stars.

Annabelle cries out and I hear her cutlery fall to her plate.

I take a deep breath and fix steady eyes on my little sister. "Go upstairs, Moo Moo."

Her bottom lip quivers. "Brody."

"I'll come see you again soon, okay? We can go out on the horses."

She hesitates.

"Go!"

Annabelle shoves her chair back, putting her napkin on the top of her plate with shaky hands. She aims a glare at our parents before leaving the room. It's not until I hear her footsteps reach the top of the stairs that I turned to face him.

"What the fuck, Dad!" My mom flinches as I rip the napkin from my lap and toss it on the table. "Don't you ever do that in front of Annabelle!"

Mom's brows draw together, her expression stern. "Brody—"

Dad cuts her off. "Your mother asked you a simple question. Don't treat her with such disrespect again."

"I'm sorry," I say with quiet sincerity. I didn't mean to lose my shit in front of my sister. "I guess I just got sick of all the crap."

"You little sonofabitch!" Dad shoots to his feet, his chair tipping and skidding back on the timber floor with a crack. He fists my shirt in his hand and hauls me to my feet. I stumble and my elbow bangs on the table, sending my plate crashing to the floor.

"You want to go at it?" he growls. My body tenses. It's taking all my restraint to keep from shoving him out of my face. "Is that what you want? For me to smack some manners into your sorry ass? We've given you everything. *Everything!*" he roars in my face. "And you throw it back in our face by flunking out? And don't think I didn't hear about your loss to UCLA over the weekend. Everyone made sure I heard about it. It just proves you won't get anywhere if you don't try hard enough. You're an embarrassment, Son, not to mention a sore loser. Be a man and handle it rather than taking it out on your family." Dad heaves air into his lungs, his eyes wild. "Fucking useless," he snarls when I remain silent.

He shoves me away—*hard*. My head smacks into the wall. I suck in a breath, feeling my brow split on impact. When I touch a hand to it, it comes away covered with blood. Dizzy, I lurch backwards, planting a shaky palm on the wall. It smears blood in a long, messy arc.

"Hattie!" my dad yells as I blink blood from my eye. "Come in here and clean up this goddamn mess."

"Fuck you!" I slur, lightheaded and sick from the white-hot pain. Straightening my shoulders, I turn and draw back a fist, slamming it in my father's jaw. Mom screams when the impact sends him sailing into the dining table. Dishes crash to the floor and food stains his suit.

I laugh. My knuckles are throbbing and my face aches, but I don't care. All I can do is laugh, but it's not remotely funny because it feels like I'm losing it.

"Get out!" my mother shrieks at me. Her face is pinched and her side sweep of blonde hair has loosened to fall on her forehead. "Get out of our house!"

CHAPTER 9

JORDAN

Two days prior…

Fielding messages from Brody, and the subsequent riot of butterflies every time his name pops up on my phone, I cut my Saturday morning run short. I don't want to like Brody messaging me; in fact, I don't want to like Brody at all—but I do.

After a long hot shower, Leah suggests going out for a late breakfast. I know a short stack of gingerbread pancakes will go a long way toward making everything better so I agree. But it's not until we're at a table, eating, that I realize Leah's purpose for this little breakfast outing: pumping me for any and all information Brody Madden related.

It's only the day after the party, but I'm beginning to notice that people somehow know my name. They pass by our table, saying hello. I'm not a social butterfly. I'm the reluctant caterpillar in the corner. It's awkward.

One girl with a group of friends actually snaps a photo of me with her phone. She's blatant about it too. Not seeming to care that I see her do it *or* that I have my mouth stretched around a forkful of pancakes. Usually they taste like little round slivers of doughy heaven. This morning they sit like rocks in my stomach.

"So spill it, Elliott. Leave no stone unturned. I want to know *everything*."

Of course she does. Leah's dark brown eyes are round and eager as she eyeballs me expectantly. The only reason she didn't get anything out of me this morning was because Leah is as dedicated to her training as I am. Or usually am, if I don't factor this morning's pathetic effort into the equation.

I swallow my mouthful quickly, mindful that people are watching me *eat*. "I bumped into him on campus."

Leah's eyebrows shoot skyward. "Like, literally?"

Oh God, the *lies*. I grimace because it's already making me sweat. The gig will be up the moment Leah sees me leaking like a giant deceitful water fountain. Will she notice if I furtively slide a couple of napkins under my armpits? "Yes," I answer firmly. "I wasn't looking where I was going."

She'll believe that little white lie. My lack of direction and my inability to read maps is now a running joke in our circle.

"And then what?" she prompts, rolling her eyes. "Come on, Jordan. This is like pulling teeth."

I put down my knife and fork to reach for my mug of tea. "And the rest is history," I blithely reply and take a sip. It's scalding hot and burns my tongue. In fact it burns all the way down. Karma is busy taking care of business this morning.

Leah's eyes narrow. Perhaps I overdid the blithe. "Why did you never tell me?"

"I didn't think—"

"That's exactly right," she cuts me off, jabbing her fork in my face. I flinch. "You didn't think."

"Hey, Jordan." Two guys walk by our table that I don't recognize. Both give me the once-over. I'm being appraised like a prize cow. This is the point where I realize I've been thrown to the wolves. I can't even blame Brody. I agreed to this in a moronic, tequila-induced moment that now appears too late to take back.

I force a tight smile and with gritted teeth turn back to Leah. "Can we go? Please?"

"No way." She grins as she forks up a mouthful of eggs. "I only just started eating, and this is too much fun."

"I'll do your laundry for an entire month," I plead.

Leah pauses and says, "That's pretty tempting ... but no."

"You're a sucky friend."

I give up on my pancakes. Wiping my mouth with my napkin, I set it on the table and reach again for my tea.

"So you bumped into him on campus and then what? You dropped all your books and he picked them up for you?"

"Yes!" I pounce on her suggestion. "That's exactly what happened."

"Wow."

"I know, right?" I nod. "Wow."

Leah sits back in her seat, coffee in hand as she eyes me shrewdly. "So then what happened? He looked into your amazing eyes, was dazzled speechless, and then it was on?"

I shake my head, pretending amazement. "How did you know? Gosh, Leah. It was like you were there."

"Shut. Up!" she shrieks and tosses a half-eaten piece of toast at me. I'm wearing a short-sleeved blue knit top, and it attaches itself to the threads like a decorative broach.

I peel it off my chest and drop it on my plate.

"Give it back here," she commands, stretching her arm across the table.

I hand it back over. "You're not actually going to eat that after you threw it at me, are you?"

"Of course I am. It didn't drop on the floor, and your shirt is clean."

I glance down where crumbs and butter now smear the thin blue wool. "Not anymore it's not."

Leah takes a huge bite and waggles her eyebrows. Around a mouthful of toast, she asks, "So did you two get it on last night?"

"What? No!"

Her eyes round in genuine shock and her smile drops away. "No?"

I spend the rest of breakfast dodging Leah's probing questions. When she finally announces she's done, I stand and race for the door. The morning sunshine hits me right in the eyes, and I slide my sunglasses down to block the glare.

Leah catches up to me, linking her arm in mine. "What are we doing today?"

"Hibernating," I answer quickly. This morning gave me insight on how bugs feel under a microscope. The scrutiny is wearing and my right eye has begun to twitch. I reach beneath my lens and rub it, trying to make it stop. "I have reading to do."

"Wow. Study. You're super fun. I'm not sure my heart can take it. Let's go shopping first."

I recoil. My bank account is reasonably healthy, but it needs to stretch my entire senior year. Not to mention my mode of transportation is already close to falling apart. "You've seen my car, right?"

"Hon, everyone has seen your car. It's the eyesore of Texas. The CIA are tracking it on satellite, waiting for authorization to take it out." Her eyes light up as we walk along the pavement. "Maybe Brody will buy you a new one now that you're dating. He can't have his girl driving a death trap, can he?"

"I'm not *his girl*. We haven't even gone on a single date yet. Technically that means we aren't really dating at all."

That was probably my first real truth of the morning, and Leah completely ignores it. Instead, I'm dragged from shop to shop, trying on outfits I can't afford. It's midday when we both declare we've had enough. With my stomach growling, I leave Leah inside the store and order two fruit smoothies from a nearby vendor.

I turn around while I'm waiting and get shoulder-checked by a redhead with an attitude problem. "Hey!" I cry out when I stumble and land on my ass with a painful thud.

The girl beside the redhead giggles, but the glare I get from the girl who knocked me down is scalding. I remember that glare from the party last night. Lindsay, I think Jaxon said her name was.

Leah charges out before I get to my feet. "What the freaking hell is your problem?" she screeches, getting right in Lindsay's face.

The sweet Asian man making our smoothies races around his cart toward me. He helps me stand while Leah and Lindsay yell obscenities at each other. My stomach rolls the moment I put pressure on my left leg. My ankle is beginning to twinge, sending out a mayday that something is seriously wrong.

"You don't belong here," Lindsay hisses at me, her nostrils flaring. I don't doubt she means what she says. "And I don't know what you're playing at, but you don't belong with Brody either. You're just a new toy that will soon lose its shine. Just give it a few days."

"Just like you wore off so fast he didn't even look your way at all?" Leah interjects.

"Look," I say, swallowing around the worrying pain shooting up my leg. Damned if I want Lindsay to know she's done some serious damage. "Maybe I do belong with Brody, maybe I don't. Either way, it's none of your business."

Lindsay scowls. "This isn't over." With her pleasant threat delivered, she stalks off, not even waiting for her friend to catch up.

"Wow. I was wondering if I should envy you, getting to enjoy that masterpiece of male perfection," Leah says as she stands there, hands on her hips as she watches the two girls disappear inside a store, "but I take it back." She turns to me, doubt in her eyes. "How does it feel to be the most hated girl on campus right now?"

"Is that a pep talk? Because you suck at it."

"Girls," the vendor mutters from beside me, shaking his head like we're an alien species he'll never figure out. "You ok?" he asks me. "You still want smoothies?"

"Yes, please," I reply weakly. "But change the order to double chocolate."

I shift slightly and wince. Leah glances down and her eyes widen on my ankle. "Oh no. No, no, no. Please tell me you didn't—"

My eyes fill with tears faster then I can blink them away. "I did."

"That bitch! I'm going to rip her apart."

Leah whips her phone out and stabs a finger at the screen.

"What you are doing?"

"I'm calling Hayden. We need to get you home and get some ice on that ankle." Leah presses the phone to her ear and stares down at my swelling ankle. "Maybe it's nothing serious. Rest it a couple of days and it'll be completely fine."

I shift some weight on my leg to test it. An explosion of fireworks shoots up my calf. I suck in a sharp breath, wincing.

Leah tries for a reassuring smile but it looks grim. "It's gonna be okay."

I spend the afternoon on the couch, my ankle elevated and regularly iced. Hayden keeps me company. With a nice dose of painkillers under my belt,

I thrash him at baseball on the PlayStation while Leah ducks out on a mysterious errand.

Vengeance was a fire in her eyes when she left, and it's only when I'm distracted—worrying she's out on some one-woman vigilante mission—that Hayden manages a win. He leaps up off the couch with a roar and the entire apartment damn near shudders.

"Enjoy the moment while it lasts, He-Man," I tell him when he starts rolling his hips and arms in a victory dance.

Halting mid-step, Hayden points his controller at me, his excitement palpable. "Let's go again!"

He slams back on the couch with force, and it jiggles my ankle.

"Arrghhhhh!" I shriek.

"Sorry, sorry, sorry," he chants, tossing the controller to the side and readjusting the ice that slid off to the floor.

Leah chooses that moment to return. Her arms are laden with glossy shopping bags, and there's a bright, determined gleam in her eye that makes me nervous. The last time I saw that look, I was dragged to a frat party in a purple 'fuck me' dress and look how well that turned out.

"What's in the bags?" I ask.

Retaking his seat beside me, Hayden eyes her loaded arms with the hopeful eyes of a kid at Christmas. "It's bags and bags of black lacy underwear."

Leah's grin is smug as she dumps them on the kitchen counter. "Nope."

His smile falters a little, but hope remains. "Red lacy underwear?"

"Nope."

"Pink?"

"Nope."

Hayden rattles off all the colors of the rainbow while she digs inside one of the bags.

"Nope, nope, and nope," she replies.

All his hope slowly dies out, leaving behind the wounded expression of a kicked puppy.

What she plucks out is a stretchy black piece of fabric, and instantly I know what it is. The dress she tossed over the fitting room door when we were trying on clothes. It's a deceptive piece of material. It looks like a bit of scrap, but after tugging it on I almost didn't recognize my own body. It has a high neckline, but it shows a mile of leg, gives me a waist, and dips so low at the back it's almost obscene.

"You didn't," I breathe.

Lean grins, victorious. "I did. I also…" she pulls out item after item after item, "…did this, and this, and this." Out comes tiny, cuffed shorts the color of ripe lemons, two blouses, a white maxi-dress that cinches at the waist with a brown leather belt, and more.

Tears prick my eyes. She must have spent a fortune. "You can't, Leah," I protest while my internal voice screams at me *she can, she can!* "Take it all back."

Opening the kitchen drawer, she comes out with a pair of scissors. I watch as she neatly begins snipping off tags and cutting through receipts. "Oops. I'm afraid I can't do that."

"Leah …" I trail off, speechless.

"That crazy bitch doesn't think you belong with Brody? We'll show her just how much you do, and then her eyes won't be the only part of her that's green. The second he sees you in that black dress for your date, he's going to swallow his tongue."

My stomach sinks like lead as she folds all the clothes in a neat pile. It doesn't matter what I wear because I don't belong with Brody. I never will. Not even if I wanted to. I'm only here for senior year and then I'm gone. Everything I'm making here—this little life inside an even smaller apartment, new city and soccer team, friends I'm growing to love harder than I thought possible—is all temporary.

After we have dinner, Leah helps me hobble to my room. My painkillers are wearing off, but I don't take anymore. I just want to sleep. Stretching out on my bed, I open my laptop to check my emails first. What I find is over a hundred Facebook friend requests, emails inviting me to parties, and emails calling me a whore. With a shaky hand I slam it shut and shove it away.

It takes over an hour for me to find sleep. The moment I do, Brody wakes me with his phone call, drunk and belligerent. I want to care that they lost their game, but he's being a dick. After the day I had, his attitude is like the cherry on top of a shit cupcake. When I hang up, I'm glad that Monday is still two days away. It will give me time to calm down.

The next two days are spent at home resting my ankle. It's not until Monday night rolls around and Brody's a no-show that I realize the battery on my phone is dead. After charging it up, I try calling him, but he doesn't answer. Brody set about this whole dating farce and now what? He gives up on being tutored before we've even started? I'm fuming mad.

It's not until Tuesday that I see him next. I'm seated in the quiet study section of the library. He stalks past, carrying a stack of lecture notes in his hand, noticing no one. He's wearing a Colton Bulls cap that hides his eyes, and his skin is damp from the outside heat. For some reason my heart starts slamming in my ribs and it gets hard to breathe. Rage. It's all that anger oozing from my pores like lava. In fact it's an exercise in restraint not to stick my good ankle out and trip him up, or toss the heavy text on my desk at his head.

"Brody," I hiss loudly when instead I should just let him go. If he doesn't want to be tutored I can't force him, but sometimes I can be a dog with a bone. Winners aren't quitters, though I'm not sure I'd classify this as winning.

Brody halts at my voice and turns. I suck in a sharp breath. His left eye is a rainbow of purple and red and so swollen it hurts just to look at it. A split brow is held together with butterfly tape and his bottom lip looks busted.

"Oh my god, Brody."

"Jordan," he says quietly and presses his lips together like he has no idea what to say. The move makes him wince, and he touches a hand to his mouth before meeting my gaze.

The teasing sparkle in his eyes is missing, and my anger disappears like vapor. "What happened to your face?"

Brody shrugs. "Training." He puts his sheaf of papers on the desk and crouches next to me, bringing me a little higher than eye level. He has to look up a little bit. "It can get a little rough."

I don't believe a word. I have a brother. I know the difference between training and a fistfight. My gaze drops to the knuckles on his right hand. They're swollen and red. "Just a little rough, huh?"

Brody puts a hand on my knee. The touch is intimate and sends my pulse rocketing right through the ornate ceiling of the library. "Sorry about last night." He waves a hand briefly at his face. "I was a bit sore. I should've let you know I couldn't make it, but I thought you were avoiding me. I tried ringing you yesterday but it kept going to voicemail."

"Oh. Well I admit I needed some time to cool off after your phone call on Saturday night, but I wasn't avoiding you. My phone was flat."

Brody grimaces. "Sorry about that. I was an asshole."

"You were."

He gives me a rueful grin. "Well at least we can agree on something. So can we reschedule the tutoring?"

I should say no, but I can't. I'm his tutor. The whole point of this is to help Brody in any way I can. And we both need to start taking it more seriously. "Thursday night," I tell him. "My apartment."

Brody exhales sharply. Rescheduling was obviously a chore he's happy to be done with. "Great. Now will you tell me what Lindsay said to you on Saturday?"

"She didn't say anything I can't handle."

His jaw ticks. Obviously it's not the answer he wants. "Tell me what she said, Jordan."

I shift my leg from underneath his grip and his hand falls away. "Brody, you're a popular guy. There are a lot of girls who aren't going to be happy with the idea of you dating me. They'll get over it, so just let it go."

Brody stands slowly, his wide shoulders looming over me. "I'll let it go. For now. But if anyone ever threatens you, you tell me and I'll handle it."

"I can handle myself. Don't treat me like I belong to you."

He leans over and takes my face in his hand, the other he props on the arm of my chair. His palm is calloused and scrapes my cheek, but his touch is gentle.

When he speaks, his voice is low and his eyes dark. "How should I treat you?"

Want makes me shake. I have to fist my hands so they don't reach for him. "Like your tutor."

Brody's palm slides away, but his gaze on me remains, eyes hungry. The heat in them swamps me like a blanket, so thick and heavy I can't get any air. "That's no fun at all."

"Neither is pretending to date someone."

"Speaking of, maybe we should drop the pretense and make it real." He straightens and takes a couple of steps back. "See you Thursday."

There's only one thought flying around in my head as my eyes follow him from the room.

I'm in trouble.
Big trouble.

CHAPTER 10

BRODY

"Hat and sunglasses, Mr. Madden."

I slouch back in my seat and glare at my uncle as I take them off. I set them on the desk and when my gaze returns to the front, he's staring hard at my bruised eye, his expression grim. Thursday afternoon and it's still a riot of color, but at least the swelling has gone down some.

He gives the room his back and shuffles some papers on his desk before pausing for a moment. When he faces his class again, he speaks quietly, beginning his lecture.

Jaxon passes across the attendance sheet, and I scratch out my name with a quick hurried movement. The desk beside me is empty. Has Jordan forgotten where the room is again? Already my lips begin to twitch. I hang on to the sheet so she can sign it when she arrives.

When I realize I'm sitting forward in my seat like an eager student, my eyes on the doorway, I sit back and fold my arms. Totally cool. Abso-fucking-lutely.

"Miss Elliott."

My eyes cut to the door so fast I get whiplash. The fact that she's rushing through the entryway with flushed cheeks and a harassed expression doesn't surprise me. She must feel my hot and heavy stare, because her eyes make immediate contact with mine across the room. Jordan Matilda Elliott is ice cream in the middle of a heat wave. I want to lick every golden inch of skin I can get my tongue on. Her cheeks redden further, and I know everything I'm thinking is written on my face for the whole world to see.

Jordan looks away and I draw a breath, feeling lightheaded. All the blood in my body has headed south, and from what ... seeing her walk in a room? I'm toast. Cindered, charcoal-covered toast. What happens if I actually manage to touch her for more than just a second? Will I pass the fuck out? I need to get a hold of myself.

"Sorry, Professor," she begins. Her hair is freshly washed. It keeps falling like a shiny, damp curtain in her eyes. She tucks it behind her ear with impatience. Is it really as soft as it looks? "I got—"

"Save your excuses and take a seat," he interrupts.

My pretend girl has not learned her lesson from last class, but our Professor has let her off easy. I catch her eye again, and jerk my head at the free seat beside me. Her gaze sweeps the room and my brows furrow. Is she planning on sitting somewhere else? There are only two other seats in the class. One is three rows down by the window, next to a girl tapping a pen in time with her foot and drinking a can of Red Bull. The other is in touching distance of Kyle Davis. So help me God if she sits there I will cause a scene.

Her gaze comes back to mine and my brows rise coolly. *Dating, remember?*

Without benefits, her narrowed eyes reply as she starts toward me.

I grin. *We'll see.*

"So you and Jordan really are a thing?" Jaxon asks from beside me.

"All you need to know is that we're exclusive," I reply, my eyes on Jordan. She shifts between seats, dodging books and discarded bags with ease as she makes her way toward us. Her legs are deliciously bare thanks to a skimpy pair of shorts the color of the sun. They're definitely soccer legs, and I can't wait to see how she uses them on the field ... and in bed.

I glance across at Jax, reminded of the way he acted with Jordan at that damn party. He's got a gleam in his eye. The one that usually takes out a female at a hundred paces and leaves her begging for more. My eyes narrow. "And so help me god," I add, "if I catch you putting your hands on her, you'll wake up an amputee."

Jaxon's mouth falls open, incredulity bright in his eyes. "Are you listening to yourself?"

Of course I am. I sound completely irrational. I don't care. My eyes return to Jordan, giving my cousin my back. It's then that I notice she's favoring her left ankle. There's a small hitch in her stride and a pinch between her brows. She's hurting.

"Are you okay?" I ask when she slides into the vacant seat beside me.

"Good morning to you too, Brody," Jordan replies and puts her bag on the floor beside her. She leans over and tugs out her books, notes, and a pen.

"Good morning, Jordan. Are you okay?"

When she straightens, I place a palm on her bare thigh, letting it slide inwards and tighten possessively. Her skin feels just how it looks—warm and smooth. I bite back a groan.

Jordan jerks with surprise the instant I make contact. Her knee cracks the desk above it, and she shoots me a glare. "What the hell?"

"We're dating remember?" My hand lowers to rub her banged knee soothingly. At least I hope it's soothing for her, because it's not for me. I have no doubt I'm the only student to ever get a boner in Business Law and Ethics. I lean her way, keeping my voice low. "You're supposed to *like* me touching you."

"I wasn't expecting it," she hisses, glancing quickly around the room before looking back at me. "You just groped me out of nowhere with your octopus hands and now everyone is staring at us."

"Newsflash. They were already staring at us, so hurry up and kiss me hello."

"Um … what?" She's looking at me like I just asked her to get up close with an alligator.

I let go of her leg and straighten in my seat. My retreat comes with an audible sigh of relief from Jordan.

"Am I not your type?" I ask quietly, sliding the attendance sheet across her desk.

She picks up her pen and signs her name below mine. Her handwriting is neat and tidy, a complete contrast to my messy, illegible scrawl. "I don't have a type."

"All women have a type." My grin is smug. "I'm yours, aren't I?"

With a roll of her eyes, Jordan passes the attendance sheet to the guy sitting on her right. "No, you're not my type at all."

"Ha!" I jab my finger at her in victory. "So you totally do have a type."

She pauses and gives me her full focus. "Perhaps I do, and conceited jocks aren't it."

"Lucky I'm not conceited then."

I don't miss the twitch of Jordan's lips and my grin widens. Dismissing me, she shifts her focus to my uncle and begins taking notes on the ethical guidelines he's outlining.

"So is that all there is to know about you?" Jordan asks me, though her eyes are on her page as she keeps writing. "You don't like chocolate, your middle name is Abraham, your dream is professional football, you're persistent, you like to think you're not conceited when you totally are, and..." she glances pointedly at the blank page in front of me "...you don't take notes in class."

"Notes?" I kick back in my seat. "That's what I've got you for."

Her mouth falls open. "Is that the real reason you didn't show up Monday night? Because you think I'm going to do all the work for you?"

The real reason? My face hurt like a bitch and my mood was shit. After leaving my parents' house, I went to the gym and lifted weights until I felt numb. And when I got home at one in the morning, I still couldn't sleep. I lay there questioning why I bothered. Why I worked so hard. I don't need to prove anything to my parents, or anyone else. I know that in my head, so why can't my heart let it go?

I meet Jordan's eyes, keeping my voice low. "It's not easy accepting that you need help. I hate that I struggle to read," I confess. "And it's not just that. I can't take notes either. Listening is a huge issue for me. I can't compute the words fast enough. They go in, but before I've had time to process them, let alone write them down, my professors have already moved on and I lose them."

There's no pity in Jordan's eyes, only that determination that's always there like a cold fire burning. "I'm sorry it's not easy for you," Jordan says quietly. "You can copy my notes down later. And next time just record them on your phone or laptop. I know it takes more time, but it's just something you have to do."

Something curls around my heart and squeezes. I know I've made some kind of choking noise when Jaxon kicks me with his foot. "Dude, what is wrong with you?"

"Nothing." Clearing my throat, I pick up my pen and pretend to focus, but I can't. When I tilt my head to look at Jordan again, she catches me and smiles.

"Brody. Jordan," my uncle calls out.

I jump at the sound of his voice. Students swivel in their seats to stare, and a smirk appears on Davis's face. I lean back casually in my seat.

"Would either of you care to correlate ethical behavior with the practice of multi-national corporations sending profits offshore?"

No. Hell no. Jordan's smart enough for me not to hesitate throwing her under a bus. "I'm sure Jordan would love to answer that question."

Jordan shoots me a glare and my lips twitch in response.

"Reputation?" she says to our professor, the word coming out more like a question than an answer.

"Expand."

She clears her throat. "Well, sending profits offshore is a tax minimizing regime, right? That's millions of dollars lost in American tax dollars, and directly affects the services the governments provide to us. What they're doing might be legal via tax code loopholes, but it's unethical, and it's harming their reputation. Customers are boycotting these businesses, forcing them to adhere to an ethical standard or face having it hit their bottom line."

"Good." His eyes scan the room. "Can anyone tell me what other ethical issues are facing big business today?"

When the lecture is over, I snap my books shut with relief and shove them inside my bag. Students stand en masse, shuffling their way outside while I wait for Jordan to get her things together.

"Brody, Jordan, can I see both of you, please?"

Jordan stands. Resting her bag on her desk, she begins filling it. When she's done I snatch it up and carry it down the front of the room for her. Davis sits off to the side. He's lingering at his laptop like a festering blister that won't go away, his fingers tapping a steady rhythm on the keyboard while pretending not to watch us. I shift forward a step, blocking Jordan from his view. It's a subtle move but when his eyes cut to mine I know he doesn't miss it for what it is.

He smirks.

My hands fist.

"How's the tutoring going?" Patrick asks quietly, looking between the both of us.

"Good, Professor," Jordan replies quickly. The back of her hand brushes mine and the knot of anxiety growing in me loosens.

"Brody? Is it helping?"

I shrug. "I guess we'll find out after midterms, right?"

The lines on his forehead deepen. "If either of you have any problems, or it isn't working out, come see me."

He nods a dismissal and we both turn to leave. "A quick word, Brody?"

I halt, telling Jordan to go when she hesitates. Her gaze shifts quickly between my professor and me before leaving the room. My irritation ramps up a notch when I notice Davis slip out the door behind her.

"Brody."

I drag my eyes away and give him my attention.

"What happened to your face?"

"Nothing. Just an injury at training."

My expression is neutral yet he cocks his head, narrowing his eyes in a look that says *I know you're lying.*

"Is that all?" My brows rise coolly. I don't want to talk about it any more than necessary. "I need to eat before I get to training."

His jaw tightens, but he nods his head at the door. "Go."

Jordan is waiting for me when I leave the room. The pleasure dampens when I see Kyle by her side, talking to her. "Get lost, Davis," I snap.

"I was just checking to see if Jordan has a study partner for the case assignments." He rubs his brow with his middle finger. "No one wants their grade jeopardized by studying alongside a dumbass."

Asshole.

In my mind I'm grabbing his throat and slamming him against the wall. In reality I'd get pulled from the next game if I did that. Davis knows it and follows up his comment with a wide grin.

I take a step closer, pleased at the three-inch height difference when he has to look up. My shoulders are wider and I roll them deliberately. "Jordan's study partner is none of your concern."

He shrugs, and like I haven't even spoken he looks to Jordan. "You know, as the teacher's aide I could help you out."

I glance at Jordan. Her eyes are on Davis like he's a cockroach that won't die. "I don't need your help." She takes my hand in hers, her grip tight. I give it a squeeze, liking her response.

"Don't be so sure about that." He turns to leave, adjusting his bag over his shoulder. "You have my number if you change your mind."

She has his number? My eyes narrow.

"Stay away from Jordan," I call to his back as he walks away.

He turns, brow arched, walking backwards. "Don't you think that's her call?"

"You only want her because she belongs to me."

Kyle shakes his head. "Wow, ego much, Madden?"

"Fuck off, Davis." Carter shoulder checks him as he walks toward us. Kyle scowls at Carter's back before disappearing in a sea of students. Carter gives me a fist bump and winks at Jordan. "Yo, pretty girl."

"It's Jordan."

"What?"

"My name," she says, her hand still tucked warm and firm in mine. "It's Jordan."

Carter smiles and lays an arm across her shoulder. "Ahh, Madden's girl." He nudges her with his hip. "You two left the party early, huh?"

"Knock it off, Carter." Letting go of Jordan's hand, I steal the football from under his arm and smack him on the head with it.

"Dude!" He snatches it back and spins it in his hands. "You guys coming to lunch? I'm so hungry I could swallow a burger whole."

"I'd pay money to see that." Eddie interjects when he and Jaxon appear behind Carter.

"How much?" Carter's tone is all business and they begin to haggle as we walk out to the quad. I retake Jordan's hand in mine, and we follow behind while they discuss terms.

"What was all that about?" Jordan asks me.

"What, me and Davis?"

"Yeah."

I stop suddenly and give her my back, leaning down a little. "Climb on."

"What?"

"Climb on and I'll tell you."

"But—"

"Hey, Eddie!" I call out. "Catch!" I grab Jordan's bag before she knows what I'm doing and toss it at him. He catches it without missing a beat. I do the same with mine and he shoulders both, waiting for us.

"Hurry up and do what the man says, Jordan," Carter orders impatiently. "I've got a bet to win."

"This better be a good story," she mumbles and climbs on my back. Her small hands link around my shoulders, clutching me tight. I'm inhaling deeply as I grab underneath her thighs, holding her firm to my back as I straighten. Jordan smells so damn good.

"Don't drop me."

I grin and lean backwards, pretending to stumble. Jordan lets out a little squeak. Burying her face in the back of my neck, she clings tighter. I'm still chuckling as we come out of the underpass and into the quad. The grass is kept green and lush, and the sun is shining bright on the students milling around talking. Most are piled in groups as they sit on the ground eating lunch.

Jordan sighs when the warm sun hits us. It's not a tired sound, but a peaceful one. I turn my head to look at her. Her profile is all I can see, but it's enough. Her lashes are dark and long and her lips slightly parted, inviting a taste. I lick my own and try focusing on something else. "So how did you roll your ankle?"

A grimace forms. "How did you know?"

"You think I don't notice those beautiful legs of yours when you walk in a room? I saw you favoring it. You know I told you not to text and jog." I grin teasingly. "You fell in a ditch, didn't you?"

"Something like that," she mumbles and a flush lines her cheekbones. "So what's the beef with you and Kyle Davis?"

Jordan's rubbing against my back in the best possible way, with each step I take. I pause briefly to hitch her a bit higher. "We went to the same high school together. He used to play football—wide receiver like me— but he was never that great. He worked hard but the talent was never there. When someone started tampering with my gear, I had a fair idea it was him, but—"

"He tampered with your stuff?"

"Yeah. I'd find straps cut on my shoulder pads, my cleats missing, tears in my gloves. That kind of stuff. Not a huge deal, but enough to get me into shit with Coach because it made me late for training and games."

"Why didn't you say anything?"

I huff bitterly, shaking my head. "Is that what you'd do? Go running to your Coach?"

"No," Jordan admits. "But I'd want to kick his ass."

"And then I'd get cut from the team for fighting. A lose-lose situation."

"So what did you do?" she asks, lifting an arm around my shoulder to brush hair from her face.

"I didn't do anything. Carter did," I reply, jerking my chin in his direction. His arm is slung around his on-and-off again girlfriend, Lara, as they walk across the quad. They're off right now, or so I thought, but that doesn't stop her looking up at him right now like he created Earth. "He got video of Davis in the act and threatened to put it on YouTube if he didn't quit the team."

"And he quit? Just like that?"

I nod. "He quit. But not just like that, because now he's an eternal thorn in my side. He's biding his time, nursing his grudge." My jaw tightens, my expression grim. I didn't miss the gleam when Davis looked at Jordan. He knew I saw it. "Stay away from him, okay?"

"That won't be a hardship," Jordan says. Her voice is close to my ear, and I fight a shiver. I like the husky way words roll from her lips, no matter what she's saying.

"I mean it, Jordan." My tone is rigid. The thought of him anywhere near her makes me tense.

"Of course."

"Good." I pause for a breath when we reach the other side of the quad. The dining hall is to the left, following a long sweeping path. To the right is the Liberal Arts building. "You having lunch with us?"

"I can't. I have American History." Jordan squirms a little, indicating she wants down. I have no intention of letting her go. Instead, I stand there, enjoying the wriggle of her body against my back. "You can put me down now, Brody."

"I'm afraid I can't do that," I say with grave seriousness, and my hands tighten around her firm, tanned legs. "You need to rest your ankle as much as possible."

Preferably while attached to me.

"Well I have to get to class."

"Eddie," I shout because he has Jordan's bag. He halts on the path toward the dining hall and half turns. I jerk my head in the other direction. "This way."

He shrugs and heads for us.

"Why are you taking American History anyway?" I ask while we wait. "That's a freshman class."

"It's part of my transfer."

Eddie catches up and we head in the opposite direction. I have to hitch Jordan up a little again, and she protests.

"Want me to carry you, Elliott?" Eddie asks. "Madden looks plain tuckered out."

"Are you calling me a heavyweight, Eddie?" Jordan loosens an arm from around my neck and punches him in the bicep.

"Arrghhh!" Eddie cries out like a wounded elephant and grabs his arm. He rubs it, his bottom lip poking out. "Your girl is vicious, Madden." He gives Jordan a wink. "I was only trying to point out that I'm a way better ride then he is."

I shove Eddie with my shoulder. With Jordan on my back it puts me off balance and we teeter precariously. Her hold on me tightens until I regain my footing. He teases her during the rest of the walk to the Liberal Arts building. When we arrive, my hands loosen on her legs, and she slides slowly down my back. I turn until we face each other.

I've placed Jordan right at the front door, and it forms a blockade at the entrance. Freshmen squeeze their way around us. All of them early and no doubt eager to make a good impression. I don't notice them. My eyes are on the lock of hair that's fallen on Jordan's face. I reach out, my intent to tuck it behind her ear. The strands slide through my hand like water, glossy and sleek.

"Brody." My name on her lips is breathy and her eyes on mine wide. Just that slight intimacy right out here in the middle of everyone is affecting her as much as me.

I can't believe how easy she makes me lose focus.

My pulse is hammering.

It's not good.

Not.

Good.

I force myself to back up a step.

At the same time, Eddie hands Jordan her bag. She takes it, clutching it to her chest. It's a barrier, warning me from getting too close.

"I'll see you tonight." Jordan clears her throat. "For the tu— For the, you know. Tonight, okay?"

I give her a brief, casual salute, already walking backwards. "Tonight."

CHAPTER 11

JORDAN

Paige comes at me hard, putting on the pressure and forcing me to make a move. With half an hour left in our Thursday afternoon training session, Coach has split the team in half and set us loose in a short scrimmage. Our team captain is taking *scrimmage* seriously. Off the field, Paige is funny and likeable. On the field she's a goddamn ninja. Before you can blink she's in your face, her eyes narrowed in a murderous glare—like the ball's her baby and you're a homicidal kidnapper. It's intentionally off-putting, but I just grin at her as I dribble the ball toward the goal, cocky and confident on the field. I was born with a soccer ball at my feet. I grew up with my brother and his friends coming at me, trying to steal it away in our backyard games. Nothing Paige can ever do will put me off.

My ankle is strapped and Ibuprofen is busy taking care of the pain as I tap the soccer ball with the instep of my right foot, feinting left. It's a classic move, but it's one Paige anticipates. So when I actually go right, she comes with me like a buzzing mosquito out for blood.

Knowing I need to find empty space, I stop the ball with my boot before passing it backwards. Leah's wide open and takes possession with ease. I signal her behind my back, indicating wide left is where I want it. With Paige having no choice but go hard at Leah, I run for open space.

Leah puts her boot behind the ball and punts it up the field. It flies up and over, landing a few meters ahead of me with perfect precision. I run straight into the bounce, using my knee to gain control before kicking off with my left boot to keep it moving. An opposing midfielder comes at me and I pass the ball, running forward to find more space. It's passed back with a smooth roll, and I draw back my boot, sending it sailing. It screams passed the goalie and slams into the back corner pocket of the net.

"Whoooooooop! Elliott!" Leah shrieks. A body crashes into my back, and we go down in a flailing pile of limbs.

"Get off me!" I yell when more bodies land above me, crushing me into the ground. My voice is a muffled shriek thanks to the forearm wedged in front of my mouth. I'm tempted to bite it, but it's the only thing between me and a face full of dirt.

Eventually I'm freed and flop onto my back, the late sun still packing enough heat to leave me gasping. I suck in a few deep breaths of air, ignoring the screaming twinge in my left ankle while everyone else regains their feet. It hurts more than it should, but I can't afford to rest it.

The piercing squawk of a whistle cuts through laughs and team banter. I lift my head. Our assistant coach is waving us over. Paige stands above me, blocking the setting sun. She holds out a hand and I take it, letting her haul me to my feet. I get a hard slap on the back that makes me stumble forward.

"I'll get you next time, Elliott."

"You'll have better luck catching a bullet with your teeth," I retort.

"Har, har," she replies, slinging an arm around my shoulder and jostling me as we walk off the field. I grimace, ducking my head as slivers of pain shoot up my leg. "You Aussies are so full of shit."

Leah comes up on my left, and Paige cranes her neck to look at her. They share a meaningful glance, something I'm not privy to but get the feeling I'm about to be.

"So." Paige's gaze returns to me. "There's a little something Leah and I need to know."

"Oh?" I raise a questioning brow, but I have a good idea what's coming and brace accordingly. "Need to know or want to know?"

"Need to know, of course," Leah replies for the both of them.

Paige sniggers and while I'm rolling my eyes, she clears her throat pointedly. "We all know Brody Madden is a prime piece of real estate, right?"

Her logic is flawless. Every single inch of Brody is prime. I'm trying really hard not to notice. Actually that's a lie. I don't think I'm even trying. He keeps giving me glimpses of the man underneath the brash exterior, and it's reeling me in like a hooked fish.

My response is a sigh. That's all I've got.

Paige continues. "Well what we want to know is—"

"Need," Leah interjects. "Need to know."

"Right. What we *need* to know," Paige corrects, "is just how prime he really is."

"How prime?" I reply, my eyebrows high. "Really? That's what you both need to know?"

"Stop holding out on us." Paige grabs her crotch in an obscene gesture as we reach the edge of the field, joining the huddle of our teammates. "The junk, Jordan," she says bluntly. "How prime is it?"

They break out in laughter and our assistant coach shoots us a glare.

"Get a hold of yourself," I mutter to Paige, because she's the one making the most noise.

"She already has," Leah replies, now in the throws of a choking fit.

"Oh good lord," I mutter.

Coach Kerr blows her whistle. The ear splitting peal slices through the afternoon air and silence reigns instantly. When she pulls it from her lips, her nostrils are flared. "That was sloppy play! You need to sharpen up," she snaps, chopping her hand against her open palm to emphasize her point. "Jordan scored that last goal because you had unmarked players. Unmarked players!" Coach is frustrated because it's the one point where our team is falling down. "Mark. Your. Player. I want you on your opposing mark like a fly on shit. Don't leave them open to score goals. Don't let them breathe without you in their face. Make them work for it. Make them run hard. Wear them down while trying to find that goddamn empty space. They'll make mistakes, and that's when you strike."

A collective expression of shame sweeps across our tired, sweaty faces.

"If you want a soccer career outside of college, you need to remember that every game counts. Every training session counts. Every pass of the ball counts. Every step you take on that field," she points directly behind us, "counts."

Coach Kerr is right. There's no room for slacking off. I've left Nicky behind for this. It's made me selfish, but it's all I've ever wanted. Training is a priority. Games. Everything else has to fit in around it. Life, people, family, friends. They fall by the wayside in the push to the top. Being the best comes with sacrifice, but if you can live with giving up everything but the game, you're in with a fighting chance.

"Breathe it," Coach demands. "Sleep it. Dream it. Eat it. And yes, shit it. Tomorrow night is game night. Let's show them that *we* are the team to beat." She pauses for a moment, her eyes sweeping over her team with fire in her eyes. "Now get back out there. I want you running extra laps tonight."

My stomach sinks. My ankle throbs. It's taped up beneath the thick, knee-high socks we wear, but it's swelling and needs elevation, not further punishment.

"How many?" Leah dares to ask.

"Until you either vomit or your legs give out."

We're dismissed and run out en masse to begin our laps. No one speaks. We're too exhausted. Our energy stores are depleted and there's nothing extra to give. I run the laps but my mind is begging and pleading for me to stop each time my left foot jolts into the ground. I run until the twinge in my ankle morphs into screaming pain. I run until I have nothing left.

When I'm home and showered, I burrow into my bed. Ibuprofen is now my best friend and I partake liberally. Rest tonight and tomorrow and I'll be playing in Friday's game. It just means keeping Leah in the dark. My ankle hasn't healed like it should've by now, and if she finds out she'll pitch an unholy tantrum.

Ten minutes later, after excessive banging of pots and pans, she's rapping on my closed door. It's her turn to cook, and my stomach is a growly lion because I didn't have time for lunch.

"I'll be out in a minute, Leah," I call out, my voice groggy as I roll over. I stifle a groan when my ankle shrieks in protest.

The door clicks open and I burrow in further.

"Just ten more minutes," I promise from beneath the safe haven of my sheets.

"Ten more minutes?" comes the distinctly amused male voice. "Just what are you doing under there? And can I join in?"

My heart is an instant jackhammer despite having done nothing but lie in bed. Oh no. *No, no, no.* That needs to stop. The little hitch in my breath? The screaming butterflies that tickle my stomach? Just … no.

The bed dips beside me. The sudden heavy weight on the mattress forces my body to roll sideways toward it. *Damn you, gravity.*

"I was sleeping," I finally manage to mutter as I furtively check my watch. I haven't been in bed ten minutes. The pain meds had me knocked out for an entire hour.

"Are you sure? I need proof." My sheets are ripped away unceremoniously.

"Hey!" I cry out.

Bright light hits me, revealing Brody perched on the edge of my bed. He's wearing sweatpants, a snug college tee shirt, and a teasing smile. His body is angled toward me, one hand planted flat on the bed near my left hip. My pulse thumps as I stare at it, mesmerized. Is there nothing sexier than football hands? I think not. His are big and tanned, boasting thick veins that pop over wide knuckles and trail up along the land of hopes and sexy dreams. Blinking, I drag my eyes upwards from thick muscled forearms.

Brody's watching me, his teasing smile morphing into heat and mischief. He cocks his head, dark brown eyes pinning me to the bed. He looks like the Big Bad Wolf, the kind of guy my brother always warned me away from.

I scrub a hand over my face in a vain attempt to restore semblance to my chaotic insides. It doesn't work. I can't pull myself together when he's looking at me like that. "Let me just go wash my face and we can start the tute. I need to wake up a little."

I go to move but Brody takes up a lot of room. His frame dwarfs my tiny bed. I pause and give him a look that says *please move.*

He grins unapologetically.

"Can you move?"

Having to force those words past my lips is *not* a good thing.

Thankfully Brody stands, backing away a little with his palms up. He jerks his head at the bedroom door. "So go."

I quickly swing my legs over the edge of the bed. "Sonofab—" I suck in a sharp breath.

His teasing smile is gone in an instant, replaced with an expression of concern. "What the hell, Jordan?"

My stomach rolls and I can't hide the grimace.

"Your ankle?" he asks.

Not pausing for an answer, Brody slides one of those delicious hands down the bared length of my left leg. His palm scrapes smooth skin, and I can't fight the shiver. My body erupts in goose bumps when he reaches the swollen joint, encasing it with his fingers.

He presses down around the injured area. "How does that feel?"

I grit my teeth, a light sweat breaking across my brow. "Hurts."

"Dammit, Jordan." He fixes me with a scowl. It does nothing to lessen the ache pulsing between my legs. "You trained this afternoon on a rolled ankle? I thought you were supposed to be smart."

"Of course I trained," I snap. "You think I want to miss a game? Coach would bench me with an injury like this."

"You deserve to get benched for doing something so …"

"So, what? Stupid?"

His lips press flat. "I hate that word."

"I'm sorry," I reply, shamed at my insensitivity. "I won't use it anymore."

Brody takes one of the pillows from behind me. Lifting my leg gently, he places it beneath my left foot. He sets my leg back down with care, but it still tears a pained moan from my throat. "You're a liability to your team playing with an injured ankle, Jordan."

I let out a frustrated huff. "What, like you've never done it?"

"Are you fucking kidding me?" Anger radiates from Brody's dark eyes as he stands, his jaw ticking. "Do you have any idea how many times I've trained with injuries? How many games I've played with cracked ribs, strains, sprains, and concussions? I know what it means to be benched. There's always another player there itching to take your place, prove their worth, prove they're better than you."

"Then why are you so angry I trained with mine?"

"Because you have a choice. I don't!" His voice rises like thunder until it vibrates right through me, making me shake. "Football is all I have!"

"I have a choice?" I burst out, my own frustration rising by the second. "I didn't give up everything and come halfway across the world to get benched for an ankle sprain!"

"You're lucky, Jordan. You've got a brain." His finger jabs at the photo on my corkboard that I tacked up only yesterday of me with my parents. It makes my gut clench to see us smiling happily at the camera, the snapshot a daily reminder of how easy it is to lose what you care for most. "You've got a fucking family. You've got the world at your feet. A smart girl with talent who looks like you? Scouts are gonna be busting down your door to get at you. You just … you … " A frustrated groan slips from his lips. He grabs at his hair and stalks for the door.

"Where are you going?" I demand when his hand circles the handle. I push up on my feet and pitch forward, my ankle giving out beneath me.

Brody moves fast, grabbing underneath my armpits before I crumple to the floor. "Dammit, Jordan."

Anger has him breathing hard. I meet his eyes to find him staring down at me. It freezes me in place and desire slams me like a freight train.

When he eventually speaks his voice is hoarse. "I wasn't leaving. I was going to get you a first aid kit. You need some ice and a bandage."

Making sure I'm steady, Brody's hands fall away and he leaves the room like Satan's on his heels. I sink to the edge of the bed, brushing hair from my face with a shaky hand. When he returns, he's carrying a first aid kit in his hand.

He crouches at me feet.

"I can do it," I squawk, my voice like a crazed bird. In my defense, I have Brody sitting back on his heels, taking my leg in both hands and resting my foot on his knee.

"Let me," Brody says quietly, his head bowed as he takes a bandage from the kit by the floor on his left. Unwrapping it from the package, he begins winding it around my ankle. After a few turns, he looks up from beneath thick lashes. "Not too tight?"

I clear my throat. "No. It's good."

He returns to his task, extending the bandage up the length of my calf and back down as he speaks. "Are you worried about scouts, Jordan?

Because you don't need to be. If they see something they like, they'll come back."

I'm tempted to throw out a cavalier comment and hide the fear. If I don't acknowledge it, it doesn't exist, right? I even go so far as to open my mouth before I snap it shut.

Brody's head is bent at his task, fingers nimble and brow furrowed in concentration. There's sweetness beneath his cocky exterior. I don't see him share that with anyone else, but for some reason I'm given peeks. Instead of turning away, I look, and now it's all I can see.

"Getting this international sports scholarship was like winning the lottery." Brody pauses and stares up at me, his eyes dark and troubled in the waning light. "I've come from having nothing, and now I'm on the verge of having almost everything, and I know I'll never get another chance like it." Like always, the thought overwhelms me. I turned my head away, staring blindly at the wall over Brody's shoulder.

BRODY

I set Jordan's foot on the floor and push up on my knees. It brings my face in line with hers. Taking her chin in my hand, I drag her gaze back to mine. The searing blue in her eyes is dull and tired. "Is that what today was all about?"

Jordan's lips press tight for a moment. "I'm scared," she says. "Sometimes the pressure gets too much, and I push myself too hard." Her eyes search my face. She's waiting for me to brush her fears off as trivial, but I don't. How can I, when the same fear echoes inside my own heart? "I'm so scared I'm going to mess it up."

"Why?" I push, forcing her to give me more. "What's gonna happen if you mess up?"

Jordan hesitates so I take her hands in mine, linking our fingers and resting them on her thighs. She stares down at them as she speaks. "I don't have it all. I have my brother and I have soccer, and that's it. He gave up so much to get me here. I was the one with the talent and the drive to succeed. He went without so I could benefit, every decision revolving around my future. And he put me first because his belief in me is as sure as his belief in the sun rising and setting each day."

Jordan has someone who believes in her. Isn't that half the battle? I swallow bittersweet emotion. My father can't wait to see me fall. To say I told you so. I'll never understand it, and yet I'll do anything to prove him wrong. Whatever it takes. And sometimes that scares me more then failing does.

Rather than offer up empty platitudes that help no one, I grab the neckline of my shirt. It musses my hair as I drag it over my head and toss it on the floor. Jordan's gaze drops to the ink on my chest, the tattoo placed to the right of my heart where I see it in the mirror every day.

> I fight to win
> To conquer
> I will persevere
> and use my fear
> And with the grace of God
> I will triumph
> over failure
> Rise
> beneath defeat
> And I will
> *fly*

I watch her silently. Jordan lifts her arm and my lungs constrict when her fingers touch my bare skin. Her fingers trail across the swirl of black letters as she reads them. Her simple touch is intimate. Reverent. It sends goose bumps skittering across my chest. Her pretty blue eyes lift to meet mine and a wordless understanding passes between us. "You fly too?"

I nod, struggling to ignore the heavy pounding of my heart. "Out there on the field, the game is everything. It builds you up, breaks you down, and it bleeds you dry. But I love it. It's the only place I'm free."

Jordan's eyes drop again to the tattoo. She covers it with the flat of her palm as though absorbing the words into her very skin.

"Who wrote it?"

She's the first person to ever ask the question. "I did."

"It's beautiful."

You're beautiful.

I shift closer. I feel like I'm falling. The weightless sensation is all her. Jordan is all I can see. My hands take hold of her hips, fingers tightening as I fight the feeling. I take a deep breath and count to ten. It doesn't work. When I try again I reach fifteen before giving up. It's not working because I don't want it to. I don't want to stop the way she makes me feel.

"You believe in God?" she asks me.

"Of course." I lean in, breathing softly against Jordan's lips, and nudge her nose with mine. Her body trembles, revealing her nerves. "I need to believe in something."

Her fingertips touch the soft curls of my hair before sliding around the nape of my neck, firm and warm. She holds my eyes and I can't look away. "Then believe in yourself."

"You can't say shit like that." Her bottom lip is lush and full. I nip it sharply with my teeth, relishing her sharp intake of breath.

"Brody." She pulls back, her rejection coming through louder than a boom of thunder. It makes me want to pitch a tantrum like a kid who's just been told Christmas is cancelled. "Why can't I say stuff like that?"

I meet her eyes, staring into an ocean of blue. "Because I'll only let myself down."

Needing a minute, I push up off my knees and walk to the desk pressed up against the window. The blind is open but my eyes are drawn to the pile of books sitting neatly in the middle. On the top rests a copy of *The Cat in the Hat* by Dr. Seuss. I pick it up and flick through the pages, letting it distract me.

"Bed time reading?" I glance over my shoulder at Jordan, waving the book.

Her expression becomes stern as if she just put on her tutor hat. In fact, I know she has when she follows it up with, "That's your first lesson plan."

"What?" My brows shoot skyward. I drop the book like a hot potato and turn around.

"You heard me."

"I'm not sure I did. Is this some kind of joke?" I fold my arms, tension pinching my expression. "Give the dumbo a kid's book and have a laugh while he stumbles over the easy words?"

Jordan's brows form a thundercloud on her forehead. "That's not it at all," she snaps. "Easy and similar sounding words are often the hardest to read. It's a book that will give me an understanding of where you stand with your reading levels."

"So you can judge my levels of stupidity, you mean?"

"Brody!"

I draw in a breath, letting it out in a sharp huff through my nostrils. Jordan's eyes are steady and resolute. She's not backing down on this. Best just to get the next excruciating hour over with and leave, tail tucked firmly between my legs.

"Fine." I pick up the damn book. "Let's do this."

With the book in hand, I move over to the bed. Jordan's reclined against a couple of pillows but shifts sideways, freeing up space. I know she expects me to simply take a seat beside her. I don't. If I have to read Dr. Seuss, I'm going to do my best to enjoy it. Before she can blink I'm stretched out beside her. It's a risk. Jordan no doubt has a kick on her that could send me flying clear across the room. But she's also injured, so I'm taking advantage.

Turning my head, I offer a grin.

"Comfy?" she asks, sarcasm loaded in her tone.

My boxer briefs are getting tighter by the second so that's a no. Her vanilla scent surrounds me, and I press my nose into her neck and breath deep. Giggles erupt from deep in her chest and she pushes me away.

"Ah ha! She's ticklish."

The book is forgotten in an instant. Grabbing a fistful of hair, I yank it out of the way and lick her neck in one long stroke. Instead of a laugh, her eyes flutter closed and I get a deep, husky moan. For a moment I'm stuck, riveted in the sound. I'm not falling for Jordan. I'm plummeting hard and fast, and the feeling is indescribable.

"Brody." My name is a rasp on her lips, and I rock my hips against her side, instinctively seeking relief. She tilts her head, giving my mouth access to the long line of her throat. "The book."

"Fuck the book," I say on a groan and take her earlobe between my teeth, nibbling as my hips rock harder. The book drops carelessly to the floor, and I cup her jaw, holding her to me so I can taste her skin.

"Stop," she gasps.

I freeze, biting back a groan of frustration. Drawing away reluctantly, my hand slides from Jordan's face. She turns her head on the pillow, her cheeks flushed.

"I'm your tutor. I have a responsibility to help you, not make out with you."

Begging is a first for me, but today I've discovered I'm all for it. "You can do both."

"Come on out, kids!" Leah's holler echoes through the closed bedroom door. My head drops to Jordan's shoulder and I'm ready to cry. "Dinner's ready and it ain't gonna eat itself."

"Be there in a minute!" Jordan shouts before looking back at me. "I'm not going to be one in a long line of your girls, Brody. I'll help you with your grades, but you can find some other girl to suck your dick."

Her words are a slap in the face. Is that all she thinks I care about?

"I'm sorry," Jordan says instantly. "I didn't mean that. I just … I can't do this."

She's out the door before I can reply. I follow her out, my stomach in knots as we sit down to dinner.

"What's wrong?" Leah asks. I look up from my dinner plate. Leah sits opposite me at the tiny table, brows high. I've been pushing food around, tuning out their chatter. "You got a beef with the beef?"

"No, it's great," I lie. It tastes like week old sweat socks, or would if I'd ever chewed on a pair, but it's no worse then anything Jaxon or Damien would ever cook so I'm not complaining.

Leah's expression is doubtful. "You think so?"

Jordan snorts. "If Brody likes the taste of leather."

Leah juts her chin out and jabs her fork at Jordan before turning it on me. "I was out here slaving over a hot stove while you two got your freak on behind closed doors. I hope y'all choke on it."

Jordan and I share a quick glance while Leah stabs at her beef, shoving it in her mouth and chewing furiously. After a long moment and an audible swallow, she stands and grabs at our plates. "Who wants pizza?"

With dinner settling in my stomach, I'm reading through the Dr. Seuss classic at Jordan's desk. My pace is painfully slow and the book is tricky. I grit my teeth every time I stumble, which is often. It has a snowball effect, leaving me tripping over every sentence.

Midway through I slam it closed and spin around in the chair. Jordan's reclined on the bed with her ankle elevated on a pillow, clueless to all the dirty thoughts that hit me just from staring at her.

"Break time?" she asks.

"You think?" I roll shoulders damp with sweat. I was already agitated. Now I've had enough. I'm so done. I toss the book on the desk and turn back to Jordan. "What's the verdict?"

She untucks her hands from behind her head and pushes up on her elbows, her eyes narrowing. "The verdict is that you're lazy."

I huff at her bluntness. "Don't hold back or anything."

"Sensitivity isn't going to help you right now. Reading for most people is like riding a bike. It's a skill they never lose. But for dyslexics, it's something you have to work on every single day. You should know that."

"I do know that. But who has the time to stretch out in bed each night with a copy of *War and Peace*?"

Jordan shakes her head. I'm not just irritating her with my bitching, I'm irritating myself. "It doesn't have to be a classic. You can read the back of the cereal box for all I care. Just read. That's your task. I want you to read for a half hour every day. I want you to highlight all the words you have issues with and I want you to write a small paragraph summarizing what you read so I can look over it."

"What?"

"You told me you struggle with the words sinking in. Learning to summarize what you read will help you with that."

Read the back of a cereal box for all she cares? I hide a smirk. If that's what she wants, I'm going to find the most downright raunchy erotic story I can find.

Let's see you look over that.

Jordan edges gingerly off the bed. Her expression is less pained, but I half stand from my seat, ready to help. "What do you need?"

"The bathroom," she pants, rising to her feet and putting all the pressure on her right foot.

"Do you need help?"

"Do I … No!" She waves me away, limping steadily out the bedroom door. She's only gone a minute when the laptop on her desk begins dinging relentlessly. Is it some kind of alarm? I swivel around and lift the lid. When it opens, the screen lights up and a guys face appears on Skype.

Shit. I press a couple of buttons, not knowing how I've managed to answer a call just by opening her laptop.

"Hello?"

The voice is Australian, deep, and suspicious, and lines of irritation decorate his forehead. Jordan said she wasn't dating anybody, but I never considered the idea of her having a guy back home waiting for her return. I'm considering it right now and it's not sitting well with me.

"Who are you?" he demands to know, his tone rude and growly.

I reach up and tilt the screen. All the better for him to see my glare. "I'm the guy Jordan's dating. Who the hell are you?"

He rears back like I just punched him clean in the face. It's semi-satisfying in a virtual kind of way. "You're *what?*"

His eyes shift to somewhere over my right shoulder, and I feel Jordan at my back. "Jordan who the hell is this guy?"

"Nicky?"

There's a lot of love and happiness in that single word. It sets me on edge.

"Were you limping just then?" he asks, his brows drawn with concern.

"Just a little," Jordan replies, leaning over my shoulder to speak with him. "I rolled my ankle. Not bad or anything," she adds hastily when he opens his mouth. "I'll be fine to play tomorrow night."

"Tomorrow night?" I swivel sideways in my chair, an *oh hell no* expression on my face. "Baby, are you crazy?"

Jordan's eyes go wide at the endearment. I admit it slipped out unintentionally but I can't deny its brilliant timing.

"Baby?" comes the echoing growl from the computer.

My grin is slow and lazy. Jordan's gaze drops to my mouth, those wide eyes now narrowing to slits.

"Jordan?" We both turn back to the computer. Frosty blue eyes glare back at us from the bright screen. "You let this asshole near you?" Nicky's voice gets louder as he directs it on me. "You touch my little sister and I will reach right through this motherfucking computer and punch your goddamn dick off!"

Little sister?

I scratch uncomfortably at the back of my neck. This has now officially moved into awkward territory. I really should feel a situation out before I charge right into it like an ignorant asshole.

"Nicky!" Jordan snaps. Her face looks hotter than the sun. If I touched her cheek right now I'm sure it would scorch the skin clean off my fingers. "Brody, this is my twin brother, Nicolas Elliott. Nicky, this is Brody Madden. He's a senior here at CPU. And we're not dating," she adds. "I'm his ..." Jordan breaks off, right before she can spit the word *tutor* out. She fixes me a look of hard-eyed frustration.

"You're his *what*?" Nicky prompts.

I clear my throat and face the screen. "We're working on an assignment together."

"And you need to do that in Jordan's room?"

Who does he think he is? Her father? I lean back in my seat, arms folded and casualness oozing from every pore. "That's right."

"Oh good lord," Jordan mutters from beside me. Putting both hands on the back of my chair, she rolls me to the side and out of view of the webcam.

"Hey!" My arms unfold, flailing as I career across the floor. I set my feet down and halt the momentum.

Jordan doesn't even spare me a glance. "Nicky is everything okay?"

"I don't know. Is it?"

She lays her palms flat on the desk, the move taking the weight off her injured ankle. "Why are you being such an ass?"

"Because I don't like you having strange guys in your room. You need to focus on school and soccer. Not Texan dickheads who go to college just so they can make notches on their bedposts."

I'm already rolling my way back toward the desk when he lays out his insult. Grabbing the laptop, I turn it in my direction. Nicky's face comes into view. "Texan dickhead?" I growl.

Jordan grabs it back, turning this ridiculous conversation into a laptop tug-of-war. "I'm working my ass off here on my grades and soccer." She bites off each word, her temper straining on a very short leash. "You need to trust that I'm doing the right thing."

"I'm sorry you think I don't trust you, sweetheart." His fingers trail down the screen as though he's tracing the contours of her face. That one gesture reveals the enormous depth of love he has with his sister. For a moment I envy it. My time with Annabelle is rare and limited, and I wish it were more. "It's everyone else I don't trust."

He says the words to Jordan, but he's looking at me when he says them.

"I have to go, Nicky. I'll talk to you tomorrow."

"Jordan—"

She shuts the lid of the laptop, cutting off the call. The room is silent while she hovers over the desk like she's taking a minute to regroup. When she's gone through whatever's in her head, she lifts it and looks at me.

"You know this whole dating farce is ridiculous."

I shrug. "You're right. It is."

She blinks. I've thrown her with my agreement.

"People won't care that you're being tutored."

"I care." I fold my arms, my jaw set. "My life isn't fodder for everyone to speculate on."

"But dating me is?"

"Not if it's real."

"Brody—"

"You took a huge risk travelling halfway around the world for something you believe in. You won't take a risk on me?"

Indecision fills Jordan's expression and she sinks to the bed behind her. She chews on her bottom lip. "It's not a good idea."

My lips curve slowly. "Some of the best ideas never are."

CHAPTER 13

JORDAN

Brody: *Tell me ur not playing.*

I read the text message, my stomach in flutters just from seeing his name pop up on the screen of my phone. Arriving in Texas, I had a plan that didn't include sexy, haunted football players. I'm strong and determined. Ambitious. With Brody I'm weak and that burns me. I tried aloofness and cool detachment, but it was a last ditch effort, like scooping water out of a sinking ship with my bare hands. It was when I read the words inked so beautifully onto his skin that the water closed over my head. My ship was sunk.

Now we're *officially* going on a date. When or where, I don't yet know. But it's happening. The thought makes my pulse pound anew and my head throb with foreboding. No good can come of this.

Jordan: *I'm not playing.*

Shoving the phone back in my bag, I take a seat at the bench in the locker room and begin the process of strapping my ankle for tonight's game. I wind the sports tape thick and tight, doing it fast in case anyone starts asking questions. Grabbing my socks, I slide the left sock on first, pulling it up to my knee. I jam my shin guard inside, resting it firm and snug beneath the tight-fitting sock. Then I repeat the process on my right leg. After sliding on my cleats and tying the laces, I stand, stomping hard on each boot to get my feet comfortable and check the solidity of my ankle tape.

My phone beeps again.

Brody: *Why don't I believe u?*

Jordan: *You don't? I'm so hurt.*

Gathering my tape, hoodie, and headphones, I shove them in my bag along with my phone and tuck it away in my locker.

Rolling my shoulders, I draw air deep in my lungs and jog out onto the field. The sky is clear, the horizon a deep orange as dusk strikes. The lights of the stadium are bright, illuminating the grass in a brilliant, rich green. Pre-game anticipation is thick in the air, stirring the nerves in my blood.

I'm the last one out. The team stands in a huddle by the goal posts waiting for instruction. I pick up my pace. We have just under an hour before kick off to warm up, run drills, and give pep talks.

Leah's eyes follow my arrival, narrowing in a glare that spells trouble. When I reach her side, her voice is an angry hiss. "I can't believe you."

"That seems to be going around a bit at the moment. What can I say?" I shrug and grin, but it's more like a baring of teeth. "I'm pretty unbelievable."

"It's not funny, Jordan. You should be benched."

"Can you say that a little louder?" I ask as I begin stretching out my left calf muscle.

"You should be—"

I cut off her shout. "I wasn't being literal."

"No, you were being a dick."

Leah gives me her back, dismissing me. There's nothing I can say. I won't be benched. After ten minutes of stretching, my eyes scan the bleachers and slowly widen. Half the seats in our modest stadium are taken, the rest filling rapidly. Loud, thumping music plays, rousing the existing crowd.

Leah has already taken off, starting her warm up laps without me. I jog quickly to catch up, ignoring the burn of pain shooting up my leg. "Have you noticed the crowd?"

"I'm not talking to you," Leah replies, panting softly as her booted feet hit the soft grass in a steady rhythm. She scans the bleachers anyway. "Oh look who's here to see his girl play."

A smirk spreads across her face like butter. I follow her line of sight and my lips tighten against the wide smile trying to break free. Brody's here. He's midway down the stadium, standing in front of the first row of prime seats where our team bench is located. The Colton Bulls cap he's always wearing hides his beautiful eyes and half his face. I can't see his expression, but I can feel it. A heavy blanket of disapproval swamps me. It radiates outwards from his folded arms and tense stance like gamma rays. It doesn't bode well, not with me here warming up when I told him I wasn't playing.

A scowl fixes on my face. Who does he think he is anyway? My brother?

Behind him sits Jaxon and what appears to be half the college football team. They're all wearing team colors, which includes the addition of war paint coating their cheeks. I glance over my shoulder. The team is jogging behind the pace we set, their eyes caught on the beefcake display that is Brody and his teammates. The boys see they have our attention and perform a mini Mexican wave.

"The crowd must be here because half the football team is," Leah puffs out, a trace of excitement in her tone. "You dating Brody is fantastic for us. Wait. He looks pissed." She glances sideways at me, suspicion shooting from her eyes like darts. "Why does he look pissed, Elliott?"

I purse my lips, not as easy to do as one would think while jogging warm-up laps.

"Ellioootttt," Leah drawls in a warning tone.

I exhale a loud puff of air. "Because I might have told him I wasn't playing."

"Awesome. You're starting your relationship off on a foundation of lies."

Oh you have no idea.

"Calm down, Dr. Phil," I retort as my booted feet sink into the lush grass with steady thumps. "It's not a relationship. It's casual dating."

"It's *exclusive* dating," she corrects. "That, my sad oblivious friend, is a relationship."

"How do you even know? Did you ever even date or were you and Hayden just born in a relationship with each other?"

Leah doesn't even acknowledge my response. She glances Brody's way again. "He's crooking his finger at you. You better go over."

"What?" My voice is a whip, but I don't swivel my head. Instead, I look from my peripheral vision, trying not to be obvious. I have a game to prepare for, both mentally and physically, and he thinks I can just take time out to chat? Clearly he's never heard the word *no* in his life. I refocus on my warm-up laps, keeping my eyes trained dead ahead.

"No he's not," I say to Leah. "That's just a twitch in his finger from an old football injury. He gets that all the time." We've reached midfield now, leading the team behind us. Every step brings us closer to the subject of our conversation. I jerk my chin at the center of the field. "Let's cross here."

"Elliott!" Paige puffs loudly from behind us. She must have run hard to catch up. "I think your boyfriend wants your attention."

I growl. I literally growl. It comes from deep inside, vibrating outwards from my throat with frustration. "For the love of ..." I change direction toward Brody, over my shoulder saying, "Be right back."

Brody unfolds his arms, taking a step forward when I reach the hip-high fence that separates us. "This is you not playing, huh?"

"That's right," I snap, in no mood to argue.

He must sense it because he shrugs and says quietly, "Okay. I get it."

"Good." I nod shortly. "Is there anything else or can I go now?"

"Actually." He turns his cap around, setting it backwards on his head. Then he grips the railing and leans in, his eyes glittering gems of mischief. "You should kiss me. For luck," he adds.

The very thought has my heart thundering in my chest, leaving me dizzy. My hands grip the fence tight, keeping me from pitching over. He peels them off and takes them in his, linking our fingers.

"People want to see us together. They're going to think it's weird we're not all over each other. Just—"

Before I can second-guess myself, I free my hands and grab his tee shirt in both fists. I drag him as close to me as the fence allows and mash my lips down on his. The press of his mouth is warm and firm and shoots heat straight to my belly. Catcalls and whistles come from every direction. I shove him away with a gasp. "There."

"Oh no you don't," he mutters when I disentangle myself from his shirt to make my escape.

Brody grabs me before I get away. Planting his large hands on my ass, he digs his fingers in and drags me back. "Oomph," is the extent of my contribution when I slam against his chest. I seize his shoulders before I fall over, and he ducks his head and plants his mouth back on mine. His tongue parts my lips and sweeps inside, hot, hard, and aggressive.

For a moment I'm suspended in shock. It quickly disappears, and I don't hold back. A groan rises from his chest when I return the kiss with equal enthusiasm. My hands slide from the muscular contours of his shoulders and loop around his neck.

Brody pushes his tongue deep, kissing me like I'm air and he's drowning. I don't want him to stop. Ever. I need more because it doesn't feel enough. I know he feels the same when he frees a hand from my backside and uses it to fist my hair violently, ramping my pulse up and into the stratosphere. That's where I float, mouth fused to his, ready to perform carnal acts without a second thought about where I am or who the hell's watching.

"I think they're actually going to have sex right here in the stadium," Eddie says from somewhere very, very far away. "Is anyone filming this?"

"I'm on it," Carter replies.

Brody's hands on me gentle, but he doesn't let go. He draws his mouth from mine and I'm a panting, trembling mess with legs made of jelly.

"Jordan," he croaks, the first one to speak. He licks along his bottom lip, his eyes dark and disoriented as he stares at me, breathing hard.

I stare back, shock freezing me to the ground so I can't move.

What in the freaking hell was *that*?

The sharp shrill of a whistle pierces my skull, jerking me from my stupor. With a quick glance of my surroundings, I'm reminded of our audience and the imminence of my soccer match, and I'm horrified.

"I have to go." I extract myself from Brody's hold. He doesn't fight me and I'm thankful. I jog backwards for a moment, his eyes holding mine. I drag them away and turn, making my way toward Coach Kerr.

Damn, damn, damn, I chant in time with the rapid beat of my heart. I shouldn't have done that. Now my mind is complete mush.

"You finished there?" Coach asks when I reach her side.

I clear my throat. "It was just a quick kiss for luck."

Coach Kerr shutters the amusement in her eyes, keeping her expression stern. "Get out on the field, Elliott, or no amount of luck will help you when I bench you for not warming up properly."

I do as she says, and after a long, sweaty match, we're tied one all with twenty minutes left in the game. The opposition is relentless and unforgiving but struggles to breach our defense. Our plan from the beginning was to wear them down. It's working. Exhaustion makes their passes sloppy and their play more chaotic. Another five minutes pass before I get my break and shoot for goal.

The air burns in my lungs and my ankle screams, but adrenaline is a powerful force that won't be denied. Our team holds their collective breath as the ball tips off the goalie's fingers in slow motion, reducing momentum. The entire stadium is silent for a single pin-dropping moment as the goalie falters, once, twice, and then loses the battle. The ball hits the back of the net before dropping inside the goal.

The stadium erupts and I'm tackled first by Paige and then the rest of the team. When I emerge from beneath a crushing, celebratory pile of sweaty limbs and excited hollers, I catch the football team doing another Mexican wave in the stands, this time Brody joining in and bringing his fingers to his lips, letting out a piercing whistle.

Jubilant, I give them a quick bow and begin a jog back to position. The opposing team's defender is letting loose a litany of foul curses from beside me.

"Lucky shot," she mutters somewhere in between, her tone disparaging.

"There was no luck about it," I snap. I'm sick of her taunts. They've been constant, her sledging an effort to destroy my concentration through the entire match. "We're a fitter, better team."

With a sneering face and the referees focus elsewhere, she jabs her booted foot at my injured ankle. Her strike hits right in the tender part, and I crumple like a cheap suit, crying out as I hit the ground.

"Ref!" Paige's shout rips across the field, signaling him with her arm thrown high as she jogs toward me.

I roll over and sit up, pain seizing hard and fast. My nostrils flare wide as I breathe through it in sharp, shallow pants. Loud shouts erupt from the bleachers. I barely hear it over the roar of blood in my ears.

"Bitch," Paige growls and shoves the defender in the chest. A cheer goes up from the spectators when the girl stumbles backwards. "I saw what you did."

The whistle blows, suspending play. The referee reaches me at the same time our team physician, Emilio, does. He runs a medical practice on the outskirts of Austin, and his fierce Italian temper is legendary. He keeps it leashed as he drops to a crouch in front of me, his eyes pinched in angry slits.

"What happened?" he asks, taking hold of my left foot with care.

"What happened?" Paige echoes with a shrill screech. She faces the ref while jabbing her finger at the number five center-back, her body a tense, quivering volcano ready to erupt. "That bitch just kicked Jordan in the ankle. You need to send her off, right now."

That bitch smirks while Emilio prods at my tender ankle. It feels like it's been put through a meat grinder. I look away, hot tears pricking my eyes. I'm definitely benched now.

Paige emits a low growl from her throat. She sounds ready to morph into a beast and seek violent revenge. Leah joins her side, and half the team circles us.

"Don't tell me how to do my job," the referee barks at Paige. "I didn't see the supposed altercation, so I can't call it. Let's resume play and watch your language, or you'll be the one sent off."

"Are you effing *blind*?" she shrieks. A huge argument blows up. Shouts break out. Paige pushes the defender again when she starts returning fire. More cheers erupt from the bleachers. The girl pushes back, fisting Paige's jersey and shoving her.

"Come on. Let's get you off this field," Emilio says quickly when the confrontation escalates into chaos. "Can you walk?"

The idea of being carried off is not one I want to entertain. "I can walk."

I yelp as I'm helped to my feet. The sound is drowned out by the argument in progress. It gains momentum when the referee holds up a yellow card.

"Oh this is *bullshit*!" Paige gripes.

I don't hear the rest. My arm is looped around Emilio's shoulder as he helps me limp from the field. The closer we get, the better I can hear Brody's shout from the sidelines. My eyes find him. His body vibrates with anger. He redirects it from the sideline referee to my coach, who's busy telling him to cool it or she'll have him escorted from the stadium.

"Hell," I mutter.

My cheeks heat. He's making it worse. And when I reach the bench, claps break out as if I'm a war-torn hero returning victorious from battle. I duck my head and sit with an exhausted sigh of relief.

"This is the best shit I've seen in ages," I hear Carter say when the applause dies off. "Chick fights are hot. Way to go, Jordan!" he yells in my direction, as if I masterminded the entire altercation just for their viewing benefit.

Eddie throws down his agreement. "We need to watch more women's soccer."

"I don't know," someone else pipes in. "I haven't seen any jersey's ripped off yet."

Emilio kneels in front of me, shaking his head. Lifting my booted left foot, he rests it on his knee and begins undoing the laces. A shadow looms over us, blocking the bright glare of the stadium lights.

"Get off the field," Emilio says to Brody without looking up and slowly begins removing my boot, taking care not to jostle my ankle.

I'm sucking in a hiss of pain when Brody crouches beside me. He looks up from beneath the brim of his cap, placing his palm on my right knee. There's tenderness in his expression that melts me like butter. My eyes drop to his lips and my pulse thumps, reminded of how much damage he did to my heart with that kiss earlier. "You okay?"

"Look, bud," Emilio pauses and tilts his head, giving Brody a firm glare. "I don't care who you are. I'm the team physician and it's my responsibility to take care of my girl here. So either get your ass off the field or I'll call security."

Brody's nostrils flare. "So call security," he bites out, his Texan drawl more defined with his anger. "I don't care. Some bitch just jabbed *my girl* with a spiked cleat. I'm not going back to my seat."

Emilio appraises Brody with his dark eyes. They must reach some kind of macho understanding because he gives Brody a brief nod. "Okay. You get Jordan's cleat off. I'll get a bandage and some ice."

Brody takes our team physician's place, picking up where he left off. He sets my boot on the ground and begins peeling my sock down my calf.

"So here we are again," I reply lightly.

"Here we are again," Brody confirms. His voice is tight, and I'm waiting for him to tell me I shouldn't have been on the field to start with but it doesn't come. Instead he bends his head, intent on his task as he unwinds the strapping tape that would've given away my pre-existing injury to Emilio. He rolls it up and tucks it in the pocket of his jeans without missing a beat.

Gratitude fills me. "Thank you."

"Jordan," Brody begins and takes a deep breath. He looks away, his eyes on the distance while my bare foot rests on his leg and his hands hold my calf.

"What?"

Brody's eyes return to mine. No lecture is given. His lips curve instead. "I'm proud of you. You played real good out there."

Warmth lights me up from the inside out. Heedless of my injury, my returning smile is bright and unrestrained. "Thank you."

Emilio returns and when I'm iced and as comfortable as possible, Brody sits beside me and we watch out the last ten minutes together. Our team's defense holds and when the final whistle blows, we win 2-1.

Brody goes with Emilio to get my bag and a set of crutches so I close my eyes. Sensing company, I open them to find Jaxon standing before me. It puts me on immediate alert considering our last conversation didn't go down so well. "Are you lost, Jaxon?"

"Nope."

That single word indicates a conversation is imminent. I sigh heavily and close my eyes again. The bench shudders when he sits beside me. After a moment of silence I squint an eye open at him. "What do you want?"

Resting his elbows on his knees, he's links his fingers together. "Would you believe me if I said I just don't want to see you hurt?"

"No." I stare out into the emptying bleachers opposite me. "Would you believe me if I said it doesn't matter because I can take care of myself?" Which clearly I can't. A certain brooding, flirty footballer is under my skin and I can't dig him out. If I do something so stupid as to hand over my heart, Brody will mark it 'return to sender' and mail it back flatter than a turkey sandwich. The problem is that I'm not sure I can stop myself. "Why do you even care?" I ask. "We're not friends if I recall."

It's a cheap shot, but I'm not feeling nice right now.

Jaxon hisses through his teeth. "I guess I deserved that, but you lied to me."

"No. I didn't."

His eyes roll. "Jordan—"

"I don't have to explain myself to you, Jaxon. All I'm saying is that I never lied to you. Circumstances aren't always what they seem."

"Oh they aren't?" Jaxon sits back on the bench and folds his arms. I'm struck then by how much he looks like Brody. His body is leaner and his hair has more curl, but their eyes and mannerisms are the same. "Are you or are you not dating my cousin?"

"Is there a problem, Jax?" Brody says from behind me. His timing is impeccable.

"Nope. No problem." Unfolding his arms, he tucks them behind his head and leans back like he's enjoying himself. "I was just telling Jordan here how crazy you are about her."

"Of course he is." That comment is thrown in from Leah. I turn my head. Both she and Brody stand behind us. Leah's had a quick shower and changed into sweats, her sports bag slung over her shoulder. Mine is in Brody's hand. His other holds a set of crutches. "No one missed that kiss before kick off. I thought the stadium would erupt in flames."

Me too. Heat floods my cheeks just thinking about it. "We should get going. I need a shower."

Brody helps me with the crutches and our progress outside the stadium is slow. "Jax." He tosses a set of keys toward his cousin. "Can you bring the car to the front parking lot?"

Jaxon snatches them midair and shrugs. "Yeah sure, whatever."

We make it outside where my car is parked by the entrance, and Brody halts so fast I almost go ass backwards.

He waves a hand at the hunk of metal parked on a perfect angle. *"This* is your car?"

"Yeah, it's my car," I reply, my defensive hackles rising. "What of it?"

"It's falling apart." Brody holds out his hand, palm up. "Give me your keys."

"What? No!"

His eyes narrow and suddenly it feels like *game on.* "Fine. I was going to get Jax to drive it to the junkyard, but we can just leave it here. I can get it towed or maybe you'll get lucky and a meteor will shoot down from the sky and crush it flat."

My mouth falls open. "I paid good money for that car."

Technically I didn't. It didn't cost much at all, but when your brother works his backside off and eats cheese toasties for dinner every night just to save money to send you off overseas, you tend to appreciate the value of a dollar.

"Then you got ripped off," he retorts.

The urge to jab him with my crutch is strong. "It works perfectly fine."

His brows shoot sky high.

"Actually it makes this weird kind of juddery noise when it goes above forty," Leah contributes. "And the air conditioner doesn't work. Neither does the passenger side window. Or the remote central locking."

"Are you finished?" I snap at Leah without taking my eyes from Brody. "My car gets me from A to B like it's supposed to."

A gleaming black SUV pulls up beside us. The door opens, revealing cream leather seats and a spotless interior. Jaxon alights. With him he brings the indescribable scent of 'brand-new car.' It's heady.

Jaxon tosses the keys at Brody, who jerks his chin toward it. "Get in."

"No."

His eyes fall to my mouth for a long, uncomfortable moment. I have to stop myself from swaying forward.

"Really, Jordan. Your car isn't safe."

Neither are you.

I don't let him win and I'm not sure why. Perhaps it's my rationality clutching at the last straws I have left. Whatever it is, our standoff ends with Leah driving me home. It's a hollow victory. I got my way, but I didn't get Brody and it seems he's all I want right now.

CHAPTER 14

BRODY

The bus jolts and quakes, coming to a stop on campus Sunday night. Our away game ended with a solid victory and spirits are high. Not me. My head is all over the place.

The apartment's empty when I get home, so I go for a run to try and gain some focus. After a ten-minute warm-up, I head out. It's late, the dark streets filled with students coming from or going to parties. I keep my head down and cap low as I dodge them, focusing only on the thump of music pounding in my head.

An hour passes before I'm a tired, sweaty mess. It should've been enough to get my head straight, but it's not. I have an icy shower to cool off. With my skin covered in goose bumps, I pull on a pair of boxer briefs and grab a beer from the fridge. With Damien and Jaxon not around, it's a good chance for me to do the reading Jordan expects of me.

Setting the beer on my bedside table, I stretch out on my bed and shove a couple of pillows behind my back, resting my laptop on my thighs. I open my email first and catch Jordan's name amongst an inbox full of junk. Finding the subject line, I double-click to open it.

Brody,

We need to go through the material for midterms so we know what areas to
focus on. When do you want to do that?

Jordan

Brief. To the point. Jordan couldn't be any less personal if she tried.
Bringing the bottle to my lips, I tip it back, my throat working as I swallow
down half the contents. It cools my chest, but not other parts of my body.
My mind is stuck on our kiss. It's obvious it affected Jordan as much as
it did me. Her body trembled and the heat in her eyes almost rivaled my
own. Jordan wants me and she's denying herself. Now she's going back to
her predictable game plan of forcing distance.

Setting my beer back down, I hit reply and slowly type my response.

Jordan,

Sounds like fun. Can't wait.

But we should go on our date first.

When do you want to do that?

Brody

PS What are you wearing???

Hitting send, I go in search of reading material. I don't have any
trouble. There are so many erotic stories available on the internet I don't
know where to start. I click on the first one I find that doesn't include
weird or creepy fetishes and begin to read. I get through it, coming to
the slow realization my plan has backfired. My chest is damp with sweat,
and I'm hard like an iron bar. I let out a harsh breath and type out my
summary. It's uncensored and wildly inappropriate, but that doesn't stop
me sending it.

Her reply comes through soon after and makes me chuckle.

Brody,

Your choice of reading material is inspired and your summary graphic. Kudos
for making me blush. Unfortunately, it needs work. I've included my corrections.
Please look them over. Interested to see what you choose to read next …

How do you feel about sushi?

Jordan

PS Clothes.

Pleased she isn't trying to wriggle out of our date, I write back
immediately.

Jordan,

I hear every sushi restaurant in the greater Austin area got shut down. It's unfortunate, but what do you expect? This is cow country.

You prefer steak? Good. Let's do that.

Tuesday night.

Brody

PS What kind?

I yawn and stretch. After finishing off the bottle beside me, I toss it toward the trashcan in the corner. It hits with a loud clang. I holler a victory at the same time Jordan's next email comes through.

Brody,

Pizza it is. Thursday night.

Jordan

PS The kind that is none of your business.

Unwilling to concede a single inch. I shake my head.

Jordan,

Done.

Brody

PS From now on, everything about you is my business.

That will get her hackles rising. Another yawn overtakes me. The screen blurs before my eyes. If Jordan writes a response it will have to wait for morning. I close the lid of my laptop and set it on the floor.

My eyes blink open when the alarm pierces my deep sleep. Picking up my phone, I switch it off with one hand and rub my face with the other. It's dark out but it's Monday morning and gym time.

Before getting dressed, I take an extra minute to check my computer. Jordan's first on my mind this morning and seeing a new email in my inbox brightens me instantly.

Brody,

I should let you know I won't be in class this week. I'm doing course work from home so I can rest my ankle. It's not healing like it should and has me a little worried.

See you Thursday. Shall I pick you up?

Jordan

PS That kind of caveman talk could see you lose a couple of teeth. Just sayin'.

I chuckle under my breath as I drag on my workout gear. I can't reply right now but I will later. Jordan's not the only one concerned about her ankle. I'm happy she's taking the week to rest it. That kind of simple injury can escalate from a molehill to a mountain if it's not dealt with quickly, and in the right way.

My day goes fast but it's not until later in the night I get a chance to send her my reply.

Jordan,

I'll give you one word about resting your ankle. Good.

Two words about seeing you Thursday. Can't wait.

Three words about picking me up. No fricking way.

Brody

PS Threats of violence get me hot. Just sayin'.

Tuesday night comes and I'm tired, irritable, and can't focus. I want Jordan. Badly. I feel like a tightly coiled spring ready to explode.

Already in bed, I reach over and pick up my phone, scrolling my contacts. I've kicked off my sheets. My skin is hot and too itchy for me to find sleep. I put the phone to my ear and wait, not having a clue what the time is and not bothering to check. It could be late. It could be early morning. I don't care. I just want to hear Jordan's voice.

"Hello? Brody?"

There it is. That low, husky accent. It almost centers me it's that good. I breathe it in like I'm drawing Jordan inside my lungs. I exhale slowly and say, "Hey."

There's a pause.

"How are you?" I ask and then wince, covering my eyes with my hand. So stilted and polite. Usually I'm a lot smoother than this, but I don't want to be that guy with her. I don't want to hide behind a wall of confidence that I'm not feeling.

"Is everything okay?"

"Everything's fine," I assure her. "I just wanted to hear your voice."

Another pause follows. It's long and its silence is louder than a herd of elephants.

"Brody, that's …" Jordan sighs, the sound soft and silky. "I like hearing yours too."

I rub fingers across my lips. I can feel the smile on them. "Were you sleeping?"

"Not really. I've been sitting around for days. It's making me crazy."

Her tone is one of frustration. I know it well. Waiting for injuries to heal is an excruciatingly slow process. "How's your ankle?"

"Much better. How's your reading?" she shoots back.

"You tell me. I sent through my summary earlier. You didn't get it?"

The sound of movement comes through the phone and the beep of a computer coming online echoes. After a few taps I hear her chuckle. "Oh you mean this one, your 'Ode to Frosty Flakes'?"

I grin. "That's the one."

A few minutes of silence follow. It's a comfortable silence because I know she's reading. I can hear her breathing softly when I close my eyes and press the phone hard to my ear. It's soothing and I drift a little. She jerks me out of it when she speaks. "Have you ever tried reading upside down?"

"Ummm ..."

"I know spellcheck is your friend, but it doesn't stop you getting your words mixed up. Next time try reading your work upside down and let me know if that helps."

"Is this some kind of wax-on wax-off mumbo jumbo?"

Her laughter comes through the phone. The sound heats my skin like a brush fire. "That's right," she replies as I snuggle further down on my bed. "Just call me Mr. Miyagi."

"I'll call you whatever you want as long as I can do wicked things to you."

My tone is teasing, but Jordan's sharp indrawn breath tells me she knows I mean every word. She's thinking about those wicked things. And wants them.

"Wicked things?" she echoes.

Are we venturing into phone sex territory? My lips dry out. I run my tongue over them. "You want me to list them?"

Another pause comes, this one setting me on edge.

"I don't think so. Night, Brody."

Disappointment slams me harder than a defensive linebacker. *Damn.*

"I'd rather you show me one of those wicked things Thursday night," she adds before cutting the call and leaving me with nothing but a dial tone in my ear.

CHAPTER 15

JORDAN

Brody's palm is splayed on the small of my back. It's all I'm aware of as he steers me down the back of the restaurant, mindful of my injury. His proximity makes it hard to breathe. When I'm directed to the last available booth, his hand falls away and I slide in with a sigh of relief.

I scan the room while he takes the seat opposite. It's small and aged but it's bursting with college students—most with curious eyes that watch us with interest. The floor is black and white check, the tabletops Formica, and the booth seats bright red and a little worn. It's unpretentious and the noise loud. It puts me at ease and I shoot Brody a smile as our waitress arrives to take drink orders. I look up into the sullen face of Lindsay. Suddenly I'm thankful of the short, sexy dress Leah bought for me and the soft waves she helped put through my hair.

I look over to Brody, not realizing she worked here. "Um, maybe we should—"

"Leave?" He looks at Lindsay, his eyes hard. "Nope. This place has the best pizza in town, and Lindsay was telling me just today how much she was hoping to talk to you."

"She was?" My gaze returns to Lindsay, confused.

Lindsay clears her throat, notepad and pen poised in her hand. "I'm sorry," she says through gritted teeth. "About your ankle."

Brody arches a brow. "And?" he prompts.

Her pretty green eyes shoot sparks. "And it won't happen again."

My mouth falls open, speech escaping me. Brody knew? He reaches across the table and takes both my hands in his. "My girlfriend appreciates the apology, Lindsay. You can bring us two cokes now, please."

She makes a rapid escape and Brody lets go of me and sits back in his seat, amusement flashing across his face.

"How did you know?"

He shrugs. "I have my sources."

My eyes narrow. *Leah.* "You've probably just riled her even more, you know. She won't let this go now."

"Oh she will. I told her if she didn't leave you alone I'd have her kicked off the cheerleading team."

"You can do that?"

Brody cocks his head and drawls, "I have a bit of power to wield around these here parts."

It seems he does. "So now what?"

His eyes dance. "Do I get to tutor you on how a date works?"

I'm interested in hearing how it works for him, since he's told me he doesn't date. Leaning forward, I place my elbows on the table and give him my undivided attention. "Please. I'm all ears."

Brody shrugs. "We share life stories while we eat dinner. Then I get to take you home and you let me kiss you."

My brow arches. "Kiss me?"

Brody's voice lowers and his eyes darken. I'm pulled in like Alice falling down the rabbit hole. "Everywhere."

I cross my legs, clamping my thighs together. Holy hell, I've forgotten how to breathe. Thankfully a different waitress arrives with our drinks. She sets them down and I'm tempted to ask for the check so Brody can take me home and do it right now. Instead, I take a sip of coke. The icy drink pools in my belly, doing nothing to cool me off.

After placing an order for a pizza to share, the waitress disappears and I give Brody my attention. "So you start."

His brows pull together, his answer short but not sweet. "Born and raised in Austin. My father's a politician and my mother a society wife. Both can't stand that I play football."

"Why not?"

Brody huffs and picks up his drink. "It's a barbarian's sport."

I don't miss the hint of bitterness in his voice. "They don't want you to play?"

"Of course not, but they allow it because …"

"Because why?" I prompt when he trails off.

Brody shrugs like he doesn't care but the light in his eyes dims a little. Something inside him is hurting and I don't like it. Not one bit.

"Because it's all I'm good for."

The matter-of-fact tone tells me it's not a pity party he's having. He believes it with all his heart. "Is that what they tell you, Brody?"

"They do. But they don't need to, because it's the truth."

God help me. I swallow the ache in my throat. It slides down slowly, a painful lump that settles in the pit of my belly and makes my eyes burn.

How could they do that? And how do I tell him otherwise so he believes me? I don't understand American football, but I know it requires more than just physical talent. It requires a smart, analytical mind. One Brody has. I've seen him use it on the field and it's brilliant.

"What, you're not going to sit there and tell me I'm wrong?"

I shake my head. "No."

"No?" he echoes, leaning back in his seat when the waitress delivers our pizza. Spicy Italian scents the air between us but Brody barely notices. His eyes hold mine while she sets down a plate each in front of us along with napkins and cutlery. Her face colors when Brody eventually gives her his attention, asking her to bring another round of drinks.

"Why not?" he asks when she leaves.

"Because telling you you're wrong isn't going to make you believe it," I say as we slide a piece each onto our plates.

Taking a huge bite, he chews and swallows before replying. "What will?"

"Showing you."

"And how do you plan on showing me, Jordan Matilda Elliott?"

Swallowing my own mouthful of pizza, I set it on my plate and wipe my hands before picking up my drink. "I don't plan on showing you,

Brody Abraham Madden." My lips curve impishly as I eye him over the rim of my glass. "You're going to do that all by yourself."

"So much faith." Brody gestures with his glass like he's toasting me. "This date should come with a disclaimer."

"Oh?"

"No expectations."

"Expectation is the root of all heartache," I quote.

"Yes. That." He points at me with the hand holding his glass before he takes a sip. We work our way through the pizza and when I'm comfortably full, Brody looks at me from across the table and says, "So it's your turn now."

"Born and raised in Sydney with a soccer ball at my feet. My father was a mechanic. My mother an accountant."

The hand holding his pizza is halfway to his mouth when he pauses. Setting it back on his plate, he cocks his head and pins me with his eyes. I know what's coming and my heart sinks. His voice is soft, yet I hear it over boisterous laughter and loud conversation. "Was?"

Are all dates supposed to be so deep and meaningful? This one makes me want to run and hide. I try to keep my tone light when my heart feels anything but. "They both died. Car accident."

He's silent for a moment. When he eventually reacts, he doesn't speak. He simply reaches into his pocket and pulls out his wallet. Tossing a bunch of notes on the table, he slides out and gets to his feet. Even the way he moves off the field is poetic. Biceps ripple powerfully and thigh muscles flex. People around us stop simply to watch.

On his feet beside me, he holds out his hand. "Let's go."

"Go?" I echo, a quick glance taking in the leftover food and unfinished drinks sitting on the table.

"Yes. Go. Now."

I take Brody's hand and we head back to the car. "I'm sorry about your parents," he says, looking over at me.

"I'm sorry about yours."

Brody shrugs my comment away. "How long ago?"

I swallow. "Five years."

"And here you are."

"It's what I'd always planned for. They wouldn't want me giving up just because they aren't around to see it."

I'm so close to blubbering. I hate talking about them being gone. Brody must feel it because he changes the subject, his tone lighter. "So dating isn't as easy as it looks."

"Perhaps it takes practice."

"What are you saying?" Beeping the locks on the car, Brody grins and the somber mood we had going earlier lightens further. "We can call that our warm-up?"

"Maybe we can."

He opens the passenger door for me to climb in. "I like your thinking, Elliott."

Brody drives us beyond the city outskirts. We start passing open fields of tall grass. A light breeze is bending it all sideways in a silent symphony. It's pretty and peaceful. "Where are we going?"

"Here," he says, jerking his chin toward an empty paddock that he turns onto. The road isn't smooth and we bounce in our seats as he turns off it and directly on the field. We reach the crest of a hill where he parks and turns off the ignition.

I stare out the front windscreen. There's nothing out there. Just a rolling valley covered in grass and trees that stretch as far as the eye can see.

Shutting the door, I walk up the slight incline behind Brody. He sits down at the top of the crest and pats the grassy spot beside him.

"You didn't mention this part when you explained our date."

"I can't give away all my secrets now, can I?"

The grass is a thick blanket on the ground and when I stretch out flat, the rich, earthy scent of soil sweeps over me. My eyes lift to the sky and that's when I get it. It's perfectly clear and millions of stars are scattered diamonds twinkling above us—bright and magical.

"Besides," Brody adds as he lies down beside me and sweeps out his arm, encompassing all of it. "How do you explain that?"

He's right. You can't. "It's beautiful."

"Is this what the stars are like for you back home?"

"No. Back home it's different."

"Different how?"

Homesickness swamps me. As beautiful as Texas is, it's not Australia. Somehow the stars are always brighter where you belong. "Because there's no place like home."

"You're wrong."

I turn my head and stare at Brody. He's not looking at me. His head is tilted toward the sky, eyes riveted on the beauty above him. My gaze follows the line of his profile. From the curl of his hair to the perfect line of his nose, down to the mouth I want kissing me right this very instant.

"Home's not a place where you live. It's a feeling." His hand nudges my own. An invitation. I twine my fingers with his and he squeezes them lightly. "Whether it's where you are, like the football field, or who you're with." Brody turns his head, looking at me when he says that. It's comforting because it unites us somehow, like it's slowly becoming us against the world. "You can be anywhere, Jordan. Home will follow you if you follow your heart."

My breath hitches from the beautiful simplicity of his words. Before I can talk myself out of it, I roll over and straddle him. My knees hug his hips, and he stares up at me from my seated position. My pulse pounds a heavy beat in the silence. *Thump, thump, thump.* It's so loud in my ears I'm sure he can hear it.

"Show me," I breathe. A gleam lights his dark eyes, and he sucks his lower lip inside his mouth. He knows what I'm asking, but I spell it out anyway. "Show me one of those wicked things."

In a move that steals the air from my lungs, he takes both my hands and pulls me down against the broad width of his chest. I'm rolled over and underneath him before I can blink. The squirm in my hips is instinctive, the ache between my thighs relentless.

"Careful what you ask for," Brody says roughly, every exquisite inch of his body pressing down on mine.

"Why?"

His lips curve. "Because when I give it to you, it won't be enough."

My fingers trail down the side of his face, grazing the firm jaw, cupping his cheek in my palm. Foreboding swamps me. I'm falling hard into uncharted territory, and all I see is a broken mess at the end. How is this going to end well for either of us?

"You're an arrogant man, Brody Madden," I whisper.

He brings his face to mine, so close I see the brilliant gold in his eyes, like flecks of light in the dark. "And you, Jordan Elliott, will be the woman who brings me to my knees," he whispers against my lips.

"Show me," I beg on a shaky breath.

Brody's lashes lower and he presses a kiss to the corner of my mouth. I tilt my chin upwards, inviting more. Rather than take my lips like I ache for him to do, he shifts sideways and begins nipping at my jaw. His breath is a rasp when he reaches my earlobe, taking it between his teeth. A sharp pinch from his bite forces a whimper from my throat.

"More?" he asks, drawing back to look at me.

"Is that even a real question?"

Brody chuckles as I slide my hand up and around his nape, dragging his mouth down to mine. He groans and kisses me gently, once, and then twice.

"Brody," I whisper, and he kisses me again, forcing my mouth open hard like he can't hold himself in check anymore. My hair is loose and he fists chunks of it in both hands while his tongue rubs against mine, hot and aggressive. It's almost too much, and when I jerk away I'm left gasping.

Brody doesn't pause. He ducks his head to my neck, his tongue tasting its way down. He finds my pulse point and sucks. It's fierce and my back arches involuntarily. His mouth shifts further down, moving on before he leaves a mark.

Sitting up, he takes the neckline of my dress in both hands. Five dainty buttons hold it together. A single wrench will rip the flimsy fabric in two. He pauses and looks at me, inhaling raggedly. "Jordan … I don't want to ruin it."

My brow furrows. I glance to the hands poised on my dress. They're tense, veins straining under his skin. My head is lost in a fog when my gaze returns to his face. "Ruin my dress?"

Brody groans, a deep sound of regret and frustration. "Us."

"You don't want to ruin us?"

He draws his hands away from the neckline of my dress. "No."

"How would you do that?"

"I don't know. I just get this feeling I'm going to." He shifts away, moving off me and rolling to his back. I turn my head. Brody's gaze is back on the stars. I watch his throat work as he swallows, the pulse in his neck pounding visibly. "All I've ever wanted is to be the best. Whatever it takes. I'll do anything. That's how I'll ruin us, Jordan. How can something so sweet survive a sentiment so dark?"

I roll to my side, holding my head in my hand. Cupping his face with the other, I nudge gently until he's looking at me. "I won't let you."

Brody's voice is urgent, his eyes fierce. "Promise me."

I can't shake the apprehension. It's set in my bones and when I speak it feels like a lie. "I promise."

CHAPTER 16

BRODY

"One more," Jordan commands.

"Nooooo!" The word comes out sounding close to a girlish wail, but I don't care. My brain hurts. It's so full of ethical case law it's going to explode if I squeeze any more in.

I roll over on her bed and bury my head beneath her pillow. It's warm and soft and deliciously fragrant. My whole body shudders and I grit my teeth. I'm denying it what it wants most of all. What the fuck is wrong with me? Right now, I'll gladly ruin everything for one whole night of sinking my cock inside her. After our date we decided to take things slow, but now it's killing me.

"It fucking sucks," I mumble to myself, my breath coming in pants because my air is swiftly running out. Maybe I'll pass out and she'll take pity on me.

"What did you say?"

I tilt my head slightly so Jordan can hear me from under her pillow. "I said all work and no play makes Brody a dull boy."

"We've barely started!" I shrink from her exasperated tone. My girl is a cruel and unforgiving dragon. On the field it's a sight to behold. Majestic and fierce. Here, in the study arena, it's a harrowing and torturous experience. All hellfire and brimstone. My head is buried, yet she keeps talking. "You know if you don't go over this particular case, it'll be the one that ends up in the midterm."

Her warning is unfair, as if I'm sealing my own downfall simply by taking a well-deserved break.

"When we've finished with that," she continues, "we need to focus on your other subjects. I think we've covered a lot of ground on those, but—"

"Nooooo!" I wail from beneath the pillow. I lift it from my face and squint one eye open. Jordan's seated in her chair by the desk facing me. A heavy text rests on her lap and her arms are folded. She's silent now, her blue eyes narrowed in a cold-hearted glare. It's one that makes me want to apologize even when I've done nothing wrong. "You should teach fifth grade."

Nostrils flare. "Hmmph."

Distracting Jordan is my best shot. "Offer me an incentive and I'll do it."

She fights it, but I see a small twitch in her lips. "You mean like a dog?"

"Sure." I reposition her pillow behind my head, happier now because it's already working. "Like a dog. I do something you ask me to do, you reward me."

Jordan's brow lowers in a deliberating expression. Her mind is ticking over while she works out what she's going to do with me. Eager to help her along, I drop my hand to the hem of my tee shirt. Sliding it underneath, I run it up over my abs toward my chest. The cotton rides up along with my hand, bunching up near my pecs. They flex as I scratch idly at bare skin, pretending an itch. I look up at her from lowered lashes and swallow the satisfied chuckle. Her eyes are following my every move.

As though arriving at a decision, Jordan slams the text shut with a heavy thump and swivels in her chair, setting it on the desk.

When she turns back around, she pulls the band from the knot of hair on top of her head. It spills down, a cascade of honey over toned, golden shoulders. "What do you want?"

"What do I want?" It's a wonder my voice doesn't crack in two.

"Mmm hmm. What do you want?" she repeats, her voice low and full lips curved.

Jordan yielded too easily. A warning alert issues. It's impossible to heed. My mind is already out of control, racing from so many options I don't even know where to start. "Dealer's choice."

I want everything, so it's better for Jordan to set the pace.

She stands and my chest tightens. "You want me to choose your reward?"

"I do."

Her chin lifts in acceptance of my challenge. Reaching the end of her bed, she bends and climbs on. She lifts her eyes and the frosty blue is gone. In its place is a rich, dark lure as she stalks toward me on her hands and knees. Anticipation builds and I lick my lips.

Reaching my hips, Jordan draws back and sits. I wait, my blood a pounding roar in my ears.

"What reward could I possibly give Brody Madden that he's never had before? I'm sure everyone you've ever known has bent over backwards to give you everything you ever wanted."

Her words hit a nerve. All I've ever wanted is to prove I'm worth something, but no one can give me that. Worth can't be bought, it has to be earned. "I don't care about everyone giving me everything I want."

"What *do* you care about?"

"*You* giving me what I want," I quip, keeping it light because there are parts of me I'm not ready to expose.

Jordan lifts an eyebrow. "Is that all?"

"I care about football too."

"Nothing else?" she asks me carefully.

I sit up, resting the backs of my hands on the bed behind me. It brings my face close to Jordan's. Our chests align and her breath puffs softly against my lips. "I care about being the best."

Jordan ducks her head and nips my bottom lip. It's sharp and sweet, and I feel it everywhere. When she pulls back there's a teasing light in her eyes. "The best at what?"

A grin tugs at the corners of my mouth. "Why the best at fucking you, sweet Jordan Matilda. I care about being so good you'll never have anyone better."

It's a conceited declaration, and she tilts back her head and laughs, exposing the long line of her throat. "One day soon I want you to prove that. But not right now. You need to focus on midterms. Come on," she says and grabs both my hands. Getting off the bed, she tugs at me, trying to pull me off.

My bottom lip pokes out. "What about my reward?"

She tugs again. "You said dealer's choice and I'm hungry. So your reward is me cooking you dinner."

"I thought you were going to give me something I've never had before?"

"I am. All we have in the cupboard is stale bread, so tonight I'm serving vegemite toast. You ever had that?"

I haven't. And when we reach the kitchen, I seat myself up on the counter and watch while she takes a dark jar with a bright yellow label from the cupboard.

"Here."

She hands it over. While I'm unscrewing the lid, she takes out a toaster and loaf of bread. With the lid off, I bring the jar to my nose and take a sniff. My lips curl with distaste. It's foul. A black paste that looks dredged from the bottom of a sewer. It smells worse. My stomach rolls over with a slow, queasy thump when the stench sticks to the insides of my nostrils.

I look at Jordan, disbelieving. "You guys really eat this stuff?"

Popping bread in the toaster, she nods. "Yep. All the time."

My eyes return to the sludge in the jar.

Jordan laughs. It's a mocking sound. A dare. "It's not going to bite you," she chides. "Have a taste."

I dip my finger in. The texture is firmer then it looks. Swiping up a decent sized amount, I bring it to my mouth and lick it off. My eyes water instantly and I screw them shut while I choke it down.

"Arrghhh." The sound comes out guttural, the bitter paste killing off all my taste buds along with the ability to speak.

Jordan's cackle is loud and evil. She takes the jar from my hand and replaces it with a glass of water. I snatch it up, water sloshing the rim as I gulp it down. "You're not supposed to eat that much."

Drawing the empty glass from my lips, I rasp, "You tell me that now?"

The toast pops. Jordan gets it out and starts spreading butter all the way to the corners. Done, she picks up the abandoned jar of vegemite.

I shake my head, watching her scrape it on like she's creating a piece of art. "I'm not hungry."

She puts the toast on a plate and offers it to me. "Don't be a baby."

"I'm not," I tell her and take it from her hands. "I just don't know why you're trying to break my spirit. Between all the study and now this, I'm starting to think you have a sadistic side, and I don't like it."

Picking up her own piece of toast, Jordan takes a huge bite and chews slowly as if savoring the flavor. I'd rather she savor me. My legs are spread slightly where I sit on the counter and she steps in between them. Swallowing down her mouthful, she licks away the crumbs and leans in. The plate in my hands stops her from pressing too close. I discard it quickly and it hits the counter with a clatter. Now free to touch, I grab her hips in both hands and drag her in. She kisses me. I taste the vegemite on her lips and I don't care.

Drawing back, Jordan looks me in the eye. "You've improved so much already, Brody. I don't want to be the distraction that sets you back." She sets her toast down and with both hands free, places them on my thighs, sliding them up slowly. I steal another kiss, this time swiping my tongue across her lips. A moan escapes and I'm not sure if it comes from her or me. "Let's focus on midterms. When they're done, whatever reward you want is yours."

For weeks I put my faith in Jordan and focus like she asks. I study until I can't think straight, reading late into the night until my brain bleeds. When I'm not hitting the books, I'm on the field, training myself to exhaustion. We become ships passing in the night and our away games alternate. On the weekends Jordan is home, I'm not, and vice versa. My need for her doesn't diminish with the prolonged absences, it only grows hotter.

Jordan has more drive and determination then anyone I know. I feed from it. She makes me stronger and smarter, her faith giving me more confidence then I've ever had before. At our next home game I'm an unstoppable force, and it's contagious. My energy spreads through the team, fueling them. The crowd feels it. It crackles through the hundred thousand spectators like a thousand volts of electricity. When the clock counts down its final minutes, our victory is almost sealed. Feet stomp fast and hard around the stadium, building to a thunderous crescendo that boosts us to greater heights.

"Hut!" Carter roars above the noise, his voice harsh and forceful, veins straining in his throat.

Sweat streams down my face, red from heat and exertion. It drips in my eyes. I don't notice. I'm already moving when Carter takes possession of the ball. My teammates are battering rams, clearing my path. My cleats sink hard into the ground, turf flying up behind me when it rips from the field. Close to goal, I turn for the pass, my lungs screaming for air.

Carter doesn't disappoint. It barrels toward me, high and curved as I run backwards. Using the last of my energy, I reach up, feet lifting off the ground as I make contact with the ball. It slides into my outstretched hands right where it belongs.

Before I find solid ground, I'm slammed from out of nowhere. The power of it rattles my bones and blurs my vision. Crushed sideways into the ground, my head hits hard. The crowd roars its approval because the hit came too late. The touchdown was made. I'm home. Fucking *home*.

Content, I let my eyes flutter closed and the world turns black.

Later that evening I'm in the ER, sitting on the edge of a bed waiting for the doctor to examine me.

The hit was the hardest I've ever taken. A sledgehammer to the head so powerful I felt my brain knock against my skull. The pounding of it hurts my eyes so I close them. It doesn't dilute the pain. I shift on the bed and grunt. The sound magnifies by a thousand and the pounding flares anew.

The curtain rattles and the clip of someone's shoes announces a visitor. I squint an eye open and curse under my breath. My father has arrived. Dressed in a tuxedo, his hair is immaculate and expression aggravated.

My name comes out clipped. "Brody."

I grit my teeth. "Dad."

"You want to explain why I've been pulled out of my party's political fundraiser tonight to be here?"

My coach must have summoned him. "I took a hit on the field tonight."

"And?" he prompts.

"And it was pretty bad."

His nostrils flare and he turns his head, so furious he can't even look at me. I might not have called him here, but it hurts that he doesn't care. The victory from tonight fades, leaving me silent and hollow. I should be amazed at how quickly he can suck the life right out of me with just his presence alone, but I'm not.

Coach Carson flicks the curtain aside and steps in the room, drawing both our attention. Seeing my father, he offers a grim smile and a hand. "Mr. Madden."

Dad takes it, giving his usual firm squeeze before letting go. "Liam, please."

"Liam," Coach concedes and nods his head my way, concern furrowed deep in his brow. "Your boy took quite a knock out there tonight. Thought it best to give you a call."

"So I hear." His smile is faint and amused, reducing my injury to a minor triviality. "It's the way of these things with football, isn't it? If my son wants to play, he needs to get used to the brutality of the sport. He can't come running to the hospital for every little bump on the head now, can he?"

Coach Carson's mouth drops a little. When he closes it, a hard edge lights his eyes. It's one I know well and usually follows a set of drills that runs us into the ground. There's a little more steel laced in his words when he speaks next. "Your son is likely suffering a severe concussion. He'll need someone to take care of him."

"I'm fine," I say through clenched teeth, even though it's clear I'm not.

"Of course you are." Dad slaps a hand to the back of my shoulder before squeezing it. His fingers dig in painfully. My head throbs and bitterness swims in my mouth. "Did you win?"

"They won," Coach interjects, his chest puffing with pride. "Brody played the best I've ever seen."

My father turns his head toward my coach, still gripping me tight. "Can you give us a minute?"

Before he can leave, Eddie steps in the room, my phone outstretched in his hand. He hasn't showered. Dirt and sweat covers his face and hair sticks to his forehead. My father wrinkles his nose. Letting go of my shoulder, he takes a step back as if grime is contagious. Eddie doesn't even acknowledge him. "Jordan's on the phone."

The heavy weight on my shoulders lightens. Whatever my father has to say can wait. "Thanks, Eddie." I take the phone and put it to my ear. "Jordan?"

"Brody. I watched the game." Her voice is panicked. Jordan's away game was Friday and their flight due in at midnight tonight. I was going to surprise her. Take her home, light candles, and see if she'd let me massage all her sore spots. "Are you okay?"

My throat constricts. I swallow and find my voice. "I'm fine."

"Brody." Her voice is now a whisper, thick and hoarse. My fingers tighten on the phone. "You were brilliant. Like a comet streaking across the sky. And then you hit the ground and you didn't move."

"I promise you I'm fine. A minor concussion."

Jordan exhales harshly, the weight of her relief in the sound. "I'm on my way."

I close my eyes and the pain recedes. When the dial tone hits my ears, I open them. Coach Carson and Eddie have gone. My father remains. I set the phone on the bed and meet his eyes, bracing for whatever comes next.

"Don't ever waste my time like this again." His voice is a whip. My skin should be toughened from it, but it's not. *One day*, I promise myself. *One day I won't give a flying fuck.* "If you do, I'll give you a concussion you'll never forget." His eyes flare from my lack of response. "You hear me?"

Do I hear? The next words escape me, clear and terse and too quick to restrain. "Fuck. You."

My father's reaction is swift. He grabs a fistful of my jersey in each hand. My stomach dips with agony when I'm jerked solidly to my feet. The room spins and a groan rips from my chest.

"You ungrateful little shit," he spits in my face. "Have you forgotten how much I do for you?"

How could I? You're always there reminding me.

"Have you forgotten what happens if you don't finish senior year and graduate college?"

My teeth clench until I fear they'll crack.

"What happens, Brody, if you don't graduate?"

They'll keep me from seeing Annabelle. My parents will break my sweet little sister, and I can't let that happen. She needs me.

I meet my father's eyes. *I hate you.*

"I'll graduate," I vow.

He lets me go. I grip the bed behind me with shaky hands. "See that you do."

CHAPTER 17

JORDAN

The heat at my back is a furnace, waking me. Rolling over, I open my eyes and see Brody stretched out beside me. It's still dark out, but I forgot to close the blinds. Moonlight plays across his bare chest. It rises and falls, deep and even. A light sheen of sweat covers the smooth skin. His body takes up most of my bed. I'm wedged on the side between him and the wall so I don't fall out. My own body is damp with sweat in the cramped, suffocating spot, but I don't want to move.

Two nights ago I sat in the airport, surrounded by teammates, Brody's game streaming live from my phone.

He was a blur on the field, his talent extraordinary. You knew you were watching something special. When the ball landed in his hands, the crowd's roar raised the hair on my neck and goose bumps on my skin. The tackle came swift, from nowhere, crushing him into the ground. When the player got to his feet, Brody remained, his body limp and broken on the field like a trampled butterfly. My throat constricted, fear stealing my breath in the eerie silence that followed.

The cameras cut to the commentator seconds later, leaving me hanging. I rang Brody the moment our plane disembarked. He was awake and talking, but he lied when he said he was fine. His voice was tight, like a rubber band ready to snap. After telling him I was on my way, his exhale was long and weighty, revealing the depth of his relief. Brody Madden, the football star who doesn't need anyone, needed me.

The very thought squeezes me, making me ache as I lie in the dark watching him breathe. How quickly I've come to need him too. Brody won't leave me intact. He'll take pieces of me I'm not sure I'll ever get back, but I can't deny myself. He grounds me. The pressure I place on myself is crazy. When it overtakes me, he makes me laugh and forces me to take a step back and breathe. We're both working toward our own separate goal, but his joy on the field reminds me the journey getting there is just as important. It's not one we'll take together. Our lives will untangle after college, and we'll both move in different directions.

We're not meant to be.

The thought makes me heartsick, but it doesn't stop the craving that claws at me, unappeased for too long. I want him.

Brody shifts in the bed as if feeling my stare. My eyes flick to his face. His are open, watching me silently. The pale moonlight darkens their rich brown color to obsidian, so dark and hungry I shiver.

My pulse thumps in time with the heat building quickly between us. It sets off an ache between my thighs that screams for relief. I can't speak. My hand moves to his chest instead. I trace lazy circles over the inked skin with my finger. He sucks in a breath. It holds in his lungs when my palm slides down to his lower abdomen, trailing over warm skin and rippled muscle. His body trembles from the featherlike touch.

I swallow, hesitating, my fingers frozen above the band of his shorts. We've been on a knife's edge for weeks, the effort of restraint leaving me dizzy. With only two days until midterms, we can't afford this distraction.

"Jordan."

Dragging my eyes from the path of my hand, I glance up, searching his face.

Brody's lips are parted, lids lowered as he watches me touch him. He lifts his head off the pillow, eyes bursting with heat and impatience.

"Please," he rasps, his voice like sandpaper across my skin.

The solitary word breaks the last of my restraint. I slip a hand beneath the band of Brody's shorts. Muscles tense when my palm covers him. His cock is already hard, like silken steel beneath the straining cotton of his boxer briefs.

A strangled groan escapes his throat and the sound sets me on fire. My grip on him tightens.

Brody turns on his side, forcing my hand to slip free from inside his shorts. He scoops me up, sweeping me beneath him with little effort. My head hits the pillow, air rushing from my lungs with a gasp.

"Let me have you."

He holds the upper half of his body above me, biceps straining as he looks down at me, eyes searching for an answer. His lower half presses me into the bed, making me hyperaware of the thin barrier between his pulsing erection and the throbbing of my clit.

"Have me." My hips push up against him. An affirmation. "I'm not stopping you."

I can't.

Brody hesitates for a brief moment. He's biding his time for my words to sink in. When they do, he scoots off me and tugs me into a seated position. His gaze shoots down, and I follow it. The hem of my tank top is scrunched in his fingers. His eyes find mine from beneath his lashes. *Can I?* he asks me silently.

Please. Yes.

Brody inches the cotton upwards, slowly baring skin to the cool night air. I raise my arms, my heart pounding. At my invitation he slides it up and over my head. With a swivel, he tosses it to the floor. Turning back, his eyes drop to my chest and he exhales shakily. The heat of his stare hardens my nipples beneath the thin cotton of my bra.

The clasp rests between my breasts. Brody holds his breath when I reach up and flick it open. I slide the straps off my shoulders with both hands and let it drop to the bed behind me. The move is bold, but I feel anything but. I'm not sweet and curvaceous. My body is boyish. Firm and athletic, it's honed for sport, not pleasure.

Brody lets out a deep puff of air. Oblivious to my insecurities, his hands bracket my hips, gliding up my ribs until he reaches my breasts. His fingers are whisper light, his caress reverent as if I'm going to break. After long, agonizing moments, his thumbs scrape along the small undersides. Back and forth he goes, a slow steady rhythm designed to drive me mad.

Each breath comes harder when his hands move inwards. My back arches instinctively, thrusting sensitized nipples into his big palms. Brody's fingers graze the taut peaks and a breathless moan escapes me.

"Beautiful," he whispers, pinching them gently.

It shoots hot sparks straight between my legs. My eyes fly open. He's watching my nipples glide through his fingers. Ducking his head, Brody takes one in his mouth. He rolls it over his tongue, flicking gently. My head falls back, a sharp cry leaving my throat when he sucks it deep and hard. It hurts so good I can't stand it. My body sways and I grasp his shoulders to steady me.

Brody unlatches my nipple with a final flick of his tongue. It's only a minor reprieve because he moves to the other, giving it the same torturous attention.

My hands slide into his soft strands of hair, mussing it. I tug gently, urging him upwards. I want his mouth. Brody complies. Lifting his head, he cups my face in his palms and covers my lips with his. The glide of his tongue is hot and wet. It rubs with mine, moving harder and more insistent. He groans into my mouth, harsh and urgent. I feel its vibration when my breasts press flush against his chest.

The kiss becomes incredibly endless. Brody pulls back when I shove at his shoulders, desperate for air. My first breath is a gasp. So is his, ragged and audible in the quiet. I don't know what time it is but the world outside is asleep. There's only us.

"On your back, Jordan."

Pillows are shoved aside and I'm pushed down. Brody leans over me, dragging his bottom lip inside his mouth with his teeth. The waistband of my pretty pink sleep shorts are seized and wrenched down. I hear them hit the floor. His hands return for my panties.

My heart climbs to my throat when Brody hooks them in his fingers. Pausing, he looks at me, lust in his eyes. They watch me as he tugs at them, his pace slowing. They ease down my legs, over my feet and off, discarded to the floor to join my shorts. Calloused palms circle my calves. Skating upwards, they edge apart my thighs. Brody relinquishes his hold on my eyes and drops them.

"Oh fuck ... Jordan." His chest expands with air. "I want my mouth on you so fucking bad."

I'm exposed to his scrutiny and I don't care. I need relief. "Please."

"So hot." His voice is low and rough. Pushing his way between my legs, Brody sinks down. With unbearable slowness, he trails his tongue down my thigh. My hips jerk. Long, wet kisses travel my legs, and I want to scream my frustration.

Finally he finds his way between my thighs. The rough pads of his fingertips dig into my hips, holding me where he wants me. His breath is harsh and erratic. It puffs against the wet heat of me, making me squirm.

"Brody!" His name tears from my lips when his tongue comes out and licks me in one long stroke. My body heats up, deepening to a fever when his mouth finds my clit and latches on. My fingers rake his skin, clutching for purchase. "Oh god."

Brody's hands tremble on my hips, but he doesn't let go. Wet sucking sounds fill the air. My eyes squeeze closed and I whimper. Pleasure untethers my hold on the world. It drops out beneath me, leaving me scrambling for solid ground. I don't find it. With every hot stroke of his tongue, my grip loosens and when his finger thrusts up and inside me, I plummet into a free fall, coming hard. White lights burst bright and hot behind my eyes.

"Jordan," he growls, lapping at me one last time. "Fuck."

My eyes slide open when Brody draws back and off the bed, staggering to his feet as if drunk. He holds a hand to his head, wincing. I sit up and scoot to the edge, ignoring the throb still pulsing between my legs. "Brody, are you—"

"I'm fine." He cuts me off as he scrambles on the floor, reaching for his overnight bag. I'm positive Brody's going for the bottle of Percocet when instead he plucks out a square, foil packet.

My breath hitches audibly at the thought of him inside me. "Are you sure?"

Brody ignores my question as if it's not even worth an answer. Tossing the condom on top of the mussed sheets, his hands go to the waistband of his shorts. He shoves them down, revealing boxer briefs in tropical blue—a color that sets off the rich golden hue of his skin. Brody yanks those off next, his hard cock slapping against his taut stomach with a lewd sound as he kicks them away.

He straightens his shoulders and for a brief moment I'm afforded a glimpse of Brody entirely bare. His body is large and powerful, every muscle worked hard to distinction, strong and defined.

My awestruck stare breaks when he snatches up the packet off the bed, tearing it open with his teeth. He spits out the torn corner and grabs for the condom, his movements frantic. My pulse climbs with the need to have him filling me. While Brody rolls it down, I lean back on my elbows, letting my legs fall open shamelessly.

He looks up from his task and groans, nostrils flaring. Feverish now, he bites down on his lip, a frustrated grunt escaping when his fingers fumble.

When Brody gets it on he comes for me. His calloused palms slide underneath, scraping my skin as he grabs the round cheeks of my ass. I'm lifted and shoved back. It's a display of strength he doesn't think twice about, but it leaves me scrambling. I'm being dominated without a second thought, and I love it.

With one hand Brody lifts my left leg, pressing it toward me. The other he grabs the base of his cock and guides it between my legs. I tilt my hips and he pushes in, inch by yielding inch.

My lips part and my head falls back with a deep, loud moan. When Brody fills me, hard and throbbing, he takes advantage and swoops down, covering my mouth with his own. His hot, wet tongue plunges inside, and it feels so much dirtier when I taste myself on his lips.

I kiss him back, desperate for friction. Brody answers by drawing back his hips. He plunges forward with a breathless grunt.

"Yes," I pant, hooking my left leg around his firm ass cheeks. "More."

Brody gives me more. Over and over. Slow and forceful. I wrap my other leg around him and grind my hips, drawing ragged groans from his throat. Both his palms slam down on either side of my head, bracketing me. He looks down, his eyes boring into me with each thrust.

"Christ," he grounds out, his words harsh and disjointed. "It's never going to be enough, is it?"

It conveys my own fear when pleasure begins building again. We haven't scratched the itch. We've set it on fire. And when he reaches a hand between us, pressing his thumb hard on my clit, I lose my breath and come hard. It shudders through me, sharp and excruciatingly bright.

His hips are frenzied now, drilling hard inside me with no control. Muscles gleam, tight and slick with sweat.

"Jordan," he rasps, grinding once, twice, and he stills above me, a hoarse cry ripping from his throat. His body weakens and slumps against me.

I'm boneless beneath him, trapped by his heavy weight, hair sticking to my neck and sweat dampening my skin.

He rolls me above him and cool air sweeps over my back and down my bare legs, bringing relief.

"This," he says, his breath ragged.

I stare down into darkened eyes, my head in a fog. "This?"

Brody slides his hands down my back until I'm wrapped up tight, his arms a steel band that locks me close. "Home," he whispers and closes his eyes. "This is what home feels like."

CHAPTER 18

JORDAN

"This is what home feels like."

Brody can't unsay those perfectly uttered words, and I can't stop hearing them. The heat in his gaze and the emotion in his voice tore right through my heart. He held me like I was a treasure he feared would slip right through his fingers, leaving him helpless to stop it.

How did I reply? With nothing, because I'm a coward. I want to run from my feelings, but I'm afraid to the edge of the earth isn't far enough.

You let this happen, I growl at myself. Not that anyone will hear me if I speak aloud. It's early, and right about now is when Leah barges into my room and rolls me from bed with a booted foot. It doesn't happen this morning because I'm awake before she is. An unusual phenomenon, but midterms are over. Results are in. Today.

I skate to the edge of my bed and sit up, my pulse racing with nerves. Brody studied hard and today is the day I prove him wrong. Football is not all he's good for, and believing in himself isn't a wasted endeavor.

Getting to my feet, I dress in the running gear I set out the night before and add a warm, fleecy hoodie. It's getting cold out now, especially in the mornings. It's surreal. Summer will hit Australia in a couple of weeks.

Christmas holidays spent at the beach, the hot sun beating down, sand sticking to sweaty, sunscreen-covered skin. If I close my eyes I can almost feel it. The familiar pang of homesickness hits. What's unfamiliar is how underwhelming it is.

Not wishing to dwell on it, I leave my bedroom and make a beeline for Leah's. Hayden stayed over last night. Although I can't hear any noise, it doesn't mean it's safe to barge on in. I bang my fist on her door. "Up and at 'em, sunshine."

"I'm up, I'm up!" Leah yells back immediately.

The door flies open. She's clad in a tiny pair of Lycra shorts and sports bra, her face hidden as she tugs a fitted tank top over her head. With mussed hair, she twitches it into place and grabs her sports shoes, tucking them under her arm.

Hayden's still in bed. Naked. The sheet barely covers below his waist, affording a peek of all the glory that lies beneath. I avert my eyes. Leah's boyfriend is big *everywhere*. I have a sudden, newfound respect for her ability to walk a single step in the morning, let alone run.

Without opening his eyes, Hayden rolls over lazily and the sheet dips dangerously low. "See ya at lunch, princess," he says, yawning loudly. "Miss your tits already."

Leah sighs. "Later, big boy."

She leaves the room, shutting the door behind her. Glancing up, she halts, eyeing my fully dressed form and wide-awake state with brow raising disbelief. "Why so perky, turkey?"

"I don't want to be late for class today."

She snorts, heading toward the sofa. "As opposed to every other day?"

"Is this how we're starting our morning?" I ask as she sits and tugs on her shoes. "With lame, shitty wisecracks?"

Leah looks up, pausing from her task. "It's how we start every day."

She's right, but my anxiety levels are rising, leaving no room for clever remarks. "Well not today," I snap.

"Okaaaay then," she drawls.

We head out for our run. I set the pace. Feeling ready to bust out of my own skin, I set it hard and fast. By the end of it, Leah's gasping and my long-healed ankle injury is shooting sparks up my calf.

After a brief cool down, we stagger inside our apartment with wheezing breaths. Leah scoops up her water bottle off the kitchen counter and guzzles down half the icy contents. Drawing it from her lips, she fixes me with a scowl, still panting from our morning effort. "What the hell, Elliott?"

Tears clog my throat and nausea wells up from the pit of my stomach. Her comment is the catalyst because I don't even know what the hell. My emotions have lost touch with reality. I miss my brother with a keening ache. I want home, but the idea of leaving Brody steals my breath. I want to stay but I also want what I've worked for since forever: a place in the US National Women's Soccer League.

"Seattle Reign," is all I manage to choke out.

"What about ..." Leah trails off. Her eyes widen to saucers and the bottle in her hand falls lax. "Oh my god."

"Valeena Kelly isn't returning." The star forward for the Reign had time out in the off-season for keyhole surgery on a torn ligament in her knee. It didn't go as planned. She won't be fit enough to return. I can only imagine her devastation, but her position is a valued one and they need it filled. "I spoke to Coach Kerr after training yesterday for the second time. They want an unknown. Someone young and fresh on the team. Someone with ambition and fire."

And I'd made the sports news not long ago, an in-depth interview that pushed me right into the spotlight.

"And they want you? What about the combine?" Leah asks, referring to the campaign where players have to register and show off their skills to the coaching staff.

"They're still holding it in early February, but they're flying me out for it. They have three key players they're looking at to replace Kelly." I draw in a deep breath and let it out. "I'm one of them."

"Holy shit," Leah breathes, frozen on the spot as she stares at me. Then she yells it. "Holy fucking mother of all shit!"

Her drink bottle drops to the floor and she leaps. Her tackle sends me flying backwards. My ass hits the back of the sofa, and the force of her momentum sends us right over. I land on the soft cushions. Leah isn't so fortunate. She rolls right over the top of me and lands on the other side, hitting the carpet with a bone-jarring thud.

"Are you okay?" I gasp, hearing her wheeze from below.

A few moments later Leah's head pops up from the floor like a meerkat, a manic grin splitting her face. "A Reign," she squeaks. "I can't believe it."

Then her smile fades a little and she stills, comprehension dawning on her face. "Seattle. That's …"

A hellishly long way from here. The distance feels greater as I fight my way through rushing students, anxious to arrive at my Ethics lecture on time. Jostled from all sides, I hold my protein shake up high to keep it safe as I push my way through. I slip inside the door and my eyes seek out Brody.

He's in his seat, Jaxon laughing at something he says. Despite the cool season, he's in his usual ensemble of muscle tee shirt and shorts. It's not worn to tantalize—Brody's body temperature runs at combustible levels, making him better suited to polar ice caps and life in the Arctic—but it does anyway. The abundance of biceps and packed muscle lining his rib cage catches my attention and holds it for a long, admiring moment.

Jaxon sees me first and nudges Brody. He swivels in his seat and finds me. A curve slowly tilts his lips as he watches me walk toward him. My body clenches. Lust. Fear. Elation. Heartache. I feel it all. Everything except regret. But as I look at Brody I know that, too, will come. Later. When I'm gone. Because that's what happens when your need to be the best eclipses all else. Sacrifices are made, and those you love are always the first to suffer.

I reach the empty desk beside him and set my shake down first. Oblivious to my inner turmoil, he reaches over and swipes it from me.

"Hey!" I cry. My stomach growls with fury when he takes the straw inside his mouth and takes a deep pull. I dump my books on the desk, my bag on the floor beside it, and slide into my seat. "That's mine."

"So are you." Brody leans across, his voice low. "Can I swipe you up and suck you down too?"

Heat breaks over me in a wave, leaving me damp between my legs. Cocky bastard knows how to get to me. Too bad for him I'm learning. My lids lower. "Only if I can return the favor."

Brody sucks in a strangled breath, making him choke on the straw. Satisfied I won the round, I steal back the shake and set it on the far side of my desk. After coughing to clear his throat, he gives me a wounded glare.

"You're such an ogre in the mornings, Jordan. I'm thinking I don't like this side of you."

"Good morning students," our professor calls out, saving me from finding a suitable retort. Our eyes draw to the front. Professor Draper sets his messenger bag on the desk. Not wasting time, he opens the flap and pulls out a handful of papers. "Look what I have for you all." He turns and waves them in the air. "Midterm papers."

A collective groan fills the room.

"There have been some surprising and some disappointing results across the board. Some of you may need to think seriously about cutting your losses and dropping this class. If you believe your grade is incorrect, do not see me after class today with your complaint. I don't have time. Schedule an appointment. If anything, it will at least give you time to build your case."

Nerves churn the protein shake in my belly to curdled milk. I steal a quick glance at Brody. He appears relaxed, sitting back in his seat, his pen tapping a rhythmic tune on his desk. Only the slight flex of his jaw betrays his anxiety.

"Don't look now," Jaxon mutters and leans back in his seat on the other side of Brody.

The papers are handed off to Kyle, who begins weaving between desks as he hands them out. Student chatter fills the room, but the two us share a wordless glance.

You've got this, I want to say but my mouth won't form the words.

Kyle makes his way down the row on my right. Reaching me, he places my exam paper face down on my desk and leans in. It's uncomfortably close, and I feel Brody tense beside me. I meet Kyle's piercing green eyes and my skin crawls.

"Great job," he murmurs for only me to hear. "If only you were that smart in choosing the people you hang around with."

He straightens, tapping my paper twice with his finger before he goes to move on. Fury explodes. For a moment I can't see through the red haze. Is this how guys feel right before they go for the punch?

My outer self remains eerily calm when I put a hand on his arm, halting him. He leans back in as if I'm going to speak as quietly as he did. I don't. My words are loud enough to fill the entire room. "You want to know about choosing friends?" Silence settles around me, chatter dying a swift death. Brody shifts closer to me in his seat, the move so subtle I feel more than see it. "If you, Brody, and I were the last three people on Earth and only you knew how to save us, I would still choose Brody, because the only person you care about saving is you." Kyle's eyes narrow at my unforgiving little speech, each word getting louder and more forceful as I speak. Good. If only he'd choke on it too. "Life is too short to spend your last moments with assholes and you, Kyle Davis, are the biggest one I've ever had the misfortune to meet."

He jerks his arm from under my hand and straightens. I'm expecting an angry retort, but I get nothing. After a stony stare, a smug file forms on his lips. He makes sure we see it before he turns his back and continues down the aisle.

Jaxon busts up with laughter, but there's nothing from Brody. I take him in with a sidelong glance. He's a simmering volcano. The moment Kyle makes his way up Brody's aisle, he's going to erupt.

"Don't," I tell him.

His jaw ticks. He's staring straight ahead as if he can't hear me.

"Brody."

Nothing.

Any altercation, big or small, could end up on YouTube and go viral. It would get back to his coach, who would have no choice but to extend public discipline and suspend him from a game. I don't need to tell that to Brody. He knows it.

When Kyle makes his way up the opposite aisle between Brody and Jaxon, Brody's body tightens like a coiled spring.

Kyle slaps the paper down on his desk and continues on.

I close my eyes, relieved.

Brody held it together.

Or so I thought.

The sound of scrunching paper reaches me. I open my eyes. The exam is a crushed mess in Brody's fist, and it's shaking. An ugly feeling takes over as he stands and grabs his bag. A panicked buzz fills my ears.

"Brody!"

He pauses for a split second and looks at me. I expect anything but the blank expression I get. It sends cold shivers up my spine. I open my mouth and he shakes his head. I shut it.

"I can't be here," is all he says.

My eyes follow him out the door. What the hell just happened? I search for Professor Draper. He's standing by a student's desk, but his eyes are also on the door, his expression resigned. A quick scan of the room shows Kyle calmly walking down the aisles, dispensing papers as though he hasn't a care in the world.

"Jordan." Jaxon leans across, resting a forearm on Brody's now vacant desk. "What the fuck was that about?"

I have an idea and I'm praying hard I'm wrong. Standing, I shoulder my bag and shove my shake across to Jaxon. "Here, have this."

When I reach the parking lot, his space is empty. After trying his phone and getting voicemail, I climb in the beat up car I'm too stubborn to get rid of, shove it in gear, and head straight for his apartment. Jogging quickly up the stairwell, I bang hard on his front door.

No answer.

"Brody, it's me," I shout. "Open up!"

I bang again, pounding my fist hard on the closed door.

It's quiet inside.

Where are you?

I rest my forehead against the white painted timber, breathing hard from fear more than exertion.

"Out there on the field, the game is everything. It builds you up, breaks you down, and it bleeds you dry. But I fucking love it. It's the only place I'm free."

I rush down the stairwell and back to my car. My hasty fingers fumble with the seatbelt. "Dammit," I growl with frustration. Eventually it clicks in place, and I back out and jam my foot down on the accelerator.

Brody's car sits in the near empty parking lot of the stadium. My tires burn what little rubber they have left as I pull to a screeching halt beside it. Switching off the ignition, I sit for a moment, collecting my breath, my heart hammering. I don't know his state of mind right now and it scares me. All I know is that I can't let him push me away.

The car door creaks loud across the lot when I get out. I slam it closed, pocket the keys, and jog over to the fence. The metal chain link around the latch is loose. I slip through and make my way out onto the field. The sun is bright and the grass lush, and so perfect it's almost not real. Brody is sitting on it by the twenty-yard line.

My pace falters and I come to a halt. Unseen, I watch him. His elbows rest on his knees and his head hangs low between his shoulders. In both hands rests a football. It's pressed to his forehead like it's the only thing that matters.

Brody doesn't need to tell me he failed the test. The defeat in him makes my heart ache, and it makes me furious. He's had a lifetime of hurdles. A lifetime of those he loves telling him his dream is worth nothing. That he'll fail because he's not smart enough. Being Brody's tutor was his hail-mary pass.

And he dropped the ball.

Starting toward him, I call out his name. "Brody?"

Brody's head snaps up. His lips are pinched, eyes red. Seeing me, he looks away. "You should be in class, Jordan."

"Screw class." I kneel down beside him, tucking my legs underneath me. "Talk to me."

Taking one hand off the football, he reaches into the back pocket of his jeans, takes out a folded piece of paper, and holds it out.

I take it, unfolding it to reveal an F sitting in the top right hand corner. My mouth opens and closes, not knowing what to say. From his earlier reaction it was what I expected, but it doesn't mean I understand it.

Brody worked so hard. He *knew* the material back to front. "It's just a midterm. I'm sure you can re-take it. We can go see the professor right now and we can get it—"

"It's not the fuckin' test!" Brody shouts and I flinch. "It's not— Fuck!" His curse is a rusty sound as if ripped from his throat. He snatches the page from my hand and crumples it in his fist. "It's not this! I don't care about some goddamn fucking ethics test."

Brody gets to his feet and tosses it off to the side as he stalks away. I snatch it up, folding it quickly and jamming it in my back pocket.

I start after him. "Brody!"

He turns his head to the side but keeps walking. "Get lost, Jordan," he says coldly, tucking his hands into the pockets of his shorts. "I actually came here to get away from you, yet here you are, chasing after me like every other damn bitch on campus."

I suck in breath, hurt welling up. "You arrogant bastard!"

He doesn't stop.

"Is that it, then? You just give up?"

Brody's head lowers a little, the only sign he heard me. Yet he doesn't stop and I want to scream and stamp my foot like a damn child.

"This isn't you, Brody!"

He comes to an abrupt halt, pausing for what feels like long, endless minutes. When he turns, his eyes are hard and unfeeling. I brace, now knowing that when Brody said he'd ruin us, he believed it with all his heart.

"This is all me, baby." He spreads his arms wide and chuckles like it's all a big joke. Like *he's* a big joke. Hot tears prick my eyes. "What you see is what you get. A big, dumb jock. It doesn't matter what you do, Jordan, or how hard you try at making me someone I'm not, or even how much you make me work. Up here…" he taps a finger to his temple "…is all broken. You ain't ever going to fix it, so maybe you should just stop trying and leave me the fuck alone for a change." Brody swallows and stares somewhere over my shoulder, not even able to look me in the eye. "I just can't fight anymore. I can't."

A pained whimper escapes my throat. I know the hurt is clear on my face. I hate that his eyes harden further when he sees it.

This time when he turns and walks away, I let him go.

"Well, Nate, I don't know what's going on with Madden out there on the field, but he's off tonight. The one thing about this well-rounded receiver is that he always plays with his heart. I'm just not seeing that magic tonight."

"True, John. This is a well-loved player who goes out and gives one hundred and ten percent every single game. He's consistent, he's strategic, but he's also the heart and soul of the team. There is no doubt this kid is headed for the NFL. He's the kind of player that every team needs. He's passionate about the game, and tough, and the players really respond to that, but his lack of fire tonight is sending discouragement through the entire team. Let's hope he can dig deep for the next half hour."

I curse.

Snatching up the remote, I switch off ESPN and toss the remote on the coffee table. The back casing flies off when it skitters across and smashes to the floor. Its two little batteries pop out and roll underneath the small entertainment unit.

Hayden glares balefully from the opposite end of the sofa. I throw my hands up. "I can hear you thinking it so just bloody well say it."

The words break free like a dam bursting. "What did you do to him?"

"I didn't do anything!"

"Maybe that's the problem," he mutters under his breath.

I push up off the sofa and head for the kitchen. Comfort food is the only answer. Stretching high, I open the cupboard above the fridge. I feel around for my stash of Cadbury Caramello: a family block of chocolate filled with sticky, oozing caramel. It's the last one from a food care pack that Nicky sent me, and I've been saving it for a special occasion. Apparently it doesn't get any more special than this.

My hand encounters empty shelf. It's not there. My anger rises like a lit match on kindling.

"Leah!" I screech. She's in the shower, hot steam misting out from beneath the closed door. "Where the freaking hell is my chocolate?"

The door flies open and she pokes her head out. Her hair is wrapped up in a towel, turban-style. She peels it away from one ear. "What?"

"My chocolate." I fold my arms, ready to rip the whole thing from her head if I find out she's eaten it. "Where is it?"

Her eyes cut to Hayden. His widen and he shakes his head. "Hayden ate it."

"I did not!" He points his finger at Leah and looks at me. "It was all her."

My phone rings, saving them both. "This is *not* over." With that ominous warning, Leah locks herself in her bedroom, and Hayden gets down on the floor by the television, digging for the runaway batteries from the remote.

Rummaging through my bag, I find my phone and check the display. Jaxon. Frowning, I hit the answer key and put it to my ear. "Hello?"

"Jordan." His voice is loud. With the noise of music, tinkling glassware, and laughter in the background, I figure he's at a bar somewhere. "Did you see the game?"

I grit my teeth. "I saw enough."

"Enough to know what's going on with Brody?"

"You too?"

"Me too?" he echoes.

"You think the way he played tonight is my fault too?"

"Well … partly, yes."

I turn and lean against the counter, my fingers tight on the phone. "That's so unfair!"

"So Brody failed his midterm and then you both don't speak to each other for three whole days. It doesn't take a genius to figure it out."

"You know he failed? And figure out what? Stop speaking in riddles."

"Of course I know he failed," he says impatiently. "Brody clearly has issues. And when something upsets him, he just pushes everyone away. He can do that with me because I'm family. I'm not really going anywhere, you know? You're good for him, Jordan. Don't let him do that to you, okay?"

"I tried, okay? It just pushed him further away. I'm not sure I can help him."

"You tried once. If that's your definition of trying, then it's pathetic."

"Nice," I bite out.

"Please, Jordan?" The background noise softens, and I know he's stepped outside. "Brody doesn't listen to me. I'm a straight-A student. He thinks I won't understand."

"Understand what?" I ask, cautious.

"Understand what it's like being dyslexic," he says.

I sag back against the kitchen cupboard behind me. "You know that too?"

"Of course I fucking know that too. He just doesn't know I know. Maybe he thinks I'll think less of him for it, which is dumb."

"Don't—"

"I know, I know. Don't say dumb." More silence. "Come by tonight. After the game."

I give in and agree to stop by. Eleven p.m. finds me at Brody's door in a pretty white dress belted at the waist, the thin straps making me shiver. What am I thinking? That I'll sway him with a bit of skin? I'm a fool. This proves it, but it's too late to run back and put on the hoodie and gym shorts I feel so much more comfortable in.

Taking a deep breath, I rap sharply on the front door.

No answer. Again.

Dammit.

Pulling out my phone, I stab at the keys, typing a new message to Jaxon. The amount of time I've given up to help Brody when I should be focused on my own future scares me. Has it all been for nothing?

Jordan: *Where are you?*

BigBananaBoy: *On our way now.*

I shake my head at the name Leah used to add Jaxon as a contact. I never got around to changing it.

Clattering feet and drunken male laughter echo up the stairwell, setting my nerves on edge. Being out so late and alone is probably not smart.

Jordan: *I might just go.*

BigBananaBoy: *No! Don't leave. Be there in ten. Promise.*

The noise level rises, the stairwell ejecting a boozed-up pile of guys into the hallway. I press my back against the door behind me and fold my arms, doing my best to appear unobtrusive.

A soft, taunting laugh sweeps over me as they stagger their way along the wide corridor. My eyes flick to the group without turning my head. Prickles of apprehension rise on my skin when I see Kyle amongst them.

"If it isn't Brody's little soccer star," he slurs, his alcohol-glazed eyes roaming over me. "And don't you look super sweet tonight."

He steps up in front of me, bathing me in beer fumes. I keep my head up, my gaze straight ahead while his drunken friends continue their merry way down the hall.

"What's the matter, darlin'?" He brushes the backs of his fingers across my cheek.

"Don't touch me." I jerk my head away, leaving his hand suspended in the air for a moment before it drops by his side.

"Did that dumb asshole lock you out?"

Anger churns my stomach, making my hands shake. I curl them until the nails bite into my palms. "Call him dumb one more time." I lift my chin, meeting his gaze with hard eyes. "I dare you."

Kyle laughs. "You're feistier than I thought." He presses his forearm against the door above me, bringing him closer. "But you shouldn't care so much. Brody isn't the nice guy you seem to think he is."

"Why do you even care?" Wedging my arms between us, I shove him away.

He staggers, pressing a hand to the wall behind him to right himself. "I don't." His lips press to a thin line, his irritation spilling over. "I'm just tired of that self-righteous prick getting everything he ever wanted."

"Because he got everything *you* ever wanted you mean?"

"Yes," Kyle hisses. Lurching back toward me, he jabs a finger in my breastbone hard enough to bruise. "Someone needs to take him down a peg or two."

"And what?" I snap. "You decided you were the man for the job?"

"See? I knew you were a smart girl," Kyle croons and cups my right cheek in his palm. "I like smart girls."

"Yeah?" I yank his hand away. My legs are weak and shaky beneath me, my show of bravado beginning to fade fast. "Because for someone who's supposedly intelligent enough to be Professor Draper's TA, you're a bloody idiot."

"An idiot?" Kyle cocks his head, and for the first time he looks unsteady, like something inside his head is out of balance. A tendril of real fear snakes up my spine. When another set of echoing voices reach us from the stairway, he takes a wobbly step backwards. Relief sweeps over me.

"I'll be seeing you in class," he says, and my eyes follow his retreating back down the corridor. He disappears inside the same apartment as his friends, and I gasp my next breath, hunching over because I can't suck it in.

I can't do this.

I can't be the strength Brody needs. I barely have enough for myself.

I start for home, my head down as I rummage for my phone. I don't get far. Jaxon emerges. Brody and Damien spill out of the stairwell behind him, drunk and singing about swinging from a chandelier. It should be funny, but all it does is break my heart. Brody is slowly ripping apart at the seams, and all I can do is run away.

Brody's song cuts off when he smacks into me. He startles for a moment, color draining from his face when he sees me. Then his eyes devour me, unable to get enough. I want to do the same. It's been three days since he walked off the field, yet it feels like a lifetime ago.

"Brody."

My voice is low, but he jerks like the sound is a slap to the face. "What do you want?"

My eyes flick to Jaxon, who gives me an encouraging thumb's-up. I shake my head and turn back to Brody, in no way encouraged. "I want to talk."

"No," he says, his tone rough and sharp. He cocks his head. "But we can fuck if you want."

Damien chokes on a laugh. I have to bite the insides of my cheeks to force back the tears. The man in front of me feels like a stranger. I want to shake him and find the real Brody inside. "Please. Don't. This isn't you."

"Christ, Jordan. You're starting to sound like a broken record." Brody rolls his beautiful eyes theatrically. "And you're wrong. It *is* me." He smiles sardonically, slapping Damien on the back when he edges his way around us. "Right, Damien?"

"Don't include me in your domestic, dude." Damien holds up his hands, walking backwards toward their apartment door. Jangling a set of keys in his hand, he points them at Brody. "This is why you don't do a chick more than once."

Jaxon takes a step in my direction and mouths, *I'm sorry.*

I shake my head. There's nothing I can do. Not when he's like this. Belligerent, drunk, uncaring.

When I brush past Brody to leave, his fingers snake around my bicep, a steel handcuff that locks me in place. He brings his face to mine, so close his eyes are all I see. They're dark and unwavering, and so cold I ache from it.

"Let it go," he whispers harshly. His eyes drop to my lips for a split second before returning to mine. "You tried, but I'm letting you off the hook. I'm not your problem anymore, Jordan. Go find someone else worth saving."

CHAPTER 19

BRODY

I rap on the door of my family home with shoulders hunched and eyes hidden behind dark sunglasses. Of course when I downed half a bottle of Jack last night I hadn't been thinking about the horse ride I promised Annabelle today. My mind had been stuck on my confrontation with Jordan last night. Her disappointment was so thick I could taste it.

Jordan's expectations had been too high. It only made the fail that much more spectacular, not to mention *humiliating*. And like the dick that I am, I handled it with all the finesse of a ball fumble at the Super Bowl.

Jamming hands in the pocket of my jeans, I turn and blindly face the street. Mr. Lewis is trimming the edges of his lawn like he does every Sunday. The old dude is a neat freak—never a leaf out of place or a blade of grass straying from formation. I have him pegged as retired military, but it's unconfirmed. He's never given me the time of day, not in the fifteen years since he and his wife moved to the neighborhood. Maybe it's because my father's a politician, or maybe he sees me as your stereotypical self-entitled jock. Either way, I don't blame him. I'd keep clear of our family too if I had the choice.

Yet I don't see old man Lewis move slowly down the drive, weed whacker steady in his hands. I see honey hair and rich golden skin, blue eyes fierce and infused with emotion. I see an angel sweet enough to tempt the devil from the dark side. *And now she's gone,* I remind myself, my mind going to our argument from last night.

"I'm not trying to save you," she told me.

My callous reply echoed down the hall for everyone to hear. Only it was just us. Jaxon and Damien disappeared inside the apartment, leaving Jordan and me to fight it out. "Then you should have no trouble leaving, should you?"

Her spine snapped straight, her strength bottomless. I had no idea where she dug it from. It made me want to shake her. *Lose control, Jordan. Shove me. Curse. Shriek and call me names. Make it easier for me to push you away.*

Jordan jerked her arm free of my hold. She didn't come at me. Of course she didn't. Her integrity was stellar. It only lowered me further.

"Goodbye, Brody," she forced out through gritted teeth.

Turning, she walked away, her long-legged frame striding toward the stairwell and out of my life. This was what I wanted. But it wasn't. "Wait!"

Jordan halted and looked at me. Her eyes were overcast, their light hidden behind a thick cover of cloud. Behind her the hallway was dark and empty, the lighting for shit. I knew the parking lot was no better. I walked toward her. "You came here alone?"

"Yes, I came here alone."

My jaw tightened. "Don't ever do that again."

Brushing past her, I moved inside the stairwell. Jordan clattered on the steps behind me so I knew she was following. "Contrary to what you might think," she said to my back, her disdain abundantly clear, "you don't actually have the right to tell me what to do."

I snapped like a rubber band. With an abrupt turn, I halted on the step, my fingers curled on the handrail because fuck it; I'd had too much to drink and I'd probably tip over. Jordan faltered, stopping before she smacked into me. With me one stair below, it brought us to eye level. "You came here uninvited, alone, late at night, in the damn dark! What were you thinking? Oh, wait," I bit out and she backed up a little, "you weren't!"

I was riled but I didn't want an argument, so I gave her my back and kept moving, my pace down the stairs a clipped jog.

"What was I thinking?" she hissed, her indignation rising as she jogged after me. "That you were handling this like a bloody man-child!

Is pushing everyone away and getting drunk the only way you can cope with disappointment? Was failing that exam really the end of the world?"

"Yes!" I shouted. We emerged into the cool night, and I spun around. We glowered at each other for a bitter, heated moment. "*My* world! *My* football career. I've barely kept my head above water through college," I continued to yell. "Three long, hard years of my GPA sitting on a knife's edge. If I fail, my eligibility to play is gone."

Jordan took a step toward me. "So get an academic waiver! Meet with the university president. Speak to Professor Draper and retake the goddamn test." She jabbed me in the chest, hard and forceful. "You have options, and instead of using them, you blow a game and drown your damn sorrows with beer kegs like it's all too hard."

"It *is* too hard!" I shouted. "I did everything you asked of me, and I *still* failed, so what's the point of retaking the test? This isn't some feel-good movie where I graduate because you tutored me for a few months. In real life the guy doesn't get the girl and the team doesn't win the championship. Real life is ugly and raw, and it fucking sucks."

"So you're just going to give up?"

"Goddammit, Jordan!" Frustration blackened the edges of my vision. "I'm not giving up. I'm trying to accept my limits!"

Fed up, I snatched the keys that hung slack in her fingertips and started for her car. My legs moved sluggishly. Admitting defeat hadn't made me lighter. It was a cement brick around my neck, weighing me down.

"I'm sorry!" Jordan's voice cracked. If I was wondering how far I could push until she broke, this was it. "I'm sorry," she whispered.

I stopped in the middle of the parking lot. My head tipped back and my eyes closed. All my anger fell away, disappearing into an abyss. Resignation rose in its place.

When I turned, Jordan was frozen to the pavement. Shadows cast half her face in darkness, but pale lamplight exposed the glimmer of tears. One spilled over. Bile climbed my throat as I watched it trail down her cheek. I swallowed the bitter taste and forced myself to speak.

"You believed in me. You made me believe in myself. Damn you for that."

Old man Lewis breaks me from last night's memory by revving his weed whacker. My eyes follow his progress. He reaches the end of the drive, his edges now in impeccable formation. After cutting the motor, he glances over. For a fleeting moment he stares, brows drawn as if I've presented him with a puzzle.

Surprised, I lift a hand in casual salute. He doesn't acknowledge me. Striding back toward his open garage, he hangs his weed whacker up on special built-in rungs and takes down his leaf blower.

Hearing the door open, I turn back. Hattie greets me with a smile, bright yellow dish gloves covering her hands.

"Hey, Hattie."

She steps off to the side, letting me through. "Mr. Brody."

"Just Brody," I instruct her like I always do.

Hattie nods her usual agreement, but she never cedes. "They're at a charity luncheon today," she informs me, anticipating my question.

My next breath is a little calmer when I step inside the sterile foyer.

"Is that Brody?" Annabelle shrieks from upstairs.

My heart lifts. "Yeah it's me," I call back. "You ready to go?"

My sister's room is the only space in the house that doesn't feel cold and empty. The walls are baby pink. Lacy frills cover her bed, hand-painted fairies trim the walls, and a chandelier dripping in pink crystals hangs from the ceiling. When it comes to Annabelle, it's not about spoiling her every whim, it's about promoting all things 'pretty.' With the redecoration complete, she messaged me a photo. *It looks like Tinkerbell threw up in my room. I hate it.*

"Oh she's ready to go, alright," Hattie mumbles under her breath. I catch a slight twitch in her lips before she disappears down the back of the house.

"Hurry up, Annabelle!" I call out, anxious to leave. "The stables are expecting us."

Annabelle's mare is kept at Mallory Ranch and Stables. Our parents actively encourage extracurricular activities, like horseback riding alongside her ballet. She's undertaking equestrian jumping, a second language, and deportment lessons. It all sounds good in theory, but it leaves me sick inside. My sister is outspoken with a bright, happy spirit, yet they're slowly breaking it down and grooming her as a future trophy wife.

"I'm coming! Hold your horses," she replies with a snorting giggle.

Moments later she's making her way down the stairs, her back straight, chin high, and hand trailing the banister like a beauty queen entrance. My mouth falls open. It's not the blouse, jodhpurs, and riding boots that capture my attention. It's her face. It's a festival of color.

Her mouth cracks a bright, practiced smile. The move showers her outfit in a rainbow of glitter dust. My lips press together. *Do not laugh. Do not fucking laugh.*

"Wow, Moo Moo." I scratch at my chin as I stare, at a complete loss. "Are we off to Mardi Gras or something?"

I shouldn't have said that. Annabelle falters, her bottom lip aquiver. "You don't like it?"

"It's um …" I clear my throat. "Aren't you a little young for makeup?"

She huffs. In no way deterred, she pushes off the bottom step and collects her bag from the entryway table. "You sound like Mom."

"You used mom's stuff?"

Annabelle's grin is one of satisfaction. It means she left behind a mess big enough to cause grief. "Yep."

My keys jingle as I pluck them from my pocket. Insisting Annabelle wash her face will only make her heels dig in further. "Do you have a death wish?"

"Don't be dramatic." She rolls sparkle-encrusted eyes as we leave, calling out a quick goodbye to Hattie before I pull the door shut behind us. "She won't kill me. She might poop a brick though."

I beep the locks. "Poop a brick?"

"Yeah, you know," she says as we both climb in the car. "Hershey squirt."

My mouth falls open. "Hershey *what?*"

"Freak out! It means freak out." Annabelle shakes her head as I back out the drive. "You need to get with the lingo. You sound like old man Lewis."

"Don't call him old man Lewis."

"Why not?" she shoots back.

"Because it's impolite."

We drive past our aforementioned neighbor. He's busy blowing grass clippings off his driveway. With the wind picking up, it pushes them across to my parents' lawn. A check of my rear view mirror tells me the old man is pretty pleased about that.

"You call him old man Lewis."

I glance across at my sister. "Because I'm a disrespectful college kid. You don't want to be like me."

Annabelle is unusually quiet on the forty-minute drive to the stables. It's unnerving. When we arrive at the property and select a trail, she's still mute. Riding out side-by-side, I glance across at her. She's chewing her lip, worrying off the red lipstick that's too old for her young face. Whatever is on her mind, it will build up and explode if it doesn't come out soon.

"How's school?"

Her voice is curt. "Good."

"And your friends? Rachel?"

"Good."

"Hell," I mumble under my breath. It has to be boys, which perhaps explains the attempt at makeup. How do I broach *that* topic? I'm not the freaking parent here.

"Is anyone bullying you?" Because little boys can be dicks when they like a girl.

I wince behind my sunglasses. Last night proves it doesn't change as they get older. They just grow into bigger dicks.

"… my older brother."

I miss Annabelle's reply. "Sorry?"

"I said," she enunciates louder, "that no one would dare bully me. Not with the Great Brody Madden being my older brother."

The Great Brody Madden. I snort at the ridiculous term, but inside it worries me. Public perception can change at the drop of a hat. You play a good game, you become a god. You play a bad one, you get raked over the coals—so do those close to you.

My hands tighten on the reins. "You'll tell me if that changes, right?"

"Yes, Brody." She rolls her eyes and glitter mists the air. "I'll let you know if you stop being great."

"You know that's not what I mean. I'm being serious here. I don't want anyone bullying you if I have a bad game."

"No one is being mean to me," she snaps.

We reach the halfway mark of our trail ride, and I'm yet to unearth the issue. Granted, I haven't dug far but she's eight. If it's not school, friends, or boys, what else could it be?

"Moo Moo …" I start and sigh. My horse snorts loud beneath me, no doubt feeling my frustration.

"Do you have a nickname for her too?"

"Do I what?"

Annabelle's eyes drop to her reins and her bottom lip pokes out. I brace accordingly and the little bomb she drops doesn't disappoint.

"For your girlfriend." Her voice is small, like she's trying to stop the hurt coming out. It might as well be a shout. My throbbing hangover reaches new heights. "The one you never told me about."

Hell. It was never my intention to keep Jordan from Annabelle, but Jordan is mine—just like football is. Something just for me. Jordan and football on one hand, family and its drama and responsibility on the other—a subconscious division.

"How did you know?"

Our dad enforces a blanket ban on social media and ESPN.

"Rachel's dad," she answers.

Of course. Her friend's father is a zealous fan. Phil watches sports religiously. All kinds. He's a big guy, brash and rough, but also warm and lighthearted. On the several occasions I've met him he's spouted detailed opinions on my recent games. While I don't take his unqualified advice on board, it only makes my father's lack of interest sharper.

"They had ESPN on," she adds. "There was a special on the upcoming draft."

"And you watched it?" They listed me as a first round draft prediction. They also delved into my personal life, broadcasting a dynamic little slide show of Jordan and me together. Funny photos lifted from Facebook. Us leaving Eastside Cafe holding hands. That kiss on the soccer field right before Jordan's game.

"Yeah I watched it. Jordan Elliott." She clucks her tongue, urging her horse into a fast clip. "Sounds like a boy's name."

"Be nice," I snap, catching up to her.

"Why should I? You're keeping stuff from me. Did you know she's poor?"

"What?"

"Dad did a background check."

Hot and cold chills prickle my skin. "He what?"

"You heard me. Do you think she's after your future millions?"

"Do I ... No! Dammit, Annabelle. You're being ridiculous."

She reins in her horse, her glare blistering my skin. "And you're being a tool."

We've reached a standoff. Both horses rest on the trail, tails twitching as they sense our combined aggravation. I stifle a sigh. "I'm sorry I didn't tell you about Jordan. It's a little complicated."

"Complicated how?" Annabelle digs her heels in. It seems we're not moving until this gets hashed out.

"Jordan believed in me." It's not until I say the words out loud that I realize how good that belief made me feel.

Her chin juts out. "And I don't?"

"I know you do, Annabelle. It's just ..." I wanted her to always believe in me.

"You know how Mom and Dad are. How they see me. I wanted to keep Jordan away from that. From their hateful words and their constant disappointment. I don't want her to see me the way they do."

"I don't hate you." A little yellow butterfly flitters between us. Her eyes catch on it and hold, following it until it disappears behind a tree. When her eyes return to mine, they're wide and childlike. "And I'm pretty like she is too, right?"

The reason for her painted face becomes clear. "Is that why you're wearing makeup, sweetheart? You think if you put all that stuff on your face people will like you more?"

Her chin juts out further. "Rachel says you're gonna ditch me now you have a girlfriend."

I stifle a deep, disgusted sigh and hold her gaze, my words firm. "I'm not going to ditch you, Annabelle."

Her brows rise, unconvinced.

How am I supposed to undo years of damage my mother has caused in just a few minutes? Jordan would know what to say. A master of the right words at just the right moment, she would be good for Annabelle. The perfect role model.

Hearing voices and hoof clops coming up behind us, I take both reins and cluck the horses. We begin moving again.

"Jordan doesn't wear makeup." Not often, at least.

I glance at my sister. Her eyes are fixed ahead, but her shoulders straighten. She's listening.

I forge ahead. "She reminds me of you. Jordan speaks her mind. She's smart and intuitive. Whenever a subject gets too stressful, she cracks a joke, making everything lighter. We both like sports and talking about it and playing it. She's so talented with a soccer ball, Moo Moo. When I watch her play …" I get lost in her. Completely and utterly lost. And when I think of all the time she spent on me when she could've been training, it feels squandered. A wasted effort. Yet I wouldn't take back a minute of it. "She has a big smile and an even bigger heart, and I like being with her because of that, not because of what she puts on her face."

That's it. I've got nothing else.

"Are you going to marry her?"

I almost laugh out of shock, but Annabelle's expression is solemn. My lips press together. I've thought about it. I know I want Jordan in my future, but the driving need to prove myself overshadows everything and I can't make it stop.

"No, sweetheart." My denial weights me like an anchor. "I'm not."

We finish our ride and head home. Another wave of glitter decorates the atmosphere when Annabelle gets out of the car. "Are you going to wash that stuff off your face now?"

My sister's lips twitch. "I don't know. I think Mom should see it first."

"I'm not sure that's smart." Pocketing my keys, I follow her up the porch.

"Smart is for nerds. I'm a lady in progress."

My voice is stern. "Annabelle."

She grins. "Kidding!"

I fold my sister in a hug, picking her up. Our size difference is almost comical. Her feet leave the ground and bump my knees. Bony little arms wrap around my neck, squeezing tight. Mother of god, she is so fucking precious it makes me ache.

"I love you, Moo Moo. Don't let them change you, okay?"

Putting her back down, I placed my hand on her back and propel her inside the house. I follow behind. Annabelle's eyes flare wide. "What are you doing?"

My steps are stilted, my voice tight. "I'm walking you inside."

"You should go, Brody."

"It'll be fine," I lie. "Just run upstairs and wash your face, okay?"

"Annabelle?" Our father's voice is empty and devoid of warmth, even for his own daughter. "Is that you?"

"Brody," she whispers, but I can't placate her now. Fury is building quickly, making me shake.

"Go!"

She jogs up the stairs, her thin little legs carrying her quickly away. Moments later my father appears in the entryway, the click of his polished shoes loud in the silence. Each deliberate step grates on my ears. His suit jacket remains in place, his tie a perfect Windsor knot that I've never managed to master.

His nostrils flare, the only indication of his displeasure at my presence. "Son."

My father's displeasure means nothing. I'm not here to ruffle his perfectly aligned feathers. I'm here to rip the fuckers out. My voice comes out somewhere between a growl and a hiss.

"You motherfucker."

He halts in front of me, brown eyes the same as mine narrow. I've always thought brown eyes resembled warmth, like the heat of whiskey sliding down your throat, but his aren't alive—they're an emotional vacuum.

"A background check?"

His jaw tightens. He knows. "I've never begrudged you your whores, Brody, but who you choose to date in an official capacity—"

I cut in. "Is none of your business."

"—reflects back on all of us. Neglecting to inform my office was a gross oversight. Your choice was made with a serious lack of judgment, and it doesn't surprise me."

"A serious lack of judgment? You know nothing about Jordan!"

"I know the facts. I know you need to choose someone who fits in with our way of life. Voters won't like seeing my son dating a foreigner. It's not good for the polls. If you need help, contact my office and I'll have my secretary arrange a vetted list."

He turns to leave, dismissing me.

My temper rips apart at the seams. "Jordan is not a *business decision!*"

He turns back. *Click, click, click,* he strides toward me, teeth bared and temper flaring. "I give you the best chance at an education and what do you give me? Nothing!" he roars, the veins in his throat bulging dangerously.

My back remains straight beneath his onslaught. "The least you can do, *Son*, is what I tell you to do!"

"Screw you, *Dad*." My glare is white-hot, rage boiling over. "You've given me nothing that matters. Nothing!" I shout, jabbing a shaking finger at his chest. When it comes to Jordan he has no say. I don't want him anywhere near her, tainting her with his hate. She's everything he's not, and that can't change. Not ever. "And Jordan…" my bellow tapers to a hoarse whisper and my hand falls to my side "…she's given me everything that does."

And I did more than just throw it away. I crushed it into the ground.

CHAPTER 20

BRODY

Gym shoes squeak, and the sound of boxing gloves connecting with flesh echo through the large space. Loud grunts and laughter compete with thumping heavy metal music and the thick stench of sweat in the air.

Coach believes in keeping our workouts well rounded. The weekly sparring is brutal and this morning's session couldn't have come at a better time. My life is a cluster fuck. I'm hopeful a few sharp jabs will knock some sense in my head.

"What's the matter, pretty boy?" Carter punches his boxing gloves together and comes at me, no hesitation. "Scared?"

I take a deep breath and slam the bars shut on my emotion. We're both stripped down to gym shorts and headgear, our bodies a sweat-slicked mess. The prominent quarterback boxes balls-to-the-wall, but he hasn't brought me down yet.

Carter swings a right hook, his big weighty bicep coming at me so fast it's a blur. I twist out of reach and his fist connects with air.

I give him a mocking grin, displaying my bright blue mouth guard. Carter and I are of similar build, our strength a comparable match, but where he's quicker, I have more patience. The best way for him to lose his cool is for me to throw out a few taunts.

"This isn't shadow boxing, dude. You hit like a girl."

"Yeah?" He taps my cheek with his glove, the move designed to irritate. It does. I jerk my head out of reach. "Well, you look tired, princess. And you hit like a jellyfish."

My bright red boxing glove connects with his ribs. He grunts, his abs tightening to lessen the impact. "Jellyfish that, asshole."

Wedging gloved fists between our chests, he shoves me away. I brace and he stumbles backwards. Using the time to recover, I wipe perspiration off my brow with my forearm.

When Carter reaches the border of the mat, I put my head down and charge, tackling my teammate until I drive him right off the edge.

"Brody!"

I turn my head at the shout. *Bam!* Carter's fist is a sledgehammer. My vision dims and pain ricochets around my head like a ping pong ball. Before I can blink, my body hits the mat and Carter's laugh comes from somewhere very far away.

"Goddammit," I slur, shaking my head to clear my vision. It lights upon gleaming black dress shoes first. My eyes follow them up, past the highbrow suit, to my uncle. His nostrils are flared and disappointment oozes from his every pore.

My pride smarts as I get to my feet. It's not easy, but he doesn't help me for which I'm grateful. Standing, I hold up a palm to Carter to take five. He shrugs and walks off the mat, swiping his water bottle off the floor.

Pulling a hand free from my boxing glove, I drag off my headgear and take out my mouth guard, giving my uncle a hard stare. "What do you want?"

He gets straight to the point. "I want to talk about your grade."

My eyes do a quick sweep of the training facility. No one's paying us any attention. "I'm in the middle of a boxing session. Now's not the best time."

"When is a good time?" he snaps. "Because I've given you plenty of it to come see me and you've pulled a disappearing act. What's going on, Brody?"

I note the impatient glance he gives his watch. "Nothing's going on," I retort, which is the absolute truth. "So don't let me waste what little time you have spare."

"Your sarcasm is duly noted and unnecessary. I'm trying to help you here."

Dumping my gear, I lean over and collect my towel and water bottle off the floor. "Hmmm ... And last time you tried that it worked out so well."

Patrick steps away from the mat as I move off it, slinging the towel around my shoulders and using the end to wipe my face. "You know when you act like this you remind me of your father."

I shrug, pretending the barb hasn't hit its intended mark. Tipping my water bottle back, the cool liquid washes away the heat of his insult. I swipe the back of my hand over my mouth. "Like father, like son, huh?"

"You have no idea," he bites out.

His tone is bitter and grief darkens his eyes for a single moment. Something niggles at me, a murky whisper. It's gone before I can make sense of it, but whatever it is lodges a sick feeling in my gut. "Am I missing something?" My uncle doesn't meet my eyes. "Something about my father?"

"Your father ..." Patrick begins and presses his lips together.

"My father ..."

"Your father doesn't deserve you," he says, finally looking at me. "And I think he's an absolute fool."

I stare at my uncle for a long, hard moment, shock rooting me to the floor. His unexpected compassion is like water in the desert. My eyes prickle with heat. I take a deep breath and blink because boys don't fucking cry.

"So what if he is?" My voice is thick and scratchy. "It doesn't change anything."

"Exactly. He'll always be there telling you how you don't measure up. He expects you to fail. He wants it just for the fact it will prove him right. So what are you going to do, give up and let him win?"

I lift my chin. "I'll do whatever it takes to prove him wrong."

"So work harder on the final, Brody."

Frustration has my teeth grinding together. "How can I possibly work harder? I've never studied so much in my damn life. I had that midterm in the bag. I *knew* the damn answers and I still failed."

"What happened with Jordan and your tutoring?"

A lump fills my throat. The ache of missing her is sharp. The way she smells of warm vanilla. The smile reserved just for me that lights her eyes. The furrow she gets between her brows when she loses patience with me. I swallow a mouthful of water and toss the bottle on a nearby chair. "It didn't work out."

Patrick exhales forcefully, his aggravation coming through loud and clear. I hate this—being the errant child he has no clue what to do with. I want to lash out and tell him I can handle it myself but clearly I can't.

"You've barely given it a chance. You can't expect miracles overnight, Brody." He reaches inside his jacket pocket and hands over a blank white card. "Here."

I take it, brows drawing as I flip it over. One word is neatly printed on the back. *Dyslexie*. Shaking my head, I look at my uncle. His expression displays the same slick confidence as my father, only his comes with conviction rather than the cool superiority I can't stand—like he actually believes in me.

"It's a font. Look it up."

My brows rise in silent question.

"Normal font is designed to be aesthetically pleasing, but this one not so much. It's slanted to dissimilate letters and words."

"Dissimilate?"

"Make similar looking letters and words different. It's supposed to be easier to read. Studies show that eighty-four percent of dyslexic readers can read text faster than standard font with fewer mistakes." He shrugs as he says it, like it's not a big deal when it possibly could be. "I'm using it to write your finals paper, so I suggest you start using it too."

Another glance at his watch. "I have to get going." Patrick picks his briefcase up off the floor and gives me a hard stare. "You can do this, Brody. Keep up the tutoring and use the damn font. If you don't, I'm speaking to your coach and you're off the team."

"Thanks," I mutter, my voice bitter with sarcasm.

"Don't thank me." His shoulders lift in a shrug as he turns to leave, over his shoulder saying, "Thank Jordan."

"Wait." My eyes follow his retreat for a single moment. "What?"

"The font was her idea," he calls back, not pausing as he strides from the room.

Of course this has Jordan written all over it. Defeat is not in her nature. She might now cross the road if she sees me walking down the street, but this proves she hasn't given up on me yet. Maybe the only way to fix us is to show her I haven't given up on me either.

I flick the card with my thumb and forefinger and grin, feeling lighter already.

Just you wait, Jordan. I'm coming for you.

Weeks later I'm at my study desk in my room, cramming hard. I check the time on my phone. My stomach sinks. Five minutes to midnight. I have two finals to sit for tomorrow, one of them for my uncle's class.

My eyes are gritty, my body tired and battered from training, and nothing short of a miracle will help me pull this off. Two back-to-back away games, endless drills, and late nights watching plays has taken all my time, leaving none to look over the new material. We have one more game before the playoffs. My focus is on the National Championships and on my team, who are depending on Carter and me to carry them to the top. Hell, so is half of Texas. And here I am stuck in my room, forcing myself to study for an ethics test that has the power to wreck everything.

I throw my pen down. The new font has made a huge difference in typing study notes but what I'm reading comes from the textbook, which is no help. My shoulders and chest are tight with frustration. I rub at the ache, trying to ease it somehow. All the lightness from two weeks ago is gone. I've never felt lower than I do right now. The pressure is crushing.

My throat feels thick and my eyes burn. I can't do it.

I look to my phone, my heart an aching lump in my chest. Notifications are piling up on the screen. None are from Jordan. Her silence has never been more deafening then it is right now. I haven't opened Facebook in days. Social media is low on my radar. The speculation on Jordan's and my relationship has become public fodder. For a brief time we were the new golden couple, now we're strangers, causing the scrutiny to intensify.

A sharp knock on the door jerks me from my spiral. I swivel in my chair, annoyed at the disruption.

Damien's propping up the doorframe, body swaying and eyes bleary. After a night of drinking he's in a complete stupor.

"Dude," he slurs and blinks excessively at the books spread over my desk. "Studying? Come have a drink with us."

Male and female voices drift from the living room, loud and rowdy. Damien has brought his party home with him. Not long ago I would've joined in, but their laughter projects down the hall like fingernails on a blackboard. I grit my teeth. "I can't. I have to get this done."

He blinks again as if seeing two of me. "Well hurry up, then."

I shake my head. The thought of being surrounded by a group of drunk and carefree people turns my stomach. "I'm pulling an all-nighter on this."

Damien shrugs and disappears. I go back to my books but my eyelids are weighted down with bricks, so heavy I can't fight against it. Before I know it, my forehead hits the desk and I'm out instantly.

A hand shaking my shoulder wakes me. Disoriented, I lift my head as Damien dumps something on my desk in front of me. He gives my back a slap and disappears again. Taking a deep breath, I swipe both hands down my face before I reach for my phone. Four a.m. stares back at me like death knell. I've been out for over four hours.

"Fuck," I snarl, glaring at the books spread over my desk. God, just once I wanted to get this right, but it feels hopeless. I've started my whole life off on the back foot and haven't managed to catch up since.

Furious with myself, I sweep out an arm, shoving everything off my desk. Books fall in a thumping heap on the floor. It's not enough to soothe the raging beast. I grab one at random and start ripping at pages. My chest heaves as the paper shreds into ribbon beneath my fingers. I scrunch them and reach for more, growling with frustration. "Fuuuuck!"

Picking up another book, I throw it at the wall. It dents the plaster before dropping to the carpet, right next to the little white bottle Damien delivered. I scoop it off the floor. The contents rattle against the opaque plastic as I bring it close and read the label.

Adderall, I mouth silently.

Clearly I've read it wrong. I blink and process the words a second time. It still says Adderall. Unscrewing the lid, I peer inside. It's full. A full bottle of pills. *What the fuck, Damien?*

I bellow his name.

Sinking to the bed behind me, I stare at the bottle, unable to release the tight grip my hand has on it. I know what it is and what it does.

As professional athletes we're always lectured on the use of banned substances. Adderall is a form of amphetamine and forbidden, yet the drug is popular on campus because it gives you the same euphoric high that intense exercise does. It helps you focus and concentrate. It improves performance on the field. It does everything I need it to do.

Let me help you, the bottle whispers in a dark, seductive voice. An ugly desperation fills me. Like black, smoky tendrils, it coils its way up my spine and over me, imprisoning me in its inky darkness. I can't succumb to it. Damn Damien for putting this temptation in my path. My hands shake as I find strength to screw the lid back on.

Damien pokes his head in my door. "What's up?"

"What's up?" I growl, holding up the bottle. "You're giving me drugs, bonehead, and you ask me what's up?"

His voice lowers. "It's just Adderall. Everyone takes it."

"I'm not everyone." I pinch the bridge of my nose. Frustration has my head pounding so hard I fear an aneurysm. My life is balanced on a knife's edge right now and my *friend* is offering me amphetamines? Not only that, the deep murky recesses of my mind are totally on board with the plan. What the fuck is wrong with me? "I'm a goddamn football player. I can't take that shit."

Damien moves further into my room, shutting the door behind him. "When was your last piss test?"

I fall back on my bed and throw an arm across my eyes. Maybe if I can't see the bottle in my hand I'll forget it's there. "Why does that even matter?"

"It doesn't. You hardly ever get tested anyway, right? No one's gonna know if you take a couple of pills to help you out. You've been biting our heads off for two weeks. You *need* these. You're tired and stressed and playoffs are just around the corner. Keep going like this and something's gonna give. Just take a couple." Damien shrugs like it's no big deal. "What's it gonna hurt?"

Drawing my arm from my eyes, I look from Damien back to the pills still clutched tight in my fist. I desperately want to believe what he says— that I *need* these. What other choice do I have? "How long do they stay in your body for?"

He shrugs again. "I don't know. A couple of days maybe? Just drink a load of water and take a handful of aspirin to clear it out."

Someone in the living room calls Damien's name in a long, drunken slur. He leaves and I go back to staring at the bottle with tired, gritty eyes. Is it worth the risk? I know the drug policy back to front. A first positive test means mandatory drug evaluation and counseling, but it doesn't mean getting kicked off the team.

Before I can second guess myself, I unscrew the lid and shake two pills into my palm. They're tiny and don't seem enough. I shake out a couple more. Picking up the lukewarm Gatorade on my bedside table, I swallow them down. Recapping the lid, I shove the evidence in my top draw. My actions have my heart pounding like I've just played the game of my life.

Resting my forearms on my knees, I hang my head low and take deep breaths as a sense of wrongness fills me. I shake it off and get to my feet. It's too late for regret. The amphetamines are slowly dissolving and entering my bloodstream. There's no going back now.

CHAPTER 21

JORDAN

Heading for the dining hall, I pick up my pace. Leah's walking with me, filling me in on the movie she saw with Hayden last night. I don't hear a word she says. I'm not sure I even recall the title. I'm too agitated and hungry. I've forgotten to bring lunch. Again. I can't afford to keep buying it, but if I don't eat this minute I'm going to start chewing the pages of my textbook.

This forgetfulness isn't me. Neither is the lack of focus. Yesterday I forgot my lucky cleats for practice, and this morning I blanked out in class. It's Brody. I just can't stop thinking about him. He's always *there*. Even in sleep. I wake in the mornings feeling alone, my skin feverish and my body aching.

"Goddamn flu," I grouch and sniff, checking for a stuffed nose.

Leah's prattle halts mid-sentence, her expression skeptical. "The flu? Since when? You never get sick."

"I am now," I snap.

"Flu my ass." Her eyes narrow on my face. She's taking in my dark circles and wan expression like a crime scene investigator. "You've got Madden fever."

"Don't be ridiculous." I quicken my pace, trying to outrun her imminent lecture. Everything was fairy dust and rainbows when Brody and I were dating. Now Leah mentally castrates him every time they cross paths. I was sparing on the details of our separation, but Leah's blame is placed solely in Brody's corner, which is where it should be. The jerk.

As if hearing my insult, Brody calls out my name from somewhere behind me. My heart leaps instantly, its beat evolving from fast to erratic. Students walking in front of me turn at the sound. The entire campus knows his voice. Hearing it speak my name is no doubt too good to ignore. Are they hoping for a spectacle? I don't turn around. I have no intention of giving them one.

I keep moving swiftly along the path, my eyes fixed on the dining hall looming ahead like it's the Holy Grail.

"Jordan! Wait up."

His voice is light as if he's happy to see me. It's hard to believe. The last time we spoke he pretty much told me to *get lost*. The humiliation still smarts my skin like sunburn.

"Please!" Brody calls in a near shout, drawing even more attention.

My pace quickens further. I'm almost at the dining hall entrance when my arm is grabbed in a big, roughened palm. I'm spun around and slam into a wide, solid chest.

"Oomph!"

I'm given mere seconds to take Brody in before he grasps my face in his hands and crashes his lips down on mine. Shock stiffens me for a moment before my body takes the wheel and returns his kiss, reacting to him the way it's never done for anyone else. It only makes me angrier.

"Stop," I gasp, ripping my mouth away. "What are you doing?"

"What does it look like I'm doing?" he replies. Licking his lips, he stares down at me like I belong to him, which I don't. Before I can shove him away, he's kissing me again, his arms sliding around and locking me in place with iron strength.

His hot tongue rubs with mine, and I damn near combust. God he feels good. I missed this connection—this sense of belonging that snaps into place, like where I am is right where I'm meant to be. My arms wind around his neck of their own accord. He groans at the submission, a deep sound of lust and satisfaction that turns my bones to water.

What the hell am I doing?

"Stop!" I jerk backwards, struggling from his embrace.

Brody's arms slide from my back to my hips but he holds tight. I pause my efforts and glare, my face burning with indignation. His hair is a tousled mess, his cheeks tinged pink, and dark pupils dilated. He looks wild and beautiful, like electricity is wired in his veins.

"Let me go, Brody." A lump forms in my throat. I don't want him to let go. "You can't do this."

"Do what?" He grins irresistibly. "Kiss you? Because I already did."

His widespread fingers dig in deliciously and tug me closer, pressing a growing erection into my lower belly. My body throbs in response, a sweet ache building swiftly between my thighs.

"And I'm going to do it again." He smacks his lips playfully against mine. "And again." Another loud kiss lands on my mouth. "And again." Brody's lips come down for more. His carefree mood is infectious, making my outrage hard to hold onto.

"Stop," I hiss before I lose it altogether.

"You heard her," Leah interrupts from somewhere on my left. Brody's head snaps in her direction. "Jordan's not some toy you can just pick up and put down at will, Madden."

His voice sobers, annoyance creasing his brow. "Give us a minute, would you, Leah?"

Leah is far from done. "No."

Brody huffs, nostrils flaring. "Goddammit, Leah. Can you just—"

Her chin juts out. "No."

I'm thankful for her strength right now. It bolsters my own. "Leah's right, Brody." His attention snaps back to me, tension gathering in his frame. "You can't keep doing this. I've worked my whole life for the opportunity to be here, and it needs to be my priority. My life and career is all mapped out." I breathe in Brody's familiar scent, his body warm and protective. I want to bury my face in his neck and inhale deeply, letting the comfort of it settle in my bones. He's right. This is what home feels like … but I have to let it go. "And you're not part of it."

His intake of breath is sharp, piercing my ears. "You don't mean that."

"Of course she does."

"Leah." My voice shakes. I stare down at my feet, blinking rapidly. "Can you go get me a sandwich before they're all gone?"

My appetite has disappeared, but Brody and I need a moment alone.

Her voice takes on a warning tone. "Elliott."

I force a reassuring smile that doesn't fool anyone, least of all me. "Grain bread if they have it," I add.

Leah shakes her head but walks off. When she disappears I look back to Brody, finishing what I need to say. "I can't keep up with you, Brody. One minute your high and the next low. All I ever did was help you, and you threw it back in my face." It hurts to keep talking, and I have to force myself. "I can't do it anymore. I need to be selfish now and focus on myself. Please understand that and just let me be."

"I can't do that. I know I fucked up." Brody shakes his head, the pink tinge on his cheeks now ashen. "Jordan." My name is a rasp on his lips. "I'm sorry. I just needed time before I came to see you. There was something I had to do first."

Reaching behind, he tugs a folded piece of paper from his back pocket. "I got my results on the finals back." Unfolding it, he shoves it at me.

"You ..." I pause, my eyes catching the grade on his printout. I look up from the fluttering page, meeting his eyes. "This is what you had to do first?"

A happy smile curves his lips. "Yes."

I feel myself responding. It's impossible not to. "You passed."

His grin widens. "I did."

Elation bubbles up inside me. I want to grab Brody in a tight hug and laugh and dance up and down. Instead I take a step back, tucking my hands inside the back pockets of my denim shorts to stop myself reaching for him. He doesn't need me anymore. "I'm so happy for you, Brody."

His expression falls and his tone takes a bitter edge. "That's it? You're *happy* for me?"

I shake my head. "I am. Wow. You got a B plus. That's ..." So much higher then an F. Almost unbelievable even. In fact, the huge difference between the two grades hardly makes sense at all. I shrug it off, focusing on Brody's expectant expression. "... incredible. You're incredible."

"No I'm not. You are. This is all you, Jordan. I couldn't have done this without you." Brody steps forward, bridging the gap. His voice lowers to a soft plea. "I *can't* do this without you."

"You can." A sob threatens to break free of my chest. "You just proved it."

His eyes widen, panic filling them. "No, Jordan—"

"Here's your sandwich," Leah growls and slaps it against my chest. Her timing is impeccable. I grab the plastic wrapped bundle before it drops to the ground. "Now let's go."

My hand is snatched and Leah's pulling me away. My legs feel like lead as she steers me back down the path. A quick glance over my shoulder shows Brody standing there, staring after me. His arms hang slack by his sides, the page still fisted in his hand.

Cracks form in my heart. "I'll see you, Brody."

Later that night I'm lying in bed with a textbook, pretending to myself that I can study with eyes red and swollen from a crying jag. A half-empty tub of caramel chunk ice cream rests on my bedside table. It's my favorite flavor and never fails to fix any problem, yet tonight it leaves my stomach churning. *Screw you, Ben and Jerry's. You had one job to do.*

With an aggravated sigh, my eyes shift from my book to the page resting on the bed next to me. It's the failed exam Brody tossed away on the field all those weeks ago. The paper is a little battered but appears harmless nonetheless. The trouble is that it's not. I've been harboring suspicion over Brody's midterm all afternoon. Going from a failed grade to a B+ is a quantum leap. As I stare at it, my suspicion only deepens.

Was Brody's grade sabotaged?

It's the question of the hour, and one I've been pondering since I got home and dug the midterm out from beneath a pile of books. Seventy percent of the test is multiple choice. If Kyle fudged his answers, I have no way of knowing, but I can't let this go. Brody deserves vindication. But pointing an accusing finger isn't going to do any good. Neither is telling Brody. He will hunt Kyle down and pummel that snide toolbag into the ground. As much as I want to see that happen, the last thing Brody needs right now is negative media attention and suspension from the team. This is a matter that needs kid gloves. It also needs proof before I start throwing accusations about Kyle to Professor Draper.

Half an hour later my eyes are pinned on the ceiling as an idea takes root. It's not one that sits well with me. In fact the very thought is going down worse than the Ben and Jerry's did, but I can't see any other option.

My phone vibrates with a text, the angry little sound making me jump. The brightly lit screen highlights Brody's name. A shuddery sigh escapes my lips.

I lie there for a minute, pretending I'm not thinking about what's in the message. Another minute later and I know it's ridiculous. I won't sleep if I don't read it. It will niggle at me like a festering sore.

Brody: *Knock, knock.*

My brow furrows. What the hell does that mean? Is Brody at the door? It's been two minutes since the message alert. With a pounding heart, I scramble from my bed and leave my room.

"Shit," I mutter. Racing back, I grab the test paper and shove it underneath my mattress. I head back out, grabbing my cotton robe as I go. The living area is dark. Leah's gone to bed, thank god. While I appreciate her mama bear protectiveness, it needs to loosen a notch before she strangles me with it.

Shrugging on the robe over my plain white tank top and panties, I tie the belt and pad over to the apartment door. Undoing the locks, I open it a fraction and peer out into the brightly lit hall. Emptiness greets me. There's no one there. Disappointment slugs me in the gut. God. This is crazy.

Once back in bed, I settle the sheets around me with forced calm and pick up my phone.

Jordan: *What are you doing?*

Brody is waiting for my reply because his answer is instant, complete with his usual errors.

Brody: *Ur supposed to answer with whose there.*

A joke? I'm getting a random joke? There's no fighting the smile that tugs at the corners of my lips. I know I shouldn't reply but it's easier said than done.

Jordan: *Who's there?*
Brody: *Beets!*
Jordan: *Beets who?*
Brody: *Beets me!*

A chuckle escapes me.

Brody: *Knock, knock.*
Jordan: *Who's there?*
Brody: *Yah.*

Jordan: *Yah who?*

Brody: *I didn't no u were a cowboy!*

I barely have time to shake my head at that before the next one hits.

Brody: *Knock, knock.*

I glance at my textbook and sigh deeply. Whatever game Brody's playing, I don't have time for it.

Jordan: *Brody, I can't keep doing this all night …*

Putting down the phone, I pick up my book and flick to my page as another alert comes through.

Brody: *Last one, I promise.*

I give in because I'm a total fool.

Jordan: *Who's there?*

Instead of a text reply, Brody rings me instead. I waver a very short time before hitting answer.

"Fuck it, Jordan," he's saying before I get out a simple greeting. Leaning forward, I grab for the blanket at the end of my bed. Lifting it up and over myself, I burrow down against the storm his voice sets off inside me. "I don't care about jokes. I care about—" He breaks off, creating a charged silence. I sit and wait, breathing heavy under the heat of the blanket. "Pizza."

"You care about pizza?"

He clears his throat. "I do."

"That's good, Brody. We all have to care about something."

His chuckle comes through the phone. "Christ, I have mad skills with a football, but when it comes to you I have no idea what I'm doing."

His vulnerability tugs at my heart. It makes me protective. It makes me want to rip Kyle Davis's intestines out through his throat and strangle him with them for all the torment he's caused Brody. *Soon,* I promise myself. "Maybe you could start by telling me what you're trying to do."

"I'm trying to ask you to come out for pizza with me after your soccer game on Wednesday."

"Brody—"

"Don't answer yet," he says quickly. "I have a bedtime story I want to tell you first."

"A bedtime story?" I echo faintly.

"Yes. A bedtime story."

"Well, okay then."

"Once a upon a time, there was a little boy called Brody." Delight curls my lips. Bedtime stories bring out my inner child, and Brody can be a bit of a closed book. The opportunity to hear snippets from his youth is one I'm not turning down. "Before he ever picked up a football he knew he loved the game, but he wasn't ever allowed to watch it.

"One day when he was six, they were driving past the local high school and a game was on. He rolled down his window and fell in love. The atmosphere was intense, the crowd, the chants, the *fun*. He could smell popcorn and hotdogs, and fresh cut grass. But most of all he could see the home team. They were worshipped like gods and treated each other as family. Brothers. They belonged to each other and to the game.

"The little boy craned his neck as they went by, sucking all that in so he could play it back later in his head. He snuck in to watch their next game, and the next, and the next, until he knew without a doubt that football was going to be the best thing that ever happened to him. But no matter how much he begged, or how many bargains he tried making, his parents wouldn't let him play. The little boy was destined for a more conservative future in politics.

"But the older that little boy got, the more they realized he wasn't going to be anything more than an embarrassment so they gave in."

Understanding hits like a lightning strike. Brody hides his dyslexia because it's an embarrassment to his parents. Something to be ashamed of. And that shame is so deeply ingrained inside him he can't let it go. My eyes burn. "I hope that little boy grew up to realize his parents were wrong."

Brody replies and his voice is stilted and thick, as if the words are hard to get out. "He didn't. The problem is that these two people are the ones he's been trying to please all his life. He knows he never will, not as long as he plays football, but maybe one day he'll be great, and what they think won't matter so much anymore."

My lips tremble and I press them together.

"But then something amazing happened."

"What?" I ask, needing to hear something good.

"Not what, but who. What this little boy didn't realize, was that it wasn't just football that was going to be the best thing that ever happened to him."

My breath catches. "Brody."

"This little boy grew up and he met a girl. She was the first person to see all of who he was, and still believe in him, even when he didn't believe in himself. She was smart, and pretty, and god, so wholesome he wanted to defile her with wicked words and hot sex. But this girl was far too serious, so he made her laugh and taught her that it's okay to sometimes let go." Brody takes a deep breath and lets it out. "This girl was utterly perfect, and he was so scared of disappointing her like he did his parents, that he fucked up by pushing her away before it happened."

Silent tears fall down my cheeks. One after the other they drip from my face and plop onto the sheets below me. I sit up in my bed, wiping them away with my palm. I realize this isn't a game Brody's playing, yet he's won regardless. He's under my skin—a part of me now—whether I want him or not. And I want him.

"You know what I think?"

"What?" he asks.

I affect a casual tone, but inside my heart is racing. "I think that if the boy told this story to the girl, that she would get it, and that if he still wants to take her out for pizza, she'd tell him her soccer game starts at three o'clock so don't be late."

I can hear the grin in his voice when he says, "Yes, ma'am."

A teasing smile forms on my lips. "And if he still wants to defile her, well … he should know that turnabout is fair play."

A pained groan comes through the phone. He releases a harsh breath. "It was the knock-knock jokes that did it, wasn't it?" I laugh and he groans a second a time. "God, Jordan, I love that sound."

I suck in a breath. I don't want to wait. I want Brody *now*.

"Hell," I hear him mumble softly.

"Brody?"

"It's late. I've kept you up. Goodnight, Jordan," he says and then I get dial tone. Just like that he's gone, but as I set my phone on the bedside table, the smile on my face is still there.

CHAPTER 22

BRODY

"Why the hell are we still doing this?" Damien grumbles. "Jordan already agreed to go out with you tonight. We don't need plan B anymore."

Eddie shoots him a glare. Being the size of a mountain, his intimidation factor is usually off the charts. This afternoon it does nothing because Eddie, like the rest of us, is dressed in a cheerleading outfit. It comes complete with a skirt *and* the pompoms we lifted from the squad room. "Shut up, assface. Brody's trying to be supportive of his girl."

Damien snorts. "Just turning up to watch Jordan play should be enough."

A growl emanates from Eddie's chest. Plan B was his idea, generated from the locker room after training when we were high on endorphins. Now he believes after the entire hour we put in to practice our routine, we need to see it through. "Love is all about grand gestures. You wouldn't understand."

"You're a hopeless romantic, Eddie, but we love you anyway." Carter grins and slaps Eddie on the back as he steps up to the side of the field. He has two miniscule pigtails of hair tied up in ribbons, the only one willing to take it that far. It was hard enough finding a supersized skirt in our college colors that would fit Eddie.

With the game starting in fifteen minutes, we're up soon. As the eight of us—including Jax and three other guys from the team—group by the sidelines, we start garnering attention. Necks strain in our direction and cameras start clicking. My Texas Bulls cap sits on my head, hiding my face. I set it backwards and turn, giving those closest a wink and a wave. Delighted laughter rings out at my gesture.

When the two soccer teams emerge from the locker rooms, the announcer comes on with perfect timing. His voice booms around the stadium gleefully. "We have something very special for your pre-game entertainment this afternoon, folks. Everyone please welcome to the field, The Colton Bullettes!"

"We're up," Eddie informs us and gives Damien a shove in the back. He stumbles on to the field.

We jog out behind him to the symphony of catcalls, unrestrained laughter, and suggestive hollers. I raise one pompom-ed arm up high and shake it, playing it up for the crowd. A breeze ripples down low across the field, fluttering my skirt. My motherfucking *skirt*. Damien's right. Of all the dumb things I've done, this is up there.

We get in position by forming a line, legs shoulder-width apart, and hands on our hips. "Shake It Off," by Taylor Swift blares out from the stadium speakers, filling the huge space with loud base and a girly pop sound. Cameras flash and I cringe. It's not going to be pretty. There is no doubt this will cause a social media firestorm.

Our routine begins and already Carter bounces the wrong way. Eddie slaps him on the ass and he turns quickly. Our hips are grinding and pompoms waving when I risk searching out Jordan. Her team is lined up on the sidelines. Most are dying of hysterical laughter. She has a hand covering her eyes as if she can't bear watching, but her fingers are spread as she peeks through them, her gaze fixed on my every move. When she sees me looking, the smile that breaks across her face is brighter then sunshine. I wink playfully and grin. She laughs hard and shakes her head, her face bright red.

We finish up our routine with the big finale, which is four of the guys crouching down, and the other four leaping over the top. It's basic leapfrog and as a wide receiver, it should be a skill I can handle in my sleep. Hell, even a five-year-old could ace the move, but I'm too busy watching Jordan. My aim is off when I leap over Eddie's mountainous crouched form. I end up with my legs half wrapped around the back of his neck and we both go down.

Eddie squeals like a girl. "Get your motherfucking balls off my neck, you sick bastard!"

He rears up and I overturn and hit dirt. "Oww, dipshit!"

When I get to my feet, I brush the grass from my face and bow to the spectators. Jax saunters over, gasping with laughter. He slings an arm over my shoulder as we walk off to thunderous applause.

"Dude," he says when he catches his breath. "I nailed it. You, not so much."

I look across at Jordan. She's jogging into position on the field, her expression serious. Their team is down to the wire. Winning this game will take them to the semifinals of the NCAA National Championships. A quick glance in my direction shows laughter in her eyes and color blooming on her cheeks. "I got out of it what I came to do."

"You have it bad, cousin." Jax pulls me into a chokehold. "Just remember it was me she wanted first."

His obnoxious comments usually roll off my back, but this one sets my teeth on edge. I shove him off, my voice hard. "Fuck off, Jax."

The unexpected anger throws me off balance, but Jax only laughs, unfazed. "But it's you she loves for some weird, unfathomable reason."

The very idea sets my heart thumping at a furious pace. I rub a hand across my chest, trying to soothe the frantic beat. "Maybe."

We reach the edge of the field and Carter holds up a hand, giving me a high five. "Dude, what's with your eyes?"

I shrug. "Nothing, why?"

Jax turns for a look, his expression morphing to a puzzled frown. "They're red. And your pupils are huge. You feeling okay?"

Shit. I've been lethargic all week. Not the kind of tired that's fixed with a nap, but an exhaustion set deep in my bones. The bottle of Adderall was still in my drawer. I've taken the pills on and off over the past month, and taking a few more earlier today didn't feel like such a big deal. I wanted tonight with Jordan to be perfect. And doctors prescribe these pills, so how dangerous can they be? "I'm just tired."

The lie makes me uneasy. Damien and I share a mutual glance. He reaches over and slaps my back. "Dude. You're good, right?"

"Hell yeah." I grin but it's more a baring of teeth because I hear his underlying question. Damien gave me that full bottle with no intention of asking for it back. It makes me wonder how many he has, and where he got them from. It's something I ought to question, but there's too much on my plate right now. Besides, Damien and I have known each other since high school. He's not a damn drug dealer. "Everything's coming up daisies."

The game is finished and I'm leaning up against the brick wall of the building opposite the locker room. I'm doing my best to appear unobtrusive and failing because of the damn skirt.

My gaze is pinned to the locker room door. Even though I know Jordan's not the type, I'm not willing to risk a change of mind and have her sneak out. She's the last one to emerge. The moment I see her everything else fades. Her eyes lift, clear blue hitting mine. Pink tints her cheeks and a slow smile forms. It rocks me down to my toes. Fuck, but I don't know how she undoes me this way. I unravel completely.

I give her a small wave. It's a casual gesture that hides the welling emotion. She starts toward me. She looks beautiful with her hair out. Shiny waves spill over her shoulders and down her back. A black sweater hugs her top half and form-fitting jeans encase her legs, hiding nothing. God willing, I'll be peeling those off later tonight and sinking myself inside her.

Jordan takes in my unchanged outfit as she gets closer and bites down on her bottom lip. "Ummm ..."

I have a change of clothes in the car, but it can't hurt to tease her a little first. I run a hand up one thickly muscled thigh and the hem of my skirt lifts suggestively. Is there anything more attractive then the hairy leg of a man in women's clothing? "You like?"

A huff of laughter escapes her lips.

"I'm very expensive." I purse my lips and scan her body. "But for you, twenty dollars."

Jordan stops in front of me, brows high as she readjusts the heavy sports bag slung over her shoulder. "Are you hustling me?"

I cock my head. "That depends."

"On?"

I sweep a hand down over my body. "On whether you want this fine specimen of man taking care of you tonight."

Jordan's lips part and she takes a step forward, closing the distance between us. There's cockiness in her stance, and so much heat in her eyes it burns me to ash. "You plan on manhandling me?"

My breath comes a little faster and heat tightens my groin. "I do."

Jordan leans closer and my mouth goes dry. "Good."

Our date is a blur. We talk and laugh, and we share a beer in celebration of Jordan's win—an advancement into the semifinals next week: Pride swells in my chest over her talent. Jordan's played a huge part in putting the Colton Bulls soccer team on the map this year. Her passion is appealing and so goddamn sexy. She glows with it. When our waiter comes to take our food order, I can't drag my eyes from where she sits across from me. I simply tell him we'll take a large pepperoni pizza "to go." I want her to myself.

We reach my car and I open the back door and toss the large box on the seat. It's already forgotten when I slam the door closed and turn, finding Jordan right behind me on the sidewalk.

She's waiting for me to pounce. It's my usual *modus operandi* with her. I can't help it. Jordan brings out the caveman inside me, but this time it's different. This time it feels so much *more*. Simply grabbing and taking feels wrong.

I reach out, my palm gently cupping Jordan's face. My fingers skim down her cheek, the whisper of a touch on her soft skin. She shivers visibly and let's out a shaky breath. I can't describe the craving in my chest right now. It's so far beyond anything I've ever felt before that it's an effort to go slow.

"You're extraordinary, Jordan Matilda Elliott," I say quietly.

Jordan chuckles lightly. "I try."

I know by her flippant tone that I've flustered her. Lighthearted humor is how she creates her little barriers when I've overwhelmed her. I like it. And I like that I see it for what it is, because it tells me I need to push a little harder rather than back away.

"You don't even need to try." My hand slides around the back of her neck and tugs gently, bringing her face to mine. "You just are," I say against her lips.

My mouth brushes hers. She brings her hands between us, lightly fisting my shirt when I go to draw away. I'm pulled back and her lashes sweep upwards, her eyes wide and searching mine.

Then Jordan does something that almost brings me to my knees. She wraps her arms around me and hugs me. I've grown up in a family where love and warmth is non-existent. Where emotional abuse and harsh words are an acceptable form of affection. How did Jordan know how much I needed this when even I didn't know?

Her lips brush my ear. "You are too, Brody."

My body begins to quake. I snake my arms around her lower back and hold on.

"Are you okay?" she asks.

I bury my face in her neck and breathe deep, closing my eyes because I'm so in love with this girl I can't even see straight. "If I wasn't, I am now."

Eventually, I let her go so we can leave. When we're inside the car driving to her apartment, I take her hand in mine. Linking our fingers, I rest them on my thigh and ask about her life in Australia.

She turns her head to stare out the window. It's a touchy subject. She misses home and Nicky, but I want to know everything. "Did you ride a kangaroo to school?"

She groans and rolls her eyes.

"I assume that's a no?"

"Despite what people might think, kangaroos don't roam the streets willy nilly."

I laugh. "Of course they do. I saw it on the internet, so it must be true. And did you just say willy nilly? What does that even mean?"

Jordan glances over at me, her lips twitching. "It means you won't see them bounding across suburban streets when you're out for a walk."

"Say no more. You're ruining the fantasy," I tell her, bringing her hand with me when I change gears. "So your brother. You said he's in construction, right?"

Jordan stiffens. I feel it when her hand tightens in mine. "He is."

"How did he get into that?"

"Family friend," she says.

It's obvious she doesn't want to talk about it, but I do. "Is that what he's always wanted to do?"

"No." She pulls her hand from mine, withdrawing like a damn turtle back in its shell. "It's not what he ever wanted to do."

Pulling into the parking lot, I apply the handbrake and switch off the ignition. It leaves nothing but heavy silence between us and a light ticking sound of the warm engine cooling down.

"He was a better soccer player than I was."

I twist in my seat to look at her. "Was?"

She swallows visibly, her eyes falling to where her hands fidget in her lap. "If my career was going to the stratosphere, his was going to the stars." A tear rolls down her cheek and plops on to her jeans. Another one follows. She dashes it away with her palm before it falls.

I feel it. Her distress. It squeezes my chest, and now I'm angry with myself for pushing too hard. How are you supposed to get the balance right?

Yanking out the keys, I get out of the car. Walking around the back, I reach the passenger door and open it. "Jordan."

Her lips are a tight white line that trembles. She shakes her head and I know speaking right now is too much.

"Baby," I whisper. Taking both her hands I pull her from the car and fold her in my arms. I can only hope it offers her the same comfort it does for me, because I don't know what else to do. I don't know how long we stay like that, with Jordan crushed to my chest. A minute. An eternity. All I know is that I'll never tire of holding her this way.

"He was driving the car," she eventually says, her voice muffled because her face is buried in my neck.

The car? For a moment I don't get it, and then the light goes on.

"We were only sixteen, not long having had our learners permits. Nicky loved driving. He pestered our parents all the time to go. It was night when it happened, and the streets quieter then. Mom decided to go with them last minute. She needed something from the store. I can't even remember what, but I remember her picking up her purse, joking that dad would get the wrong thing like he always does." Jordan takes a deep, shaky breath but keeps her head buried. "Another car barreled straight through an intersection and slammed into the passenger side. My parents were killed instantly. Nicky's left leg was broken in three different places. Otherwise he was okay, physically. But he was trapped in the car. Nicky couldn't move." The absolute horror of what her brother went through sickens me. Jordan burrows in further and my arms around her tighten. "He was stuck in that damn car and couldn't do anything."

Apologies feel useless right now, but it's all I have to offer. "I'm so sorry."

Jordan pushes from my embrace. Her head is downcast as she wipes her face. "It was five years ago." She shrugs and finally looks at me. "You think it would hurt less by now, but Nicky ... His leg healed, but not his heart. We never had much, not even insurance, so he gave up soccer. School too. He took the construction job so he could take care of the both of us."

Respect for her brother hits me hard. The inner strength it would take to give up your dream and hand it over to someone else. That's not huge. It's *enormous*. And now Jordan's doing everything she can to be worth the sacrifice. My lips graze her forehead.

Jordan lets out a shaky breath and lifts her chin. "Will you come up?"

A faint smile reaches my lips. "Don't expect me to say no."

When we reach her room, I have a plan. Slow and tender. But Jordan blows it out of the water. She shuts the bedroom door behind us and peels away her sweater. She comes at me, unfastening the back hook of her bra and flinging it away. At the same time, she splays a hand against my chest and shoves. It's not enough to push me down, but I get the hint and sink to the edge of the bed.

"I thought you wanted to be manhandled?"

"I do," she says, tugging her jeans down. It's an effort, one I'm thoroughly enjoying watching. Peeling one leg off of her right foot, Jordan goes for the other and pitches forward.

We fall back on the bed with her landing on top of me. Before I can grab skin, she's rolling off, panting as she pulls the other leg over her foot and throws her jeans to the floor.

My cock is already hard. She's driving me insane and all she's done is rip her clothes off like a maniac.

"What's this?" I ask, taking in her black lace panties—what little there is of them. It's not her usual practical attire. The little black scrap is provocative and indecent. It sets my pulse skyrocketing, but it's anger that drives my next question. "Have you worn these for anyone else?"

Jordan pauses at my tone and looks at me. "What?"

The sudden surge of anger is irrational, but I can't seem to get a handle on it. "You heard me."

"Brody," she breathes. Untangling her long legs, she gets up off the bed. Her black sweater is half hanging from the bedside table. She picks it up and shrugs it back on.

My fisted hands rest on my knees, knuckles white. Sweat dots my brow and my heart is pounding a hard unnatural beat. What the fucking hell is wrong with me? "I'm sorry."

CHAPTER 23

JORDAN

Brody's jealous outburst is like icy water dashed in my face. I turn and look at him. His head is downcast and jaw tight. I don't understand his anger. No, I haven't worn this underwear for anyone else, not that I'm telling him that because it shouldn't matter. In actual fact, the bra and panties are new, and the guilt from the reckless purchase left me sick. My pillaged bank account was left devastated, but I told myself it would be worth it to see Brody's face.

Brilliant plan, Jordan, I snort to myself.

Not that I expected *this* reaction. I should have. Lately, when I expect Brody to go right, he goes left. Down? He goes up. The unpredictability is insane.

"Save it," I tell him.

Yanking on the handle, I throw the bedroom door open and stomp toward the kitchen, my heart pounding a furious beat. I'm only in my sweater and tiny scrap of black lace, but it doesn't matter because Leah is at Hayden's apartment tonight.

"Jordan," Brody calls out and follows behind me.

My eyes land on the pizza box we set on the kitchen counter earlier. Perfect. That's exactly what I need right now—carbs and calories. Ripping open the kitchen cupboard, I grab plates. They make a loud, satisfying clank when I dump them on the counter.

"Jordan, I'm sorry," Brody implores from behind me.

"I heard you the first time," I tell him, my voice terse as I rummage for paper napkins. I'm not sure we have any. Hayden goes through them like candy because he never stops eating. It stupidly fuels my anger. I spin around hard. "Maybe you shouldn't waste your apologies. At the rate you're burning through them, you'll have none left soon."

Brody flinches at my snide tone. I barely notice. I want to throw the entire pizza box at his head, delicious carbs be damned. I don't. Coming from a family that's never had much, the idea of wasting food makes my toes curl.

"Are you going to start trying to control everything I wear from now on? Because if you're going to be a jealous dick all the time, I'd really like a heads-up on that."

"Shit, Jordan." He rakes fingers through his hair, leaving it in messy tufts on his head. "No. I would never do that. I love you in anything you wear. And those panties ..." He exhales audibly, waving a hand at them as if he has no idea what to say. "I *am* a jealous dick. The thought of another guy seeing you the way I do makes me see red."

This argument is as ridiculous as his outburst. "I don't plan on any other guy seeing me this way!"

We stare at each other for a beat of silence. After a moment, Brody ducks his head. He looks up at me from beneath his lashes, a stupid grin pulling at his cheeks. "You don't?"

Damn him. "No!"

Brody takes a step toward me. His eyes fall to my mouth, and down lower. I take a step back. My lower back presses into the counter behind me. There's no more room for me to move.

"You have no idea how happy that makes me," he says.

The acute relief in his voice deflates my anger like a limp balloon. It annoys me because I *want* to be angry. I want to make him work for my forgiveness, but how can I when all he has to do is smile like that to get it?

Brody takes two more slow, deliberate steps forward, his eyes holding mine, using them to pin me in place. It ramps up my pulse. I'm being *stalked*. "Let me make it up to you."

I don't need to ask how. Brody's intent is written all over his face. The way he looks at me, like nothing else exists for him, sets off a heavy, pulsing ache between my legs. My body responds to him so easily, and it's scary. I want him, but I never expected this level of *need*. This thing between us is a freight train. Nothing seems able to stop it. Not me. Not him. Maybe not even distance.

I barely process the thought with Brody now standing in my space, his wide shoulders crowding me. His massive hands settle on my hips.

I let out the breath I've been holding.

"Let me."

One of his palms slides around my belly and down, gliding lower until he's cupping me over my panties. He rubs his whole hand between my legs, back and forth, back and forth, a slow steady rhythm designed to send me mad.

Brody's chest expands as he breathes in deep through his nose, keeping himself in check. His eyes are watching me, reading my reaction.

My lips part and a small moan escapes. *Touch me. God. Please.*

That's all it takes.

He wrenches my panties aside, and a thick finger glides through the slick, swollen heat of me.

"Fuck." His exhale is harsh and he groans. "Jordan."

The relief from his touch is instantaneous. *Yes. God, thank you.* But it's not enough. My hips rock forward, a silent demand for more. His lips land on mine, tongue thrusting inside my mouth at the same time his finger pushes inside me.

The invasion forces a pleasured whimper from my throat. Brody swallows the sound, kissing me so hard it almost hurts. My hands grab his shoulders, holding on before I buckle beneath the pressure.

He draws back, panting, long enough to rasp, "Your sweater. Get it off."

I barely get it past my shoulders when his mouth latches onto my nipple. Brody sucks it deep in his mouth, all the while his finger keeps up its steady assault, plunging inside and then pulling out to stroke over my clit, again and again. My breath hitches at the relentless onslaught. I wrench the sweater over my head and it drops to the floor, already forgotten when he picks me up and sets me on the counter.

"Oh god," I gasp as he sucks open, wet kisses down my belly.

Brody drops lower, spreading my thighs wide. His gaze settles between my legs and he bites down on his lip.

I squirm. "Brody. Please."

His eyes lift, lust-filled and dark. They hold mine as he takes the thin, elastic strap of my panties in his fists and drags them down and off. His eyes drop. I'm completely exposed, wearing nothing while he's still fully dressed. I don't care. I need him, any which way he wants to give himself to me.

Brody dips further down, between my thighs. Rough palms glide along my outer legs. He urges them over his broad shoulders. I comply, squealing when he grabs hold of my waist and stands. His strength is immense, each defined muscle bunching tight as he takes my weight.

My ankles lock around him, my thighs bracketing either side of his head. I dig my fingers into his hair, clinging unsteadily on his shoulders. Right before I think I'm about to pitch to the floor, he turns and shoves my back against the high kitchen cupboards behind me, his breath warm and harsh on my clit.

"I want to eat you every which way, Jordan," he tells me in a tone that leaves no doubt he means what he says. A single moment later he strokes me with the flat of his tongue. I moan long and hard, my head falling back and hitting the cabinet with a *thunk*. "Oh god."

My hands shift to his shoulders. The rounded muscles are solid and thick beneath my grasp—straining. My fingers dig in hard and he grunts a sound of pleasure as his tongue plunges deeper inside me.

I know I'm safe—Brody's hands on me are hard and secure, yet I still feel dizzy and overheated. My head is near the ceiling and my heart pounds feverishly. My gasps and moans get louder and closer together as his mouth feasts on me, his tongue lapping steadily as my orgasm approaches.

"Need you, Brody," I pant, because I desperately do. I need his body naked and locking me tight before I come apart at the seams.

He moves steady and slow, lowering me back to the counter with another grunt. Released from the tension of holding on, my thighs tremble. Brody steps back, grabbing at the neckline of his shirt and tugging it over his head.

"Hurry," I urge, though I don't think he can move faster than he already is.

Brody tugs a condom from his pants pocket, and I'm thankful he's being smart because I'm too impatient to care. He tears at the little foil packet desperately, fingers fumbling. "Dammit," he mumbles.

"I need to go on the pill," I tell him, impatient.

"Do that," he says, managing to get the condom free. Holding it in one hand, he uses the other to undo the button and zipper on his jeans. Shoving them down his thighs, he pulls his thick cock free of his underwear and rolls it on. "Next week. I'll come with you."

I shift forward on the counter, spreading my thighs in invitation. He moves between them. Our breath comes in pants and my gaze drops, settling on the swollen head of his cock pushing inside me. With an agonizingly slow thrust, Brody fills me. Our chests press together, both our hearts thumping a manic beat. Then he stills and bows his head, resting his forehead against my breastbone. I feel his breath on my naked skin, hot and heavy.

He swallows, his voice choked. "Nothing feels better than you, Jordan."

Without lifting his head, Brody pulls out slowly and thrusts back in, sinking himself deeper.

I rake fingers through his silky hair and whisper his name, my eyes burning with sudden emotion. How could I let this happen? I fly halfway across the world chasing a dream and end up with the hottest, brightest, sweetest love I'll ever have the chance of knowing. Brody is exciting and turbulent, charming and sexy, and deeply tortured down beneath the surface.

The man buried inside me right now is wildly imperfect, and I want forever with him.

I wake late in the morning. A simple shift of my hips and I'm groaning. I ache everywhere, but it's a delicious ache. It's the kind that only two bouts of incredible sex can produce. Drawing in a deep breath of air, my lungs expand as I roll in bed, stretching sore muscles and seeking out Brody.

He's at my desk, idly swinging in the swivel chair. My laptop sits open. He's talking to someone in between taking bites of the cold pizza slice resting in his hand. My brow furrows. Is he on the phone? I shift up on one elbow, tugging the covers up with me.

No doubt hearing the sheets rustle, Brody turns and a smug grin lights his face. Instantly, I'm wary.

"Oh, she finally wakes," he says.

"That must have been one hell of a soccer game," my brother responds. Brody stifles a snort.

What in the everloving hell? My eyes snap to the computer screen. Nicky waves. It's summer time there and the ends of his hair look dipped in gold from the sun—bright and brilliant to my tired gaze.

I rub a hand over my eyes. Have I woken to an alternate universe where my brother and Brody have become best mates overnight? It seems so.

Taking a huge bite of pizza, Brody holds out the slice in my direction. His eyes are wide as he chews, his face overly bright as if he hasn't slept at all. He swallows. "Want a bite?"

"No," I croak, though secretly I do. Cold pizza for breakfast is a shameful weakness of mine and I'm starving, but I have no plans to languish naked in bed, eating pepperoni and cheese while my boyfriend and brother chat in the same room together. It's weird. And wrong. And did I mention weird? "What's going on?"

"We're just catching up," Nicky tells me in his pleasant 'isn't this fun' voice.

My stomach growls. I ignore it as I look between them both. "Yeah? Catching up on what?"

"Surfing," Nicky says.

"Soccer," Brody answers at the same time.

My suspicious glare deepens.

"Well. Good chat. Gotta go. Congrats on the win, Barney." After casually throwing out that horrific childhood nickname as a tactical diversion, Nicky leans in and taps the keyboard, abruptly ending the Skype call.

Brody sputters a laugh, spinning his chair back in my direction after closing the laptop. "Barney?"

My chin juts out and I fold my arms.

Without any warning, Brody dives on the bed and I'm smothered beneath an enormous two-hundred-odd-pound mass of delicious man flesh. He draws back and I manage to suck in a quick lungful of air before he attacks. Grabbing both my hands, he pins them above my head. He rips the sheet away with his free hand, exposing my naked torso to the cool air. The rough pads of his fingers glide down my ribcage, deliberately hitting all my ticklish spots.

I shriek and giggle. When they brush over a soft nipple it responds instantly, peaking and sending delicious sparks of pleasure straight to my core. My back arches and my laughter dies out, a moan breaking free of my throat.

"Mmmm ..." Brody draws out the sound, his gaze locked on my now hardened nipple. He traces the peak with his finger, teasingly slow, before drawing away. I squirm, my chest rising upwards, chasing more of his touch. "You like that..." he looks up from my breast "...Barney?"

"Brody." I try to say his name in a stern voice, but the cheeky glint in his eyes sets off another peal of laughter.

"I'm dying to know," he says before sucking the nipple inside his mouth. His tongue swirls languidly and my breath hitches. It pops free and he finishes his sentence. "How you got that particular nickname."

Brody frees my arms and instantly I'm covering my breasts with my hands. "I'll never tell."

He pouts. "I have ways to make you talk."

I'm sure he does. In fact, I know he does when the rest of the covers are ripped right off the bed and tossed carelessly to the floor.

"It's cold," I complain, yet my body is already beginning to heat as Brody slowly begins to torture me, touching me everywhere, driving me to the peak of orgasm before withdrawing, not letting me reach that lovely crest my body so desperately needs.

"Okay," I gasp eventually. "I'll tell you. Just ... let me come, damn you."

He lifts his head from where he's now licking the crease of my thigh. "Tut tut, Barney. Ask nicely."

A laugh escapes me. "Please! I'll do anything you ask. Just stop calling me Barney!"

"Anything? Okay then." Brody latches onto my clit instantly, sucking with his mouth and swirling his tongue.

From somewhere in the room his phone rings. He ignores it completely.

Keeping his relentless rhythm, Brody doesn't stop until I see bright white spots behind my lids.

"Oh my *god*," I cry out on a long, keening moan.

His phone rings again as my legs flop uselessly on the bed. I am so done. "You should get that."

Brody draws back, his hands scraping down my thighs as he rests back on his heels. He's shirtless, an impressive erection straining the crotch of the jeans he's wearing. "It can wait."

"It sounds important."

His hands pause in the act of undoing his zipper. "It's a ringtone. How can it sound important?"

"Because whoever it is already rang twice." Whenever someone rings like that, it sets off a panicked flutter in my chest that something is wrong. "Just answer it," I urge.

With a roll of his eyes, Brody climbs off the bed. Lifting up on both elbows, I watch him stride over to my desk. He picks up the phone where it rests beside my laptop and checks the screen. His brow furrows. "It's my uncle. Professor Draper."

Being his uncle, the reason for the call could be anything, yet my stomach ties itself in knots. "Are you going to call him back?"

Brody rubs the back of his neck, and I know he's feeling the same tension I am. "Later. After the game."

"No." I shake my head. His next game is two days from now. "You should just do it now. Get it over with."

When he just stares unhappily at the screen, I scoot off the bed and quietly pad over. Coming up behind him, I rub his shoulders and he lets out a deep sigh.

"If it was anything urgent he would've left a message," he reasons.

Taking the decision out of Brody's hands, his uncle rings again.

"Answer it."

Brody grits his teeth, but he hits the little green button and puts it to his ear. "Hello?"

I can't hear the professor talking. Instead I turn my head to the side and rest it against his back. My hands move from his shoulders and down, sliding around his waist until I'm hugging him from behind. He settles into my hold as if he likes it, his free hand coming to rest on mine, his way of telling me to stay put.

"What about it?" Brody asks, his body going tight.

There's a pause where his uncle speaks again. As he listens, Brody's body locks tighter, his chest beginning to rise and fall in a heavy rhythm.

"Fuck," he bites out.

My eyes flutter closed. Whatever it is, it's not good. I knew it wouldn't be, and Brody's physical reaction confirms it.

"I can't. I have training all day. In case you might have missed it, we have an important game in two days."

Another pause.

"Fine," Brody grounds out. "I'll be there in a minute."

He hangs up the phone and tosses it back on the desk.

Sighing deeply, I draw away, letting my arms fall as I take a step back. He turns, his expression pained as he faces me. "I failed the course."

My indrawn breath is audible. "Brody."

Brody shrugs, but I can see the slight tremor in his lips. He's struggling to hold back the wave of frustration. *One step forward, two steps back.* He casts his gaze down, blinking hard as he chokes out the next words. "I passed the final, but the midterm and casework grades weren't enough. It's going to lower my GPA and I'll lose my eligibility to play football."

Taking hold of his arms, I tug them toward me, wrapping them around me. "So what do we do now?"

Brody huffs a bitter laugh and shakes his head, somehow holding it together. "Never say die. That's your motto, right?" His hands glide down, setting off shivers as he cups my bare ass. "You should have that tattooed right here." He squeezes firmly.

I moan. I can't help it. Even now, with this devastating bit of news, my body can't get enough of him.

Brody responds by dropping his head to my neck, planting kisses along the line of my throat. "I need you," he rasps, ignoring my question about where we go from here. "Right now."

He trips me backwards toward the bed and pushes me down. I fall back on it with relief. I would've expected Brody to push me away with anger, but instead he's pulling me closer, his need so palpable it makes me ache.

"Yes," I tell him. "Now."

He tears his zipper down. A bare second later Brody's lifting my legs. Curling me into a ball; my lower half rises up and he pushes his thick cock inside me. It's not sweet or intimate, but rough, and it feels good. He pumps hard and fast, driven by an animalistic need. All too soon, he's groaning my name, his hips slamming against my ass. I don't come, but I don't care. Brody took care of me earlier. This is his turn.

Brody lets go of my shins and my legs fall open. He drops down between them, his skin sticky as he lands on top of me. My hands run down the damp skin of his back, soothing and gentle as he sucks in air. "I'm sorry."

"No more apologies."

He shakes his head. Planting his palms flat on the bed above me, Brody pulls out with a regretful groan and steps back off the bed. "I have to go." Tugging up his pants, he yanks the zipper closed.

"You never answered me before. What do we do?"

"*I* have to do extra credit, make up the grade before he turns them in to the college."

It makes sense. Brody's lucky the professor is his uncle and willing to extend the offer. But we're in the middle of championships. There's no time to do what I know he has to. I sit up on the edge of the bed. "What can I do?"

After tugging his shirt down and into place, he leans over and smacks a loud kiss on my lips. "Baby." He draws back and looks at me, his hands on my knees. His cheeks are tinged pink, but the exhaustion in his eyes worries me. "I've got this. All I need is to hold you at night. Can I do that?"

I have to fight to keep the waver from my voice. "I'm all yours."

When he leaves, I make for the shower, my anger rising steadily. If Brody hadn't failed that midterm, he would've passed the course. All I can think right now is that this is on Kyle, and I need to put my plan into action. Tonight.

BRODY

After leaving Jordan's apartment, I head straight for my uncle's office, eager to get this meeting over with. After passing the final, I hadn't even considered failing the course. The news was a monumental blow, but right now I'm calm. It's at odds with the way my temper has been raging out of control of late. I need to track down Damien and ask him about the side effects of these pills. Something I didn't even think about before I started chewing them down like candy.

My knuckles rap sharply on his door.

"Come in," Patrick calls out.

After taking a deep breath, I turn the handle and step inside. My uncle looks up from his desk, pulling his glasses off and tossing them on top of a pile of papers. He stares at me for a long, hard moment. "You look like crap."

I'm sure I do. I haven't slept a single wink in over twenty-four hours. I don't feel tired though. It's like I've had a solid eight hours already. My body isn't giving me any signs that its sleep deprived, and that's a huge positive. I have training all day and we're down to the wire. Every minute has to count, but I know I've got it covered now thanks to Damien.

I smile lazily, taking a seat opposite my uncle. "Well I feel great."

His eyes narrow as they look me over. My body shifts uncomfortably beneath the scrutiny. "What the hell are you taking, Brody?"

Fuck. How does he know? My knuckles turn white as my grip tightens on the arms of the chair. I force a confused furrow to my brow. "What do you mean?"

Patrick pushes back his chair. Getting to his feet, my eyes follow as he stalks around the desk. Stopping in front of me, he leans down and gets right in my face. "You think I don't recognize the signs of drug abuse? You look exhausted, and yet you're wound up tighter than a spring. I've been through law school, Brody. I've seen it all, and everything I've seen?" He leans in further, eyes flaring hard and fierce. "It never ends well."

A huff of laughter escapes me and I roll my eyes. "Seriously. Drugs? I don't—"

My uncle pushes back, his voice a harsh command, veins straining his neck. "Shut the fuck up!"

I sit back in stunned silence as angry tension forms in the room. Patrick swipes a hand down his face, shaking his head. "What are you taking, Brody?"

My jaw tightens. "I'm not."

"Don't argue with me. You're my nephew. I know you better than your own damn father does. I know you're taking something. Whatever it is, you need to stop. Taking pills not medically prescribed for you is wrong." Disappointment radiates from him in waves. "It makes you a cheater, Brody. Is that how you want to get ahead? By cheating?"

My lips press together. Patrick is making a mountain out of a molehill. A couple of pills is *not* drug abuse, nor is it cheating. Not when I'm behind the eight ball to start with. All Adderall has ever done is offer me the fair chance that being dyslexic never did.

"Damn it all to hell, Brody!" he growls when I remain tightlipped. "You're a college athlete. A football star. Hundreds of thousands of fans think you walk on goddamn water. What would they think if they knew?"

"It was just a couple of pills," I tell him. But it wasn't just a couple. My hands shook when I opened the bottle this morning and found it almost empty. I don't even remember taking that many. "For study. That's all. No more."

My uncle returns to his seat, his sigh deep and heavy. He looks at me, and judging by his expression I know he wants to believe in me, to give me the benefit of the doubt that I simply don't deserve. "Promise me that's it."

I look him in the eye and I lie. I don't have a choice. I won't get through the next few days without taking more, not now with this extra case work to deal with. It lets me see everything in color, get shit done, and feel great while doing it. Right now it's my savior. My ace in the hole. My motherfucking touchdown.

I *need* it.

After a full day of training and watching play, I slide inside my SUV, my body bruised and aching. I toss my phone onto the passenger seat. It lands on the folder my uncle gave me this morning. Two case assignments. Both will take multiple hours each to research and complete. I know I'm lucky being given the chance to make up my grade, but bitterness fills me anyway. What comes easy for everyone else is ten times harder for me. I want it to be over, but I have one more semester to complete before I can graduate. And I *have* to graduate. My father prides himself on being a man who always follows through with his threats.

Jamming the keys in the ignition, I start the engine. Now that I'm physically sitting down, exhaustion overwhelms me. It's been thirty-six hours since I last slept. My body is crashing hard. I tip my head back and close my eyes, just for a minute.

A rap on my window rouses me with a jolt. Swiping a hand across my face, I use the other to depress the button. Cool air rushes in, doing its best to wake me and failing.

"Coach," I slur, my voice too weak to say more.

"Madden." His brow furrows as he ducks his head, looking in at me. "You okay, son?"

"Fine. Just tired."

"Good." Coach nods. He knows he's been pushing us beyond hard. For him our fatigue is a badge of honor. "You're on curfew. Get home."

My phone buzzes as I pull out of the parking lot. I ignore it. My calls and messages of late are all junk: sponsors wanting to talk brands, agents providing unsolicited advice on my future career in the NFL. It should get me excited, but I don't have time to appreciate the position I'm in right now, nor sit back and appreciate how far I've come. All I can do is focus on each day as it comes, and maybe, hopefully, I'll come out unscathed on the other side.

After packing a bag, I take one more pill before shoving the bottle inside it, hiding it beneath a pile of gym gear. Done, I head back to my car, tugging my phone out as I jog down the stairwell to let Jordan know I'm on my way.

A message from Jax sits on the screen. It lists the address of a frat house well-known for it's back-to-back to parties.

Jax: *Dude. You need to get here, pronto.*

I shake my head, not bothering to reply. Instead I turn my phone on silent. My cousin knows I'm on curfew. He also knows I'm back with Jordan, so why would I want to be partying the night before a big game?

Beeping the locks, I open the passenger door of my SUV and dump my bag. My phone vibrates with another message as I walk around the front to the driver's side.

Cursing under my breath, I check the screen, my brow furrowing. Jax again, sending a photo. Keys jangling in my hand, I pause by the door and flick it open. My eyes strain, making out the dark figures. The moment I realize what I'm seeing, my heart begins to pound a furious beat, slamming so hard against my ribcage it hurts.

I reach breakneck speed getting to the party, taking corners too fast, tires squealing. Leaving my car double-parked, I make my way inside, silently fuming. I move through partygoers, guys giving me backslaps left and right, hitting me with advice on how they think I can improve my game. I dodge them all as I search for my cousin.

When my eyes find Jax, he's leaving the kitchen for the backyard, Damien right behind him. I shout his name, pushing through people to reach him. He turns, relief lighting his face like neon when he sees me. It only ties my stomach in tighter knots.

"Where is she?" I ask when I get close, my voice harsh.

He shakes his head. "I don't know. They both disappeared."

They.

My stomach churns. The image of her and Kyle, heads bent close together, so *intimate*, is burned on my brain. The faint smile on her face is soft and tempting, and one that should be meant only for me.

JORDAN

After checking two previous parties, I find Kyle at the third one, drunk off his face.

Good. This is going to be a walk in the park.

Angling myself in his line of sight, I wait for him to notice me. He does. His eyes lift and scan the room, doing a double-take and coming back to me. He looks around, seeking out Brody. When he doesn't see him, his eyes shift back to me with purpose, and he makes his way toward me. I knew he would. Any opportunity to get me onside and piss off Brody is one he's going to take.

"Jordan," he says, reaching my side. I force a smile to my lips. "You're off leash tonight I see."

Har, har, you tool.

Knowing I need to keep this believable, I roll my eyes. It would rouse suspicion if I suddenly began fawning over whatever it is he thinks makes him so much better than everyone else.

"Drink?"

I shrug. "Sure, okay."

Kyle tips his head toward the kitchen. "Follow me."

After handing me a cup of beer, he grins, swaying slightly. "So where's Brody tonight? Is he sitting at home waiting for you, or did you finally see the light and ditch the dumb fuck?"

Oh, I am going to nail your goddamn ass to the wall.

"We're on a break."

Kyle's brows rise as he leans back against the counter behind him, using it to prop him upright. "Well, I sure am sorry to hear that," he replies, his expression telling me he's anything but.

I cast my eyes down because I can't stand looking at him. Not that he notices. With Kyle drunk, it's easy to engage him in meaningless conversation, slowly drawing it around to the teacher aide work he does with Professor Draper. A subtle ego stroke never hurts. "The professor's a busy man. You must do a lot of hard work for him."

"I do." Kyle cocks his head. "Hey, I have to use the bathroom." His eyes scan the room slowly. "It's a bit wild in here tonight. Come with me?" He winks. "I'll keep you safe."

In hindsight, it's the exact moment the player became the played, but my mind doesn't register anything except what I came to do. All I want is to catch Kyle in his web of deceit and fix the grade he sabotaged. "Okay. Thanks."

Setting my empty cup on the bench, I follow him up the stairs. Knowing I might not get another chance, I use it to hit the record button on my phone before tucking it back in the pocket of my skirt. The bathrooms have queues, so I think nothing of it when I'm led to the third floor. He opens the door and I step inside, halting when I realize it's a study and not a bathroom.

I spin around as Kyle shuts the door behind us. His smile is slow and lazy. It sets my heart thumping with rapid beats of apprehension. "What are you playing at, Jordan?"

God I must suck at this. *Show no fear,* I command myself.

"Playing at?" I cock a brow coolly, folding my arms. "What are *you* playing at, Kyle?"

"It's not *what* I'm playing at, but who. And it's Brody, babe. Who else?"

Annoyance rips through me and I shake my head. "Why?"

Kyle takes a step toward me, eyes glinting. I stand my ground, forcing myself not to take a step back. "Did you know Brody and I go way back? We went to primary school together. We even ended up in the same peewee league. And even then he was always so damn entitled. In that big fancy house with his mom and dad, his nice clothes, always wearing the best of everything. Nothing secondhand for him, only high-end brand-named football equipment would ever do." He takes another step. "As if that wasn't enough, his coach, and all his teachers, gave him a free ride through school while I had to work my ass off. Bumping up grades faster then a fat kid eats candy. No doubt getting paid off. You know what that made me?"

Kyle is right in my face now, a smile on his lips. Hate and bitterness ooze from it like black tar, raising the hair on the back of my neck.

I glare, my voice a scathing attack. "A resentful, jealous little dick?"

He chuckles. "Pretty much, but who cares?" Kyle's expression is modest when he shrugs. "I'm just the guy making sure Brody gets what he deserves, or in this case, doesn't deserve."

"And he didn't deserve to pass the midterm?"

"Are you fucking kidding me? What a coup, earning that teacher's aide position for the same course Brody's taking. I couldn't let an opportunity slip by to fuck with his grade."

My heart pounds so hard I fear I can hear it. "You fudged his answers?"

He shrugs. "Honestly? I would have. Sadly, I didn't need to do a single thing. Brody failed all by himself."

"I don't believe you."

Kyle laughs. "Come on, Jordan. I wouldn't lie to you." He leans down, putting his face right near mine. "I like you."

"Well I don't like you."

This whole idea of mine is a complete bust. My bicep is grabbed when I brush past.

"Where do you think you're going?" His fingers dig into the soft flesh of my upper arm and I cry out, trying to yank free. Kyle twists the arm around behind my back. White spots dance behind my eyelids, the pain so excruciating my voice fails. I'm spun around, my feet tripping over each other as he shoves me face first into the couch.

"I think hanging around dumb assholes has rubbed off on you." He grabs my other arm, clamping them both together behind my back, leaving me incapacitated. His hands begin roving over my skirt. Patting at my pockets, he reaches inside and grabs my phone. He checks the screen, hitting the stop button before tossing it away. It hits the floor and skates across the sleek timber, out of reach. "I'm a bit smarter than the average guy, in case you haven't noticed. And yes, I did fuck with his grade." He smirks. "What are you going to do about it?"

"Fuck you!" I shriek, panting and trying to kick out with my legs.

Kyle grunts when I catch his shin, but the effect is that of a pesky mosquito and does nothing. His hand slides up my leg and underneath my skirt, grabbing at my panties. "Get off me you sick fuck!"

BRODY

Damien shrugs at me. "Maybe they went upstairs."

His offhand comment has my hands curling into fists.

Jax elbows him sharp in his side. "Ow!"

"You're an asshole," my cousin adds.

"What? Why?" Damien shrugs again and downs the remains of his beer. Tossing the empty cup in the direction of a big open bin nearby, he smirks. "Maybe they did."

Jax and I share a mutual glance. Judging by his unhappy expression, he suspects Damien could be right. Not saying a word, I turn and make for the stairs at the back of the house, taking them two at a time. They're both behind me when I reach the second level, stalking down hallways and shoving open doors. I'm panicked by the time I reach the third and top level of the house without finding either of them. I'm reaching for the handle of the second door when I hear a loud sob and Jordan shout, "Get off me you sick fuck!"

Heart in my throat, I shove the door open. Kyle has Jordan pinned against a couch, her skirt pushed up around her hips and a hand in her panties. Her face is mashed sideways into the cushion, but she's squirming hard and manages to get an arm loose and elbow him in the gut.

"You bitch!" he snarls and rounds a hard open palm to the side of her face, the sound a loud crack in the small room.

Burning rage blinds me. Its onset is so swift and hard it overtakes my body completely. I barely register what I'm doing when I pick Kyle up and throw him across the room. The sound of his body slamming into the wall fuels my anger. He hits the ground with a grunt and rolls on to his hands and knees.

Reaching Kyle's side, I kick him hard in the gut. He cries out and drops instantly, rolling to his back and gasping for air. It's not enough. I want to fucking *kill him* for putting his hands on Jordan. Without another thought, I'm on him. Straddling his body, I smash a fist in his face, my knuckles burning from the impact. It's a good burn. I want more of it. I want motherfucking *blood.*

We lock in a furious struggle and my elbow cracks him in the eye. He falls back with a howl, disoriented and weakened. Not giving him anytime to recover, my fist smashes him in the face again. The bones in his nose crunch beneath the impact and blood spurts hot and wet, oozing down his face in a river of red and covering both of us.

Jordan says something, but I can't hear it over Kyle's loud groans. He locks his legs around me and twists, shoving me sideways onto the floor. My head hits the timber boards. It leaves me dizzy for a moment, and I miss seeing the roundhouse punch Kyle aims. It lands on my jaw and my gut twists with pain. *Motherfucker.*

"Brody!" Jordan cries out.

But I don't hear anything. All I see is that snake in the grass with his hands on my girl. My eyes fly open, landing on Kyle. "I'm gonna fuckin' kill you," I slur.

I roll and take him back down. My fists pummel hard, hitting anywhere and everywhere I can reach. I'm in a zone of bloodlust and there's no breaking free of it. Loud shouts come from behind me. I don't know how many hands grab hold, dragging me off Kyle's prone form.

"You sonofabitch!" I yell, my voice hoarse and chest heaving with rage as they hold me back. "Why? What did I ever do to you?"

Kyle groans, struggling to move. No one offers to help him.

Suddenly Jordan is right there and whoever has hold of me lets go. My jaw locks and my eyes burn as I take her in. Her makeup is smeared and her hair's tangled. Her right cheekbone is bruised and beginning to swell, and the beautiful light in her eyes is just ... gone.

"Jordan," I croak, my heart cracking into a thousand pieces. I don't know what to do, how to fix what Kyle did, and put everything back the way it was. The arms I wrap around her feel weak and useless. She buries her face in my neck, hot tears plopping thick and fast on my skin. "Are you okay?"

Unable to speak, Jordan simply nods as I stroke a trembling hand over the back of her head.

"Did he touch you?"

"He ... He ..." Jordan licks her lips and swallows, her fingers clutching at my shirt like she's drowning. "He grabbed my panties. All he managed was to rip them aside and then you were there."

My arms on her tighten. A minute later and god knows what could've happened. "I told you to stay away from that asshole, Jordan. Why were you with him?"

"I'm sorry," she whispers. "It's all my fault. But he messed with your grade, Brody."

"He what?"

She draws back and looks me in the eye. "The midterm. I knew it. All I needed was for him to admit it. I tried to record it on my phone. God, I thought it was a great plan but he knew. Somehow he knew."

A sick feeling lodges in my gut. My eyes fall to where Kyle's trying to pick himself up off the floor. His hand slips in blood as he rolls onto his hands and knees.

BRODY

"Get her out of here, Madden," Jax says.

I look from him back to Kyle. His face is a mess. I did that. Satisfaction and shock both hit me at once. I've punched a few guys in my life, but nothing so violent as this, and never over anything more than a bit of bullshit. This is a full-blown assault. Kyle didn't stand a chance. I've always been bigger than him. Faster. Stronger. But he deserved it and then some. Jesus fucking Christ, who cares about the grade, his hands were *touching* her.

I want to rip into him all over again, but Jordan has hold of my shirt, her teeth beginning to chatter. She needs somewhere safe and familiar. Jax is right. I need to get her home.

"We'll take care of this," he adds.

We share a quick glance, my gratitude deeper than the damn ocean. I nod and croak, "Thanks, bud."

We leave out the back way and walk around the house where my car is still double-parked out front. The drive back to Jordan's apartment is quiet. My right hand rests on her thigh, reassuring her I'm right here. Jordan does nothing more than glance at it before returning her gaze out the window. She's a zombie right now, and I don't know what to say or do to bring her back to life. My heart aches. My knuckles ache. Every part of me motherfucking aches.

"I'm okay," she says into the unforgiving silence. Her eyes are still trained on the dark scenery passing us by, so she must be feeling my constant, worried glances.

"No. You're not."

Jordan lets out a low, shaky breath. "I am."

"It's not your fault, baby."

She presses her lips together.

"I don't care about what he did. I'll make up the grade. Kyle Davis has always been a thorn in my side. I'm used to it."

"You shouldn't have to be used to it!"

I shift my hold on her thigh and take her hand in mine. It's cold. I give it a squeeze. "I've never had anyone fight in my corner the way you do." I bring her hand to my lips, giving it a kiss. She looks across at me. "Granted, I do *not* like the way you went about it, but thank you all the same."

A tear spills over and tracks down her cheek. She wipes it away with her free hand. "I'll always fight in your corner, Brody."

When we get inside her apartment, Hayden and Leah are snuggled on the couch. An action movie is playing out on the television and they're bickering over a bowl of popcorn. Both their heads turn in our direction.

Leah frowns, her eyes narrowing slightly. "Where've you be—"

Jordan pastes an overly bright smile on her face and cuts her off, pulling free of my hold. "Just going to have a quick shower."

Leah's gaze cuts to me, her eyes narrowing further as Jordan makes straight for the bathroom. I shake my head, silently telling her to let it go.

When I follow behind Jordan, she shuts the door in my face, calling out, "I won't be a minute."

Shit.

I rap on the door. "Jordan."

"I won't be a minute," she says, her voice a little harder, and I hear the lock click in place.

I turn around. Leah and Hayden are both watching me. Leah grabs for the remote off the coffee table and hits pause on the movie. Setting it back down, she hands over the bowl of popcorn to Hayden. He grabs it with a monkey grip, his expression gleeful. With his giant paw of a hand, he shoves in a huge mouthful while Leah gives me her full attention. "What the hell, Madden?"

"Babe," Hayden mutters, popcorn falling out of his mouth and littering his shirt. He picks up the fallen pieces and shoves them back in as he speaks. "Don't get involved in their domestic. It's none of our business."

"Jordan isn't feeling well," I tell them.

Leah's expression turns a little alarmed at the mention of illness. "What happened?"

Hayden gives me a sympathetic shrug. "Dude." He holds the bowl out toward me. "Popcorn?"

"No," I tell him, not moving from the door. "Thanks."

Hayden kicks his feet up on the coffee table, shoveling in another mouthful for himself. "So. Big game in a few days, huh?"

Big game is an understatement. It's the National Championship game against Kansas State. Win this and it will be the first time CPU has ever won a conference title in two straight years. It's the biggest game of my life, and I can't even think about it right now. "Yeah."

"At least it's not far to go."

The game is being played in Waco, Texas. It's a short bus ride, but we arrive days earlier. Our team has media to deal with, press conferences, a fan meet-and-greet, breakfast functions and dinner functions, and god knows what else. "No, not far. What about—"

I'm cut off by the sound of a loud sob penetrating through the door. I don't even knock. Grabbing the handle, I shove hard, putting my shoulder into it. The flimsy lock buckles, letting me through.

What greets me makes my throat close up. Jordan is sitting naked in the bottom of the shower. She's closed up in a tight, vulnerable ball, her face pale and all the fight in her gone. The shock from Kyle's attack is wearing off.

I get inside the shower. My shirt and jeans stick to my skin as I reach down and pick her up. She can't curl any tighter as I clutch her against my chest and step out from under the water.

"Brody," she sobs, trying to speak.

I brush my lips over the top of her head. "Shhh."

Half-resting her on the basin, I loosen my hold and reach for a towel. Sliding it off the rack, I use it to cover her shivering form. "Let's just get you warm and dry."

I carry Jordan to her room. When I set her on the edge of the bed and go to draw back, she clings to me like a koala. "Don't leave."

I fix my eyes on hers. "I'm not leaving you. I promise. I'm just getting out of these wet things. Okay?"

Jordan presses her lips together and nods. She lets me go, and I draw back and tug my tee shirt over my head. It drops with a wet *plop* on the floor.

It's not until Jordan starts rummaging inside my bag for dry clothes that I remember the pills. It doesn't take her long to find the bottle, holding it up to read the label. It's too late for me to snatch them from her.

"Brody," she whispers.

With her back to me, she sinks to her knees and unscrews the cap. Two solitary pills rattle around inside it. *Two.* That's all I have left, and I barely remember taking them at all.

I swallow the guilt. "They're not mine."

Jordan shakes her head. "Please don't lie to me."

"They're not, I swear."

"Fuck you, Brody."

Her harsh curse shocks me. "Excuse me?"

"You heard me." Getting to her feet, Jordan caps the lid and turns to face me, her eyes furious. "Fuck you!"

"Jordan—"

"Shut up!" she screams and throws the bottle at my chest. It bounces off and hits the floor. "Did you take all those pills? Is this why you did so well on your final? Why you're suddenly getting amazing grades and killing it out on the field? You know what I thought?"

She's looking at me the same way my father does, with anger and a whole boatload of disappointment. Fuck it hurts. I lift my chin and fold my arms, bracing for the worst of it. "What did you think, Jordan?"

"I thought your hard work was paying off! That I was helping! But it wasn't either, was it?" Jordan shouts. Bending down, she snatches clothing at random, shoving it all inside my bag. Doing up the zipper, she straightens and smacks it hard against my chest. "Get out."

Frustration flares as I grapple with my bag before it drops to the floor. "You have no idea what it's like for me."

"I have a goddamn clue!"

"You know what? Screw it." I start for the door, too pissed off to care that I'm still wet and only half dressed. I scoop up the pill bottle on my way out and wave it her mockingly. Her eyes narrow.

Jamming it inside my bag, I seize the door handle and turn, meeting Jordan's fiery gaze. "You're so fucking perfect, sweetheart," I sneer. "No one can live up to your impossible expectations, least of all me. I'm tired of trying. I'm just so fucking tired of it all."

Jordan's intake of breath is sharp. Her face screws up and fat tears begin to fall one after the other down her cheeks. I pause in my tracks, a lump filling my throat.

"Go!" she chokes out.

"Jordan—"

"Get out!" she shrieks, choking on a sob. Covering her mouth with her hand, she gives me her back. "God, I'm so stupid. How could I not see?"

I let go of the door handle, my arm falling limply by my side. "I can't leave like this."

"You can. The door's right there." Jordan turns and waves a hand at it. "Use it."

"No." I drop my bag on the floor and take a step toward her. "You know I told you I'd ruin us."

Jordan stares at me stonily, her eyes red. "You did."

"And you promised you wouldn't let me," I say quietly.

"Because it hasn't ruined us," she spits out, dashing away her tears with the backs of her hands. "It's ruined *you*."

I shrug helplessly. "You're right. It has. And you're better off without someone like me, but the truth is, I'm better off with someone like you, and I can't give you up." I take another step, reaching up to brush the backs of my fingers gently against her swollen cheekbone. She flinches, jerking her head out of reach. My arm drops, hurt burning a giant hole in my chest. "I love you, Jordan."

Jordan stills, my declaration hanging in the air between us as she stares wordlessly. I take her face in my hands, my fingers trembling against the damp pink of her cheeks. I'm laying myself bare for this girl, and my timing sucks, but it's too big for me to hold in any longer. "I love you. You're my home, and I'm yours." My eyes burn at the thought of losing her. "Don't ask me to leave. Please."

"I love you too," she whispers through tears, and damn it feels good to hear it, to know I'm not alone in this. "But you need to go."

The words chill me to the bone. "Why? Because I took a few pills?"

"Because you're a liar and a drug cheat, Brody." Despair washes over her face. "Because together we're a volatile mess. And because you're wrong. My expectations aren't too high. All I ever wanted was for you to be the best you could be, and for a moment I thought you were truly starting to believe in yourself enough to do that. But it was all a lie. You don't believe in anything except a little bottle of pills." Jordan steps around me and walks to the door. I turn as she takes hold of the handle and opens it wide, her jaw trembling with an effort to hold herself together. "Please go."

My heart splinters into a thousand tiny jagged pieces. It's the worst pain I've ever felt in my life. "I can't."

"Please," she whispers.

I take a ragged breath and walk to the door. My whole body is vibrating with the need to grab hold of her and not let go. It takes everything I have not to do it. Bending down, I pick my bag up off the floor. I sling it over my shoulder and straighten. All the while Jordan doesn't look at me, as if the sight of me makes her sick.

Reaching the doorway, I pause, staring straight ahead into the darkened living area. "I'm so sorry."

"Me too."

With morning comes a new kind of hell. My phone rings early, waking me from a shitty sleep. Last night's events hit me in a rush, and it's all I can do to take a breath. Realizing it could be Jordan, I snatch the phone from my bedside table and read the screen. My father. God, he has the worst timing in the history of the world. I toss the phone somewhere on my sheets, letting it ring out.

With a groan I fall back on my pillow and cover my eyes with my forearm. I'm losing Jordan and I can't handle it. I have to stop taking the pills. All I need is to just keep those last two saved for finishing the case studies, and I'll be as good as gold. No more after that. Then I'll talk to her and everything will be fine. I can fix this. I have to.

My phone rings again. I snatch it up again, hitting answer this time. "Goddammit, Dad!"

"This is how you answer your phone?"

He sounds as pissed off as I do, and I don't care. "Nope. That's a greeting I reserve special just for you."

My father makes a strangled sound of anger. "I want you home. Now."

"Dad, what the hell?" I pull the phone from my ear to check the time. Six fucking a.m. "It's early and I have training."

"Not anymore you don't."

"What?" I sit up in bed. Coach will be furious if I'm late to practice. "You can't—"

"We both know very well I can. Home," he enunciates loudly. "Now."

When I get dial tone, I turn and smash my fist into the pillow with a frustrated growl. There's nothing I can do when he says jump, except ask how high. I drag myself from bed. After throwing on my training gear, I stick my head in Jaxon's room. It's empty. His bed is unmade, but not necessarily slept in. Not unusual, but after leaving him to deal with Davis last night, it leaves me edgy not to find him home.

Arriving at my parents' house, I pull in the drive. Even at this early hour old man Lewis is out working in his yard. I slam the car door, not bothering to give him my regular casual salute. I just can't be bothered.

Reaching the porch steps, I notice the door slightly ajar and raised voices. My brow furrows when I hear both my father and uncle caught in a loud argument. I move to the door and pause.

"Brody will be here any minute. I'm sure he has a brilliant explanation," my father says, his sarcasm crystal clear. "Assault charges, for fuck's sake. There's no way Jaxon did this. It has Brody written all over it."

"Are you kidding me? This has *you* written all over it." That comes from my uncle and he sounds pissed. "You've done that boy no favors with your violent temper and your contempt."

"I gave him a roof over his head and food in his mouth!"

"You gave him nothing!" Patrick roars and I flinch. "Brody is troubled and I've waited far too long to step in. I should've done it a hell of a lot sooner. He's failing classes, taking drugs, and getting into fights! *You* raised him to be this way."

"Drugs? Oh hell no—"

"Enough!" Their shouts are bouncing off the walls, and I can't take it anymore. I push open the door and step inside, finding them both facing off in the hallway. "What's going on?"

My father flares his nostrils as he looks at me, hands on his hips. "What's going on is that I've just spent the past two hours cleaning up your mess. Kyle Davis laid assault charges against you last night after you beat the hell out of the kid. Jaxon took the fall for you."

"Jax was arrested?" My blood boils. *Fucking Davis.*

"He spent the night in lockup, but we got the matter cleared up," Patrick says. "Jaxon's on his way home. Speaking of..." he glances at his watch "...I need to get home as well." Giving my shoulder a firm squeeze, my uncle looks at me. "Brody I don't know what Kyle did, but I can't believe all this was over nothing. My door's always open for you if you want to talk."

He leaves and when the door clicks shut behind him I turn to my father. "How?" I ask. "How did you clear it up?"

"We had to pay people off." His voice rises. "Including Kyle Davis, who blamed the whole incident on you." He bridges the distance between us, getting in my face. "And he wasn't cheap, so you owe me for this."

My eyes narrow. "I *owe* you? I would've taken the charges. I didn't ask you to fix it. You fixed it for yourself and your goddamn political career so don't even try pretending otherwise."

Dad jabs a finger at me. "You watch your mouth. My *political career* pays for the clothes on your back."

Tugging my tee shirt over my head, I shove it against his chest. "Here." He grabs it, his expression pissed. "Have it back. You can have them all back. That's how much I care about what you do for me."

I start for the door.

"Where do you think you're going?"

"Training," I say without looking back.

"Like hell you are," Dad growls.

My bicep is grabbed and I come to a grinding halt. I half turn, the fury emanating from my father palpable. "You can't just—"

His palm cracks hard across my face, cutting off my comment. My head snaps sideways and pain blooms across my cheekbone. "Don't you dare leave when I haven't finished speaking to you."

"So finish," I say to my dad as I shove him backward, hiding the pain from his slap. Violence is the only form of communication we've ever had. Why change things now?

CHAPTER 26

BRODY

When I get home Jax is spread out on the sofa wearing last night's clothes. He looks a little rough around the edges, though I'm sure I look worse.

"What the hell happened to you?"

"My father," I say, my voice flat.

Jax pulls himself to a sitting position, his jaw ticking. I get in first before he can ask questions. "How was the chain gang?"

"Oh, it was the best." He shifts sideways and stares hard at my face. "I almost became Big John's bitch, *and* I made friends with the local roaches. The mattress smelled like a rotting corpse and the tap water tasted like piss. And because of your father, I have no criminal record to show for any of it."

"Ripped off," I joke and chuckle, which causes my ribs to throb like a bass drum. With a groan, I sink to the sofa and meet Jaxon's eyes. "You know, when you said you'd take care of everything, I didn't mean for you to throw yourself down and sacrifice your butt virginity to Big John."

Jax huffs a short laugh and shakes his head. "Well after all that he didn't ask me out, so I guess I'm feeling a little let down." He looks at me with an expression of mock hope. "Maybe he'll call later."

"I'm sorry."

"That he didn't call?"

"Yeah. Maybe he has a brother."

"Little John?"

I laugh and it sends a stabbing pain down my left side. I suck in a sharp breath. My father had followed up his slap to my face with a sharp jab to my ribs after I'd shoved him away.

"Hell." Jaxon reaches across and yanks my arm away, revealing my swollen torso. All the previous amusement slides from his face. "Bud, that looks painful. You need a hospital?"

"No hospital."

"You should go anyway," he argues, already up and heading for my room. I follow behind. He opens my dresser drawer, pulling out a tee shirt and sweatpants. "We can go in the back entrance. No one will even know you're there." Jax dumps the clothes on my bed and reaches for my arm. "At the least they can give you some strong drugs for the pain."

Drugs for the pain. Why didn't I think of that? I tug the clothes on, slow as an old man.

"Shit, Brody. You can't play like this. Can you play like this?"

"Sure I can. It happens all the time. Tony Romo played through a broken rib and punctured lung."

"Jesus you guys are fucking crazy. You want me to call Jordan?"

My stomach clenches into a tight, hot ball of misery. "No."

His brows rise. "No?"

"She's gone, Jax."

"Gone?"

Giving him my back, I pick up my phone. It's been on silent and a pile of missed calls and messages from my coach glare back at me from the screen. I'm not sure what excuse to give him for missing training today, but whatever it is, I know it has to be damn good. Tucking it in my pocket, I swallow the huge lump in my throat and answer Jax. "Yeah. You know, the soccer finals in Florida. She'll be gone a week."

"Oh right. For a minute I thought you guys were off again."

I don't answer because I can't. I don't know what the hell we are right now. I keep fucking it up, and I don't know how to stop.

"You want to tell me what your father was pissed about this time?" Jaxon asks when we're in the car and speeding toward the hospital.

"Me breathing," I mutter under my breath.

"Davis, right?" Jax shakes his head, white-knuckling the steering wheel. "That dick needs to drop off the face of the earth."

The next day in training my rib is strapped tight as a damn corset, and I'm flying high on Percocet. Two pills instead of one takes me to cloud nine. It's nothing like Adderall. The pain meds dull my senses, but man is it beautiful coasting up there in the sky. Nothing hurts. Nothing matters. Even my battered heart stops bleeding. It's just me, the ball, and an endless field of green. Beautiful.

I don't even have to come up with an excuse for my absence yesterday. Coach Carson spoke to my dad, who told him I was involved in a minor car accident. Coach had the hospital records faxed to the team doctor, who checked me over himself. His face was all skepticism, but he kept silent. They want these championships as much as the team does. On the day of our game, I'm injected with a high dose painkiller and sent out on the field with a slap on the back. I play high as a kite. I play rough. I play like a man with nothing left to lose.

We win but for the first time ever I can't summon any joy. The slaps on the back, the celebratory hugs, and the wide grins are all forced. I limp off the field a broken man. It's the highest point of my football career, and the lowest I've ever felt. It scares me when I start questioning why I'm doing this at all. But what would I do without it?

Later that night we celebrate at the bar. It's loud and rowdy, and girls cover every single surface. Their makeup is bright, their dresses short and body-hugging. They keep grabbing my hands and trying to shove them up their skirts. I used to think it was hot to be wanted this way, but now it just makes me sad. I don't want anything to do with any of them. I just want to drink. I want oblivion for a while.

I'm four beers in when Jordan rings. I get up quickly, pushing through people to get outside. The air is ice cold, and my breath puffs out in white clouds when I answer. "Jordan?"

"Brody."

All it takes is her speaking my name and a rush of calm washes over me. A smile forms on my face. Hugging my body, I lean up against the outside wall of the building, keeping my head down low to avoid unwanted attention. "Hey you."

When she replies, her voice is soft and low and brings goose bumps to my skin. "Hey yourself. I just …" She pauses for a moment and then exhales a shaky breath. She's nervous, like she doesn't know what to say. "Congratulations on your win today."

My smile widens. "You watched the game."

"How could I not watch it?"

"It wasn't my best play," I admit.

"Your average play is better than everyone else, but you played like you were injured."

Avoiding the question, I check my watch. "What are you doing up so late?"

"I can't sleep."

"No? Why not?"

Jordan pauses for a long moment, almost to the point I think she's either fallen asleep or hung up and I'm too out of it to realize. "Because you're not here."

I hug myself tighter. "Jordan—"

"I'm so sorry."

My brow furrows. "For what?"

Jordan laughs and the sound is high and nervous. "I had this whole thing in my head of what I wanted to say to you, and I can't remember any of it."

A drunken group of three approaches me, roaring our team song. I wave them away and turn, giving them my back. "So just say anything."

"I'm scared."

I press the phone harder to my ear, needing to hear her better over the loud noise of the bar that's filtering outside to the front entrance. "Why?"

"You're messed up, Brody, and I don't know how to help you. You saw what happened. I found those pills and I freaked out. I love you, and instead of helping you, I made you leave."

Turning, I press my forehead against the rough brick and close my eyes, my stomach a queasy lump. "Because I lied to you."

"You did."

There's a long pause and I don't know how to fill it.

"Are you still taking that stuff? Are you taking anything else?"

"No! I—" Jesus, I have a hospital prescription for Percocet and my team doctor prescription for the same thing. I'm swimming in pills right now. But it's not the same thing. I need these. My face hurts like a bitch, my rib is throbbing, and my body took a huge battering at the game. I put a hand inside the pocket of my letterman jacket. My fingers curve around the bottle, holding tight, and my voice is a rasp when I speak. "I'm not taking anything."

"I don't know if I should believe you."

"I deserve that."

"Brody ... why?"

My throat closes up. I stare down at my feet. "Because I'm not good enough without it, and please don't try and tell me I am. It's a fact, Jordan. It got the job done when I needed it to..." my tone hardens a little "...and I'm not going to apologize for that."

"I'm not asking you to," she snaps in response.

My voice rises. "Then why are you calling me? If you want to let me go, then just fucking do it. Don't string me along with your pity calls." It hurts too damn much when I'm already hurting enough.

"I don't want to let you go, but we're no good together!"

"Goddammit!" Turning, I ram my fist into the brick wall of the bar. Jordan's cries reach me through the roaring pain that ricochets up from my knuckles. "Don't cry. Baby ... please." Reaching in my pocket, I thumb open the cap of the bottle and palm a pill, swallowing it dry without a second thought. "We can be good together. We've just never had a chance."

"Will we ever have it?"

"We have to. I love you, Jordan. I'm not letting you out of my life. Not ever."

After a shaky breath, she says, "I should go."

"It's the pressure," I blurt out, desperate to keep her on the line, just for a minute longer. "It's really bad right now, but it won't always be there."

"What are you saying? We should put our relationship on ice for a while?"

"No ice, Jordan. Just ... one day at time." Which is more than I have any right to ask, but I'm asking anyway because what have I got left to lose? I can deal with anything if I know I have Jordan at the end of each day. "Let's just do that."

"Okay," she agrees quietly and my shoulders slump with relief. "One day at a time."

CHAPTER 27

BRODY

A week later I'm watching Jordan's team bus pull to the curb, returning them to campus from the airport. I'm anxious. I know I am. But the Percocet keeps it buried well below the dark, murky surface where it can't touch me. With hands jammed in my pockets, I watch as she bounds down the steps behind her teammates, her cheeks flushed pink with elation because they won their semifinal, moved up to the championship final, and then won that too.

A beanie covers her head and silky waves ripple over her shoulders and down her back. Her face is turned and she's laughing at something Paige is yelling from behind her.

When she turns back, her eyes catch mine and she sobers instantly, pausing on the bottom step. I didn't tell her I'd be here. I wasn't sure I would be. But it felt right and I didn't want to wait, so here I am.

Her clear blue eyes run over me like she hasn't seen me in years. It gives me hope. Tense shoulders ease beneath me, and I breathe out in a rush, my lips curving slowly. "I hope it's okay that I'm here."

Paige gives Jordan's back a nudge and she steps off, walking toward me. When she reaches my side, she lifts a hand, her eyes on my bruised face.

"You're hurt."

Gentle fingers trail down the side of my face. All her teammates pour out of the bus, swarming the pavement, excitedly hugging family and friends, but I don't see them. It's just the two of us.

"It's nothing." I take her hand and move it away from my face, linking our fingers. "Just the price of the game."

"It looks sore."

"It's fine. I can barely feel it."

Jordan starts pulling away, her gaze caught on the driver removing luggage from under the bus. "I should get my bag."

"I'll get it." I know which bag is hers and find it quickly. Picking it up off the ground, I sling it over my shoulder and turn, nodding toward my car parked by the curb. "Can I take you home?"

Affection warms her eyes. I'm trying this 'one day at a time' thing, and I know she sees and appreciates it. "That would be nice."

We start for my car, walking side by side. Her hand slips in mine, fitting perfectly. My fingers close around it, and my heart expands when she squeezes gently, silently telling me we might just be okay.

I bring her hand to my lips, kissing the back of it as we walk. "Congratulations on the Championships. I knew you'd do it."

Jordan grins. "It still hasn't sunk in."

"Well, I know just how to celebrate," I tell her with a wink, letting go of her hand to tug the keys from my pocket. I beep the locks.

"Oh?" Jordan arches a brow at the innuendo in my tone. "And that is?"

I open the rear passenger door and toss her bag on the seat. Slamming it closed, I turn and grin. "With champagne of course. Why? Were you thinking of something a little more ... intimate?"

Jordan grabs the handle and jerks open the passenger door, but not fast enough for me to miss the flash of disappointment in her eyes. "Of course not," she mumbles, sliding inside the car.

I chuckle to myself as walk around to the driver's side.

I wake early to filtered sunlight and my body spooning Jordan in a warm cocoon. Pushing up on an elbow, I rub my face. We're still wearing our clothes from yesterday, but sometime during the night Jordan grabbed the blanket from the end of the bed and pulled it up over both of us.

Shifting hair away from her neck, I lean close and press my lips to the bared skin. It's impossible not to. Jordan gives a sleepy moan and my cock twitches. When I'm with her I only ever feel good. I want more of it. My lips trail down, nibbling, until I reach the point where her neck meets her shoulder.

She rolls over, blinking lazily, a smile curving her lips. Last night we drank champagne, ate vegemite toast, and talked about nothing in particular. It ended with us lying in bed watching a *Game of Thrones* marathon on her laptop. Blood. Violence. Nudity. It was awesome. I'd never seen the show before, but I was now a convert. Kicking back in bed together and watching Jon Snow fight the good fight against the White Walkers felt so normal. I loved Jordan giving me that because my life felt so far beyond normal right now.

"If this is one day at a time, I like it," she says with a voice husky from sleep.

"Me too."

Jordan's eyes roam over my face. "I like waking to your pretty face too."

I roll my eyes with disgust. Her response is to giggle, and my heart soars at the lightness in the sound. "I think the correct term is manly and sexy."

"Uh huh." She shakes her head, serious. "Pretty."

Not taking kindly to the term, I launch myself at Jordan. She responds with a shriek, her knee coming up instinctively to block me. It gets me in the ribs. I fall back with a hard grunt and a muttered "fuck."

Her face looms over me, mussed tendrils of long hair spilling on my neck and chest, tickling my skin. "I'm sorry."

"I'm not." I tug at her arm and she collapses on top of me. I hide the wince of pain and stretch up, capturing her lips with mine, holding them for a long, hot moment. She draws back and I see her eyes are filling rapidly. "Hey. What's wrong?"

"You, Brody. That Skype call you had with my brother. You were arranging for him to be there for my finals in Florida."

"All I did was Skype him to tell him the dates and chip in with the flights. Nicky arranged the rest. It was nothing."

I know the ache from having no family at your games. At least with Jordan the only barrier was distance and that's something easily fixed. Her brother and I are Facebook friends now. I saw Nicky's posts from his visit and having him there meant the world. I could see it in Jordan's smile from the photos.

"You gave me a week with my brother. That's not nothing." Jordan pushes up off me, sitting up on the bed. "I wanted to ring you a million times to thank you."

"Oh?" My brows wing up. "That's funny because I didn't see a million missed calls on my phone."

"I know. I'm sorry. I just thought it would be easier to wait until I got home." Jordan cups my cheek and leans close, pressing a soft kiss to my lips. Drawing back, she looks at me. "Thank you. So much." Her eyes shift to the clock on the bedside table. "Don't you have training? You have a bowl game to prepare for."

I kiss her again. "It can wait."

"Tell that to your coach."

Jordan's right, but I don't want her to be—especially when she climbs off me and stands. The sports shorts she's wearing are a shade of orange so bright I feel blinded. I still look anyway, because the mile of leg they're pretending to clothe requires a certain level of inspection and appreciation. I watch them walk away, carrying Jordan to the door. "I'll make you a protein shake."

I don't protest her leaving, only because her protein shakes are morning miracles. She adds honey and banana, and something she calls *Milo*. It's some kind of crunchy chocolate powder she has her brother ship in special from Australia. She can have her vegemite, but I'll eat that stuff from the tin until I'm sick.

When the room is clear, I roll from bed and reach for my jacket hanging off Jordan's desk chair. I shrug it on and after using the bathroom, I stand at the basin, palm a couple of pills from my pocket, and shove them in my mouth. Turning on the water, I lean over, drinking straight from the faucet as I swallow them down.

After washing my face, I straighten, both hands braced on the vanity, and look myself in the eye. I look fine. A little bruised, but all that dark shit eating at my insides isn't showing on my face. Good.

JORDAN

Brody's team loses the bowl game. It was close, yet he blames himself when he shouldn't. Something's not right with him. Even now, with both of us back in the thick of study and training for our respective combines, I feel dark clouds hovering above.

As I sit here on the edge of his bed waiting for him to get back from the gym, I'm contemplating ransacking his room. He said he wasn't taking anything. I should believe him. A small part of me doesn't want to know, and I hate that part. How easy it would be to just bury my head in the sand. I'm one week out from trials with Seattle Reign. Career comes first, no matter what. Focus. And besides, soon Brody and I won't have this time together anymore. Should I spoil what little we have by voicing my fears?

Yes. You should, my inner voice argues.

Screw it. I'm reaching for the bottom drawer of his bedside table when he walks in the room, tossing his gym bag in the corner. I snap back on the bed, my heart hammering.

Brody faces me, freshly showered and already peeling off his clothes. A grin lights his face, his eyes bright and alert. I give him a tentative smile. Happy seems to be tonight's mood of choice.

"Let's go out," he says, and gives me his back as he opens a dresser drawer and pulls out a pair of pants.

"Out?" I ask, dubious. It's late and I had plans for an early night.

Brody turns, tugging them up his legs. "Somewhere nice." Leaning over, he presses a quick, hard kiss to my lips. I'm surrounded by the scent of fresh soap before he draws back, taking it with him. "We'll stop by your place so you can change."

It doesn't take Brody long to railroad me into going. Just under an hour later I'm seated opposite him at a restaurant table. I look away from the waiter pouring expensive wine in my glass and take in the pale timber floors, warm lighting, and nearby diners watching us with recognition in their eyes. There wasn't much time to make an effort with my appearance, but at least I had that stretchy scrap of black fabric to wear thanks to Leah. The dress is making its debut tonight, and Brody hasn't been able to drag his eyes off me from the moment I walked out with it on.

When my gaze turns his way, he's still watching me intently. "I'm not sure we should be here." My eyes drop to the menu as the waiter leaves us. No prices are listed. "A steak probably costs more than my car."

A smile tugs at his lips. "A Happy Meal would cost more than your car."

"That may be true, but it hasn't let me down yet," I boast.

He finally looks away, his gaze turning out the window. "Not like me, huh."

"You didn't let me down. But what you did? That's not who you are. I'm sorry you felt taking pills was what you had to do. I just don't want you to do it anymore."

"I won't do it anymore." He closes his menu and rests it on the corner of the table. Swallowing hard, his eyes lift to mine. "Okay?"

I want to believe him. So much I ache with it. "Okay."

The waiter returns to take our orders, and halfway through our meal, Brody puts down his knife and fork and clears his throat. "How's your fish?"

"Incredible," I reply. It's cooked perfectly and full of flavor, which surprises me because this is Texas, the unofficial meat state. "How's your cow?"

Brody's eyes crinkle and he looks to the half-eaten slab of beef on his plate. "It's good." His gaze circles the room before returning to me, and he runs fingers through golden-brown tufts of hair. "You're probably wondering why we're in this place, huh?"

"I am," I reply. Brody's gone to some effort bringing me to one of Austin's best restaurants. It's sleek and upscale, with candlelight adding an air of romance. "I know we've been taking things slow so maybe it's so I'll put out?" I joke.

I wait for a teasing response but none is forthcoming. When he speaks, there's a deep chord of sincerity in his voice. "You're not ready. And I'll wait however long it takes until you are."

"I don't want to wait anymore."

The acknowledgement has my body breathing a sigh of relief. I know

Brody's is too because he's half lifting out of his chair before I finish speaking. "I'll get the check."

I laugh and wave my fork in his direction. "I'm still eating!"

He grumbles and sits back down while I take a big mouthful of fish, now in a hurry to leave too. Brody watches me chew hurriedly and laughs. It's deep and ripples across the table. It dies off suddenly and I look up, finding him staring at me with a strange look in his eyes. "Jordan." Taking a deep breath, he blurts out, "Let's get married."

My breath stills, my limbs freeze, and underneath it all my heart pounds a wild, staccato beat. Carefully resting my knife and fork down on my plate, I give him my full attention. His expression is bright with hope and more than a little fear. "What did you just say?"

"Marry me." He reaches over and grabs my hand, dragging it closer to him. His palm is clammy and squeezes mine tight, my fingers crunched in his grip.

Butterflies riot in my stomach and my mouth opens and closes. Marriage is something for the future. I don't know what it takes to be ready for such a step, but whatever it is, I don't have it. "That's crazy."

"I know." He takes in my expression of disbelief and firms his lips. "But it's the good kind of crazy, right?"

"Brody ..." I shake my head. "Why?"

"Why?" He sets my hand free and thumps back in his seat, breaking our connection. "You seriously need to ask that?"

"We're going from one day at a time to getting married?"

His jaw tightens. "I don't need to do *one day at a time* to know I want to be with you the rest of my life."

Tears prick my eyes. I feel the same but what he's asking is impossible. I look somewhere over his shoulder because I'm a coward, unable to bear seeing the hurt I'm about to inflict. "I can't, Brody. I'm signing with Seattle. I'm leaving."

"I know," he says quietly. My eyes shoot to his and I see heartbreak hiding behind them. "I already know. And I'm not going to lie. It hurts you're not signing closer. The Houston Dash would jump to have you. But here's the thing. I'm proud of you, Jordan, and I'm not going to hold you back. This is your dream, and who the hell am I to take that from you? Or put restrictions on it. I know I won't be able to wake up to you every morning, but at least I'll know I have you in my life. I need you in my life."

I swallow, not knowing what to say, so I stall, a nervous huff of laughter escaping my lips. "I haven't even met your family."

"And if you're lucky, you never will," he replies, his eyes darkening into a hard glare. "I'm not asking you to marry my family, Jordan. Just me."

I should say no. That would be the logical, smart thing to do, and I've always been logical and smart. We're both young. We both have careers. We haven't even graduated college. Yet I can't bring myself to form the two-letter word. I swallow, my mouth dry. "I need to think about it."

After a pause, a smile tugs at the corners of his lips. "That's not a no."

JORDAN

"What?" The word explodes from my brother's lips via the screen of my laptop. "Fuck no!" He leans in, as if seeing the furrow of fury on his brow up close will force me to comply. "You are not marrying some college footballer. This is not going—"

I cut him off when he begins to finger jab, warming himself up to a full-blown rant. I should've kept my mouth shut and spoke to Leah about it instead, but marriage is a life altering decision, and one I wanted my twin to weigh in on. Just not so heavily. "I knew I shouldn't have told you."

Nicky rears back like I punched him clear in the nose. "I'm your twin. You should be telling me everything." His eyes narrow. "What else aren't you telling me?"

"I'm not keeping anything from you," I lie, because really, there are just some things you can't share with a brother, twin or not.

He shakes his head. "The time for your career is now, while you're young. You won't get another shot at it, and if you don't take that shot now, you're going to live a life of 'what ifs' and regrets, and you'll always look back wondering what could've been. How far you could've gone." My stomach sinks because I know his words come from his own experience. He gave his shot away for me, and now his mind will always wonder what could've been. "Relationships, marriage, all that bullshit can wait. Soccer can't, Jordan." He rakes fingers through his hair and sits back in a huff. "I can't believe I even have to tell you that." My lips press together in a tight line. Nicky's right. I can't believe he has to tell me either. "When did he ask you?"

"Dinner two nights ago. It was completely out of the blue. We've never even talked about it before then," I add, so he knows I wasn't keeping him out of the Elliot Circle of Trust.

"And what did you tell him?"

"I told him I'd think about it."

Nicky curses under his breath but I still hear him. "And after you thought about it, you told him no, right? Tell me you said no."

For a second I want to show defiance and tell him I said yes, just because I hate the way Nicky acts like my parent. Sometimes it would be nice to have the fun-loving, mischief-making twin back that he used to be before we lost everything. Instead my eyes drop to the keyboard. "I said no."

"Good." He tips his head back against his high-back chair. "I don't want to hear any more about it."

With Nicky's words reverberating in my head, I focus on nothing but soccer for the next week. Every morning I wake exhausted, as if I've done drills in my sleep. Trials with Seattle Reign go better than I hope and my spirits are high when they call to discuss a contract. It's really happening. I'm moving to Seattle at the end of the semester, the very next day in fact, and going to training camp with the best team in the NWSL.

Brody trains just as hard for the draft, and we keep up the tutoring. It's not a huge success. There are some beautiful highs and very ugly lows, but he scrapes by in the last of his subjects. At least he doesn't have the dark cloud of Kyle Davis hanging over his head. Brody won't talk about it, but I know Kyle tried laying charges of assault that didn't stick. Jaxon told me. What else happened I don't know, except Kyle didn't spend his last semester at Colton Park University. The college grapevine says he finished up his final semester in San Antonio. Good riddance to bad rubbish.

With the end of senior year arriving, Brody is the number six draft pick in the first round, signing with the Houston Wranglers where he can remain relatively close to his sister. It's a big deal. Huge. And the media storm rains down, leaving us with little time to talk about our future.

It's when I'm at Austin airport, having come full circle, that the magnitude of leaving Brody hits. He's dropped me off and gone to park the car. Tears burn my eyes as I check in at the counter.

"Fuck," I mutter coarsely and wipe fingers beneath my eyes. Any other word simply won't do. Not for this.

"It's teeming rain in Seattle," the ticket lady tells me with a sympathetic smile. "I'd be crying too."

"It is?" I didn't even know but it feels fitting.

"That your man?" she asks. I turn my head. Brody's standing off to the left of the line behind me, stuck signing autographs. He gives me a wink from under his cap, but I see the frustration in his eyes. Our time is now measured by mere minutes and strangers are stealing it away from us. "Mmm-mmm, he is *fiiiine*," she drawls. "I've seen you both in the papers. Such a cute couple." I'm handed my ticket. "Be a doll and get me his autograph?"

I force a smile, tugging at my ticket when she holds it hostage. "I'll ask him to stop by your counter on his way out."

Her eyes light up. "Do that." My ticket is released. "And if Darlene is on the counter while I'm on break," she calls after me, "tell him she can buzz me from the rec room!"

My back is turned and I'm already walking away, but I wave my ticket in response. Brody's eyes lift as I stride toward him. He's different from the day I first met him over a year ago. He's a little older now, bigger and harder, his body automatically adopting the role of seasoned professional football player he's just signed on to be.

He's still surrounded by people, a pen in his right hand as he signs someone's plane ticket, but Brody's dark brown eyes lock with mine, not letting go of them. He gives back the autographed ticket to the man beside him wearing a Wranglers tee shirt. The man grins, slapping Brody on the back before turning away, and the next fan takes his place.

"Getting a drink," I mouth before reaching his side, nodding my head toward the café on the left.

He nods, resigned.

I buy two Gatorades, dropping them in my carry-on along with my purse. Shouldering the bag, I turn back. Another crowd of fans has him surrounded like the last chip at a seagull party.

"Sorry guys." Handing over another autograph, he pushes through them, his lips pressed tight in a polite smile. "Really. I have to go."

Brody finally reaches my side, all golden skin, intense eyes, and light brown hair curling from beneath his cap. His presence is extreme, a giant magnet that draws everyone toward him like metal. Eyes follow him, and the more zealous fans begin their approach. He latches on to my elbow and steers me toward my departure gate.

"All set?" he asks, moving us along quickly, his vibe screaming 'back off and leave us the hell alone.'

"Yep," I say, aiming for casual as we reach the gate, but the solitary word comes out a hot mess, strangled by the huge lump in my throat.

"Baby." His voice cracks, and my bag drops to the floor by my side when he wraps me in his arms, holding me so tight my feet lift off the ground. I burrow against Brody's chest and his body shudders. "I don't want to let you go."

"I'm sorry." Tears stream down my face now, a tidal wave of emotion I can't hold back. My eyes will be red, my face splotchy, and I'm no doubt leaving a trail of snot all over his shirt. I don't care. I hold on like there's no tomorrow. "I'm sorry, I'm sorry, I'm sorry," I chant into his chest where my face is mashed. "I've changed my mind. I'm staying. I'll tell Seattle I made a mistake. Houston Dash will still take me. I won't leave them any choice."

He huffs a sad laugh, his warm chest vibrating against my cheek. "You know I want that. More than anything. But Seattle won't wait for you. I will." The announcement booms around us that my flight is boarding. "You know you have to go," Brody says, yet his arms lock tighter, belying his words.

"Six weeks."

His clamp on me loosens, just enough for him to draw back and look down into my eyes. Six weeks is how long his pre-camp training is. When he's done I'm flying back into Austin. But just for the weekend. After that, training begins to get serious. For both of us. He nods. "Six weeks."

My flight is called again.

"Brody," I whisper. This is it. I'm not ready. My breath hitches, and both my head and heart begin to thump in perfect symphony. From this moment our relationship status is on long-distance time. Phone calls. Skype. Messenger. This is our life now. Indefinitely. "I love you."

"I love you too. So much." Brody ducks his head, his lips meeting mine in a long, deep kiss that leaves me hot and flustered. "We can do this." He slips a piece of paper into the pocket of my tiny denim shorts.

I glance down as he tugs his hand free from the tight confines. "What's that?"

"A message from Leah. She wants you to read it the second the plane lifts off the ground, okay?"

Leah.

I lower my head and nod. My best friend blubbered when I left this morning. In a fit of nostalgia, she insisted I leave the apartment the same way I arrived. So I did. A final match of MLB with Hayden ensued. He asked me what goodbye was in 'Australian.' I told him, and after getting squeezed by the great, big, bloody Viking, he said, "Hoo roo, mate," and grinned. "Have a good one."

My eyes swam in response, blurring him in front of me.

After giving Leah back my key, she crouched, wrapped both arms around my legs just under my butt, hoisted me up, and carried me out the door. No spills. We rolled my suitcases down the tiled stairs together, the wheels hitting each one with a loud thump. Reaching the parking lot, we hugged for an eternity while Brody stowed my bags in his car.

I'm jolted from the memory by Brody whispering, "Go," in my ear. He nudges me in the back, toward the boarding ramp. "Seriously. Go, before I stop you."

My legs move on autopilot, taking me down the ramp to the airplane door. I don't look back, even though I know he's standing there. I feel him watching me, his words lingering in my head. *We can do this.* Apprehension prickles along my skin. I'm not sure we can. Nothing between us has felt one hundred percent since I found the bottle of Adderall in his bag. I tried talking to him, but we were both so busy.

Busy is no excuse, my inner voice chides.

And the voice is right.

I'm not sure I tried hard enough.

My stomach dips when the plane lifts off the ground. Remembering the note, I tug it from my pocket. *Elliott. Look out the window to the airport parking lot. Leah xo*

I turn my head but we're climbing and I can't see the airport behind us. After a few minutes the plane banks right and I see it. A giant, white banner held out by a bunch of human specks. Leah must have used at least six king-sized sheets to make it. It jiggles up and down, and I've no doubt the entire soccer team is there, waving it above them.

WE LOVE YOU,
ELLIOTT!
KICK ASS, GIRL!
XOXO

A smile breaks across my face, even as tears burn my eyes. I love Leah. I love that Leah has Hayden. And I hate leaving them both. But the memories hurt beautifully. When I can no longer see them anymore, I tip my head back against the seat and close my eyes.

Five weeks pass as I learn my way around a new city. My limited knowledge of Seattle is that it always rains—daily downpours that turn streets into raging rapids, with natives dressed in raincoats and galoshes, running along the sidewalks holding inside-out umbrellas smashed by gale force winds.

There was a minor sprinkle on my arrival, sort of a 'welcome, here's some light precipitation in honor of your arrival,' but since then it's been the Sahara freaking Desert. I'm unprepared for the dry air that sears my lungs, and the warm sweeping winds that toss the soccer ball in every direction but where I need it to go.

My contract provides accommodation. Unfortunately it means sharing a two-bedroom apartment with Dani, the Reign's team goalie. I've taken the room Valeena lived in until injury forced her from the team. Dani takes it as a personal insult. My arrival is not met with a welcome mat, but more of a 'screw up and I will cut you' mentality. Fortunately, she's never here, and I spend my nights on Skype with any friendly face willing to talk to me: Nicky, Leah, Hayden, Paige, and Jaxon, but most of all, Brody.

Sitting on my bed, pillows propped behind my back, I take in the four barren walls of my room. I can't bring myself to decorate the space and pretend it's home. Without Brody, Seattle will never be home. It's merely just another stepping stone in my career, the same way Texas was supposed to be.

Opening the lid of my laptop, I click on Skype, dialing Brody for our scheduled call. He answers almost instantly—his chest bare and lower half encased in nothing but black football pants. My blood hums at the display and a whimper escapes my lips. I'm awarded a bright smile, making me hate myself and what I'm about to do.

"Bitch," I mumble under my breath.

But this is what sacrifice means. This is what it takes to be the best. *He'll understand. More than anyone else, Brody will get it,* I tell myself. It doesn't stop the sharp pang of guilt.

"One more week," are the first words from his lips.

I give a faint smile of apology. "About that ..."

When I trail off, his brows pull together.

I glance down at the keyboard, noting my letter E has a smudge on it. I rub at it, slowly realizing it's not a smudge. The key's worn. Huh. I guess E is my most popular letter.

"Jordan?"

I draw a deep breath of air into my lungs and speak in a rush. "I'mnotgoingtobeabletomakeit."

Flicking my gaze up quickly, I gauge his reaction. It takes a moment for my rushed words to sink in. I know the second they do. He doesn't move. He doesn't flinch. The happiness in his eyes simply disappears.

"I'm so sorry. We have an exhibition match, and—"

Brody holds up a palm, cutting off my hurried explanation. "I understand."

Just like that. Like I knew he would.

"How's camp going?" I ask, changing the subject.

He rubs a hand across his brow and then down the side of his face, scratching at the faint gold stubble on his jaw. There's weariness in the gesture. "It's hard. These guys are good. Damn good. I knew they would be. This is the pros, right? But shit, Jordan, sometimes I wake up wondering what I'm doing on the team. What do they want with me? It's a whole other league to college. I never expected to feel that. Not with football. It's what I'm best at. *All* I'm best at."

"Brody." I shake my head, unable to believe what I'm hearing. "You need to give it time. You're on the team because they saw something special in you. I'm not sure I can even explain what it is. It's like you're made up of puzzle pieces, and when you're on the field they all click together, creating a beautiful picture no one can look away from."

Brody quirks a brow. "You mean *you* can't look away from. Because I'm hot." He nods his head and rubs his chest suggestively, his hand sliding across a thick wall of muscle to circle a nipple with his finger. "You know you want some of this."

I laugh out loud.

"Laugh it up now, chuckles, because you won't be later at the pathetic orgasm your vibrator gives you." His lids lower. So does his hand. "Nothing beats the real thing."

I squirm uncomfortably on the bed, the pulse between my thighs now a raging ache.

"Hurry up and get some time off, baby." Brody draws back a little, and I see his palm stroking along the swollen crotch of his fitted football pants. I suck in a breath. "I need to fuck you."

Four weeks later I get two days. I book my flight online, pack a bag, and leaving an hour earlier than I need to for my flight, I instruct the cab driver to drop me off at Northgate Mall. Shrugging my carry-on bag over my shoulder, I make my way inside, straight toward Victoria's Secret. Once inside I stop dead. Lace, satin, and silk assault me no matter where I look, and the prettiest man-child I've ever seen sweeps toward me with fixed purpose. He's taking in my deer-caught-in-headlights expression and appears ready to wrestle me to the ground. Maybe it's a slow sales week.

"I know you," he says.

"You do?" I ask as my elbow is grabbed and I'm hustled right into the belly of the beast.

"My boyfriend watches all kinds of sport. It's his religion," my accoster explains excitedly, jostling racks of underwear with his hands. "Even women's soccer."

His slight insult is one I'm used to hearing, so I grit my teeth and smile. He introduces himself as 'John Darling, the underwear stylist, but everyone just calls me Darling, or Johnny.'

"So today you're looking for …" he trails off, waving a hand for me to expand.

My face heats with the intensity of a brush fire.

Johnny nods knowingly. "Something sexy." He strides off. I think I'm expected to follow, so I do. "What kind of sexy are we after?"

"There are different kinds?"

Brows wing up. "Of course." Johnny expands. "Innocent sexy. Hardcore sexy. Flirty sexy. First date sexy. Third date sexy. We've been together too long sexy," he rattles off and sucks in a breath to continue. "We've been apart too long sexy, I—"

"That one!" I shout, relieved there's a sexy in there somewhere that fits my exact needs.

Johnny pauses to confirm. "We've been apart too long sexy?"

I nod. "Yes."

"Oh my god." His eyes brighten. "That's the best kind of sexy."

"It is?"

"Uh huh." Johnny starts toward the racks. I follow. He starts shoving hangers of bras and panties at me without questioning my size, leaving me to assume he's an underwear savant. I grab them before they fall. "It needs to make an impact. Sex factor ten. Something his eyes can devour in a matter of mere moments before getting down to business. It also needs to be a little bit filthy, and a lot more flimsy," more scraps of lace hit the growing pile in my arms, "because that's when the ripping can commence."

Oh my god. My eyes drop to the mountain of lingerie. "I don't have time to try all this on. I have a flight to catch."

"A flight." Hands flutter and his next words sound winded. "How fucking romantic." Johnny grabs everything back from my arms, leaving one solitary bra and panty set. "That one it is."

He divests me of my bag and directs me to the fitting room. "Let me know when you have it on so I can check the sizing."

I put the bra on. It's sheer, edged in black piping with cups that barely cover my nipples, and decorated with embroidered red roses. The matching thong is a tiny mesh triangle, a strategic rose, and three black straps that go around each hip. It's romantic, a little exotic, and says 'I love you and want to fuck you,' all at the same time.

"How are you doing?" Johnny sing-songs through the door.

"It's perfect."

"Of course it is."

"Can I wear it now?"

"Of course you can. I'll go get the scissors and we can snip the tags off for you, sweets."

It's midnight when I place my bag on the floor by the hotel room door and knock. I'm in Tennessee. Brody's Houston team is facing the Titans in two days for the first exhibition match of the season. I'll be watching the televised game. It's highly probable Brody won't get any field time—he's second string wide receiver now—yet his nerves are at fever pitch. It's clear in the way he clenches and unclenches his fists when he talks about it.

With no answer, I knock again. Harder. My arrival is a surprise, so I send up a quick prayer that he's in. After a few moments the door swings open. Brody's hair is mussed, and he's wearing nothing but a pair of shorts and a sleepy, irritated scowl. It disappears quickly and he breathes my name, taking me in like I'm an apparition.

Darkened eyes lower over the black knit dress I chose to wear. It has a high button neckline and a short skirt—perfect for the occasion. When they rise, his gaze lands on my chest, caught by the action of my hand. It's attending to the task of undoing the first three buttons, revealing the suggestion of cleavage, sexy lingerie, and a clear message. "Did someone call for their room to be serviced?"

"That would be me," Brody says to my boobs. "But I think they made a mistake."

I slowly unfasten another button. His lungs expand. And hold.

"Oh?" I prompt.

"It's not my room that needs servicing." Licking his lips, Brody's gaze flicks up. My heart hammers at the lust in his expression. "It's me."

The next button goes with a slightly shaky hand. "Then we have a problem."

"We do?" he asks.

I cock my head. "I'm not that kind of girl."

A grin splits Brody's face, and he gives a husky laugh. Grabbing my wrist, he hauls me inside his room, bringing my bag with me. "Yes you are."

But the laughter dies out when the door shuts and I'm slammed up against it, face first. The move is wired with sexual aggression. His arms come around me, his body pushing me into the door. The last of the buttons are ripped away in his impatience. Torn from the dress, they bounce to the floor unnoticed. His breath harsh and hot against my neck, Brody yanks the top half of the knit down, freeing my upper body.

"Jordan," he rasps, his hands everywhere, pulling at the cup of my bra, pinching a nipple, the other yanking up the hem of my dress, shoving it to my waist with no finesse.

My panties are pushed aside and thick fingers probe, finding me swollen and wet, which I have been from the moment I boarded the plane. A growl leaves his throat and before I take my next breath, the blunt head of his cock pushes inside. Pulling back, Brody drives forward until he's all the way in.

My hands splay flat against the door as we both pause, panting, reveling in being joined after so long. He draws out again, pushing back in with a grunt. We don't make love. We fuck. Hard. When it's over my legs give out and we sink to the floor, Brody's arms still holding me from behind, his cock still inside me.

He nips at my earlobe, taking it between his teeth. "Again."

"Again? Now?"

Brody grinds his hips, and every exhausted nerve ending in my body reignites. "Yes now."

CHAPTER 29

BRODY

Jackson Reynard is one of our starting receivers, and he's so good I never see field time. Until now. He's blown out his knee. It's not career ending, but it's bad.

I had to step up and the pressure was too much. I walk off the field after ending the worst game of my entire football career.

It sends the media into a frenzy. My teammates are questioned on my play. My coach is questioned on signing me. My college games are rehashed on ESPN, each play picked apart by a panel of commentators in minute detail. The general consensus is that I choked. I got to the big leagues and couldn't handle it. The kid needs time. But time is a luxury in professional football. It's something a rookie doesn't get. We need to come out shining like a diamond. If we don't, we don't play. If we don't play, we don't get better. If we don't get better, we don't get endorsements. We get traded. And eventually we fade from the limelight and just become some guy that played pro ball once.

The media got it partly right. Only it's not the football I can't handle, nor is it the attention that comes from playing professionally. It's everything else. But I'm trying. I haven't taken a pill in three weeks. I need to prove to myself that I don't need them. The withdrawals leave me shaky. I'm tired but finding sleep is hit or miss. It's not a detox. To use that word would lay claim to me being an addict and I'm not. I'm just cleaning up a little.

Soon after I'm subjected to a urine test. I stand in the cubicle pissing into a small container while sending up a prayer of thanks. The timing is a miracle and the relief leaves me sick.

My next game I play better, but only marginally. I can't find my focus. The next there's more improvement, but not enough. I'm not playing anywhere near my best level without enhancements, and pushing through the pain from every bruising hit I take is wearing me down.

Breaking down, I go back to the Adderall. It turns me into an improved version of myself, like a smartphone upgrade. It's still me. I'm still the same person. I can just do more. The only issue is the insomnia.

After talking to the team physician, explaining my exhaustion and inability to sleep, he prescribes Ambien. Two weeks later I play like a god. I back it up brilliantly the week after that. Another week later I get Jordan for four whole days. It feels like Christmas and my birthday all rolled into one.

With two days off from training, we spend it traversing Houston—holding hands, shopping, eating, being normal. We play tourist, visiting the Space Center and the zoo, and that's where our relationship hits the national spotlight.

We're stopped in front of the new gorilla habitat. Jordan is wearing one of my old western shirts over a fitted white tank top. The worn material is blue and green, and soft from countless washes. She's teamed it with her denim shorts and a pair of hot pink converse, keeping her long hair loose. I love the way she dresses—casual and cute. No matter how big her profile becomes, Jordan hasn't changed.

She has a brand new Canon slung around her neck and her eyes dance with excitement when she turns to me and lowers her camera. "Why did the Gorilla go to the doctor?"

It's a new side of Jordan I've only discovered today. Her bad animal jokes. She's had one for almost every exhibit we've seen so far today. "I don't know, babe. Why?"

"Because his banana wasn't peeling very well!"

I groan. "How many more of these do you have?"

Her eyes narrow. "Why? You don't like them?"

"Don't quit your day job is all I'm sayin'," I tease, holding up my hands.

"You couldn't handle my day job."

I arch a brow. "Oooooh, is that a challenge?"

Jordan's lips twitch. "You better believe it."

I laugh out loud. "You're on. This afternoon. You and Eddie against me and Jaxon in a soccer showdown."

Jaxon visits every other weekend, and the Houston Wranglers signed Eddie on as a linebacker. I bought a house with my signing bonus, and Eddie moved in because there's too much space for me to live there alone. It has six bedrooms—the master suite for me and Jordan, three rooms for each of our future kids, Eddie's room, and a guest room.

It's a beautiful house—one that Jordan is decorating piece by piece each time she visits from Seattle. I've no doubt she'll pick something up from the gift store here today and I'll find it sitting somewhere in the house days later. I usually hate clutter, but everything she sets out isn't just there to look good; it's a memory of our life together.

I look at Jordan, grinning. "Think you can handle it?"

Her eyes dance at the challenge. "Prepare to have your ass handed to you."

"Au contraire," I argue. Grabbing her hand, I bring it to my lips, still chuckling when I press a light kiss to the back of it. "I'll win, and my prize will be you naked in my bed alllllll afternoon."

"Keep dreaming," she retorts.

We play in the local park, and Eddie and I lose by a long, ass-kicking mile. I thought having him on my team would be an advantage, and maybe it would've been if it were football. But Eddie and I are too big. Jordan weaves the ball around us like a magician, leaving us standing there like two stunned lumberjacks, wondering how she did it. She could've taken us both without having Jax there at all.

She returns to Seattle the following afternoon, and the next day photos from our mini holiday get splashed over the media via stalking paparazzi. The one in front of the Gorilla exhibit where I'm kissing her hand goes viral. I don't know what it is about the photo. Maybe it's the light in her eyes as she looks up at me. Maybe it's the way I'm looking down at her like she's my world. Or maybe it's the way we look so relaxed and in love.

I see it first and send her the link via Facebook messenger.

Brody: *They think we're in love, but u just want my cock.*

She replies a minute later, having just changed her profile picture to the new image.

Jordan: *So true. Should I set the record straight and tell them?*

I grin.

Brody: *Maybe they can already tell by the way you walk funny.*

With two brilliant games under my belt, and the Seattle Reign's winning streak, we both become the golden couple of sport. Suddenly we're everywhere. I get my first endorsement and soon I'm shooting ad campaigns for protein supplement company, Evolution. Jordan does a 'women in sport' feature with Marie Claire magazine. They photograph her in black and white. A face shot first, her eyes dark and smoky and her hair a wild tangle. It follows with a body shot. Her skin looks dark and slick, her hair in a messy bun on the top of her head. They've shot her from the back, not a stitch of clothing on, but she's holding a soccer ball behind her with both hands, and it covers her sweet ass. With her standing on tiptoes, it highlights every sleek muscle in her body.

I send her a Facebook message the minute I catch a five-minute breather from on-field training.

Brody: *Ur a fucking work of art.*

Jordan: *Tell that to Nicky. My ears are still ringing.*

Brody: *I bet.*

But messages aren't enough. Skype isn't enough. Football keeps me busy, and right now I have the world at my fingertips, but even knowing that isn't enough.

Six weeks later I'm in Seattle, knocking on the door of Jordan's apartment. I'm exhausted, edgy, and I have to be back in Houston in twenty-four fucking hours. This is our future and it's taking its toll. My eyes burn as I stare ahead at the door, waiting. My need for Jordan is palpable. I feel it in every part of me—my itchy skin, the short puffs of air pushing past my lips, the pulsing of my blood. I'm almost hyperventilating.

Open the damn door, Jordan.

It opens suddenly and she's there, every perfect inch standing right where I need her to be. Warmth leaches deep inside my bones, calming me instantly. It's the equivalent of walking out of a raging snowstorm and into a warm, cozy log cabin.

I take a deep breath and grin crookedly. "We've got to stop meeting like this."

Jordan's response is to grab my face, dragging it to hers as I step inside, kicking the door shut behind me. She kisses me violently, pushing her tongue in my mouth.

"Missed you," she mumbles, tugging at my jacket. "How long do we have?"

"Hours," I manage to get out before her mouth is back on mine, my arms grabbing at my own clothes, helping her. "Just a few hours."

When I realize her own shirt is already off, my arms slide around, fumbling the clasp of her bra with shaky hands. It drops and my palms fill with her tits. She moans, tilting her head back. I take advantage, covering her neck with wet, open kisses.

I go for the button on my jeans, and Jordan bats my hands away. Dropping to her knees, she undoes the fly with hasty fingers, revealing my boxer-briefs. She tugs those down too and my cock springs out, filling her palms. My body shudders. Opening her mouth, she takes me in. Wet heat surrounds me, and warm hands grab my backside, pushing me in further.

"Fuck." I groan.

The sucking and licking sends me rock solid, and Jordan whimpers around my cock. It's like a fucking steel pipe in her mouth. Mere seconds later my body tightens with the sweetest agony, my balls pull up, and I'm coming down her throat. "Sorry," I rasp, my legs unsteady. "Sorry. Fuck."

Jordan pulls away with a final lick, and I blink down at her. A tear trickles out the corner of her eye. *Shit, did I hurt her?* I drop down in front of her. Another one escapes and I catch it with my finger. "Baby?"

Like the word is a catalyst, a sob rips from her throat. My jaw trembles and I wrap my arms around her curled form, dragging her against my chest.

"I h-h-hate this," she stutters through sobs, her pain stabbing at me like a thousand knives. "I thought I c-c-could do this, but I ... but I c-c-can't."

"You can," I tell her, desperately needing it to be true. I'm not the strong one here. Jordan is. She always has been. Jordan is like the strongest oak in the forest. Nothing can fell her, yet here she is, half-naked in my arms and falling apart. It's breaking my heart.

Later that night we lie in bed facing each other. Jordan stares at me as I play with a lock of her hair, watching the honey strands slide through my fingers. "If this is what it takes to be the best, then I'm not sure I want it anymore," she croaks.

"Sure you do." I pause my hair playing and look at Jordan. Dark circles line her eyes and there's a sadness in them I've never seen before. "We'll get used to living this way," I reassure her. "It's not permanent."

But my words don't ring true. At least not inside my own heart. I don't want to get used to living this way. It's hell. And this situation stretches like a long road ahead of me, so dark and bleak it may as well stretch forever.

Jordan slowly drifts off to sleep, but I don't. I lie there wide awake, so many pills coursing through my system I feel I'll never sleep again.

Eventually my phone beeps. The first alert on my alarm, reminding me I have an hour left before I have to leave for the airport. I pick it up to turn it off when I realize it's not the alert, which isn't due to go off for another ten minutes. It's my little sister Annabelle who I haven't spoken to in months. Why is she calling me at three a.m.?

My chest pulls tight with dread. I shoot up in bed and quickly hit answer. "Moo Moo?" I answer quietly.

"Brody," she responds, her voice timid.

Swiping my boxer-briefs up off the floor, I tug them on, leaving the bedroom as I speak. "Sweetheart. Is everything okay?"

A little hiccup escapes her throat.

"Annabelle?"

Another hiccup hits my ears. I pad silently out into the hallway, pressing my back against the wall as I wait for my sister to say something. "No."

"Moo Moo, what's wrong? Talk to me."

"You left," she squeezes out, her voice getting louder as she speaks until it ends on a shrill shout. "You left me and you never came back!"

Oh God. Fucking shit. What do I say? I tried. I tried calling. I stopped by the house more times than I could count, but I wasn't allowed through the door. I stalked her school, but parents kept shooting me suspicious glances and I kept getting told to move on. I didn't know what else to do.

Hanging my head, I run fingers through my hair, mussing strands that are long overdue for a cut. "I'm so sorry."

"You're not sorry. You're not! Otherwise you'd be here. I hate you!" she shrieks. "I hate you, Brody, and I'm glad you're not here! You—"

A muffled sound comes through the line. "No!" Annabelle screams. "Give it back!"

"Annabelle?" I cry out.

My father's voice comes on the line. "Lose this number," he orders tersely and then I get dial tone.

The arm holding my phone drops by my side and I slide down the wall, planting on my backside. My lungs drag in air, but it feels as if I can't breathe. I've held it together for so long. So long. I can't lose it now. I know if I do, I won't ever find my way back. I'll vanish somewhere inside myself where no one can reach.

Hold it together, I order myself, blinking fiercely.

I sit there until the second alert on my phone goes off. When it does, I stand on autopilot and walk back inside the bedroom. Jordan's breathing is deep and even, the dark circles beneath her eyes more pronounced in the pale moonlight. Finding my clothes, I dress quietly and grab my bag. When I'm ready to leave, I lean over the bed and press a light kiss to her forehead.

Hailing a taxi, I get in and direct the driver to the airport. As we zoom off into the quiet, dark night, I pull a pill bottle from my bag. It's labeled as 'Percocet' but that's not what's inside. I shake out a couple of downers along with some Ambien, trying to counteract the effects of Adderall so I can sleep. It works. After boarding, I pass out on the flight home.

"What the fuck did you give him?" Jaxon shouts somewhere near my ear.

At least I think it's him screeching like a pissed off barn owl. My eyes are closed and opening them is a feat of mammoth proportions. So I don't. I shoot out an arm and swat at where I think he might be. My efforts prove futile when I encounter air and I giggle. Then I giggle because I'm *giggling,* and only girls do that.

"I'm a fucking girl," I slur.

"Jesus Christ," Eddie mutters. He's my best bud. My roommate. Together forever. "In electric dreams," I wail loudly, breaking out in song. It's an oldie but my sister loves the song. Fucking loves it. I know that's supposed to make me sad, but I giggle again.

A hand smacks me across the face, cutting me off. It doesn't hurt. I can't feel a thing. I'm epic. I'm *Captain America.*

"Don't fucking touch me," I warn whoever it was. Just because I can't feel shit doesn't mean I'm everyone's punching bag.

"What did you give him?" Jax growls.

"Just some ecstasy," Damien says.

"Ecstasy," he echoes flatly. He says it again, only this time he shouts it. "Just some fucking ecstasy? You gave Brody hard drugs?"

His voice reverberates through my head like a gong. "Cool it, Barn Owl."

My eyes flutter open. Jaxon is standing above me. His face is screwed up and red, veins popping on his neck. He looks a bit angry. "Barn Owl?"

"Dude." I cover both ears with my hands. That's when I realize I'm flat out on the floor in the living room of my house. I look from Jaxon to Damien, who's hovering on the other side of me. Damien shrugs. I tilt my head and look in front of me. Eddie's standing at my feet. I'm surrounded by morons. I look between Jax and Damien again. "What are you both doing here?"

Jax scowls. "We've been here all weekend."

I scowl. "Well how would I know? I've been in Seattle with Jordan."

He shakes his head. "We were here before you left, remember?"

"Shit, you're wasted," is Damien's epic contribution.

"And it's your fault." Jaxon jabs a finger in his chest. "I can't believe you gave him ecstasy. What are you doing with that shit? And why the hell are you giving it to Brody? It's going to fuck with his head and fuck with his career." Jaxon plants both hands on Damien's chest and shoves hard, shouting, "What the fuck were you thinking?"

I roll over and my face encounters carpet. "Ugh." Getting up on my hands and knees, I start crawling away. It's a slow process and I don't know which direction I'm headed in. Hopefully it's the kitchen. I'm thirsty. Really thirsty. Like I could drink all the water in Lake Michigan.

"I wasn't, okay?" Damien shouts back. "He needed something and that's all I had!"

Suddenly I'm airborne. Eddie has me in a fireman's hold and he's carrying me somewhere. My room, I realize, when I flop down uselessly on my bed.

"You're an idiot!" Jaxon yells, their argument going strong from the living room.

"What the hell is going on, Madden?" Eddie asks.

"My dad's an asshole, is what's going on." My teeth feel funny. I lift a hand to rub at them but my muscles are lax and my arm flops by my side. I continue talking. "I fucked up. Remember that time I beat the crap out of Davis? Well apparently that was the last straw. That and the drugs. I'm bad news, Eddie." He lifts my legs, swinging them over the bed. They collapse down on the sheets as if they aren't connected to my body. "Dad won't let me see my sister anymore. Maybe he's right. I'm no good to anyone. Not even Jordan. She's an oak tree. Did you know that? Don't tell her I told you." No girl wants to be compared to a tree. It's not sexy. "She tutored me because I'm stupid." My eyes close, bringing blessed darkness. "I think that's about it."

I pass out.

The whole drug mess causes a falling out between Jaxon and Damien. Both he and Eddie ban Damien from our house and from my phone. They blocked him on my social media. I'm cut off and I hate the panic it sets off in my chest. I can't be who everyone needs me to be without a little help.

I track down Damien on Facebook and send him a message.

Brody: *Sorry bout the shit storm bud.*

Damien: *It's cool dude. I fucked up.*

I type my next message, my fingers shaky on the keys.

Brody: *No. I did that all by myself. Do me a favor?*

Damien: *Sure.*

Brody: *Thanks bud. I need something.*

It takes him a half hour to respond. The wait leaves me coiled tighter than a spring. When his message finally comes through, the coil unravels, leaving me almost buoyant. A satisfied smile forms on my face.

Damien: *What do you need?*

Five weeks later, following a torn ligament during game time, I'm blindsided with another drug test.

This time I fail and all hell breaks loose.

CHAPTER 30

JORDAN

Tucking the phone between my chin and shoulder, I rummage through the kitchen cupboards. I can't bring myself to call them *my* cupboards. Or *my* apartment. Nor is Seattle *my* city. It's a beautiful place to live, but I'm struggling to do this again. Start over. Open myself up to new friends when I'm missing the ones I've left behind.

"… and Hayden agreed," Leah says in my ear. "I mean, the place has six bedrooms and it's right on the beach. It's perfect. So are you in?"

"What a bloody jerk," I mutter under my breath, ignoring Leah's question as my agitation bubbles over.

"Elliott?"

"I'm moving out," I growl, slamming shut the last cupboard. My Milo is gone. It's not sitting where I left it yesterday morning. It's vanished. My last tin of beloved crunchy chocolate powder has simply ceased to exist. My eyes narrow on the rubbish bin. Dani's taken great pains to make my stay here a living hell. One guess she's tossed my Milo in the rubbish just because she knows I can't live without it.

"What's she done now?"

"What hasn't she done?" Putting the lid on the blender, my finger jabs high speed and the blades roar to life. "She's deliberately trying to piss me off!" I shout over the screaming noise.

"You can't move out."

"Why not?" I yell.

"Because that's what she wants you to do."

"So?" I switch the blender off and the apartment settles into stillness. "She wants me to move out. I want to move out. Something we're actually both in complete agreement with."

My phone beeps. "Hang on," I tell Leah. "I have another call."

Putting her on hold, I answer an incoming call from Jaxon.

"What are you doing awake?" I ask. Putting the phone on the bench, I hit speaker and turn, grabbing a cup from the cupboard as I speak. "You do realize it's just after five in the morning, don't you? I know how much you need your beauty sleep, Jax."

"Har, har."

"If this is about Dani, I've told you, I'm not giving you her number. Seriously. I'm doing you a favor," I tell him as I pour the thick protein shake out. Emptied, I carry the blender to the sink. "She's scary. She will sleep with you—"

"Elliott."

"—and then she'll rip your head off and feed it to her young. Is that what you want? Because from where I'm standing—"

"Elliott!"

Turning on the tap, I start rinsing off the blades, which is more than Dani ever does. "What?"

Charged silence follows. Flicking off the hot water, I turn back, brows drawn as I walk over to my phone. "What is it?"

"How soon can you get here?"

There's something off in his voice. Something that makes my heart begin to pound. *Thump, thump, thump.* I stare at the phone. It stares back at me, a coiled snake waiting to strike. "Get where?"

"Houston."

"Why?"

"I can't talk about it on the phone."

I forget about Leah waiting for me on the other line. "Is Brody okay?"

"Define okay."

Fear makes my voice sharp. "Is he hurt, Jax?"

"No."

"Then what's going on?" Resting my backside against the kitchen counter, I fold my arms and stare at my feet. The left one is deep purple and green—bruised from being stomped on in training yesterday. "Why do you want me in Houston? I have a game in two days."

"Fuck your game." Jaxon exhales sharply. "Brody needs you."

"Did he say that?" I ask, and immediately regret my question. If Jax says Brody needs me, then I know he means it. I should be pushing off the counter right now and heading for my room to pack a bag, but I can't just up and walk out on the team right before a game. I'm contracted to play. It's not that simple.

"Brody happens to think your soccer is more important than he is right now. But it's not, is it, Jordan?"

His voice is a steely reprimand. "I'll be there as soon as I can."

But getting away before the game proved impossible. With current team injuries, my team would be left without a striker if I didn't play.

Heading from the field with another solid win under our belt, I shower quickly. Pulling on a pair of Seattle Reign sweats, I tug a brush through my wet hair, arrange a taxi, and head straight for the airport.

I send Jax a message before boarding to let him know I'm on my way. Brody doesn't know I'm coming. I've been trying to call him ever since I heard from Jaxon, but he's not answering his phone. With no one telling me anything, my anxiety levels are through the roof by the time my plane touches down in Houston.

The taxi drops me in front of Brody's house later that night. It's gated for privacy, but beyond the imposing barrier lies a welcoming house with a wide timber porch and lush, expansive gardens. There's a pool out the back and enough yard space to kick a ball around. The outdoor seating area boasts a weatherproof sectional, an outdoor kitchen, and a mounted flat screen television so all sports coverage won't be missed if Brody's either cooking on the grill, or swimming in the pool. It's idyllic and geared toward outdoor living, with French doors along the back of the house, always kept open to meld the indoor with the out.

The house is a home. *My home,* and not because I helped him furnish it, but because Brody lives there.

Using my key, I step inside, walking through the dark-timber floored entryway down to the back living area. I drop my overnight bag on the sofa and look around. Thanks to a regular cleaner the house is spotless, but it's quiet.

"Hello?"

Jaxon steps through the laundry door which sits off the side of the kitchen. His hair is mussed. Not the messy, sexy kind that takes him hours to achieve, but dirty and lank. He glares at me through exhausted eyes, looking nothing like the flirty, carefree guy I met in college.

"You're here," he says.

"I'm here."

"Two days was the best you could do."

Jaxon's anger is gone, replaced with flat disappointment which somehow feels worse. "Yes. It was. I told you they'd be short a striker and—"

He cuts me off. "And nothing. Clearly you have your priorities, and Brody isn't one of them."

My jaw ticks. "Are you finished? Because I'd like to know what the hell is going on. Where's Brody?"

Jaxon stalks to the kitchen counter. "You want to know what's going on?" Bending low, he opens a bottom cupboard. Straightening, he sets a white, opaque pill bottle on the bench top with a loud *clack*.

My blood chills to ice as I stare at it. *Oh no. Please.* My eyes hold Jaxon's for a long moment, willing it not to be true, but all I see is resignation in his expression. Reaching across the counter from the opposite side, I take hold of the bottle and read the label, mouthing it silently. *Ambien.* Sleeping pills prescribed by the team doctor.

But Jaxon isn't finished. He sets another bottle on the counter. I put the Ambien down and pick the next one up. Percocet. Another medically prescribed drug. Before I can blink, Brody's cousin sets another bottle down. Adderall. Then he tosses two separate plastic packets next to the growing hoard. They both hold more pills. Unlabeled ones. I close my eyes, devastation rocking me down to my very toes. Jaxon is quiet. When I open them I pick the sleeve of pills up, flipping it over in a shaky hand.

"What are these?" I croak.

Jax shrugs but his eyes are red and he's battling the urge to cry. "Who the fuck knows? Uppers, downers, all kinds of fucked-up shit."

Deep, jagged cracks form in my heart. It hurts. It *fucking hurts* knowing he put all these deadly chemicals inside his beautiful, strong body—

tainting it. That he would do this to himself. My eyes fill and a fat tear spills over, splattering to the counter below. My gaze falls on the Adderall. I pick it up. It doesn't rattle, indicating the little plastic bottle is empty. I meet Jaxon's brown eyes. "He was taking these in college."

"I know. For study, right?"

"But he stopped," I whisper, putting the bottle back down as a sob builds inside my chest.

Jaxon shakes his head.

"He promised me!" I cry out, my stomach rolling with pain. I point at the Adderall and shout, "He promised me it was a one off. I believed him!"

Did you believe him, Jordan, really? Or did you just want to?

Oh god.

"Brody lied to you. He lied to all of us."

The sob escapes. I sweep out an arm, scattering everything on the counter to the floor. "Why? Why would he do this?"

But I know.

He's never deemed himself good enough. Not his entire life. Adderall was the temporary fix, giving him a reprieve from the struggle—only it escalated into this … this goddamn drug-infested nightmare. Why didn't I see? Why didn't I let myself see?

My stomach cramps with regret.

I was too busy worrying about myself and my own future. Jaxon is right. Brody needed me, and I wasn't there for him. I was never fucking *there* for him.

Jaxon reaches for me and I push him away. Wiping tears with a shaky hand, I croak, "Where is he?"

His gaze moves toward the stairs. "In his room, sleeping."

I spin hurriedly, starting for the master suite. I need to see him. I need to see he's okay.

"Jordan, wait!" Jaxon calls after me. "There's more." I keep walking up the stairs, not sure I can handle more. "He failed his last drug test."

I pause on the middle step and turn, sucking in a breath.

Oh no.

Brody.

"What are they going to do?"

Jaxon runs fingers through his filthy hair and pulls them away with a grimace. "They've put him in an intervention program."

"And what's that?"

"It means he has to see the Medical Director to determine whether he needs treatment or not. If not, then he's subject to regular testing for ninety days."

"That's it?"

He gives a single nod. "That's it. Oh, and the media doesn't know, thank fuck. If this got out, his dad would rain holy hell down on his head like you would not believe."

I've never met Brody's father, but I know Jax is right. The last thing Brody needs is this getting splashed all over the papers.

Making my way up the stairs toward the bedroom, I push open the door. It's dark in the room, but I hear the rustle of sheets and see a body turn in the bed. "Jordan?"

My name is hoarse on Brody's lips. Making my way across the thick carpet, I reach for the bedside lamp and flick it on. Warm light floods the room. I turn to face Brody in the bed. His cheeks are flushed, his usually intense eyes dull and unfocused. "What are you ..." Brody trails off when his gaze meets mine.

He knows then that I know. I see the burst of anger and the bitter twist in his lips. Brody turns his head, nostrils flaring and body rigid. He's bracing. Waiting for the same reaction he got when I first discovered Adderall in his gym bag.

Sitting on the edge of the bed, I take his hand. The muscles along his forearm pull tight, bunching with tension, as I drag it toward me. I turn it over and rest it on my thigh, exposing his calloused palm. I don't know what to say. I don't know how to fix what's so clearly broken inside of him.

I begin to trace the lines on his hand. It relaxes in my grip, and that's when I feel the slight tremor beneath his skin. I open my mouth and speak, forcing out calm words instead of the hysteria I'm feeling. "They say your entire life is mapped out on the palm of your hand." My finger trails along his heart line—the line at top, directly below his fingers. "I had mine read at the markets once."

A moment of silence follows. Then Brody turns his head, looking from his palm to my face. I don't know if the disbelief in his raised brows is from me talking about mumbo jumbo fortune telling, or the fact that I'm not yelling at him. "You believe in that shit?"

"I'm not really sure. At the time it was a bit of fun. Who would you marry? How many kids? That's what my friends wanted to know. All I wanted to know was if I'd succeed in soccer. She said my success was tied deeply to my line of destiny."

My eyes follow Brody's own line. It runs deep from his head and his heart line. "Your line is the same as mine," I tell him, tracing it slowly with the pad of my index finger.

"What does it mean?"

I give him the answer she gave me. "It means success will be achieved at the end of your life."

"That's good, right?"

I pause the trace, recalling her exact words. *It depends on the definition of success, child. The word can mean many things, not necessarily what it means to you, and its meaning can change multiple times during your life.*

At the time, I brushed her cryptic words off. It couldn't mean anything else but soccer. I never longed for success in anything else, and I never would, I was sure of it.

"It's good," I confirm.

The best way to answer your question is to look at why you want to succeed, she told me at the end of the reading. *To be the best of course,* was my flippant reply. I love the game. It's where I want to be, and it's natural to want to succeed in your chosen career.

But maybe it's not everything.

Why do I want to succeed?

Nicky's face floods my mind. For my brother. To prove his sacrifice for me was worth it. That I'm worth it. But at what cost? My own happiness?

My soccer career is right where I want it to be, slotting in neatly with my very own definition of success, but I have nothing else. I don't have my friends and family by my side; I'm unable to set down roots in a strange city; and the man I love is slowly, but surely, falling apart.

I'm not happy, I'm heartbroken.

"What?" he asks, breaking me from my introspection.

Taking a deep breath, I keep going, following along the lines of his hand. "Your heart line touches your life line."

I read up a little on palmistry after my reading. Enough to know it indicates a heart too easily broken. And the curved indention is fragmented, representing deep emotional trauma. *Oh Brody.*

"And it means what?" He huffs a bitter laugh. "Let me guess. That I'm weak and mediocre. Unable to succeed at anything without the addition of chemicals."

"Of course not. It doesn't mean anything. It's palm reading." I twist my torso so I'm facing him directly, and I take his hand in both of mine. It's cold and dry. I begin to rub, trying to warm the chilled skin. "Brody—"

"Don't placate me, Jordan." His voice is sharp, and he tugs his hand free of my grasp. "On the surface, we both appear the same. But we're not. We're opposites, you and I. I'm weak. But you..." he shakes his head "...your strength is like the sun, Jordan. It feeds me. And if you don't let me go, I'll just use it all up until you have nothing left."

"Brody." Seizing his chin, I drag his face until he's looking at me. "I'm not letting you go. It's you and me, and we'll be strong together, okay?"

Doubt and bitterness shadow his eyes. "How can we? You're there and I'm here. There is no *together.*"

Dropping my arm, I sit back and lift my chin. "I'm quitting Seattle."

"Don't be *stupid*, Jordan," he spits with anger. I flinch from his word choice. Knowing it's a word he hates makes the use of it that much worse. "Seattle is your dream. And not only that, you have a contract."

"Contracts are made to be broken."

"And how do you think that makes me feel?" Brody shouts and jerks up in bed, pushing away from me. "That you quit your dream because I got busted for drugs? Fucking pathetic, that's how! Poor Brody takes a few pills and his girl has to drop everything to come running to his side and take care of him."

My own anger riles in response. "I'm not quitting my dream! I *want* to be with you. And I can still play soccer. Houston Dash will take me, I know it. I can move here and—"

"Bullshit!" he roars. Brody scrambles from the bed, naked, and wrenches open a dresser drawer. Seizing a pair of boxer-briefs, he turns, jerking them on as he speaks. "The fact that you said *move here* rather than *move home* just proves it!"

"This is home!" I shout. Standing from the bed I jab a finger hard into his chest, right where his heart thumps visibly underneath. "Here. You."

My arms fly out in a sweeping gesture. "Not this bloody house. Not Texas. Not Australia. You!"

Brody glares for a long, hard moment, his chest rising and falling erratically. Slowly, his dark brown eyes lose their hard edge. "Finish your contract, Jordan. No team will want you if you break it. When you're done, we'll talk then."

What he says makes sense, but I don't want to finish it. I bloody well don't want to. Instead, I want to drag him to Australia, away from all this. We can live by the beach, pretending it's just the two of us without any cares, or obligations, or any need to prove our right to exist. But it's not that easy. *Life* is not that easy.

I take a step toward him. "On one condition. No, two," I correct. "Two conditions."

Brody exhales heavily. His hands reach up and rest on my hips, tugging me closer. "What?"

"A holiday. When the season ends, we spend four weeks in Australia, away from everything. Friends, family, social media. No phones. No television. No football. Just you and me."

"I can do that." He nods jerkily and begins to shiver, goose bumps breaking out across his bared chest. They overtake his whole body. Only it's not cold. The air circulating through the open window is almost too warm.

"What's the other condition?" he asks, appearing oblivious to the way his body betrays him with its need for drugs. Does he even realize he's shaking as if he were standing naked in the Arctic?

"You have to stop." My eyes burn, filling rapidly as I watch him break apart before me. "All these chemicals you're putting inside your body scares me. It scares me so much. Please," I beg, my voice cracking as I swallow an emotional lump the size of a boulder in my throat. "Don't do this to yourself. Promise me you'll stop."

Brody's jaw trembles and when he blinks, a solitary tear falls, tracking slowly down his cheek. "I'll stop," he whispers hoarsely. "I'll do the drug counseling session. And I still get to play. I'll work hard," he vows. "I promise. I'm not addicted, Jordan. I'm just..." Brody presses his lips together, looking over my shoulder as if the words he seeks are written on the wall behind me "...I'm just trying too hard."

Another tear falls. Reaching up, I wipe it away.

He stares down at me, trembling violently. "I promise I'll stop."

But the words he speaks are just that. Words. They're meaningless without actions to back them up.

CHAPTER 31

BRODY

I wake in a scorching sweat, my stomach churning like I'm sailing through raging seas. Jordan's lying across my chest, blistering my skin with her body heat. Bile rises quickly. I swallow, but there's no stopping it. Gagging, I shove Jordan off and stumble for the bathroom. Dropping to my knees, I grab the toilet bowl with shaky hands and heave. Last night's dinner comes charging out like a bull at a gate.

"Ugh." I spit in the bowl, hocking out the bitter taste from my mouth.

My stomach contracts again, pushing out every last bit of food until nothing is left. Breathing heavy, I sit back on my heels and groan.

A cool, wet towel brushes the back of my neck. It's a little sliver of heaven in this hellish morning. I turn my head and look at Jordan. Even feeling half dead, she stirs my blood. She's wearing plain white panties and a loose, hot pink tee shirt that hangs off a beautifully toned shoulder. Jordan's perfect, and I'm a fucking disgrace. I hate her seeing me this way.

"Get the fuck out."

The faucet gushes cool water and Jordan wets the towel again. "No."

"Don't you have somewhere to be?" I rasp, my throat stinging from the acid that raged through it just moments ago. "Like Seattle? You've been here two days already. That's enough."

Jordan brushes the back of my neck again with the cool towel. I hold back the moan. It feels amazing.

"I can't leave you like this."

"I'm not a damn toddler." Pushing unsteadily to my feet, I reach across and open the glass shower door. I flick on the taps and cold water blasts out from the showerhead. Shoving my underwear down and off, I step beneath the icy spray and hiss when it hits my overheated skin.

When I turn to close the door, Jordan's still standing by the sink, wringing the towel in her hands. I love her so damn much it hurts, and god, I want her to stay. But not now. And not like this. She deserves better. Putting her through this makes me nothing more than a piece of shit. I don't want her here when I'm like this.

"Would you fucking go already, Jordan? Book your flight back to Seattle. I don't want you here when I get back from training."

I slam the shower door closed.

My backside jars as I slam it down on the bench in front of my locker. Dropping my helmet at my feet, I hang my head and pinch the bridge of my nose. Today I trained like a newborn holding a football for the very first time. I've lost confidence in myself and what my body can do, and I have no clue how to get it back.

Eddie drops down on my left and the entire bench shudders beneath the force. His meaty paw slaps me in the back, shoving me forward a couple of inches on the seat. "What a shit show."

I wipe my brow with my forearm. It comes away grimy—a testament to every body slam I took out there on the field, my face spending most of its day mashed in the dirt. "Thanks for the pep talk, Eddie."

He leans over, droplets of sweat scattering to the floor as he starts untying his laces. "Pretty words aren't going to fix anything."

"Well damn, there goes my poetry reading session this afternoon."

After peeling away his socks, Eddie stands and starts tugging off his equipment. "Jordan went home today?"

"Not home," I correct him, resting my elbows on my knees and lacing my fingers together to hide the tremors. Jordan didn't wait until after I left for training to leave. When I stepped out of the shower she was already gone. "Seattle."

He grunts, wrapping a towel around his waist. "You're a dick."

"Christ, Eddie!" Jerking to my feet, I kick the base of my locker and face him. "I get it, okay? You're not my number one fan right now!"

His hand wraps around my throat, and I'm slammed against the locker before I can blink. Eddie jabs a finger right in my face. "No, you're the one who doesn't get it, you fucking motherfucker." His eyes are red and rife with emotion. "Everyone's pussyfooting around you because you keep going off like a firecracker on the Fourth of July. I'm tired of it, and I'm not the only one. Someone needs to give you a 'come to Jesus' talk, and I hereby nominate myself."

Unpeeling his fingers from my neck, I shove him off me. "Yeah? Well save your breath. I'm retracting your nomination, asshole."

"Really?" he growls. "When you get home today, take a look in the mirror. A good, hard look. When you're done, you can come tell me who the asshole is here." Eddie stalks off toward the showers and pauses for a moment before turning back. "I don't get it. Are you trying to make it harder for yourself?"

"Yes." I roll my eyes. Slumping down on the bench, I give him my back as I tug off my cleats. "That's exactly what I'm trying to do."

"We want to help you, but you're pushing us all away. Jordan didn't just go back to Seattle, you forced her to go. That's your usual MO. To deal with it yourself. Well guess what, you keep doing that, and one day you'll wake up alone. A drugged-out fucking waste of life that nobody gives a shit about. Or worse, dead."

Eddie's stomping feet take him away and the locker room settles into silence. Grabbing the back neckline of my jersey, I tug it over my head and off, tossing it to the floor. *Fuck him. Fuck Eddie, and fuck Jaxon for bringing Jordan home, and fuck everyone.* Of course I'm dealing with it myself. It's *my* problem. If everyone left me alone, I could focus on fixing it.

I ignore Eddie after showering. He doesn't seem bothered. He jokes and laughs with other teammates as if I don't exist. When I'm dressed, I leave for my drug counseling session. Our team physician passed on the address. It was written on a scrap of paper along with name McDougall. After killing the engine, my fingers tap restlessly on the steering wheel as I stare at the house in front of me, wondering if I read the address right.

The fact that it's a house throws me—a nice house with leafy trees, garden flowers, and a porch. It's private and discreet. You would never guess the reason I was here. And perhaps that's the point. Stories like mine keep the media fed. You're the carcass and they're the vultures, and they will gleefully pick you apart until nothing remains except bones.

Huffing loudly, I get out of the car and step up onto the porch. After knocking, the door opens and I'm greeted by a guy, big and fit—almost my size. Maybe forty if that, he's barefoot and wearing worn jeans, a black tee shirt, and a sauce-splattered apron with the silhouette of a dachshund in tartan print that reads, "Are you looking at my McWiener?"

As pissed off as I am to be here right now, I can't help the laugh that escapes me. I clear my throat. "Dude. Cool apron."

Holding a wooden spoon aloft, he glances down as if forgetting he's wearing it and laughs. "Shit. It's my wife's."

He catches my brows flying upwards.

"Aaaand I'm not sure that makes it sound any better." Just when I'm ready to ask him if I have the right house, he checks his watch and then points the spoon at me. "You're Brody Madden."

"And you…" I take a step backwards "…look like you're in the middle of cooking dinner." Jerking my thumb in the direction behind me, I keep talking. "So I'm gonna go, and maybe—"

Transferring the spoon to his left hand, he holds out his right before I can make an escape, cutting me off. "Doug McDougall."

My lips press together. Stepping forward, I take it, giving it a firm shake. "Great name, Doug."

"The best, thanks to my parents' perverse sense of humor," he jokes and lets go of my hand. Stepping aside, he leans against the open door to let me through. "Though mostly I get McDee or Big Mac."

I follow him through a cluttered hallway to a kitchen out the back. The whole vibe of his house is more well-lived-in rather than untidy. It's comfortable. Like Doug is—a man who appears confident and relaxed in his own skin. It makes me wonder how it feels to be that way.

"Did I get the time right?" I ask when he heads straight for a big steel pot resting on a gas cooktop. Doug plops his spoon back in, giving it a messy stir.

"Yep. I'm just running behind thanks to afternoon traffic. It's my turn to cook and it's chili night. Not to mention my wife will bitch me out if she doesn't get fed." Doug tilts his head to look at me as he stirs. "You like chili?"

Usually, but today the scent has my stomach rebelling. "Sure."

Setting down his spoon, Doug turns and rests his back against the kitchen counter. Crossing one leg casually over the other, he says, "So. Brody. Tell me why you're here."

I fold my arms and sidestep his question. "You ask me that like you don't know."

He waves a hand. "I got the official spiel, but I want to hear it from you. Humor me."

"I'm only here because I'll get suspended from play otherwise."

"I see."

It's the first 'therapist' sounding statement to pass his lips and my nostrils flare. "What do you *see*, Doug?"

"I see that you're here because you have to be, not because you want to be. I see that football is important to you, Brody. More so than yourself." He cocks a brow. "How the hell is that going to work out for you?"

"What do you mean?"

"I mean, you care more for football then you care for yourself. How are you going to get better if getting better is not your highest priority?"

I shake my head. "I'm not sick."

"Okay." Walking to the far end of the counter, Doug picks up a piece of paper from a crowded pile of books and folders. He hands it to me. I grab it before it flutters to the ground, looking at the page. It's a bill for his electric.

My brows rise when he takes a step away, shifting back to his leaning stance against the counter behind him. "And I'm holding your bill because?"

Doug's shoulders lift in a casual shrug. "I just wanted to see how deep your tremors were." And he's right. The paper is shuddering in my hand like an earthquake just hit. He cocks his head, ignoring my curse as I slap the bill down on the counter. "And when I asked if you liked chili, your face took on the color of my lawn. Combined with the circles beneath your eyes and the epic lines of irritation on your face, I'm going to go ahead and call bullshit. You're sick, Brody, but not the kind you can easily see because the sickness is in your head and your heart. Your body is simply the one paying the price."

"Call it whatever the hell you like. All I did was take a few damn pills." My chin lifts. "I don't need to be here."

Doug picks up his spoon again and turns to stir the chili, giving me his back. "So leave," he says simply.

Tugging my car keys from my pocket, I crunch them in my fist so hard it hurts. When I start down the hallway, he doesn't stop me. But before I reach the front door, he calls out, "Can I say one thing before you go, Brody?"

Turning, I see Doug standing at the kitchen entrance, lips pressed together and disappointment in his eyes.

"Sure." My arms sweep out expansively like I'm doing him a huge favor. "Why not."

"Prove yourself wrong."

I shake my head. "That's it?"

"Yep. That's it."

Grabbing the handle, I wrench open the screen door and step out. Dusk has fallen, streaking deep pinks and orange across the sky. It's vivid beyond belief, but I don't notice the beauty as I head toward my car, the screen slapping shut behind me. Cool air has hit the sweat dotting my forehead and my shivers are almost unbearable.

"I'm sure I'll see you again soon!" Doug yells after me.

Sure. Soon. Good joke, Big Mac.

I fume the entire drive home. When I walk through the door connecting the garage to the living area, I find both Eddie and Jaxon sprawled on the sofa, *Pitch Perfect* their movie of choice. Both sets of eyes hit mine expectantly.

With a huff, I throw my gym bag on the floor and head for the kitchen. I come back with a lemon-lime Gatorade because it's all my body can handle right now. Flopping on the recliner, I lift the bottle to my lips and suck half of it down in one hit.

"Well?" Jaxon prompts.

My gaze shifts from the television to the sofa. Both sets of eyes are still watching me. Eddie's are wary, no doubt waiting for my Fourth of July explosion.

"Well fucking what?" I snap, cringing inside because every word out of mouth lately is a curse. I'm sick of hearing myself.

311

Eddie huffs and goes back to watching the movie. He's sick of hearing me too.

"How was it?" Jaxon asks.

My eyes hit the ceiling. "How the fuck do you think it was? I had the time of my life," I bitch. "*Dirty Dancing* has nothing on me."

Eddie's gaze is still on the TV but his lips twitch.

"What?"

"*Dirty Dancing*," he replies. "Best. Movie. Ever."

Getting to my feet, I grab my bag, muttering, "Wankers," as I head for the laundry, using the curse word Jordan sometimes mumbles when people annoy the absolute living crap out of her.

"What's a wanker?" I hear Jaxon ask Eddie.

"I don't know. Google it."

JORDAN

It's night, and late, and I'm the only one left standing after training. The white floodlights are still on, illuminating the empty field. After running drills, I'm kicking the ball against the brick wall of the training sheds.

"Jungle" by X Ambassadors blasts through my headphones as I punt the ball back and forth, my breath coming hard and sweat dripping down my face. I'm in the zone, that precious headspace where you feel like you could keep going forever. So I push harder. Another half hour and my legs are screaming for a break. I'm running my body ragged to stop myself from worrying about Brody. It's the only way I can find sleep at night.

Did he go to his counseling session? Is he training? Is he still taking drugs? My chest aches, bringing back the painful emptiness that kicking the ball had managed to deflect.

I rip the headphones from my ears, leaving them to rest around my neck as I bend down and swipe the soccer ball from the ground. Nearing the locker room, my phone dings from the pocket of my soccer shorts. I tuck the ball under my left arm and pull it out. The message is from Brody. It's just gone midnight, which means it's two a.m. back in Houston.

Brody: *U know I luv u rite? More than anything.*

A sob wrenches from my chest. Just like that. One simple message and I'm an emotional basket case. I heave my soccer ball at the wall of the sheds with a low growl. "Damn you!" It smacks against the bricks and the sound echoes through the still night.

I begin stabbing at letters on my screen, typing an angry response. Then I delete it and shove my phone back in my pocket. Our ups and downs are too frequent. Is it really worth the fight anymore?

Picking the ball back up from the ground, I stalk inside the locker room. My phone dings again as I'm pulling out my gym bag.

Brody: *I luv u like a squirrel luvs his nuts.*

A wheeze escapes me, the sound caught somewhere between a sob and a laugh. I ignore the message. I'm not doing this again. Deciding to shower back at the apartment, I grab all my things and leave.

There's nothing more from Brody through the next day, but later that night another message comes through.

Brody: *I luv u like a hobbit luvs second breakfast.*

My lips pinch together. I don't know if I'm angry or trying to fight the silly grin. *Not doing this again,* I remind myself. Another one comes through the next night.

Brody: *I luv u like Kanye luvs Kanye.*

That one draws a giggle, but I still don't reply.

Brody: *I'll keep going til u talk 2 me.*

He carries through with his threat, his next message coming early in the afternoon. We're in the middle of dissecting plays for the upcoming game with the Boston Breakers. Foreheads are drawn in concentration as we stare at the whiteboard, following the strategy our coach is busy outlining. Soon the board is a mess of arrows and squiggles, becoming almost impossible to decipher. My phone dings. All eyes turn to me in collective irritation for breaking their focus. Mumbling an apology, I retrieve my phone from its hiding place beneath my folder and swipe the screen with a furtive gesture.

Brody: *I luv u like a condom luvs lube.*

My shout of laughter draws the wrath of my coach. "Elliott!" he barks. "Turn that phone off or I'm flushing it down the toilet."

There's no question he means what he says. I've heard rumors he's done it before. Fumbling in my haste, I quickly switch it off while he glares, watching me.

It's not until I return to the apartment later that night that I remember to switch my phone back on. There are two messages from Leah, one from Nicky, and one from my agent, marked urgent. I ignore them all in favor of the newest message sitting in bold from Brody.

Brody: *I luv u like a couch potato luvs his remote.*

How many of these does he have? My phone dings again as I'm mid-giggle. I open his next one.

Brody: *I luv u like the sun luvs the day.*

That one makes me sigh, and before I can stop myself my fingers are on the keys typing a response.

Jordan: *You got me in trouble.*

Brody: *She speaks!*

Jordan: *Coach threatened to flush my phone down the toilet.*

Walking to my bedroom, I shut the door behind me. Climbing on the bed, I shove pillows behind my back and curl my legs up close.

Brody: *Nooo! Tell him if he breaks ur ph I'll break his face.*

Jordan: *Sure. Because violence is always the answer.*

Brody: *It is when someone comes between me getting to talk to u.*

Jordan: *That's the problem though, right? You never really TALK to me.*

After leaving the ball in his court, I wait for ten minutes, using the time to scroll through Facebook, liking and commenting on various pictures. But Brody doesn't respond. Bitter disappointment fills my mouth. I slap my phone down on the bedside table. He always does this. Draws me back in, but only so far before he slams that invisible wall down so hard my teeth clack together.

Grabbing a clean towel, I shove my bedroom door open and head for the bathroom. Dani's occupying the full length of the sofa, caught in the throes of a *Nice Girls* marathon. *Ha!* Maybe if she pays attention it might give her some pointers.

"There's no hot water," she calls out, her lips stretched in a smile of mock sympathy.

"I don't care," I retort, even though I do. I'm not so tough that cold showers don't make me squeal like a kid, but maybe the cold water will cool my temper.

It doesn't. I stomp back to my room, and after snapping a brush through my hair, I stomp to the kitchen. Taking my caramel chunk ice cream carton from the freezer, I rip off the lid, grab a spoon, and head back to my sanctuary.

"You'll get fat," Dani warns as I move through the living room.

I stop dead and stare. "Are you kidding me?"

"Nope," she replies, taking me literally. "Have you read how many calories are in that carton?"

After careful consideration, I decide against emptying said calories on her head. My ice cream is too precious. Pinching my lips, I keep moving. When I reach my room she calls out, "What did he do now?"

With an irritated growl, I shut the door behind me. Setting the carton on my bedside table, I see a message from Brody waiting on the screen of my phone. I snatch it up.

Brody: *So lets talk.*

Dropping to the edge of my bed, I'm tapping out a reply when he sends another.

Brody: *Skype?*

I set my phone down and grab my laptop off my desk, bringing it to bed with me. Resting it on my thighs, I open the lid and sign in.

Jordan: *Good to go.*

Moments later the call comes in. I hit answer and wait for the video to kick in. When Brody comes on screen, I stare for a moment. He's wearing his ball cap backwards and stubble lines his cheeks. His face is tanned, so I know he's spending all his time outside training. Despite the rough edges, he looks fit and healthy, not at all like someone addicted to drugs. Aren't they supposed to be pale and thin? Unable to function? If the pills hadn't come to light, would I have ever known?

Brody grins when I appear, his eyes crinkling in the corners. "Babe," is all he says. Then the background behind him starts shifting. He has the laptop and he's walking with it. "Sorry. My laptop was in the living room." The image bounces as he jogs up the stairs and walks into his room. After setting the laptop on the bed, he flops down in front of it.

"You look so good," I say, trying to hide my surprise.

"And you look so damn edible." Brody's eyes roam over me, darkening. He runs his tongue along his bottom lip. "I like that shirt you're wearing," he adds. I glance down. It's an old shirt, worn for maximum comfort. "But it would look better on the floor."

BRODY

The sound of her laughter floods my body with warmth. "Jordan, I—"

She leans forward expectantly and my words break off. Lifting my cap, I toss it away, scrunching fingers through my hair. I promised Jordan I'd talk and now I don't know what to say.

She speaks for me. "I miss you." My heart gives a sharp pang. Her mouth tilts at the corners as she adds, "I miss you like a squirrel misses his nuts."

My laugh feels bittersweet. "You liked those?"

Jordan holds up her thumb and forefinger to the screen until they're an inch apart. "Just a little bit."

I smile faintly. It wavers and silence falls. Not an awkward one, but one where the cold reality of what I've done sits between us. I know it will only get worse until I give Jordan the explanation she deserves.

I draw a deep breath in and let it out slowly. "You know I told you I'd do whatever it takes to be the best. Well …" I press my lips together.

Jordan draws her knees up to her chest and wraps her arms around them. I know the gesture. She's subconsciously protecting herself, expecting what I say to hurt.

"They made me better."

"The drugs?"

I nod my head in answer. "They did for me what I couldn't do myself."

"Brody—"

I cut her off. "Don't." Pity or meaningless platitudes is the last thing I need to hear right now. "It's the truth. When I was seven years old, my father said to me 'you're too damn stupid to do anything else so you better make football count,' and I believed him." An intense burning pain spreads through my chest—strong enough to take my breath away. "Only I couldn't even do that."

Jordan shakes her head vigorously. "You can. You never believed in yourself, Brody." Her lips press in a thin line. "It all started with that bloody midterm. If Kyle hadn't messed with your paper, you would have passed, and none of this would have ever happened!"

"It would have," I admit both to her and to myself. "You're right, Jordan. I never believed in myself. If I did I would have questioned my grade. I'd have never taken the Adderall. And maybe I wouldn't have hidden my dyslexia like a shameful secret. Instead, I put myself in a position where I couldn't find a way out," I say quietly. "I pushed, and pushed, and I took drugs, but it got me where I needed to be. Is this what it takes to make football count?" I stare down at my hands, absentmindedly rubbing the callouses on my left palm. "Because it fucking sucks." My eyes lift and deep cracks form in my heart, making me crave the euphoric numbness that Percocet always gives me. "I'm losing you, and—

Jordan cuts me off. "You're not losing me, Brody."

"Are you sure about that? I've already lost my little sister. I can't lose you too."

She sucks in a sharp breath. "Annabelle?"

A scowl forms on my face. "Dad won't let me see her."

"Since when?"

"Since I gave Kyle Davis what he had coming." My jaw tightens and my tone turns bitter. "I'm a bad influence. They don't want me anywhere near Annabelle."

Jordan's voice trembles with hurt. "Why didn't you tell me?"

"Because I don't want you exposed to *them*!" I sit up on the bed, swiping a hand down my face. "I've tried so hard to keep you separate from my family. You don't want anything to do with them, Jordan. Trust me. My parents aren't warm like you are. There's no love. Or joy. It was like growing up inside a cold, barren wasteland. When they look at me, they don't see *me*. They see disappointment." My lips press together. I focus my eyes on the wall above the screen of the laptop. "And I keep pushing you away because …" My words die off, my body growing tense as I force myself to look at her. "I don't want you to see me the same way."

Her next words are a knife to the chest.

"I am disappointed, Brody, but there's a difference." She keeps talking but I don't want to hear it. "I'm not disappointed in you, or who you are, only in what you did."

If she says I'm better than this, I'm going to lose my shit. Only she doesn't. What she says next hurts more than I thought possible.

"If you couldn't get drafted into the big leagues without drugs, then maybe it's not where you're supposed to be."

CHAPTER 33

BRODY

"You good to go?" Eddie calls out.

Sliding the zipper closed on my sports bag, I call back, "Be right there!"

Loud thumps tell me he's jogging down the stairs. When the sound of the fridge being raided reaches my ears, I quickly slide open the bottom drawer of my bedside table and reach for the little bottle. Unscrewing the lid, I palm a handful of Adderall and tip my head back, tossing them down my throat.

The fridge door slams shut as I'm swallowing them dry. "Hurry up, Madden!"

"Yeah, yeah!" I call back, my heart pounding hard in my chest.

Taking the pills—especially still under stage one of the substance abuse program—is a risk the size of Mount Everest. But with a home game in just a few hours, followed with a bye and four days in Seattle with Jordan for her finals, it's a risk I'm willing to take—more so than ever in the wake of her words from last week. *Maybe it's not where you're supposed to be.*

Jordan couldn't be more wrong. Everything I've been through to get to this point would all be for nothing otherwise.

Grabbing my bag, I sling it over my shoulder and jog down the stairs.

"Yo!" Eddie appears in the living room and fastballs me the car keys.

Stretching up, I catch them and my ribs give a twinge. The entire length of my torso is black and blue from training this week. It's par for the course, but when I walk in shirtless to my trainer's office an hour later and tell him I need something for the game, I'm jabbed with a shot of Toradol—a non-steroidal anti-inflammatory. When injected, it becomes an amped up painkiller, used to reduce pain sensitivity and leave you playing like a fearless machine.

Numbness floods my body, and I walk back to my locker with the knowledge I'm doing what I have to do. As a pro player, the hits come harder and the injuries more frequent. You need to have an edge, take risks, and show you can play with pain, otherwise they'll replace you with somebody who can.

Eddie's grin is wide when I return to my locker.

My brows rise in question as I shove my shorts down and off, tossing them in the direction of the open shelf. "What?" I ask, yanking my football pants out.

His grin widens further, bright enough to take out an eye. Standing, he pulls his football jersey down over his head. Tugging it in place, he says, "You got a surprise visitor."

"Yeah?" Stepping into my pants, I tug them up my legs. "Who?"

He jerks his head toward the door of the locker room. My head turns but no one's there.

Hawk, our starting quarterback, strides past. "Yo, Madden." He gives me a playful shove and keeps moving. Turning, he walks backwards and winks. "Your girl looks hot to see you. Better go put that fire out."

"Dammit, Hawk!" Eddie bellows. The big, romantic lump scrunches his hands into fists, his expression wounded. "You ruined the surprise!"

Hawk spins on his heel, laughing loud and hard before disappearing inside the office of our head coach.

My heart leaps at least a mile in the air. I look at Eddie. "Jordan's here?"

Not waiting for an answer, I start jogging toward the outer room.

"Five minutes, Madden!" Joe Pettone, our wide receivers coach, yells out behind me.

Waving him off, I reach the outer room and stop dead when I see Jordan's solitary figure, her hands clutching a large handbag slung over her shoulder. She's wearing my football jersey, tight dark jeans, and a hesitant smile.

A rush of love hits me harder than a linebacker tackle, stealing my breath. Jordan's here to watch my game, and I'm fucking thrilled. "You're here."

Her smile falters slightly. "Is that okay? I wasn't sure if— Oomph!"

Jordan's words are cut short when my body slams in to hers. Before she can topple backwards, I'm picking her up. Her long legs wrap around my waist and her arms grab my shoulders. Holding her thighs, I spin us both around.

Coming to a stop, I bury my head in her neck and breathe deep. "You're really here."

My teeth find skin and nip gently, following a path up toward her ear. She giggles, drawing back a little. "That tickles."

"Too bad." I do it again, my tongue snaking out to suck her lobe into my mouth. Jordan jerks back, still laughing. "Kiss me."

She does. Her lips find mine, and her laughter turns to a low moan. Only when I'm dizzy from lack of air do I pull back—but not far. I rest my forehead against hers, our mouths less than an inch apart.

"I'm sorry," she says.

My brows knit. "For what?"

"For what I said. Of course you're supposed to be here. Football is in your blood. Anyone can see that. I'm just scared." Jordan's eyes fill and she turns her head, blinking. "What it takes to play at this level..." her gaze returns to mine "...it's overwhelming and intense, and so fucking hard."

My lips press together and her eyes narrow at the dirty gleam in my expression. "What?"

"You said hard!"

"Brody!"

Jordan's lips twitch and I laugh, more than happy to surface from the deep waters our heavy conversation was falling into. She wriggles and I let her slide to the ground. When her feet hit the floor, she aims a hard jab to my bicep. Her fist bounces off. "Jesus," she complains, taking in my large, rounded shoulders. Built-up deltoids are the best defense against injury for a wide receiver, and mine have never been bigger. "It's like punching a brick wall."

I grin and flex. "You like?"

Jordan's gaze lowers over my chest and ribs. "You're so bruised." Her hands skim over my skin, her touch soothing and delicate.

"It doesn't hurt." She looks at me, skeptical, but the Toradol is so powerful I could get hit by a car and barely feel a thing. "I promise."

My jersey slaps me in the head from out of nowhere. Grabbing it in my fist, I drag it from my face, revealing an exasperated Eddie. "Your five minutes are up, Showpony." He gives Jordan his attention. "I'd apologize for dragging him away, but it looks like I'm actually doing you a favor."

Dimples break out on Jordan's cheeks when she gives Eddie a laugh. I don't like it. They're *my* dimples.

"Shutting your mouth would be doing us both a favor," I retort. Slinging my jersey over a bare shoulder, I take Jordan's hands in mine and tug her close. Seems I can't handle having her in the same room without some part of her body touching mine. "I'll be there in a second."

Eddie gives me a nod and Jordan a salute. "See you after the game, sweetheart."

"She's not your sweetheart!" I call after him, flushing with indignation.

"Dude." He holds up his hands defensively and turns, his big body disappearing from sight.

"Now," I say, looking down at Jordan with intent. "Where were we?"

"*We* weren't anywhere. *You* were too busy puffing out your chest like a peacock."

I snigger.

Her eyes roll, amused. "Yes I said cock."

My lids lower, liking the word on her lips. "Say it again."

"Do you really want to go there right now?"

Jordan's hips press against my groin, a reminder that I'm currently wearing tight football pants and no cup. It's all on display down there. I draw my hips back. "Probably not a good idea." Threading our fingers together, I finally get around to asking Jordan how she managed to be here. "You have finals in four days, babe," I add as if she didn't already know.

Heat steals over her cheeks, flushing them red. She clears her throat.

"I uh, told them I had an ankle twinge. I'm supposed to be resting it overnight."

I gasp in mock horror, clutching a hand to my chest. "You … *lied?*"

My words have her biting her lip, dragging it inside her mouth. "I wanted to see you."

"And seeing me is all that and more, isn't it?" I curl my forearm and biceps bulge.

Jordan laughs and I'm punched in the shoulder. Again. "Would you stop?" she asks.

"Can't," I say, shaking my head seriously. "You're my girl. It's programmed in my fundamental makeup as a man to show you my strength. You need to know I can provide for you."

"Okay, you prehistoric brute." My shoulder is rubbed in a placating gesture. "Use those manly muscles of yours to go forth and provide. You're taking me out after the game, and I have a hankering for Japanese food."

My insides recoil in horror. "Steak," I correct firmly.

"Sushi."

"Steak."

"Sushi."

I open my mouth and Jordan jabs a finger in the direction of the locker room. "Go!"

"I'm going." Ducking my head, I press a long, slow kiss to her lips. Drawing away slowly, Jordan turns to leave. "Hey." I pull her in close. Grasping her chin in my hand, my eyes lock with hers. "Don't be scared, okay? Everything's fine. I've got this."

Maybe my words were prophetic because I bring my best game to the field. So do the Colts. Every sack they deliver hits like a freight train. One of them breaks a rib. There's zero pain, but it's getting harder to breathe so I know the fracture is there. My body will pay the price tomorrow, but I'm in the zone right now and it's hard to care.

With a minute left on the clock, we're trailing by four points. One touchdown is all we need. I step into the huddle, sweat in my eyes and every breath harsh inside my helmet. When Hawk calls the play, my pulse spikes, forcing an adrenaline rush so hard I feel the surge in my veins.

"Hut!" we roar in unity. With a loud clap we break and take formation. My eyes focus dead ahead, tuning out the screaming, chanting sea of blue that surrounds us. The opposing linesmen stare back at me, determination making their eyes hard and dark inside their helmets. There's an endless field of green behind them. I fix on it. Nothing else exists except that empty space, and our entire team is betting against the clock, giving everything they have left to ensure I find it and bring the ball over the line.

I roll my shoulders. *This is it, Madden. Breathe and run. That's all you need to do. Breathe and motherfucking run.*

"Hut!" The ball is snapped to Hawk and both teams rush. Digging in my heels, I push off, clumps of turf flying up behind me as I sprint for the green, ducking and weaving every Colt who comes at me. A player slides and I hurdle the felled body.

A quick glance to my right shows Hawk tossing the ball to Felix Lynch, our first string wide receiver. From there, the Colts strike, expecting him to carry the ball. But it's a trick play that allows me to find the pocket I need to take possession. With the double pass in play, Lynch throws the ball down the opposite sideline. Vaulting high, the ball slides into my outstretched arms. Perfect orchestration. Wranglers supporters roar in triumph. I don't hear them. I don't see them. My task is clear. *Run like a motherfucker.*

With a final burst of speed, I reach the end zone and make the touchdown. Throwing the ball away, I leap up and fist pump the air. "Whoooop!"

"Umphf!" Eddie slams me before I hit ground. Lifting me high, he roars our victory. When I do hit the ground, Hawk runs at us both. His hand grabs my neck and we headbutt helmets with a loud *crack*. "You brilliant sonofabitch," he gasps and slaps me on the back. "Didn't think you were gonna make that catch."

Pandemonium from the crowd surrounds our team as we slowly reach the sidelines. I'm snagged by a reporter before I can go any further. Dragging fingers through sweaty hair, I tuck my helmet under my armpit and give her my attention. Holding my sweaty bicep to prevent escape, she faces the camera.

"In what will likely be touted as one of the best games of the season, the Houston Wranglers clinch a nail-biting win against the Indianapolis Colts. Here I am with man of the hour, rookie wide receiver Brody Madden." Erica looks at me. "Brody, a brilliant last few minutes. It secured a win for the Wranglers. Tell us about your final play." She shoves the microphone in my face.

Swiping a hand across my grimy face, I shrug and grin. "We knew we had to pull out something miraculous." I drag a few deep breaths into my lungs while Erica waits expectantly. "The Colts defense was like a brick wall. Our final play was the best way we knew to break through."

Erica draws the microphone back to her. "It was a thirty-five yard catch and beautiful to watch," she informs me. "I'd have to call that pretty miraculous. So do the Wranglers supporters." Erica gestures toward the screaming crowd, waving flags and banners and homemade signs, some with my name on them. "It looks like Madden Fever is sweeping the nation. How does that make you feel?"

Back slaps hit me as team members walk past. Joe gives me a noogie, making me laugh as he pulls me in for a half hug. "Insane catch, Madden," he shouts in my ear before walking off, victory making his steps light. I give my attention back to the microphone in front of me. "How does that make me feel?" My lungs expand with euphoria. How do you explain what it's like to fly? "Incredible. Playing with the Wranglers, a team I've idolized all my life, is a dream come true."

Erica smiles, pleased with my answer. "For the last two games you were a chosen finalist for the Pepsi NFL Rookie of the Week. There's no doubt you will be again this week, which will make it the third week running. How do you do it?" She brushes away a lock of hair that blows in her face. "What does it take, as a rookie, to maintain this level of play?"

Lady, you have no idea. I swallow the lump of shame. I'm not the only one who does what they need to do in order to get time on the field. "Discipline and hard work."

"What about family?" she asks, digging for a more personal angle.

A grin lights my face. "That would be Jordan. She's my biggest supporter."

"You're referring to Australian ex-pat and forward for Seattle Reign, Jordan Elliot. She's been your girlfriend since senior year of college?"

I shake my head. "She's not just my girlfriend."

Erica's brows rise in question. "No?"

"No." My heart rate kicks up and a smile pulls at my face. Jordan is going to kill me for going public with this, but I'm ready to burst after sitting on the news for far too long. It's time. Finding the family section where Jordan should be sitting, I press my index and middle finger to my lips and then hold them up high. The gesture is for her, and her alone. Jordan's mine, and I want the whole world to know. *She's my reason for breathing.* "Jordan Elliot is my wife."

Erica fumbles the microphone. Before she can recover, I lean in to the camera, salute the home viewers, and walk off.

CHAPTER 34

JORDAN

No! He did *not* just say that. I rise in my seat, my eyes narrowed on a grinning Brody as he leaves the field. I'm going to kill him. I'm going to wrap my hands around his neck and squeeze until his pretty face turns red and his eyes bulge from their sockets.

"Did he just say what I think he said?" Renae screeches from beside me. She's Felix Lynch's wife, and we've been making general small talk throughout the game. I've only met her once before, but I like her. She's loud and assertive, and reminds me of Leah. "You two are married?"

I turn toward her, my mouth open. A scant second later, my shorts begin to vibrate, alerting me to a phone call. Pressing my lips together, I close my eyes.

"You okay, Jordan?" Renae asks.

My pulse begins to race a mile a minute and a headache starts thumping at the base of my skull. "You know, I'm not sure."

The phone in my pocket continues to vibrate, the sound seeming to get louder and louder. Little dings follow. Message after message is racking up.

"Ummm ... are you going to get that?" Renae asks, her tone cautious as if she expects me to spaz out at any moment. It's possible I might. I flinch when she reaches out and proceeds to pet me, her hand stroking my forearm in a slow, soothing motion.

"No." I open my eyes. "I don't think that's a good idea."

Her expression of cautious delight changes to one of understanding. "You didn't know he was going to do that, did you?"

"No." The word comes out slow and shaky.

Her whole face lights up. "How romantic!"

"Sure." My voice begins to rise as I speak, verging on hysteria. "Everything is all crazy and romantic until someone gets maimed!"

Meaning me. Nicky is going to shit a brick. He likely already has. He's just waiting for me to check my voicemail and hear how it went down. *Hell.* "I have to go." Grabbing my bag, I sling it over my shoulder and flee the stands.

My phone gives me a reprieve as I head for the locker room. It lasts five seconds. I'll have to face the music sooner or later, but later is the sanest option right now. Winding my way quickly through hordes of people, I smack into a hard, grimy chest. Blinking, I stumble back. Before I can steady myself, I'm lifted and squeezed in a rib-cracking hug. I come face-to-face with Eddie, a grin splitting his face.

"It's Mrs. Madden!" he shouts.

"Shhhh!" I glance around. Players are heading for their lockers, and reporters and trainers are swarming the area like bees. "Keep it down."

Eddie laughs. It's a loud, booming sound that comes from deep in his belly. "I'm pretty sure the whole world knows."

My lips pinch. "Where is he?"

"Where's who?"

"Peter Piper," I hiss with loaded sarcasm. "He stole my pickled peppers and I want them back." Another belly laugh from Eddie jostles me in his arms. "Put me down and go find Brody," I order. "I have a killing to get to."

He cocks his head as he sets me on my feet. "You know, I think you're a bit pissy."

"I am?" I wave my hand in a swift circle around my face. "Because this is my expression of happy excitement." Try as I might, I can't seem to un-pinch my lips and form a smile. I raise my brows instead. "I want to go hug the man of the hour. Mr. Pepsi NFL Rookie of the Week."

My phone dings a few more times. Eddie's gaze drops in the direction of the sound and comes back up. "Are you going to get that?"

"No!"

"You know…" he cocks his head "…if anyone has a right to be pissy, it's us."

"Us?"

"Your friends." Eddie slings a sweaty arm around my shoulders and starts leading me toward the locker room. "Well, at least I thought we were." He glares down at me, making his displeasure clear. "What's the deal, Elliott?"

We reach the locker room to the loud chants of "Madden, Madden, Madden!" Eddie starts pushing me through the door, and I struggle backwards. "I can't go in there!" But it's like swimming against the tide. I'm expelled into the room like I've shot out from an overflowing storm drain.

My presence goes unnoticed as the chants continue. A champagne cork pops. The room is sprayed. Then I see him, caught in the middle of the rowdy bunch. Shirtless, soaking wet football pants, sweet sticky alcohol dripping from his chest, and a huge grin on his face. My heart pounds. He's so full of life. So happy. So *vital*. I can't shit all over that. At least not right now. I'll do it later.

Pushing my way through the fray until I stand behind Brody, I tap him on the shoulder.

He turns and his grin falters. Taking my hand in a brave gesture, Brody lifts it to his lips and presses a kiss to the back of it. Desperate to preserve my anger, I restrain the visible shiver. Instead it rocks me on the inside, all the way down to my toes.

"Marry me, Jordan."

I should say no. That would be the logical, smart thing to do, and I've always been logical and smart. We're both young. We both have careers. We haven't even graduated college. Yet I can't bring myself to form the two-letter word. I swallow, my mouth dry. "I need to think about it."

After a pause, a smile tugs at the corners of his lips. "That's not a no."

"And it's not a yes."

"Jordan." Brody reaches across the restaurant table and grabs both my hands in his. There's hope in his eyes and a doggedness that tells me he's not letting this go easily. "Your whole life you've done what you're told. Study, training, games.

You've followed the path set out for you. Don't you want to break free of that? At least a little? Life's too short to wake up at the end of your soccer career and wonder if it was all worth it." He squeezes my hands. *"Do something crazy."* The words take root inside me and my heart begins to thump. *"Make life worth living, Jordan. With me."*

How was I supposed to say no? Instead, I woke the next morning with a ring on my finger, and the knowledge that crawling off into a deep dark hole to die would be better than facing my brother with the news. I tried telling him, easing him into the idea by mentioning Brody's proposal, but he completely lost it. How could I tell him the truth after that?

Brody lowers my hand. "Are you mad?"

"Am I mad?" It's not obvious? "Your little announcement tonight has brought the wrath of hell down on both of us." Nicky would be the leading torchbearer. "We're both dead."

"And what a sweet tragedy it would be, Jordan Matilda Madden." Brody shakes his head in mock sadness, yet there's mischief glinting in his eyes. "But so be it." He spreads his arms out wide and winks. "Life wouldn't be worth living if you weren't married to me anyway, right?"

BRODY

"If that's how you feel ..." Jordan digs inside the pocket of her shorts. She pulls out her phone. Grabbing my hand, she slaps the device in my palm. "Then you can talk to Nicky."

It vibrates in my hand. I check the screen and see that possibly every person Jordan has ever met in her lifetime (and those she hasn't) has called to confirm the news. I scroll through the notifications. Nicky's only called once. It's more ominous than calling a thousand times. He's not happy. And he knows we know he's not happy. Jordan's brother doesn't need to call a thousand times to reinforce that fact. Just once will do.

Jordan wanted us to sit on the news until she could tell him in person. I just blew that right out of the water. Speaking to Nicky is the least I can do. "Sure, I'll talk to him."

Her brows rise. "Just like that?"

"We're not in shooting distance, so it should be fine. Really," I reassure her. "It's better this way."

Jordan's bottom lip quivers. We've hurt her brother by hiding the news. Possibly hurt all our friends. I pull her close toward me, heedless of my dirty, sweaty body and everyone else around us. "I'll just tell him that sometimes two people are meant to be."

Her nostrils flare in a frustrated huff. "That's it?"

I run my thumb along her cheek. My eyes follow the path before flicking up to meet hers. "It's the truth, isn't it?"

Eventually the locker room clears. Jordan's gone home to change. A big night of celebration looms. Eddie swipes his bag up off the ground and gives me a fist bump. "See you back at the house?"

I nod. "Right behind you."

He leaves, his hand slapping the Wranglers logo on inside wall before he disappears. Then, and only then, does my guard come down. Sinking down on the seat, I curl over on myself. The Toradol dose wasn't enough. Pain is seeping through. And with a sleepless night from the Adderall ahead, tomorrow will be agony.

Voices from down the hall reach the main room. Turning my head, I see the door of Joe's office ajar. He's talking with Porter, the team physician. There's no time to think through my actions. Rising to my feet, I walk down the long, wide, empty hallway until I reach medical. I grab the handle and give an experimental tug. The door is unlocked.

With a quick glance left, and then right, I push my way inside. Medications are kept inside a locked cabinet, but there's a portable kit sitting half open on the desk. I head straight for it, ignoring the heavy pounding of my heart. Digging inside, I check each bottle until I find what I need.

Leaving quickly, I pull the door shut behind me and start back down the hall. Porter appears moments later, walking toward his office. A puzzled frown creases his face. "Brody. Can I help you?"

"Nope." I hold up my opaque navy water bottle, making sure it doesn't rattle from the pills I poured inside it. "Left this in the weights room earlier today," I say, nodding behind me toward the gym down the far end of the facilities building. "Just grabbing it before I leave."

"Oh, right." Porter nods, his face smoothing out. "Good win today, son. Keep it up."

He keeps moving. Wiping the sweat of tension from my brow, I head back to the locker room. Remorse sits like lead in my gut, but it's not heavy enough to stop me swallowing a small handful of painkillers before I leave.

Parking inside the garage, I walk through into the living area. "I'm home!" I shout.

"In the kitchen!" Eddie calls back.

Dumping my sports bag on the floor by the stairs, I head for the kitchen. Jordan turns, wine glass in hand. She's wearing a strapless black dress, leaving tanned shoulders bare. It reaches just below her knee, showing off toned calves and feet encased in spiky black heels. My gaze drifts back up, landing on the wedding ring adorning her left hand. Finally. My chest expands.

"Jordan." The word comes out breathless and unsteady. Jesus. I'm getting emotional over a bit of jewelry. I clear my throat. "You look … perfect. Just …"

Shaking my head, I press my lips together.

Eddie has a wide grin. He hands me a glass of wine and leaves.

Jordan runs a hand down the inside of her thigh and arches a brow. "You like?"

"I do," I croak, taking a step toward her.

"I'm very expensive." She purses her lips and scans my body, the same way I did to her the day I wore that damn cheerleading skirt. "But for you, twenty dollars."

I take another step, slowly pushing Jordan against the kitchen counter behind her. "Are you hustling me?"

"Yes." With her left hand holding a wine glass, she presses her right flat on my chest. Feather light, it trails down slowly. My breath hitches when she reaches my hardening cock. "Is it working?"

"I don't know. Is it?" My lips curve wickedly. "You tell me."

Setting both our wine glasses down, Jordan grasps me outside my shorts and strokes with increasing pressure. A groan rises up from my throat. "I'm not sure." She tilts her head to look at me, a teasing light in her eyes. I love Jordan like this—sexy, cheeky, uninhibited. It heats my blood to a fever. "You might have to take off your pants—"

My lips cover hers, swallowing the words. Our tongues meet, rubbing together with delicious warmth. Her hands slide around my neck. They move upwards, grasping strands of hair.

Without breaking the kiss, I seize the backs of Jordan's thighs. Lifting her, I set her down on the counter. A sexy whimper escapes her throat when my hands shove the tight material of her dress up above her knees.

She pulls away with a sharp gasp. "Brody."

My palm travels her inner thigh until it reaches her pussy.

Jordan swallows and lets out another whimper. "We need to talk."

Now? I run a finger over her panties. She's hot and wet. "Later."

"Brody. We …" Slipping the panties aside, I slide a thick finger over her clit. It's slick and swollen and fucking beautiful. I let out a shuddering breath.

Jordan moans loud. Her head tilts back and I lean in, my mouth landing on her throat at the same time I push a finger deep. "Oh god."

My finger plunges in and out. I slowly add another, thrusting them both deep and hard. "Don't stop," she begs.

Sounds from the living room remind me we're not alone. "Sorry, baby. I'm going to have to stop, but just for a second."

Withdrawing my hand from between her legs, I lift her off the counter and carry her into the laundry room. Setting her on the frontloading washing machine, I step back, shut the door, and shove down my shorts. Jordan wriggles, panting as she pushes her dress up higher and spreads her thighs.

Wrenching her panties aside, I rub the head of my cock through her slick heat. When I find where I need to be, I push in, filling her in one swift stroke.

Jordan cries out.

I put a hand over her mouth as I pull out and thrust back in. "Shhh!" My eyes hold hers. I see the plea in them, dark and needy. She wants more.

Removing my hand, I take her hips, holding her steady while my own drive hard and deep. The washing machine begins to bang against the wall from the force of each thrust, but I can't stop. Grunts leave my throat.

"Brody!"

Jordan's close. Her body's trembling and her lungs are gasping for air. "Let go."

She does, and her inner walls clench so tight, I come with a surprised shout. My hips still, and with my face buried in her neck, my cock pulses its release inside her body. Drawing back, I rest my forehead against hers and cup her face in my palms, our harsh breaths mingling. "I love you. So much."

Jordan tilts her head and brushes her lips against mine. "I love you too."

After we both take a few moments to catch our breath, she slides off the machine on shaky legs while I pull up my shorts. Stumbling on her heels, I catch her before she tips over. "Whoa!"

Jordan giggles as she twitches her dress into place, her smooth hair in a tangle and cheeks flushed. "Eddie's going to know what we were doing."

"No he won't," I lie and open the door into the kitchen.

Eddie's head is buried in the fridge. Pulling out a beer, he slams the door shut and twists off the top, flicking it in the sink as we both step out. "You know I can never do laundry in there again now."

Jordan clears her throat, brushing hair from her face. "I have no idea what you're talking about."

Eddie laughs. "Sure you don't."

With head held high, she leaves the kitchen and heads upstairs.

After taking a pull of his beer, Eddie looks at me, suspicion narrowing his eyes. "You've had sex in every room in this house, haven't you?"

My answer is a grin. Swiping the beer from his hand, I follow Jordan.

"Dude!" he yells after me. "That's not sanitary!"

I find Jordan. She's in our bathroom. Her panties are kicked off and rest on the floor. Her legs are spread slightly, and she has a washcloth stuck between her thighs. Perhaps I'm oddly perverted, but the sight has my cock twitching hungrily.

Jordan glances up at my entrance, cheeks heating. "You made a mess."

I shrug and grin. "All in day's work."

"Brody!"

The washcloth flies across the room, slapping me in the neck. I laugh. Peeling it away, I rinse it off under warm water and come at her. "Let me help."

Jordan holds up a hand, warding me off. "Don't touch me. You can't be trusted."

"I won't do anything other than wipe you clean."

Her nostrils flare warily. "I don't believe you."

I make a quick sign of the cross over my heart, my lips fighting an impish grin. "I promise I won't stick my penis in your vagina."

"Oh my god," Jordan moans, exasperated.

I laugh again. "Here." I hand over the warm bit of towel and sit myself down on the closed seat of the toilet. Leaning back, I fold my arms to watch.

She folds her arms in response, creating a little standoff. "You're going to watch?"

"Are you kidding? I'm a twenty-two year old male with a cock for a brain and you're my wife. Hell yes, I'm watching."

"Brody!"

"Fine." I close my eyes. "Earlier you said you wanted to talk, so let's talk."

Silence follows. I crack an eyelid open. Jordan is staring at me, mute and apprehensive. It sets me on edge. All the levity in the room flees, leaving nothing but a thumping pulse in its place. "Jordan, what is it?"

Setting the washcloth on the edge of the basin, she twitches her dress into place. Facing me, a hesitant smile forms on her lips. "I've been selected to the Australian national team roster to play in the FIFA World Cup."

Pride has the breath catching in my throat. "Holy shit." Unfolding my arms, I rise to my feet. "This is incredible."

Jordan frowns. "I know."

"Be excited, babe." I grasp her by the elbows. "This is the best thing that could've happened. It's what you've worked for."

She pulls free of my grip. Picking up her discarded panties from the floor, she tosses them in the hamper, all the while saying, "I'm not sure it's what I want anymore."

I stand rigid, confused, watching her fuss around the bathroom, straightening towels, moving hand soap until it sits just so, basically doing anything but look at me. The heavy weight of realization lands on my chest. My hands clench at my sides and my eyes burn. It takes everything I have not to smash my fist in the wall. Why can't I ever catch a damn break?

"When do you leave for Australia?"

Jordan pauses her tidying of the sink and her eyes lift to mine. "Five days."

"And how long will you be gone?" Tension fills the bathroom, swift and silent. "Jordan?"

Her chest lifts and falls with a deep breath. "Five months."

Pain clutches at my heart. It's so long. And so far. But I told Jordan I'd never hold her back. I'm not going to start now. She needs to go into this with the knowledge I'm backing her a hundred and ten percent, not with the fear that distance will destroy everything we've built together. I lock all the hurt away inside and take her cold hand in mine. Threading our fingers together, I pull her toward me.

Her head tips back, anxiety darkening her eyes. "You can do this, Jordan. I have so much faith in you."

I'm given the briefest expression of hope before her gaze sweeps down, focusing on our linked hands between us. "There's one more thing."

"Jordan …" That's all I've got. I'm not sure if I can take another emotional hit tonight.

Her lower lip wobbles. "I don't want you at my finals."

"What? No! That's—"

She shakes her head. "You've got some spare time. You need to use it to go see Annabelle."

"Baby—"

I can't get a word in. "She's going to hear, Brody. She'll *hear* about our marriage. You need to find a way to see your sister. This rift needs healing. Now is the time to do it. If you leave it any longer, it might just be too late."

BRODY

There's no nostalgia as I pull in the drive of my parents' house two days later. Instead my skin crawls and my stomach resembles a large ball of lead. I rest my forearm on the curve of the steering wheel, my fingers tapping an anxious rhythm as I stare up at the pretentious hunk of rendered brick.

Jaxon turns his head in the passenger seat. "We going to sit here all day?"

"Maybe." I swipe a hand over my face, feeling slightly punch-drunk. I drove to Jaxon's house late last night and crashed with the help of some Ambien. The sleep didn't recharge my batteries. It was more of a fitful doze thanks to my fractured rib. I look at my cousin. "You don't have to be here."

"And miss a confrontation with your father?" He leans forward, shaking his head as he tucks his phone in the back pocket of his jeans. "Not a chance."

"I'm not here for a confrontation." That's the honest truth, but I've no doubt it's inevitable anyway.

Jax echoes the sentiment with a snort. "This is your father we're talking about." He runs fingers through his hair, grabbing at random tufts before letting his arm drop to his side. "He's a fucking douche canoe."

After drawing the keys from the ignition, my eyes catch the subject of our conversation emerging from the front door. My father's face is mottled, the anger vibrating from his big frame almost tangible. The lead ball in my stomach grows. "You're not wrong."

"Shit." My cousin's face darkens. "You owe me double for this."

Grasping the door handle, I pause to look at him, my expression incredulous, especially considering he invited himself along for the ride. "Double?"

"Yes, double. There's the small matter of you and Jordan getting married and not telling anyone," he mutters, reaching for his own door handle. "Not to mention I've had chick magazines hounding me for details of the happy nuptials."

A strangled laugh dies in my throat. "Sorry about that."

"You can be sorry about it later by fixing me up with Cherry."

"Cherry the cheerleader?"

He nods his confirmation. "One and the same."

"Done."

It's just that easy. It makes me glad to be male. The price of having a vagina meant Jordan's phone call to Leah took two hours minimum. And even now nothing is resolved. There's some kind of appeasement process Jordan seems duty-bound to follow before ruffled feathers can be smoothed. Talks of her planning a wedding celebration were made. There was mention of dresses, tent hire, caterers, and musicians. The only time I willingly stepped into the conversation was to make it clear that if we went ahead with this, it was for Jordan, not Leah, and whatever Jordan wanted, she was to have. It only set off more excited chatter, at which point I tuned out entirely.

I push all thoughts of the conversation aside and open the car door, stepping out. Fresh morning air drifts over me, ruffling my hair. But it's not the cool breeze that chills my skin, it's the level of detachment my father emanates. He's stopped in front of my car, arms folded and eyes devoid of emotion.

"What are you doing here, Brody?"

Lifting my chin, I shut the door, pocket my car keys, and start toward him, showing nothing but determination. From the corner of my eye, I see Jax follow. He stands a step back on my right like a sentinel flanking his commander. I'm grateful for his support, a silent reminder that I *do* have family at my back. "You know why I'm here. I just want to see Annabelle."

"She doesn't want to see you."

A lawn mower powers to life, the noisy rumble reverberating from across the road. I turn my head. Old man Lewis is out trimming his lawn. It's not something I've ever known him to do this early on a weekday. As if feeling my stare, he looks up and meets my eyes. They shift to my father, narrowing slightly, before returning focus to the task in front of him. I turn back. "We both know that's not true."

"Oh, but it is. You're living a whole new life in Houston. Football. Parties. An impulsive marriage to that … girl." He speaks the word with distaste. "Annabelle believes you abandoned her."

"I didn't abandon her!" My teeth clench together in an effort to leash my rising temper. *Don't let him bait you like he always does.* "You won't let me see her."

A hint of satisfaction creeps into my father's eyes. "She doesn't know that."

"You're an asshole! Why are you doing this? It's not just because I punched another student who had it coming. And it's not even about the drugs." I step forward and his hands fist reflexively. "You just used it as an excuse to push me out. I've never been good enough. Never smart enough. Never just *enough*," I shout with force. "I pushed myself every day, hoping one day I would be. And I'm almost there, right on the cusp of being fucking great at something and…" My words wither away, something inside me giving up as I stare into his stony eyes. It's like a light winking out for the very last time, leaving my heart to finally accept what my mind has known all along. "You don't care."

My father's lips pinch. "You're right." Jaxon sucks in a sharp breath. "I don't care. No one *cares*. You keep coming here causing scenes." His voice rises. "Demanding attention." Dad takes a step forward, ire building. "Making everything about you when it's not," he hisses. Planting both hands on my chest, he fists my shirt and shoves, pushing me back a step. "Well it's not about you, and I don't want you here."

"This is about Annabelle, and you keeping me from her." I yank free, my shirt twisted. "She needs her brother."

Anger sparks in my father's eyes. "You're not her brother anymore!"

"What the hell are you talking about?" Jaxon asks.

"Screw this," I mutter and start for the house, calling out, "Annabelle!"

Dad blocks me, a veritable wall of rage. Spittle hits my face when he snarls at me to shut my goddamn mouth.

"Move," I growl, "or I will fucking end you."

He keeps his feet planted on the drive, heedless of my threat. Shoving past him, I start for the door. He grabs my arm and I half turn, my fist pulling back reflexively. With a sharp jab, I punch him square in the nose. Bones crunch and pain blooms across my knuckles.

My father cries out. Letting me go, he covers his nose with both hands, blood spilling out beneath them. I didn't want this—the inevitable confrontation and violence. Why does he push, and push, and fucking push? "Why?"

Jax grabs my bicep, trying to pull me away. I shrug him off, all the hurt I pushed deep now bubbling to the surface.

"Why don't you care?" I shout as Dad wipes at his bloodied face.

"Because you're not my son!" he roars.

Utter silence reigns for a single, heartrending moment. The air gusting between us stills. My voice lowers to a whisper. "What did you say?"

"You heard me."

"Holy fuck," Jaxon breathes, his feet frozen in place. "You can't be serious."

But he is. I know he is because it makes sense. Of course it wouldn't matter what I did or how hard I tried. Why would it if I wasn't his son? There's no feat on Earth I could perform that would change something like that. "You're not my real father."

I say it more as a statement than a question, the words sounding foreign to my ears, as if someone else spoke them.

"No," he reiterates. "I'm not."

A feeling of emptiness steals over me—swift and consuming. I should feel something shouldn't I? Even just relief that I don't share the same blood that runs through his veins. But I've been sucked inside a void where it's dark and cold, and ironically it's a place more painful than anything I've ever experienced. My feet carry me forward a step. Jax puts a cautionary hand on my forearm, worried at what I'll do. But even I don't know what I'll do. Everything I thought I knew is all wrong.

"Mom. Is she …" The question lodges in my throat.

Dad wipes the back of his hand under his nose, smearing a trickle of blood. "You're hers."

"I don't understand."

"By all means, let me explain in terms you can understand." His upper lip curls with condescension. "Six months after we married, your mother went on a night out to celebrate a friend's work promotion. She didn't come home until mid-morning the next day claiming her drink was spiked. Nine months later there you were," he spits out bitterly.

I stand stoic as he speaks, unresponsive, even as his words tear into my skin. *I'm the product of assault.* No wonder I'm unwanted. I'm a reminder of something ugly and sickening. The spawn of a monster. Does that make me one too?

My voice is a whisper. "Why didn't you just get rid of me?"

His anger flares like a lit match. "It was too late! You were already there and they wouldn't abort you. And once the media found out your mother was pregnant we were stuck. We couldn't even give you away." My father comes at me, hopeless rage twisting his face.

"Liam!" My mother steps out of the house, her face ashen beneath the flawless layer of makeup. I look between them, now able to see my parents with true clarity. They both wear a picture-perfect veneer to hide a fracture so deep it won't ever heal. "Please. Stop!"

Dad keeps talking, too caught up to even hear her. "You wouldn't die like I wanted you to. Instead you thrived. A fucking virus I knew would never go away!"

My shirt is grabbed and he heaves, snarling, and shoves me backwards, slamming me hard against the passenger side door of the car. I hear my mother cry out as air leaves my lungs in a rush.

"We never wanted you," he gasps, his eyes so rabid I know he's lost touch with reality.

Jaxon seizes Dad's arms, his face white with shock. Mom cries my name, her voice desperate, begging me to do something. I'm not sure what she wants me to do. The most she's ever expected of me is to just leave, so that's what I'm going to do. I push an elbow between my father and myself, using it as a bracket so I can dig the keys from my pocket.

I'm halfway there when Dad wrestles free of Jaxon and launches himself at me. His fist smashes in my face. My head snaps back, hitting the rounded metal of the car where the roof meets the door. There's no time to recover before an uppercut gets me in the ribs. There's a powerhouse of muscle behind the punch and something crunches beneath it. A bone. Pain erupts. The intensity is like a starburst, brilliant and fiery.

But he's not done. He comes at me again, and again. I can hear Jaxon shouting. I feel like I should do something. Defend myself. But all I can hear is the words *we never wanted you*. They batter my head like a broken record. *You wouldn't die.*

Suddenly my father is gone. I stumble forward, dizzy and trying to catch my breath. Jaxon has him in an armlock. They grapple, and my cousin gets a hard elbow to the ribs. He grunts and lets go. Before I can blink I'm on the ground and a fist is coming at my face.

"Goddammit, you'll kill him!" Jaxon yells. He's trying to pull my father off me.

"No," I rasp. Let him do his worst. Lance the poison and maybe then it'll be enough. His large hands wrap around my neck and squeeze. It's a vice, making my eyes water. My air is cut off instantly. I react instinctively, clawing his fingers, my body panicked.

The sound of a gun being cocked hits my ears. "Get off of him. Now."

Hands release from my neck swiftly. Air floods my lungs, fast and sweet. I suck it in with hoarse gasps.

My eyes lift, landing on old man Lewis. Both his arms are outstretched, the gun in his hands steady as he presses it to my father's temple. "You okay, boy?" he asks without taking his eyes from his target.

I can't answer the question because I don't know.

"Get that gun out of my face," my father growls. He's frozen beneath it, sweat trickling down the side of his face.

Lewis draws it back slightly, and Dad slowly shifts away and stands.

"Jesus. Brody," Jax breathes in a shaky voice, sinking to his knees beside me. His hands hover above me, unsure which part is safe to touch.

I don't spare him a glance. My stomach's knotted with pain. I roll to my side and throw up on the front lawn. Even that simple action leaves me dizzy.

"Lay another hand on that boy," Lewis growls, forcing my father to back away, "and it'll be the last thing you ever do."

"Are you threatening me?"

"I sure as hell am."

Well, what do you know? Old man Lewis has a heart after all. "Call an ambulance," he orders Jaxon.

"No." Adrenaline pushes me to my feet. Jaxon reaches for me. I hold out an arm in warning, staggering as I back away. "Don't fucking touch me."

Passing by Lewis on unsteady legs, I give him that casual salute that I always do.

Jaxon drives us back to his apartment because I refuse a hospital, but I don't remember much beyond that point. I know he must have left me alone at some stage because I called Damien. I know I called Damien because I'm sitting on the tiled floor of the shower, an empty bottle of Percocet gripped in my hand. The water gushing from above is ice cold. It's catching me in the back of my bowed head. I blink away the water in my eyes, not noticing how they sting. My clothes are soaked, but I can't bring myself to care.

Taking a handful of Percocet gives a high like heroin so I'd chewed a large handful down to make them work faster. Today I need to feel good. Just once. But I don't. Why isn't it working? My heart is racing so hard I'm sure it's going to punch its way out of my chest, yet I'm just as empty as I was before. Maybe I need to lie down. My fingernails dig into the grout of the tiles, the only leverage I have to pull myself upright. I stagger my way to the guest room, skidding against the walls, using them to prop me up when I feel myself falling.

Slumping down on the bed, I reach for my bag and some pills. I down a couple to help me sleep. Maybe they'll stop my heart from galloping because it's beginning to hurt. Falling back on the pillow, I close my eyes but oblivion doesn't come. My arm trembles as I stretch it out toward my phone. I fumble and it drops to the floor.

"Fuck." Rolling on my side, I grab for it. It takes several attempts before I get it in my hand. Slumping back on my pillow, I dial Jordan. It starts to ring and I exhale deeply. Her soothing voice will fix everything.

"Hi. You've reached Jordan Madden." I'm frustrated at getting her voicemail, but there's a small measure of warmth hearing her message has changed to include her married name. It's something small, really, but it feels huge. Jordan is all I have now, but for how long? She keeps slipping through my fingers. I'm doing everything I can to hold on, but the fight is too much. *It's too much.* A sob rises up from deep in my chest. For the first time I can't hold it in. It rips out of me, the sound loud and broken. I fist a hand in my hair as another follows. God, there's so much pain inside it's killing me. "I'm sorry I can't answer the phone right now. Leave your name and number and I'll call you back."

A long beep follows. "Baby?" Christ I'm so fucked-up. I use my forearm to wipe the tears but it feels too heavy to move, so I just leave it there, resting across my eyes. "Sorry, I just …" The words don't come out sounding right, like my tongue is too big for my mouth. I end the call and throw the phone away, remembering she has soccer finals. She doesn't need my shit right now. Maybe not ever.

As I lie there my body begins to tremble violently and sleep still proves elusive. Did I take the Ambien? Why can't I remember? Dragging myself from the bed, I dig for the bottle in my bag. Finding it, I rise, using the wall to prop me up as I empty a pile of pills in my hand. I swallow them down. My mouth is dry and they stick in my throat. I work them down and peace comes soon after. It's a loving blanket that wraps itself around me, cocooning me in its warmth. My head tips back and my eyes close. A voice from deep inside screams at me as I slide down the bedroom wall. It has fists that bang against my chest, fingers that claw desperately, and sobs that are so deep and wounded they would break my heart if it wasn't already broken.

I ignore it as the empty bottle falls from my hand, dropping harmlessly to the carpet beside my slumped body. In a brief moment of piercing clarity, I feel my last breath coming. The pain of leaving Jordan is like a sharp knife slicing through my skin, but I can't stay. It's so beautiful where I am. So calm and peaceful. I don't have to fight here. I don't have to prove myself. Here I'm not the son my father never wanted, the brother that's never there, or the rising football star I don't deserve to be. Here, I'm not anything, and nothing has ever felt more right.

CHAPTER 36

JORDAN

14 hours earlier...

Our soccer semifinal is just half an hour away and the locker room is crowded. My stomach rolls and my hands shake. Nerves get me every game. As soon as kick off comes I'll be fine, but those final minutes beforehand wreck me completely.

Sitting down on the bench, I lean over and adjust the laces on my cleats. They're new, and a little longer than what I'm used to. After tying a double knot, I grab some black tape and wind it around each boot, strapping the cords in place. As I straighten, a pang of loneliness robs me of breath. I wish I hadn't sent Brody to see Annabelle. It was the right thing to do, but I miss him. *I miss my husband.*

My phone rings from inside my locker cupboard as I stand. My heart leaps. Brody always rings me right before a game. Flipping open the door, I take it out. It's Nicky. My heart rate slows to normal pace. "Hey," I answer.

"Jordan," he replies. There's an edge in his voice now. It's been there since the news of mine and Brody's marriage broke.

Brody said he would talk to my brother for me, and as much as I wanted him to take one for the team, it wouldn't have been right. So I returned Nicky's call later that night, my apology sounding lame and trite. My brother was deeply hurt, unable to comprehend my need to break free and do something fun and reckless.

How could I explain it to him? How could I explain the way Brody looked at me when he said 'I do' in the tiny little registry office? His eyes were dark and loving, almost fierce as he promised to cherish me forever. It was intense and romantic. For a single moment in time we were wild and free, the only two people in existence. After the clerk announced Brody could kiss the bride, his lips on mine were deliciously warm.

A smile pulled at the corners of his mouth when he drew back and whispered the words, "No regrets, okay?"

There would be no regrets. My love for him surpassed all reason and common sense. "None."

Brody nodded, satisfied. "From now on, it's just you and me."

After speaking our vows, we went to a nearby bar. It was packed, the crowd rowdy. We pushed into the thick of it and tossed back beer after beer until we couldn't see straight. We drank and laughed until the early hours of the morning. When the band began to play a cover of U2's "All I Want is You," Brody whooped, declared it our wedding song, and hauled me out onto the dance floor. I remember the click of my heels on the thick wooden floors and tipping my head back, looking at the beautiful fairy lights that covered the ceiling as Brody spun me around, laughing and drunk. It was crazy beautiful. He made my wedding night perfect.

Tears well up from the overload of emotion. I blink them back and sit down on the bench behind me. Holding my head in my hand, I close my eyes, returning to the present and Nicky's phone call.

"I just wanted to wish you luck," he says. "So … good luck."

My voice drops to a whisper, not knowing what to say. "Nicky …"

"Don't." He lets out a sharp breath. "Focus on your game."

I don't tell him the game doesn't mean to me what it used to. It's not everything anymore. "I'll see you at home in a few days," he says.

Australia isn't home anymore, but I don't tell him that either. My brother has already been punched in the gut. I don't need to kick him while he's down. "See you then."

He hangs up and I join the gathering huddle for our pregame pep talk. Our head coach gains our attention with a shout and a clap of his hands. Silence descends. Pausing, he scans our faces.

"Do you know why you're here? What you're busting your ass out on that field for?" Coach doesn't wait for an answer. He stares at each of us in turn with a hard glare in his eye. "That's what you need to remember today, because this game is already over for you if you're not out there for the right reasons. You know you're the best team. You know this game belongs to you. It belongs to your teammate beside you. It belongs to everyone who helped get you here today. To every person you love who puts up with never seeing you. To every fan who looks up to you." He draws in a deep breath of pride, his nostrils flaring and his finger jabbing to emphasize his words. "When you leave that field at the end of the game, win or lose, be sure you did everything you could and gave everything you had, because if you didn't, you've let down everyone and everything this game belongs to." His arm rises high. "Now get the hell out there, bust your ass, and prove just how good you are!" Our coach raises his voice and it echoes around each and every one of us. "Prove that you're better than even *you* thought you could be!"

It's a rousing speech. One that makes me pause. I *do* know why I'm here. For the love of the game. That's all it comes down to. But my love for Brody is stronger than even this. It's for him I'll do everything I can, and give everything I have. He's the reason why I signed a new contract with Houston Dash this morning. When I'm done with my FIFA tour, I'll be heading home. It makes my heart sing.

Unzipping my jacket, I shove it in my locker and turn to follow the team just as my phone rings again. *Shit.* I glance around the emptying room. The hell with it. I palm the ringing device in a furtive maneuver and hit answer, whispering, "I literally have five seconds."

"Then why are you answering your phone?" Brody asks, amused.

"Because I love you and I miss you, and I'm a selfish bitch because I'm wishing I didn't tell you to go to Austin. I want you here."

He laughs in the face of my misery. "You just want a fuck to pound all those pre-game nerves from your system."

My face flames because he knows how hard I like it just before a match. It loosens tense muscles and clears my head. "You know me so well."

His voice softens. "I do."

Eddie shouts something at the television in the background. My brows pull together. "I thought you'd be in Austin by now."

"No, we're heading out for pizza with some of the guys from the team. I'll leave from there."

"You'll be too tired to leave from there. You should go now."

As if on cue, he lets out a loud yawn. "I know, but I want to catch your game on the TV. If I'm driving I'll miss it."

"Jordan!"

"Shit," I mumble into the phone. "That's my coach."

"Go!" Brody booms. "Kick a goal for me."

"Bye," I whisper. Ending the call, I lose the phone and race out on the field with minutes to spare.

Just like he asked, I kick a goal for Brody. When it's done, I press my index and middle finger to my lips and then hold them up high so he knows it's for him.

Despite giving our hearts to the game, we lose. It doesn't just sting either, it burns like a raging bonfire. My first season in a professional league has ended in heartache.

Brody rings me later that night. I'm stretched out in bed, declining consolatory team drinks. With no grand final ahead of us, I have a window of opportunity. I plan to use it wisely by flying to Austin in the morning to surprise Brody, and I want to get a good night's rest.

"Did I wake you?" he whispers.

I stare up at the ceiling, wide awake. "No."

"I'm sorry."

Disappointment wells. "You can't win them all."

"Don't give that bullshit line." He's right. It's a standard one we all use to death and means nothing. "Tell me how you really feel."

"I feel like a failure." My eyes burn. "I gave it everything, Brody. I did the best I could, but it wasn't enough. What if this is it? What if this is the best I'll ever do?"

Verbalizing the fear doesn't make it disappear. It makes it real, and it makes me shake. When you work your whole life toward one true goal, the last thing you want to believe is that you'll never reach it.

"Don't ever think that or you'll choke," his deep voice rumbles through the phone. "You'll stop trying. You won't push yourself that little bit harder, and you'll turn your fear into reality. Besides," he adds. "You've been selected to play for Australia in the World Cup. Does it get better than that?"

"Yes," I reply stubbornly. "By winning it."

He laughs and there's a wealth of affection in the sound. "That's my girl."

"Brody …"

I open my mouth to tell him about signing with the new soccer team but change my mind. I'll tell him in Austin tomorrow. I want to see the look on his face when he hears the news.

"Mmm?"

"I hope you sort something out with your parents tomorrow. I know your dad is a total asshole, but you and Annabelle were close. It's not right for him to keep you from seeing her."

I feel his tension ignite from thousands of miles away. "I hope so too. I don't know what else I can do."

The rattle of a pill bottle reaches my ears. My stomach clenches. "That's not—"

He cuts me off, annoyed. "No. It's an anti-inflammatory. My body's sore as fuck."

"I'm sorry. It's just … I worry, Brody." Painkillers are a way of life for athletes, but where is the line between necessity and addiction drawn? For Brody it's already so blurred. "You promised me you'd stop taking all those pills. You have, haven't you?" My hand tightens on the phone. I hate that I have to ask him, that I don't trust him when it comes to taking medication, but I don't know what else to do.

"I don't take anything that doesn't come from the team physician's office."

Brody's response should placate me—the Wranglers team doctor wouldn't hand out anything they shouldn't be taking, or supply medications in dangerous doses—but it doesn't.

When I don't respond, he adds, "I'm not in the mood for an argument. I'm fucking tired."

"I'm not arguing with you. I just—"

"Good."

I huff. "Dammit, Brody."

After a long pause, he says, "Goodnight, Jordan."

His voice is curt. Ending a phone call with hateful words is unbearable, but there's no talking to him when he's like this.

I sigh. "I'll talk to you tomorrow."

"Sure," is all he says before ending the call, leaving my stomach in bigger knots than before he rang.

My sleep that night is fitful, and I'm grateful for the early morning flight to Austin. My goodbyes were said yesterday and my suitcase is packed. The majority of my Seattle possessions were shipped back home to Houston a week ago. My plan is to spend two days with Brody in Austin and fly out to Australia from there.

Arriving at the airport, my phone vibrates a message as I'm checking in.

BigBananaBoy: *When does ur flight get in?*

Jordan: *Midday. Why?*

BigBananaBoy: *I'll pick u up.*

The man at the counter offers a practiced smile and hands over my ticket. "Have a good flight, Mrs. Madden."

The use of my married name gives me such a thrill. I smile at him. "Thank you."

Walking toward the coffee stand, a small carry-on over my shoulder, I type a reply.

Jordan: *You don't have to. I can get a cab.*

BigBananaBoy: *I want to talk to you about something.*

That sounds ominous. After ordering a skinny chai latte, I hand money to the cashier and step aside to wait.

Jordan: *As long as it's nothing to do with your banana, then ok.*

BigBananaBoy: *You had ur chance at my banana. You blew it. And not in a sexy funtimes way :P*

I give him my standard response, rolling my eyes.

Jordan: *I was washing my hair.*

BigBananaBoy: *And you've never lived it down since, have u?*

Not from Leah *or* Paige. And enough with the banana talk.

Jordan: *Have you spoken to Brody this morning?*

BigBananaBoy: *The grumblebum is awake and angry, and he's busy letting me know just how much.*

Jordan: *Go easy. He has to deal with his asshole father today.*

The barista calls my name. I grab my cup and venture toward the departures board. My head tips back as my eyes roll down the list, searching out Austin. With a single blink, every departure time listed changes. I groan. Those closest duplicate the sound. Heavy morning fog has delayed every flight on the board.

Sipping my latte, I text Jax the bad news.

Jordan: *Flight delayed an hour. Shoot me now.*

BigBananaBoy: *Sucks to be you.*

Jordan: *Hey you didn't tell Brody I'm coming did you?*

BigBananaBoy: *You are? Take a photo. I want to see your sex face.*

Jordan: *You live in the gutter.*

BigBananaBoy: *You should visit me down here. It's filthy fun.*

Jordan: *You can have your gutter. I'm married to the newly crowned Hottest Rookie in the NFL.*

BigBananaBoy: *No fucking way!*

Yes way, because I'm staring at the magazine cover right now from the newsstand, my mouth open in shock. Brody is on it, looking like I've never seen him before. Tight black and burnt orange uniform, tanned skin, black stripes under his eyes, and a fierce glower that razes you on the spot. The photo is sexy as fuck. *That's my husband.* Pride hits me, along with the urge to snap up every copy in existence. I don't want that fierce glower aimed at anyone but me.

I have to settle for purchasing just two copies—one to keep nice and the other to read on the plane—otherwise I wouldn't fit them all in my carry-on. I go find a seat and settle in, and eventually my flight is called. Dumping my empty latte in the bin, I shoulder my bag and line up at the gate, sending Jaxon a quick message before switching off my phone.

Jordan: *Boarding now. See you on the flip side.*

But I don't see him. When I reach the arrivals zone Jaxon isn't there. Twenty minutes later and no answer from his phone, I head for the taxi zone, wheeling my suitcase behind me.

My phone rings just as the driver is stowing my suitcase. In my haste I fumble the damn thing and it drops in the gutter. My thigh muscles scream with exhaustion as I crouch low to pick it up, just missing a call from Brody. "Crap," I mutter.

Sliding in the back of the car, I get a beep from voicemail.

"Where to, ma'am?"

Providing the driver with the address of Jaxon's apartment, I hit play on the message and put the phone to my ear as we pull out of the airport. Brody's voice filters through. It's slurred and garbled, making no sense.

My chest begins to pound, my fingers shaky as I press the button to replay it. But there's no technical glitch. The message comes through again, exactly the same.

A cold sweat breaks out across my body. Not caring about surprising Brody anymore, I try calling but he doesn't answer. I try Jaxon again. No answer. Something's wrong. Very wrong. And it chills my blood. I glance up, scanning the surroundings to see how far away we are. Too far. We've barely cleared the airport.

"Please hurry," I tell the driver, my heart pounding with a fear I can't rationalize. I pocket my phone, keeping it close.

Twenty minutes later, we turn down Jaxon's street. An ambulance is double-parked in front of his apartment block, lights flashing. I want to throw up. "No, no no, no, no," I chant rapidly, my voice rising with each syllable that leaves my mouth.

"Ma'am?" the driver asks, glancing at me in the rear view mirror.

Paramedics are wheeling a gurney from the building, their pace brisk. I'm not close enough to see who it is, but my gut knows, and Jaxon confirms it by following them out moments later.

"Brody," I cry softly, grabbing for the door handle on the still moving vehicle. "Stop the car!" I scream shrilly.

He screeches to a halt, but I already have the door open. When my feet hit the ground I'm running, frantic.

"Hey, lady!" the driver yells after me, his head out the window and honking his horn. I haven't paid my fare and my luggage is still in the boot of the car. I don't hear or see him. My focus is on the gurney the paramedics are wheeling toward their ambulance.

"Jaxon!" I cry out.

He turns, his face ravaged and wild with panic.

Oh god, this is not happening.

It feels like it takes me forever to reach them, my body running through quicksand. People nearby have stopped in their tracks, watching the scene unfold before their eyes. I push through them, not even noticing when someone I knock stumbles to the side.

"What happened?" I ask breathless, jogging with the gurney as I look down at Brody. He's unconscious. A tube is jammed through a cut in his throat, blood smeared down along the incision. His neck is mottled with red and purple, his lip split, and eye swelling closed. He's a bruised mess.

The paramedics remain tightlipped.

"Please!" I shout, desperate. "I'm his wife!" I turn to Jaxon as they wheel him inside the waiting vehicle.

"I shouldn't have left him alone," Jax cries. He fists hands in his hair, tears rolling down his face. "Oh god, Jordan. I can't ..."

"Someone fucking talk to me!" I scream, frustrated and frightened. My body is shaking and my lungs have no air. I've never been so scared in all my life. Brody's body begins seizing violently. A sob breaks from my chest seeing him so broken and vulnerable.

"Ma'am," the paramedic says to me after leaping in the back of the ambulance. "Get in."

He doesn't need to tell me twice. I spring into action, jumping inside the back. The doors slam closed behind me. Moments later, the ambulance screams to life, rocking as we push our way into traffic, sirens piercing the air.

"Please," I beg again, watching the paramedic turn Brody to the side while his body suffers through the convulsions.

"What's your name?" he asks.

"Jordan."

"I'm Rafe," he replies, but I don't want ridiculous introductions. I want answers. "Jordan, your husband overdosed."

I suck in a sharp breath, watching frozen as he returns Brody to his back. There's a needle already set up in his inner elbow. Rafe hooks it to an IV with fast, efficient movements.

"No," I choke out. "You must be wrong. He wouldn't do that."

Rafe shakes his head as he hooks Brody up to machines. The sound of a pulse flickers to life inside the ambulance. It's faint and erratic. "A mix of painkillers and sleeping pills."

Oh god, Brody, why? Tears spill over and my heart breaks right down the middle as I look down at his face. "I can't lose him," I say through a sob.

"We'll do everything we can," Rafe reassures.

I hear the conviction in his voice as he checks Brody's vitals, but I'm not reassured because his eyes tell a different story. They're saying he's seen it all before. Brody is just another statistic. Another young life lost before it's barely begun.

My hands fist, fighting the urge to scream and rage my denial. There's still hope. Pushing my way in beside the paramedic, I sink to my knees beside Brody.

"Get back," Rafe orders.

I ignore him. Wiping tears from my face, I lean close and brush damp hair off Brody's forehead with gentle fingers. "I won't leave you," I croon into his ear, praying that somewhere deep down he can hear me, and that he can feel me at his side. "I promise. Not ever."

Moments later, the unthinkable happens. Brody flatlines and I lose my fucking mind.

CHAPTER 37

JORDAN

I'm hunched on the floor in the corner of the ER waiting room, my back pressed to the wall. My legs are too weak to move. I can't even bring myself to stand.

Tipping my head back against the wall, I close my eyes. I don't want to open them again. I don't want to see the world anymore without Brody in it.

Why? Why did you do this to yourself? To us?

But I know why. Deep down *I know*, my mind falling back to the day Brody showed me the tattoo on his chest.

"You fly too?" I'd asked after reading the pretty cursive script inked out across tanned muscle.

"Out there on the field, the game is everything," he told me. *"It builds you up, breaks you down, and it bleeds you dry. But I love it. It's the only place I'm free."*

I cover my mouth with my hand, my heart screaming with pain. *Is this what you wanted, Brody? To leave us all behind and be free?*

Desperate to touch him, I'd covered that tattoo with the flat of my palm. His skin was warm, his heart beating powerfully beneath it. *"You believe in God?"*

"Of course." He leaned in then, his eyes dark and honest, laying his soul bare for me to see. I'd known it right then, that Brody would have my heart, and that he would break it. Yet I gave it to him anyway. The revelation had left me trembling. *"I need to believe in something."*

"Then believe in yourself."

"You can't say shit like that."

I'd pulled back in a last ditch effort to shore up the walls that were crumbling between us, a pitiful attempt to stave off eventual heartache. *"Why can't I say stuff like that?"*

"Because I'll only let myself down."

That right there is why. He never believed. Not once. And god it hurts to know the man I love with everything I have never had faith in himself the same way he had faith in me. It rips a giant gaping hole in my chest.

The ER automatic doors whoosh open and Jaxon rushes in, dragging me back to reality. His eyes are red and frantic as they scan the waiting room. I realize that I left him there on the road. Jax is Brody's cousin and I just pushed my way in without a second thought, leaving him to find his own way here. I didn't think. I just reacted, seeing no one or nothing but Brody.

Jaxon's gaze lights on me and he doesn't pause. He heads straight for me. I suck air into my lungs when I realize I'm sitting here not breathing, a huddled messy ball on the floor of the ER.

His voice cracks. "Brody?"

I shake my head. Jax reaches out. Muscled arms wrap around my torso, lifting me with ease, they anchor me to his side as deep, jagged sobs tear from my chest. He squeezes me tight. "Tell me," he begs thickly.

Oh god.

"I wasn't there for him, Jax," I cry, dragging in deep, juddering breaths. Something happened at his father's house. A catalyst that left Brody desperate and in pain, and *alone*, and I wasn't *there*. "Brody ... he …"

My words die as my gaze falls to the ER doors over Jaxon's shoulder, the same ones a woman is walking through that I've only ever seen in photos. Seeing her in the flesh, the resemblance to Brody is clear—hair the color of rich caramel, dark brown eyes, tall. Behind her comes a man in a suit. Liam Madden. His father. His presence can only mean one thing. The media has gotten wind of what happened and they're outside.

My eyes narrow on the man who told Brody his life was for nothing, and then made him believe it with every fiber of his soul.

"You," I hiss. Rage builds until I see nothing but red. I launch myself at him, wild with rage and hate. I don't know what I plan to do except cause him pain the same way he did to Brody. Jaxon moves in, grabbing me around the waist and pulling me away.

"Jordan, stop!" he cries, panting with effort because anger has given me superhuman strength. But I can't stop. I'm lost in a world of hurt because Brody's dad is here pretending to *care* when he never has. It makes me livid.

"This is all your fault!" I shriek at him, trying to pull free. "None of this would've happened if it weren't for you, *you fucking asshole!*" My voice is shrill and I'm sobbing openly, not caring that the entire ER waiting room is silent and watching.

When Liam speaks, his voice is forceful and cold, shocking me like icy water dashed in my face. "I didn't force Brody to take drugs. He did that all on his own."

"You sonofabitch," Jaxon growls and lets me go.

Hands fisted, he starts for Liam, pulling up short when a little girl steps out from behind Brody's father. Pretty blonde curls halo her face and dark brown eyes stare right at me, wide with fear. A tear leaks out, trickling down a single, rosy pink cheek. "Jordan?"

She walks around her dad and straight up to me. She's a tiny little thing, yet the way Brody talks of her, she's an absolute hellion—full of fire and cheeky attitude. "Annabelle?"

My anger deflates and wiping my face with the backs of my fingers, I sink to my knees in front of her. It brings Brody's sister a little higher, causing her to look down at me. I open my mouth to speak but have no idea what to say.

"Is my brother okay?" she asks, her voice wobbling.

Jaxon holds his breath, both of them looking down at me. Brody's mother comes to stand behind Annabelle, placing her hands on her daughter's shoulders. I look up. Pale and distraught, Juliet Madden still radiates beauty, even now fighting back tears. Dismissing her completely, my eyes drop back to Annabelle.

"He's sleeping," is all I can say, my eyes filling again.

Her little chin lifts, but I see how much it costs her. There's so much strength inside this tiny little girl. "Is he going to wake up?"

My voice is like sandpaper as I force the words past my lips. "I don't know, sweetheart."

"Jesus, fuck," Jaxon mumbles and sinks to a chair, holding his head in his hands.

Annabelle slams her little body against me, her bony arms wrapping around my neck. I put a hand on the ground to steady myself before we both tip over on the floor. It shocks me. I never expected Brody's little sister to like me, or show affection, let alone grab for me in her grief. When I'm steady, I wrap one arm around her little waist and my free hand goes to the back of her head, brushing at the curls.

"I don't really hate him," she cries, her hot tears dripping on my skin. "I was just mad that he went away. Do you think if I could tell him that, he'd wake up?"

Shifting upwards, I slide into the seat beside Jaxon, bringing Annabelle with me. She holds on tight, and I realize her attachment stems from the need to be close to someone who loves her brother as much as she does. I know because I feel it too.

Jaxon takes her hand in his and bows his head toward me, our foreheads almost touching. "You don't need to tell him that," he says to Annabelle, "because he already knows you don't hate him."

"That's right," I say, rubbing my hand up and down her shoulder, forcing a calm I don't feel. She looks to me. "He'd never believe something so silly as all that."

"But he left."

Jaxon and I share a pained glance. "Annabelle …" I flick a glare toward Brody's father. He doesn't even notice. Juliet is hovering nearby, but he's taken a seat away from us, his phone pressed to his ear. My eyes return to Annabelle. "You have to believe me when I tell you that leaving you was not something he ever wanted to do."

She nods, unsure. "I still want to tell him I don't hate him. Just so he knows."

"Of course you can tell him," Jaxon says.

Juliet steps in. Taking her daughter's hand, she tugs her off my lap. Annabelle goes reluctantly. "Come on. Let's go get a coffee."

"But I don't drink coffee," she says as they walk away.

"No, but I do."

Annabelle glances behind her at both of us, her expression torn. Brody's little sister needs comfort, and I honestly don't know if that's something her parents are physically capable of providing.

Jaxon takes my hand when they disappear, his voice hollow when he asks, "A coma?"

I nod. "That's all I know. He … Brody died on the way here. He *died*," I choke out. Jaxon grabs me, gathering me up in his arms. This time it's for him and not me. He buries his face in my neck and my palm brushes the back of his head the same way I did for Annabelle. "They managed to revive him, but all the sleeping pills …" I trail off, shaking my head. "Jaxon, what happened? Please tell me."

Jaxon draws back, glancing in Liam's direction, but Brody's father has disappeared as well. In a rough voice he tells me the story, starting from the moment they got out of the car at Brody's parents' house, and finishing with when they left.

For a single moment we sit in silence, staring at each other. I'm angry for so many reasons I can't even count, so *fucking* angry it makes me shake. "It's my fault. I sent him there. He was coming to Seattle with me. He was going to watch my finals, and I told him no. I told him he should use his time off to try again. To see Annabelle."

"It's not," Jaxon protests. "It's mine. I took him back to my apartment and I left him there. I had to hand in an assignment. I wouldn't have bothered, but it was already overdue and Brody told me he was going to sleep. He was so calm. It was almost eerie." He wipes at his face, his head tipping back to stare at the ceiling. "Why are we blaming ourselves?"

"It's easier," I say with sorrow, my body drained.

He turns his head, looking at me. "Easier?"

"It's easier to blame ourselves for what happened, rather than believe he would do something like this to himself."

BRODY

I'm trapped beneath a thick sheet of ice and can't break my way through. I don't want to be here. The water surrounding me is cold and below me it extends into darkness, its depths infinite. There's no one else here. It's empty as far as my eyes can see.

Despite being stuck in this frozen hell, I can still hear everything above me—the beeps of machines and the sounds of people moving and talking around me, sometimes the birds, even the hot buzzing sound that sunshine seems to radiate. Jordan is up there. The sweet scent of vanilla is close. There's something warm in my hand. I realize it's anchoring me to the surface, not allowing me to sink down into the dark. Maybe it's her hand holding mine. I try to squeeze it, to reassure her I'm okay down here, but my body won't respond, and I don't know if I'm okay or not.

"Brody?"

A deep wave of warmth rolls through me. *I'm here.*

"I'm so sorry."

Her sadness filters through. *No! Don't be sorry. I did this.*

Something hot and heavy presses against my arm but I can't see what it is. I can only feel it. "Jaxon told me what happened. I should've been here with you."

I'm a big boy, Jordan. I don't need you to hold my hand through every crisis. Which is ironic really because she's up there right now, holding my hand.

"Why?" she whispers, her voice cracking. It makes me want to weep, but I can't even do that. "Why would you do this to yourself?"

I didn't know what I was doing, I tell her. It's unbearable for her to think I meant this. *Forgive me, Jordan. Please,* I beg. *It just got so hard. And it felt so good, just for once, to not be anything at all.*

"The doctors say it's up to you now, but if you don't want to be here, then … then … Dammit!" she cries. "I'm not going to tell you it's okay to go. It's not. You fight, Brody," she hisses. "You fucking fight and you don't stop fighting. I need you."

I'm fighting. I promise. My fists bang against the sheet of ice, frustration clawing at me. I'm more than a little scared. It's thick and holding fast. How will I ever get through?

Footsteps filter through above me, getting closer. A new voice speaks. It's Jaxon. "Any change?"

"No," Jordan tells him. "Nothing."

There's a pause and the rustle of paper. "What's that?" she asks.

"Trust me, you do *not* want to read this."

Jaxon sounds pissed.

"Yes. I do."

Jordan sounds even pissier.

You won't win, Jax.

I hear paper ripping, followed by more footsteps and Jaxon's sharp huff. There's silence. Whatever it is, Jordan's reading it. Then she speaks. "Drug Overdose. Rookie NFL star Brody Madden in coma."

It's a newspaper headline. *Fuck. Jax was right. Don't read it Jordan.*

"Oh god," she whispers. "They're tearing him apart."

They are? That hurts.

Don't read anymore.

"Not just him," Jaxon says, resigned.

Not just me?

"You too, Jordan. By association."

Fucking bastards! I bang my fists harder against the ice, but it does nothing.

"Oh god." Her voice shakes. "I can't read anymore."

No! Keep reading, baby. I need to know what they're saying about you.

But she doesn't. The paper makes a slapping sound as if she's tossed it away. Moments later the warmth of her hand disappears, and I feel myself sinking.

My hand is warm again and I surface.

"Did you miss me?" Jordan asks. She's trying for flippant, but she doesn't pull it off. There's too much pain there.

I did. Every minute you weren't by my side.

"There's someone here to see you."

Who?

There's warmth on my other hand. Someone else has hold of me now too.

"Brody?"

Oh god. Annabelle.

The sound of a child sobbing reaches my ears. All I can do is lie here and bear hearing them. "I don't hate you," she says, hiccupping. "I never did."

I know, Moo Moo. I love you so much.

"So you can wake up now," she adds.

I want to, I promise. I just don't know how.

"Jordan, why is he so still? And why won't he wake up?" Her voice turns shrill. "I don't like it! I don't—"

My sweet wife cuts her off. "Come here, baby."

The warmth leaves both my hands and I begin to sink, but not before I hear Jordan comfort my sister. I know she has Annabelle folded up in her arms, soothing her with sweet words. It breaks me that she needs it, but it puts me back together because they're forming a bond, and it's beautiful.

"I'm quitting FIFA."

No, you're fucking not. Christ. If I was able to do anything at all, I'd be wringing Jordan's pretty neck.

"You're not quitting."

Thank you, Jaxon, for saying what I can't.

"Brody needs me here."

"Brody would kick my ass clear across this hospital if he knew I let you quit the Australian soccer team."

Damn straight.

"Besides, you signed a contract. Those killer legs of yours are legally obliged to kick major goals on behalf of your country."

Eyes off my wife's legs, you fucking dipshit.

"Jordan?" There's a brief pause and when Jax speaks again, it's like he's talking through a throat full of crushed glass. "What if he never wakes?"

The thought sends waves of pain rolling over me, crushing me beneath them. I focus on Jordan's hand, holding onto the warmth with everything

I have. "Don't you say that," she growls, full of fire. "Don't you ever say that."

But Jaxon is right. What if I can't find my way back?

"I'm sorry, I didn't … I can't imagine a life without him in it."

"Me either," she says.

The sound of chair scraping along the floor reaches me. Then a deep exhale. "Brody changed when he took up football," Jax says, his voice close. He's sitting beside me with Jordan on the other side.

"How so?"

"He became happier, but he became harder too. Brody found something in life to love, and it loved him back, but he had to fight to hold on to it. And the older he got, the harder that fight became. The dyslexia was a noose around his neck. But it should never have been. His parents put it there, and even when the kids teased and bullied him at school, they never let him seek help. They made him feel shame. They made him feel less. It made him fight harder, yet he still managed to take joy in the smallest of things because for him they were huge. Then you came along and he changed again."

"How so?" she asks.

My eyes close beneath the water, letting their conversation drift over me quietly.

"He became more accepting of himself. More confident. You showed him he was more than football. You showed him he was worth loving for who he was rather than what he did. But then he had to fight to keep you too. All the time he was fighting."

Jordan's voice is thick. "He got tired of it, didn't he?"

"No. He's still here, so he hasn't stopped fighting yet."

"I don't want him to feel he has to fight to keep me too, Jaxon. All the more reason to quit FIFA."

"He wouldn't want that for you."

"They don't want me anyway so it doesn't matter."

Why don't they want you? I ask, joining the conversation. *They'd be fucking lucky to have you!*

"According to the social media backlash, if Brody's taking drugs, then I am too. When I spoke to my Australian coach about needing time, I could hear it in his voice. He barely restrained himself from telling me to walk."

Jaxon echoes my own sentiment. "Asshole."

"He is. But I get it. And my presence would cast a dark shadow over the entire team. How would we work together if none of them want me there?"

Fuck this. I didn't just ruin us, I ruined *her*.

I'm so sorry, Jordan.

But sorry doesn't cut it. I need to fix it somehow, and the only way I can think of is if she had no association with me. If I wasn't in Jordan's life, she would have a chance to rebuild her battered reputation.

I would have to let her go.

Pain slices through me.

Jordan gasps. "Jax, he ... Brody just squeezed my hand!"

I did?

"Are you sure? It wasn't just some kind of muscle spasm, was it?"

"I'm positive. He *squeezed* it!"

"Holy shit!" Jaxon sounds giddy. "Buzz the nurse, Killer. Buzz the nurse!"

"I am, shut up already."

Jordan sounds giddy too. The warmth leaves my hand. This time I don't sink into darkness. I'm alert. I can still hear them talking.

"Buzz it a second time."

"It's been five seconds, Jax!"

"Take his hand. He might squeeze it again."

Warmth explodes through my palm, radiating upwards over my arm and across my chest. My eyes blink open. Light burns my retinas. I quickly close them.

"Oh my god, he opened his eyes." The thud of something crashing on my left jolts my ears. "Brody?" Jordan is close. Her palm brushes across my forehead and down the side of my face. "Can you hear me?"

BRODY

Every part of me hurts. My eyes, my throat from the tubes, my ribs and face. I reach for the button to buzz the nurse, and when I realize what it is I need, I let go quickly. My arm falls back to my side on the hospital bed.

No more painkillers.

Jordan half stands in her chair. "Are you okay?"

No. "I'm fine," I rasp.

She reaches for the cup of icy water from the table at the end of my bed. "Have some water."

"No. I'm good."

Water means having to piss and getting out of bed hurts. Jordan sets it back down and wheels the table closer so I can reach for it myself if need be. She returns to the seat by my side. Tucking her legs up, she wraps her arms around them and rests the side of her face on her knees, her eyes on me.

"Do you want to talk?"

"About what? My overdose? That my real father is a sick fuck and that I'm his son? That I'm addicted to drugs?"

Jordan winces at my bitter tone, but I can't seem to help it. "I spoke to your mother."

"That must have been a fun conversation. You didn't get frostbite, did you?"

She sighs. Reaching out, she takes my hand in hers. The small comfort is everything. Her being here is everything. Jordan should be in Australia right now starting training with her new team, but she won't leave. The last thing I want is for her to go, but I'm not willing to let her stay just to babysit my fucked-up ass.

"I think she's trying to change. What your father did ..." She trails off. We all know what he did and there's no point revisiting it. "You know she's the one bringing Annabelle in to see you."

Too little, too late, Mom. "Good for her."

And there I go again with the bitter tone.

"She admitted something to me that your father doesn't know."

"And what's that?"

"That she didn't fall pregnant with you the way your dad thinks she did. She lied rather than tell him it was a one-night stand with some guy she barely knew and never saw again."

So many lies and secrets it makes my stomach knot. I don't want to hear anymore. I grunt as I shift in the bed and Jordan pauses.

"I can't go there right now," I tell her.

Pressing the button beside my hospital bed, the back begins to rise, bringing me to a reclined seating position. My ribs scream and I grimace, holding back the groan. "There's something else we need to talk about."

Jordan's phone rings, interrupting me. Reaching for it, she switches it to silent and drops it back inside her bag. When she looks back at me her lips are pinched. Stretching out my arm, I turn it over, palm up. An invitation. Her hand slides in mine and I give it a squeeze.

"You have to go."

Her chin lifts. "No."

Please don't make this any harder than it has to be. "You say that like you have a choice."

"I'm not leaving you."

She's so determined and beautiful. I'm going to miss her. So much. My eyes burn. A tear spills over and I turn my head so she doesn't see it. "I want you to."

"No, you don't. You're just saying that because you don't want me

366

quitting the team. It doesn't matter, Brody. I signed with Houston Dash. I'm staying here. Permanently."

Fuck. I let out a deep, shaky breath.

"I *need* you to go." I turn to face her and admit something that hurts. "I don't know who I am anymore, or if the NFL is even where I want to be. I can't work that out with you here. I need time for me, to work out my life and where I went so wrong."

Jordan snatches her hand away, leaving me cold. "Is that what I am? Some mistake you made along the way?"

"No!" *Dammit.* That didn't come out right. "You're not a mistake. I love you, Jordan. You're the best part of my life. But I can't be who you need me to be. Not right now. I can't pretend I'm okay anymore. I need to fix the part of me that I broke."

Hurt wells in her eyes. That I'm the cause of it burns like a hot poker to the gut. "And you don't want me here to help you do that?"

So the media can vilify you for it? Would I willingly drag you down with me? My jaw locks. "No."

Jordan stands, but not before a sob rips from her chest. She grabs for her things with shaky hands—bag, jacket, keys, some girl magazine she was flicking through earlier while I dozed. They're clutched to her chest in a messy heap.

"Jordan," I rasp with my scratchy throat. "Don't leave like this. I can't—"

She faces me. One last time I take her in—all the stubbornness and fire and beauty so bright it hurts my eyes. "I'll see you in the morning."

But you won't, I say silently as she stalks out the door.

This time when I reach for the button, I buzz the nurse. It hurts to breathe. I need a fucking painkiller. God, I need something. Anything. She comes in a few minutes later and checks my chart. Then I'm given some light aspirin which does fuck all except sit in my stomach like a lead weight.

After staring out the window into the dark night for over an hour, a rap comes at the door. I turn my head as Doug McDougall walks in, casual in jeans and a tee shirt that reads: Kilts. Because balls this big don't fit in jeans.

Funny guy. I want to laugh, but I don't have it in me. "Big Mac."

He nods. "Madden." Moving to the end of my bed, he picks up my chart and runs his eye down it, flicking pages, frowning. He looks up. "How you doing?"

"Great." I wave a hand around my stark hospital room. "Look how far I've come."

"So I see." Putting my chart away, Doug takes a seat on the edge of the chair Jordan vacated just two short hours earlier. Resting elbows on his knees, he leans forward and looks me in the eye. "Tell me, Brody. Why am I here?"

I take a deep breath. "Because I need to prove myself wrong."

He nods again, liking my answer. "Just you. No one else. When you do that, you'll find your way, kiddo." Standing, he ruffles my hair and buzzes the nurse again. "Let's get you out of here."

"You packed my bags?" I ask, flicking back the covers.

"You're all set."

A grunt slips out when I swing my legs over the edge of the bed. Doug steps back, letting me do my thing. I respect that. Panting with effort, I rise to my feet, dizzy and sore.

When I catch my breath, I look at Doug, my face grim and sweaty. *Please don't hate me, Jordan. I need to do this for the both of us. It's the only way.* "Let's blow this joint."

CHAPTER 39

JORDAN

Four weeks later
Present day...
North Sydney Oval, Australia

I step on the bus. It pulls out as I walk down the aisle checking for an empty seat. My eyes fall outside the window to my brother walking to his car.

Two years ago he waved me goodbye at the airport. I left this country with stars in my eyes and determination welded deep inside my heart. Now I'm back a lifetime later, successful, two lucrative endorsements under my belt, and utterly alone.

Finding a seat, I put my headphones on, kick back, and stare out the window into the darkness. Our wedding song hits my ears, and I realize I pressed the wrong playlist. Instead of changing it, I let it play, silent tears falling down my cheeks.

Where are you, Brody? Why won't you answer my calls, or my messages and emails? Why do you have to do this alone?

And the one that keeps me awake at night. *Are you okay out there?*

He just upped and left. There one minute, and the next … gone. An empty hospital room. An empty bed. And no answers. Nothing left behind, not even a note. Just a broken heart. I returned to our house in Houston and I waited, twiddling my thumbs, dodging pitying looks from Eddie, but I knew he wasn't coming back. Two weeks after arriving home, I booked my ticket for Australia. It was what he wanted. If he couldn't be with me, then I would at least give him this.

I wipe my face as the bus deposits the FIFA team back at the Sydney Intercontinental hotel. They laugh and joke with each other, making plans for a late dinner as we walk toward the bank of elevators, keeping me excluded. I can't bring myself to care about their petty bullshit. They don't know, nobody knows, just how incredible Brody Madden is—or what he went through.

One of the girls hits the up button on the elevators and we mill around to wait.

"Killer!"

No. Way.

I spin around, searching for the face that belongs to the American voice. It's coming from the direction of the hotel bar. I scan the busy crowd. It's Friday night. The masses are dressed in business attire, winding down after a long week of work. My eyes land on the only guy dressed in jeans and a thin tee shirt. It has no collar, so he's managed to charm his way in despite the dress code.

Jax stands when I reach him. Without a word he hugs me tight. I hang on, because somehow I'm lost here in Australia, and Jaxon is more home to me now then my own country.

"What are you doing here?" I mumble into his chest.

"I'm here to bag a hot Aussie chick."

A huff of empty laughter escapes me.

Jax draws back but doesn't let go. I look up at him. "Where is he, Jax? He's not returning my calls or emails. His social media is completely shut down. He's dropped off the face of the earth."

Without answering, he turns and tosses a few notes down on the bar. Taking my arm, he leads me toward the elevators. "Let's go to your room. We can talk there."

Taking the elevator to the eighteenth floor, we step out and walk down the hallway to my room. Swiping my card, we step inside and I dump my heavy training bag on the floor by my bed.

When I turn around, Jax is checking his watch. He looks at me, and then nods toward the bathroom. "Go take your shower. We can talk after that."

My brows rise. "Are you saying I stink?"

"To high-fucking heaven. Now go." He reaches for the hotel phone. "I'll order you up some food." Because I know he's right, I make my way into the bathroom. "Oh and, Killer?" I half turn, my hand on the doorframe. He winks. "Put something sexy on when you're done."

I shake my head as I give him the middle finger.

He gasps and holds a hand to his heart. "That hurts."

I'm shutting the door when he speaks into the phone. "Yes, room service? Can I order ..."

His words fade out as I reach in and turn the water on. After a steaming shower that turns my skin raw, I dry off, put on a tank top and sweats, and step out to five different plates of food. Burgers, steak and chips, pancakes, pasta, and a pizza. Jax grins, a beer in his hand. "I didn't know what you wanted."

"There's no way I can eat all of this," I say, looking at all the plates as I towel dry my hair.

"I'd be impressed if you did. Seriously. But what you won't eat, I will." He pats his firm belly. "I'm a growing boy."

I snort. "Hopefully you're growing a brain in there somewhere too."

"Har, har," he retorts as I settle on a slice of pizza. Nibbling on the end, I back up until I hit the bed and sit down. Jax grabs a slice for himself and takes a seat beside me, taking a huge bite. He waves his bottle of beer. "Want a drink?"

I swallow a mouthful, my eyes shifting to the little bottles of spirits over by the mini bar. Would such a small bottle take the edge off everything I'm feeling? There's an urge to find out. "Not allowed."

He shakes his head. "The life of a jock. You're all such bores, eating nothing but chicken and rice and drinking vile protein shakes."

"Hey, I'm eating pizza."

Jax looks at my small bite, and then at his slice almost gone in one mouthful. "And you're doing a miserable job of it."

I try to laugh but it falls flat.

"Christ, I flew all this way and you can't even crack a smile."

"You did fly all this way, Jax." I half turn on the bed, facing him. He's stuffing the last half of pizza in his mouth. It bulges out the sides of his cheeks. "And I'm so happy to see you, but … why are you here?"

Rather than speak, Jax checks his watch again and then picks up the remote. He points it at the television as he chews, fiddling with buttons until he finds the channel he's looking for.

"Jax?" My gaze turns to the screen and my next breath lodges in my lungs, almost making me choke. It's Brody on ESPN. He's taking a seat at a dais, his agent on his left, coach and team manager on his right. Adjusting the microphone, he leans in and looks at the cameras ahead of him.

Flashbulbs are going off in a frenzy and reporters are yelling questions. Through it all Brody holds a piece of paper in his hand, his expression unreadable to those looking at him. Except me. I know that face. He's exhausted and tense and doing whatever he can to hide it.

"Brody knows," I breathe. I look at Jax. "He knew I was talking to the media tomorrow."

"Of course he did."

Frustration builds. I stand and toss my pizza slice back in the box, my appetite gone. Turning to face Jax, I fold my arms. "And he sent you here to stop me from doing it."

Brody clears his throat. It draws our attention back to the screen, saving Jax from a response. "I'm going to read a brief statement." He exhales and looks down at his page before looking back up again. "First I want to confirm that yes, I was in hospital from excessive drug use. This has put me in a Stage II violation of the NFL's Substance Abuse Program. Second I want to stress that I acted alone. Those closest to me were not involved, nor aware of what I was taking. The NFL has issued a four game suspension, along with a substantial fine. I will not be appealing the decision. In fact…" Brody hesitates "…I'm retiring from the NFL, effective immediately. Thanks for your time."

He stands to leave. I cover half my face with both hands as I sag back on the edge of the bed, speechless with shock. He's giving up everything he worked for. His dream. *Oh, Brody.*

Reporters explode.

"Why retire?"

"Why don't you just take the suspension?"

"What drugs were you taking?"

Half out of his seat, Brody leans in to the microphone and stares out at the sea of reporters. "I've chosen to retire because remaining in that kind of pressure-packed environment would be detrimental to my recovery."

"Are you saying you couldn't handle the pressure?"

My hands fist in my lap. *Assholes! Damn them.*

"Jesus," Jax breathes as Brody sits back down.

"Pressure in the NFL is about being better, faster, stronger. Not just against the other teams, but your own. For me, I had something to prove to everyone but myself, and the problem was that I was willing to do whatever it took. That was wrong. All I can do now is apologize to those who looked up to me and expected better than what I could give."

"What will you do now?"

Brody remains strong and calm when he answers, "I don't know. Right now I want to focus on being healthy and finding what makes me happy."

"What about Jordan? Your soccer star wife has started training in Australia for the FIFA tournament. Have you split? Was your wife taking drugs too?

Brody's eyes turn hard with anger, his first full show of emotion. "As I said earlier," he bites out, "I acted alone. Those closest to me were not involved. Further, the subject of my wife is not up for discussion. Again, thanks for your time."

With that he stands and disappears from view, reporters yelling questions in his wake.

Jax and I sit there in silent unity for several moments, our eyes stuck on the screen and my heart pounding harder than a jackhammer. "Did you know he was going to retire?" I eventually croak.

Picking up the remote, Jax switches the television off, the corners of his mouth turned down. He takes his time answering, as if recovering from his own sense of shock. "No."

A stab of hurt hits me, just under the breastbone. It grows until my body quivers with it. Jax reaches for my hand. Taking it in his, he threads our fingers together, his skin warm against the chill of mine.

"Are you okay?"

"Am I okay?" How is that even a question? "Brody just retired from the NFL, and I had no idea he was going to do it because he's not talking to me. He's making important life decisions without me, and for all I know, they're ones that don't include me anymore." My voice rises, matching my hurt. I snatch my hand free and stand. "How does any part of that make me okay?"

He picks up the glass of water from the table by the bed and holds it out. "Just take a few deep breaths and—"

"I don't need to fucking breathe!" I yell irrationally. I grab the glass of water from his hand and turn, hurling it at the wall. It smashes on impact, sending shards of glass in every direction. "And I don't need a fucking drink of water!"

"Whoa!" Jax stands, approaching me like I'm a wild animal to tame. "I know rock stars like to trash their hotel rooms, but jocks? That's gotta be new."

I bring a trembling hand to my forehead, unable to deal. My eyes feel raw and bitter when they meet his. "Do you have to make a joke out of everything?"

Pausing, Jax shrugs. "It's how I cope."

"Shit." Dropping to a crouch, I wipe tears from my face and sniff noisily as I begin picking up the largest of the glass shards from the floor. Jax drops beside me, plucking up some of the smaller, sharper ones. "I'm sorry," I say quietly.

"He's doing this to protect you, Jordan."

I rise and walk to the small bin in the corner of my suite. "I don't need to be protected."

Dropping the smashed pieces of glass inside, I turn back to pick up more but Jax has got most of them. The rest will need vacuuming. He drops them in the bin. "It's what you do for those you love."

"Exactly. So why can't I do that for him too? Damn his double standards." Stalking to the mini bar, I reach for a tiny bottle of vodka. Unscrewing the cap I pour half into a shot glass from the little bench.

Jax grabs my hand when the glass is halfway to my lips. "What are you doing?"

"I'm having a drink," I retort. Shrugging free, I toss the liquid down my throat. My eyes water and I gasp at the burn. Jax raises his brows at me. I point at him with the same hand still holding the empty shot glass. "I'm also still doing the press conference tomorrow. If Brody thought speaking first would stop me, he was wrong."

"Jordan—"

"Don't even," I snap angrily.

His mouth closes and his brow furrows in obvious frustration. "Right. Well, I'm just going to use the bathroom and then I'll leave you alone."

Jax slams the door behind him. I empty the rest of the little bottle into the shot glass and down that too. When I'm done, I shuffle to my bag, pull out a pair of purple bed socks, and tug them up over my cold toes.

The toilet flushes and after hearing the sound of Jax washing his hands, the door opens. By then I'm tucked in bed on my side, lights off, covers up to my shoulders, and the late night local news playing out on the television.

For a brief moment the room is flooded with light until he flicks the bathroom switch, bringing back the low, artificial glow from the television.

"Jax?"

I sense him pause before coming toward me. He crouches by the side of the bed, bringing us to eye level. "What's up, Killer?"

"How long are you here for?"

"Two days."

"Really?" It's a thirty-four-hour round trip flight, and it's not cheap. "You flew all this way just to hold my hand for one weekend?"

Jax nods. "I did. And it's lucky because you look like crap. You're not sleeping or eating are you?"

"I'm trying but it's not working. I'm so tired." My eyes fill and my stomach gurgles, not liking alcohol on an empty stomach. "And I miss him."

I reach up, brushing hair out of my face. Jax takes over the task, tucking the strands behind my ear with care. When he's done, his eyes return to mine. "That makes you lucky. You have someone in your life worth missing."

When did Jax get so sweet? My voice lowers to a whisper. "You're going to make some girl very lucky one day."

His grin is wicked. "I plan on making lots of girls lucky."

"Thank you."

"You would be if I was the one making *you* lucky."

My chuckle is tired. "Thank you for being here with me, Jax." Moving my arm from beneath the covers, I take his hand in mine and give it a squeeze. "I'm a shitty friend right now and I'm sorry, but it doesn't mean I don't appreciate a good one when it's staring me in the face."

"You know what they're going to ask you," Coach Riley says as we walk toward the conference room, our team captain and vice-captain following behind.

"Yes, I know."

"We need to discuss how you're going to answer."

"I know how you *want* me to answer," I retort.

Coach takes my arm, forcing me to pause. I look up, my jaw set. "Elliott, I know your situation, and wanting to stand up for Brody is truly admirable, but you're just going to get sucked inside the circus. This will only tarnish your reputation further. Is that what you want?"

"It's not about what I want," I hiss harshly. "It's about doing what's right."

"Ah hell, Elliott." Coach Riley lets go of my arm and rubs his brow the same way he does every time the opposition gets through our defense and scores. He's already tried debating my stance without success. It's too late for last-ditch efforts.

I reach for the door of the private entryway and swing it wide, holding it open. "Let's just do this."

Coach walks through first, followed by our captains. I bring up the rear, stepping up onto the platform and taking a seat at the end of the long table. Nervous flurries fill my stomach as I look out at the media. They're impatient, having been kept waiting for over half an hour. I lift my chin, ignoring the flash of cameras.

Coach Riley begins with a brief opening statement. He follows it up with details of our training preparation, exhibition matches, and FIFA tournament schedule. I barely hear a word he speaks until he opens up the floor for questions.

Cameras, microphones, and eyes, all shoot my way. I brace, my heart pounding.

"Jordan, can you tell us where Brody Madden is? Is he on his way to Australia to be with you?"

I lean into the microphone and give my one word answer. "No."

Coach Riley grants a brief nod of approval before another question is yelled my way. "Have you spoken to Brody since he announced his retirement from the NFL?"

"No," I answer again.

My teammates relax beside me when I don't expand further.

"Are you and Brody still together?"

Seriously? A proud, strong man has been forced to his knees with the public reveling in his downfall and I'm supposed to just abandon him? It's all I can do to keep the tremors of fury from my voice. "Yes, of course we—"

My coach butts in. "That has no bearing on why we're here today."

The media gives him their attention. "Just how vigorous is drug testing in the Australian teams, Coach Riley? Is the entire team undergoing rigorous screening? Has Jordan Elliott been tested?"

I want to close my eyes because they were all right. I've had hate mail, vicious messages, slurs from teammates, and now the media is joining in. I lift my chin and straighten my shoulders, and as my eyes scan the room they land on my brother standing at the back. He's leaning against the wall beside Jax.

He shakes his head at me, disappointment so sharp in his eyes I feel the stab of it clear across the room. I glare for a brief second before shifting my gaze away.

"Soccer is a clean sport," Coach retorts, the veins in his neck pulsing angrily. "My girls are elite athletes who train hard and train right. If you start casting aspersions on any member of this team I'll have you thrown out of this room."

Cameras return to me when the next question is called out from somewhere in the back. "Jordan, did you know Brody Madden was taking drugs? And do you think his fine and suspension is fair, despite his decision to retire? Professional athletes are in the spotlight and should be setting an example for the younger generation. It seems to me that more should be done about the use of drugs in sport. Instead they're getting minimal punishment and having it swept beneath the rug."

The room falls silent, the only noise coming from the click of cameras and light whirr of the microphone. They want an answer and I'm prepared to give it to them. My only hope is that Brody is watching and can hear my words.

I draw a deep breath and lean forward. "It's not about what's fair. It's about what it takes to be the best, and every expectation that comes with it." I glance across at my coach. He closes his eyes for a second, resigned.

"It takes everything you have. People put you up here," I say, holding my hand up high. "But being up there is hard, and it's lonely. And if you fall, it's a long way down and no one's waiting at the bottom to catch you." My voice cracks and I have to pause for a moment. Jax gives me a silent thumbs-up from the back of the room, encouraging me to keep going. "The pressure to live up to that is immense. So immense that sometimes people do whatever it takes not to bow underneath it, or god forbid, break. And if they do, it's only because they were human. People make mistakes. Every single day. It doesn't mean they aren't strong enough, or didn't give enough. It means they gave too much and they tried too hard. It means they deserve forgiveness from those who were expecting too much, and from those who were supposed to be there supporting them when it got too hard."

Please hear what I'm telling you, Brody. I'm not angry. I'm heartbroken. I need you to forgive me for not being there when you needed me.

The media regroup and a reporter from the front catches my eye. "Jordan, how do you feel about being selected for the team?"

I break out in a blinding smile at her question. More camera flashes fill the room. "I'm excited and I'm thankful to be here right now, to be a part of the Australian soccer team, to be selected for something so great," I answer. "And when I go out there and give my best, I won't be doing it just for myself or my country, I'll be doing it for Brody too, because he's still a good person, and maybe he isn't the best in your eyes anymore, but he still is in mine." My eyes fill with tears and that's okay. I don't care if they see them. "He's still the best in mine."

My phone rings later that night, waking me from an exhausted sleep. Training that day was long and rough, and I was so glad to get back to the hotel, to have Jaxon there to laugh and joke with, and pretend for just one night that everything was fine.

I reach for the phone from the bedside table and answer without checking the screen, my voice husky with sleep. "Hello?"

"Jordan."

I hear the quiver in Brody's voice. My grip tightens on the phone. I shoot into a sitting position, wide-awake in a single instant. "Brody?"

He sucks in a sharp breath as if hearing me speak his name hurts. "Yeah. It's me."

"You asshole!" I shout. "Do you know what I've been through? You just up and left. You left me! And what, it takes me talking to the media for you get in touch? Screw you, Brody," I hiss. "If you're phoning just because you're pissed for what I said then you can just hang up right now." My chest is thumping with anger. "In fact, I'm going to do it for you."

I jab the red button, ending the call, and as I sit there in the dark, my breathing harsh and my body trembling, panic begins to claw its way up my throat. *What did I just do?* With shaky fingers, I go to my recent calls list to hit redial but the number listed is unknown. I can't phone him back.

Before I can scream my frustration, it rings in my hand. Wild with relief, I press the green button and put the phone to my ear. "Brody? I'm sorry. I'm so sorry. I wasn't thinking. I just—"

"Stop. Please."

I press my lips together. Silence reigns for a long moment before Brody speaks again. "I watched your press conference."

"Yeah? I watched yours too."

He huffs. It's followed by another length of silence. "It was …" Brody trails off before trying again. "I didn't deserve what you said, but it was beautiful."

"I meant every word."

"I know you did, baby. I know." That he understood what I was saying lightens the heavy weight from my shoulders. I slump back against my pillows, and when Brody speaks again his voice is rueful. "I should've known."

"Known what?"

"You looked so calm up there. So strong. You didn't let them mess with you. Not a single bit. I thought leaving would protect you. I know it hasn't. But you never needed me to."

"What are you saying?" Does he think I don't need him? The thought sets off a shiver of fear. I pull the covers up, burrowing into their warmth. "That you think I don't need you? Because I do. It's so dark and cold without you."

Brody chuckles. "That's because it's just gone midnight there in Australia, and it's winter, right?"

"Really? You're going to—"

"Going to what?" Brody prompts.

"Nothing." I decide to ask him straight out. "Are we done? Is that why you're calling, to tell me we're over?"

"God, no!" he bursts out. "Jordan, baby, I'm calling because there's something I need to ask you."

"What?"

Another long pause follows before he speaks, his voice low and soft. "Wait for me."

I close my eyes. "Wait for you?" I whisper.

"I know I let you down, but I'm trying to make it right. I'm getting help. I'm doing everything I can to fix the mess I made, but I've realized I can only do so much without you. Jordan … we all need that one person who sees us. The one who gives it to us straight and tells us how it is. We need that one person who isn't afraid to get in our face and scream back. That one person who won't ever hesitate to call you on your shit because they love you. That one person who'll be there for you no matter what. You're that person." He draws in a shaky breath. This is hard for him. I can hear it. And it breaks me apart and puts me back together all at the same time because I believe him. I believe *in* him. "You're it for me, Jordan. My end game. So yes, I'm asking you to wait for me. Can you do that?"

"I'll wait for you, Brody Abraham Madden." I swallow the thick lump caught in my throat knowing that wait is going to hurt. "I'll wait as long as you need."

EPILOGUE

JORDAN

Five years later...
Houston, Texas

The alarm goes off with an ear-piercing shriek. *Is it morning already?* For the love of god, I only just went to sleep. I shift my head a fraction on the pillow and it starts pounding like a bass drum. A pathetic whimper leaves my throat. I'm not even hungover, I'm just damn tired.

"Make the shrieking stop," I mumble.

A heavy arm reaches over the top of me. It's followed by the sound of a loud slap and a crash. The shrieking stops. Peace reigns. I moan my thanks.

"I love you so much," I say to my heavenly pillow as I burrow my head beneath it.

"Of course you do," my pillow replies with a deep male voice.

Interesting. I nudge the fluffy cushion with my nose and encounter armpit, the hair beneath it tickling my skin. I scrunch my nose as I roll to my back and an arm follows me, settling across my chest. The warm, calloused hand attached to the end of it gives my breast an experimental squeeze over my tank top. "The question is," the voice comes again, "just how much?"

Despite my stubborn determination to get another ten minutes, my nipple betrays me, peaking at the touch. A thumb brushes over it and the pleased groan of aroused male reaches my ears. Heat begins a steady throb between my thighs.

"Daddy!"

It's Brody's turn to whimper. His hand shifts down to settle on my ribcage with reluctance. "Pretend we're asleep," he mutters to me.

"I am asleep," is my muffled reply as I grab my real pillow and shove it over my face.

"Daddy!" The screech is getting closer, as is the sound of feet pitter-pattering across the thick timber flooring and into our room. "It's game day!"

We both remain studiously still. Brody jostles beside me, and I know it's Hadley shoving at him. She's the more demanding of our two girls.

"Wake up!" she shouts.

I swallow the chuckle when he gives up without a fight. My bed dips beside me as he shifts up on an elbow. "I'm awake, sweetheart."

"I'm not sweetheart. I'm Haddie."

"You're my sweet Hadley."

"I'm not sweet. Sweet is for girls."

I shake my head. Uncle Nicky has been getting in her ear.

"You *are* a girl," he argues.

Another shout comes from near the bedroom door.

"Avery, do not throw—" Brody begins as I'm lifting my head from underneath the pillow, just in time for a football to smack me up the side of my face. "—that."

"Game day!" Avery yells.

The alarm begins to shriek again as I fall back on the bed, holding a hand to my cheekbone. *Great.* It's going to swell and bruise, and I'm going to look like ass for Brody's big day.

"Baby, you okay?"

I open my eyes to mere slits, finding my husband hovering above me with concern furrowing his brow.

"Fine," I mutter as he reaches across me to turn the alarm off for a second time.

I'm used to it. It's just another morning in the Madden household. Chaotic. Crazy. Exhausting. That's what happens when you end up with twins. They're three years old, and still Avery won't sleep through the night. Why is it she wakes up at all hours screaming for me (no one else will do), but it's her daddy she seeks out during the day? It's unfair how he gets such a lovely, unbroken sleep, waking up all refreshed while I resemble the living dead. All I want is one night of uninterrupted bliss and when the possibility of one looms bright on the horizon, Brody takes advantage. His hands and tongue are too skilled to ignore, try as I might. In no time at all he gets me hot and bothered and suddenly I'm all, 'who needs sleep anyway?'

"Sorry, Mommy."

I turn my head. Avery is standing on my side of the bed, her curls a tangled mess and her weapon now tucked safely beneath her arm.

"No throwing the ball in the house," I instruct for the millionth time. "Who gave you that anyway?" I ask, my cheek throbbing. "Where's your soccer ball?"

Haddie bounces onto the bed, half landing on her daddy. A loud "oomphf" escapes him. "Daddy kicked it over the back fence," she informs me.

My brow arches and my lips pinch as I turn to look at him. "Oh he did, did he?"

"But I'm not 'sposed to tell you that."

Brody shrugs, eyes wide with feigned innocence as Avery climbs on the bed alongside Hadley. "I didn't mean to. I can't help it if I can kick a soccer ball further than you."

"Is that so?" I look from him to the girls. They're not identical, and for that I'm pathetically grateful. Hadley's hair is long and smooth like mine, the color a rich honey. Avery's hair is white-blond chaos. Both girls have their daddy's brown eyes and also his deep affinity for football. After having the twins, I signed a new contract with the Houston Dash and while Brody brings them to watch my home games, it's gridiron that gets them excited and jumping in their seats. "Well your daddy was telling me just last night that he was going to make you banana pancakes for breakfast this morning!"

They both clap and squeal while my husband groans. It sets our two mini dachshunds barking from somewhere downstairs. I hear the ticktack of their claws on the floor, and I know they're scrambling for the stairs. They know we're awake now and that means food.

"I'll make some for you too," Brody says in retaliation as I scoot from the bed. He knows full well warm banana is the one food that makes my stomach pitch. I'm retching at the very thought before I even make it off the bed.

"You just try it, pal, and you'll be wearing them on your face." And with that lovely threat, I escape bedlam for the sanctity of our half bathroom, shutting the door just as Thor and Jon Snow race in, hope in their eyes and tails rotating like helicopter blades.

I take a nice deep breath and lean over the vanity, inspecting my face in the mirror. The right side is swollen and red. *Awesome.* Today is going to be *great.* After a mere ten seconds of peace the door opens, injecting chaos into the little sanctuary. I actually think I might cry.

"Please," I whimper, the sound drowned out by screaming girls and barking dogs.

"Mommy!" Avery shouts, because apparently I must be hard of hearing. "Daddy said we could wear our ballerina dresses to football!"

I grip the edge of the vanity, trying to find my happy place. It proves elusive. "No, you're not wearing those to the football."

Hadley interjects. "But Daddy said—"

"—we could," Avery finishes.

Brody steps in behind the girls, taking up every inch of space with his wide frame. "I said no such thing."

"Oh? What *did* you say?" I ask, looking at him via his reflection in the mirror.

The corners of his lips quirk up. "I told them to ask you."

My eyes narrow. "You couldn't just say no?"

He takes on the expression of the walking wounded. "And break their sweet little hearts?"

"Mommy!" Hadley stomps her foot and frustration has me grinding my teeth. Why do I always have to be the bad guy? "I want to wear—"

I give both girls a firm look. "No."

Hysterics ensue. Brody ushers them all out of the bathroom. "Cartoons are on the television. Go downstairs and I'll be down in a minute to make your pancakes."

Appeased for the moment, they leave, their chatter and dog barks slowly fading. I let out a deep sigh and look again at Brody through the mirror. He steps up behind me, arms sliding around my waist and hands resting on my lower belly where a tiny bump is burgeoning. He rubs it lovingly as he lands a kiss on my shoulder. "How's our little guy doing in there?"

"You don't know it's a boy. I'm only twelve weeks along."

"It's a boy." His lips touch my shoulder again, eyes lifting to look at me in the mirror as he trails kisses up toward my neck. I tilt my head, giving him access without a second thought. "God wouldn't be so cruel as to leave me alone in a house full of estrogen."

"That's what Thor and Jon Snow are for."

Brody's hands rise from my belly, roaming up over my ribcage until he's cupping my breasts. They grew a full size after the birth of the twins and much to my delight they didn't shrink again. I have *cleavage*. "But we never win anything. We're a sucker for you girls with your pretty hair and scheming eyes."

I turn around, swallowing the sudden lump in my throat. Brody grips my hips with his big hands, drawing me toward him until our hips press flush together. "And I'm a sucker for you."

The emotion in my eyes makes his own soften in response. "Aren't you glad you waited for me all those years ago?"

I bite down on my lip, the distant pain surfacing like it always does when I think of how he almost died. The months following were the best of my career, and some of the worst of my life. The media circus eventually faded away, the next tantalizing story waiting around the corner.

Our team won the FIFA World Cup, and I gained a new kind of attention. Fox Sports did a big feature on me, from where I came from to where I ended up, portraying me as some kind of survivor. It didn't just make me cringe, it somehow made me into the darling of professional soccer.

Interviews, soccer camps, and sponsors took all my time. Wherever I went I was signing soccer balls and jerseys. It was surreal and time consuming, and I buried myself in it. We don't get paid anywhere near what male soccer players get, so taking advantage of every opportunity was a priority. I became the face of Chapstick lip balm and Nike sportswear.

My face was everywhere, and when I began my contract as a forward with Houston Dash, they welcomed me with open arms.

But I did it all alone. Brody had his own hell to deal with, pushing me out of it. It's something I'm still struggling to get past. My husband recovered, eventually leaning on me for support. He built a life with me beside him. We created a family. We forged a future that's brighter than any star shining down from the night sky. The price we paid for it was high, but our reward is incomparable. Brody proved to himself that he was worth all of it. I've never been prouder, happier, nor more in love with this man than I am right now.

My eyes begin to swim, blurring Brody in front of me.

"Don't," he says. "You waited when I had no right to ask it of you." His hands cup my face, thumbs dashing away the tears when they spill over and down my cheeks. "And when you came back to Houston, you didn't just bring yourself, you brought everything because you and the girls, this little guy…" he rubs my little bump, glancing down at it before staring into my eyes "…hell even the damn dogs, you're all my world."

"You're ours too, Brody."

He ducks his head, his lips meeting mine. They linger sweetly, but heat follows soon enough. My mouth opens beneath his and our tongues tangle.

"Pancakes, Daddy!" Hadley shrieks up the stairs.

Brody ends the kiss and draws back, pressing his forehead against mine with a deep growl of frustration.

I can't help the chuckle. "You better go. Your world needs you."

Brody spins me around and slaps my ass before giving it a loving grope. "Tonight," he vows as I lean inside the shower, flicking on the taps.

I turn, slowly pulling my tank top up and over my head, dropping it to the tiled floor. It leaves me standing in nothing but a simple pair of hot pink panties.

His nostrils flare. "You don't play nice."

"I don't," I reply, smirking as I pile all my hair up into a knot on top of my head, "but if you can't handle the game, then get the hell off the field."

Brody runs his gaze down the length of me before flicking back up, his eyes intense and hot. "Never."

BRODY

I jog down the stairs to the kitchen, the image of a half-naked Jordan still imprinted in my vision. I love my two little girls but they seriously need to work on their timing. I need to fuck my wife.

Soon, I tell myself. I wasn't making empty promises when I told her tonight. My brother-in-law is arriving for his four-week annual holiday this afternoon and jetlag or not, he's taking care of the twins. Nicky won't mind. He adores the girls. They have him wrapped around their little fingers. Me, not so much. Our relationship has travelled a long and rocky path, especially after the hell I put his sister through, but the arrival of Hadley and Avery won him over. We're a solid family unit now, and Jordan's never been happier. Of course I like to think I have a lot to do with that. Making her happy is my number one priority, and I know Nicky sees that.

Usually his visits find us out on the back deck with beers in hand, manning the grill while arguing over the merits of football versus soccer, but not tonight. I'm whisking my wife away for a surprise night in the city at a fancy hotel. Dinner, a cabaret performance, and then me, and so help me god if she snores through the show like she did the last time I organized a night out, I'm going to cry like a fucking baby.

Thor and Jon Snow scramble when I hit the bottom step and the fight is on to see who reaches me first. Jon Snow wins and he treats the backs of my calves to little licks as I make my way into the kitchen.

"Daddy!" Hadley screams from the living area. "I want chocolate chips in mine!"

"Me too!" Avery shrieks.

"Okay," I call back, willing to give them whatever they want if it shuts them up for even a minute.

I make a quick detour to the French doors that lead out onto the back deck. The dogs spin in circles while I pour food in their bowls. Jordan taught them to chase their tail for a treat. Now every time they get something to eat they orbit each other until I'm sure they're going to pass out.

When I reach the kitchen a knock comes at the door. *Seriously?* It's Saturday morning, and *early*.

"I'll get it," Hadley cries out, excitement in her voice. Any visitor is a good visitor in her eyes, and if she gets to show them her princess pony collection, it makes them a great visitor.

"You will not answer that door, Haddie," I call back sternly as I head her off at the pass. She grumbles but walks back to Avery, settling on the floor but keeping her eyes firmly fixed on the door.

Twisting the handle, I swing the door wide. Annabelle is standing on the front porch, arm up and ready to knock again. Over her shoulder I see my mother reversing out the drive, not bothering to stop in and say hello.

My parents separated not long after I left the hospital. Mom and Annabelle moved to Houston at my little sister's insistence. Liam (I don't call him my father anymore) moved on to a bigger house with a younger woman, his political career soaring despite the drug scandal overtaking the news for weeks. I don't talk to him. I barely talk to my mother. During my counseling sessions with Doug, I was told forgiveness is the key to moving forward with my life, but it's a stretch.

At the least I can understand why they are the way they are. I'm not Liam's son. Married to my mother, he was trapped into raising me, and he did it the same way his father raised him—with harsh words, a violent temper, and constant disapproval. I know my mother loved him once. She told me that years ago after one too many glasses of wine. But their marriage came second to his career and over time it molded my mom into the cold, bitter woman she is today.

I did learn something from them though. I learned how important it is to define myself, rather than let other people define me. I learned that no one is perfect. I learned how to find strength to pick myself up off the ground when I fall, and to embrace my own future in all its uncertainty.

I learned how important it is to raise my girls with acceptance. I want them to succeed in whatever they choose to do, but I also want them to fail and learn how to get over it. I want them to feel free to be themselves, and to ignore those that don't accept them for who they are.

In our house there's laughter and joy, and tears and tantrums, but most of all there's love. Our lives are perfectly imperfect, just how they're supposed to be.

"Aunt Moo Moo!" Hadley shrieks.

Both girls scramble off the floor and race for the door. My sister is instantly surrounded by screaming little banshees. She crouches and hugs them close.

"Pick me up," Hadley demands.

"Me first," Avery argues.

I grin down at Annabelle. "They're all yours," I tell her and make a quick escape for the kitchen, going straight for the coffee. Eventually my sister untangles herself, and after visiting their bedrooms and dispensing loving pats to Thor and Jon Snow, she settles into a seat at the breakfast counter to watch me flip pancakes.

"What are you doing here?" I ask, pouring fresh batter into the pan.

"It's your big game today. Like I'd miss it."

Nervous twinges fill my stomach. "It's just a football game."

"It's *not* just a football game," she argues as I check underneath the pancake to see it browning nicely. "This is the beginning of a whole new level in your career. Everyone is coming to watch. I can't wait."

After flipping it, I look up, my jaw set. "Who's everyone?"

Like my words are a catalyst, another knock comes at the door. The twins commence their excited shrieks and the dogs race from their lazy spot in the sun to the front entryway. Somehow a ball gets thrown and breaks the lamp in the corner. Avery starts to cry. And all before I've even left the kitchen.

The front door opens, bringing Eddie, Jaxon, and Carter inside.

"What the hell is going on?"

My gaze shifts to the stairs and lust punches me in the gut. Jordan's ready and her gaze is taking in the chaos where moments earlier there was peace. Skinny jeans wrap around her long legs, and a black blouse—one that's entirely too low cut so she'll have to change—shows off the cleavage she's so proud of. Tousled waves spill over her shoulders and the dark crap around her eyes makes the blue in them burn brighter. *My wife is fucking hot.*

"Come here," I order.

But Avery's already running for her, her little arms wrapping around her mommy's legs, the same ones I want wrapping around me right now. "Mommy, Haddie stole my football!"

"I did not!" Hadley yells, running over to my friends and telling them all about the banana pancakes she's having for breakfast. She then throws me under the bus by telling them I'm adding chocolate chips.

I don't miss the narrowing of Jordan's eyes, but Eddie saves me by leaning in to kiss her on the cheek. Then he reaches down and grabs Avery, picking her up. "What's going on, sweet stuff?" he asks her, settling her on his hip. He scoops the football up with his free hand and herds both twins outside along with Annabelle.

Meanwhile I watch Jaxon and Carter take turns in kissing my wife. "Are y'all done there?" I growl.

"Not quite." Jaxon grabs Jordan by the hips, pulling her toward him with a smirk. She lets out a little shriek when he dips her. Her hands grab at his shirt, clinging so she doesn't fall. "Did I hear banana was on the breakfast menu this morning?" he says, a grin on his face as he looks down at her.

Jordan bursts into laughter, but I don't get the joke. I point my spatula at my cousin. "Leave my wife alone. What are y'all doing here anyway?"

Carter slaps me on the back, reaching around the front of me to grab a handful of chocolate chips from the bowl on the counter. "Heard there was a big game today."

My gaze shifts to Jordan. "Did you tell everyone?"

"I did." She walks into the kitchen where I finish flipping the last pancake. It's a little black around the edges so I set that aside for Jaxon. Jordan takes hold of my chin, turning my face to hers. "Because I'm proud of you," she says, "and I want the whole world to know."

My lips press together. "The media is going to descend, aren't they?"

"They are, and they're going to see how happy you are, and how good you are at what you do. Your team is going to kick ass, Brody, and we all want to be there cheering you on."

I give Jordan a quick kiss on the lips. My wife is my biggest champion. She always has been. "What would I do without you?" I whisper softly.

The twins begin shrieking from outside. We both wince. Jordan follows it up with a chuckle. "Probably live a long and peaceful life."

"Peace is for old people. I'll take the chaos."

Hadley runs inside. "Mom! Eddie kicked the football over the back fence."

"Good." Jordan grins. "I happen to know there's a soccer ball in the pool house. Go get that."

Another knock comes at the door as Hadley runs back outside. Jordan goes to answer as Eddie comes back inside to get a drink, leaving me to talk with my friends about their drunken escapades last night, Eddie included. He turns from the fridge where he's grabbing water bottles, his face fire engine red as he blurts out, "I met someone."

"Who?" I ask, wanting to know who it is that managed to capture the soft gooey center of the Wranglers' biggest linebacker.

Jordan returns, bringing Leah and Hayden with her before I get an answer. "Mr. Crosby," I say, shaking his hand. Leah steps around him and takes my shoulders, giving me a quick kiss on the cheek. "Mrs. Crosby," I add. "Let me guess, you're both here for the big game."

Leah's brows fly up. "There's a game?"

"Don't tease," Jordan interjects. Her friend has always been tough on me. Not so much anymore, but it doesn't bother me. Jordan couldn't have picked a better friend if she tried. She and Jaxon barely left Jordan's side during the World Cup. I watched every televised match and I was there for the final, surrounded by a proud bunch of screaming Australians when she kicked the goal that secured the win. I wanted to go to her then, be there for her the same way she always was for me, but I couldn't move. My feet stuck to the ground and I choked, struggling with the fear that I'd left it too long, and it was too late.

In the end it was Jordan that found me. I was on the sidelines of the football field in Houston. The grass was freshly mowed and the yard lines painted a rich, brilliant white. A breeze blew low, ruffling my hair. From the bench behind me, I grabbed my baseball cap and tugged it down on my head, shielding bright afternoon sun from my face.

Jordan called my name then, the husky voice sending shivers curling up my spine. It was a voice I dreamed of hearing each night, leaving me awake and wondering if it was a sound I'd ever hear again.

I turned around and there she was. All the longing I'd pushed down for months came rushing to the surface, leaving me short of air. A few short strides and I could've touched her, but my feet still wouldn't move. I held her eyes instead, rooted to the ground as I faced my biggest fear—losing her. "Jordan."

A smile formed on her lips. It was hesitant and small, but there was hope in it, and love, and I knew then that everything was going to be okay.

A beautiful sense of calm spread through my body where there was only blind panic just moments earlier.

"Brody?" Jordan takes hold of my bicep, bringing me back to the present. "You okay?"

I nod. "I'm good."

Paige, Jordan's old college teammate, steps in the room behind Hayden and Leah and suddenly Eddie's face burns brighter. I have my answer. It's one I like.

Grinning, I load up three big stacks of pancakes and hustle everyone out in the morning sun where the outdoor seating can fit us all. After breakfast and an impromptu game of soccer in the yard, I leave them all for the game. They'll follow later.

When nighttime falls, the Houston Hurricanes gather in the locker room, tension thick in the air. It's the first game of the season and it's always the biggest. It sets the tone for every game that follows. It sends a message to fans, to the media, and to every team opposing us, that this is who we are and this is how we play.

I step inside the room, my second home.

"Coach is in the house!" says Assistant Coach Dawson in a loud, sharp voice.

The boys settle into silence when I step in front of them. "Take a knee," I tell them. They all lower to the ground and lift their heads, looking at me, waiting for me to impart some magical wisdom that will help them win the game.

For three years I coached the Peewee League and I loved it. I had the best of both worlds. It was where I first found my own passion. Where the game meant nothing else but the joy it brought to my heart. No pressure, just a field of green and a ball to run over the line.

But I was good at coaching—too good—and I got poached. Now here I am, head coach for high school football team, the Houston Hurricanes. Being offered the position set off controversial opinions across the state of Texas. Most of them adamant that I didn't deserve it, that it was the wrong decision, and that the fledging team I was charged with would suffer for it.

As I stand before the boys, taking in their expressions of determination, I know I'm not here to prove all those people wrong. I'm here because I want these boys to learn from someone who knows the pressure that awaits them in college football and beyond. There's no one more qualified than me to prepare them for what lies ahead.

I open my mouth and deliver the best words I can. "Tonight is your game. Don't let anyone in the stands or the media distract you," I instruct them, concerned with public backlash for me being their coach. "Listen to what I tell you, run the plays I call, and have some fucking fun out there!" Cheers erupt and Dawson shouts for them to settle down. "One more thing," I add. They quiet down and give me back their focus. "It's not your opponent out there on the field that's against you tonight. It's yourself. *You* are your greatest competition. How can you defeat yourself? By believing. Believe in your team," I tell the boys, my eyes grazing over each and every one of them. "Believe in why you're here, believe in what you do, and believe in yourself, because when you do, everyone around you will start believing in you too." I clap my hands and shout, "Let's go!"

The boys get to their feet, rowdy and fired up. They jog out of the tunnel, and I follow behind, cap set forward and pride in my heart. I turn, my eyes seeking Jordan in the stands. She's standing front row, Avery and Hadley in front of her, Nicky and our close friends beside her. I press my index and middle finger to my lips and then hold them up high.

She returns the gesture, a smile spreading wide on her face. Even from this far away I see the emotion burn in her eyes. It echoes in my own. It forms the image that gets splashed on the front page of the newspapers the next morning after we take a solid win against Texas City.

I skim the article as I stand at the kitchen counter, smile on my face, coffee in my hand, and my girls causing chaos around me. My life is not my past anymore, it's my present and my future, and right now? It's pretty damn good.

THE END

ACKNOWLEDGMENTS

To my readers. Your support and enthusiasm for my books continually blows my mind. Every comment, message, tag, email, and tweet, never fails to give me warm fuzzies. I'm so very honoured to have you reading and enjoying my work. Please feel free to stick around—there's more to come!

To all the bloggers who have helped spread the word about this book. There are no words to express the level of my gratitude and appreciation of your constant hard work and support. Thank you so very much.

To Max. As always, you save the day. You are my magical unicorn with your stabby wit, sprinkling rainbow dust over my words and making them glitter! Don't ever leave me (I will find you).

To my betas:

Tammy Zautner, Maree Hunter, Simone Nicole, Kim Anderson Bias, L.B. Simmons and Rachel Grey.

Tammy - I adore you. Send me the hair-colouring bill for all the greys I added to your head while writing this book (and future books to come).

Maree - your encouragement means more to me than you will ever know. You put up with all the crazy memes I continually send your way (even while you were trying to have a baby) and yet you still never stopped supporting me. That is the definition of a true friend.

Simone thank you for letting me pick your brain on all the things related to dyslexia, and for basically putting up with me. I know I'm a handful, and crazy, but you are too.

Kim, L.B. Simmons and Rachel, thanks for helping me with all things US related, including football and Texas. The knowledge and notes were invaluable, as is your support and friendship.

To Kylie at Give Me Books. What would I do without you? You ensured The End Game got the best start out in the real world that was possible. There are not enough thank you's in the world for me to send your way. I hope one will do. Thank you. Now let us drink.

To Elaine at Allusion Book Formatting and Publishing. Thank you for making my baby pretty.

And last but not least, to the members of the author groups I'm a part of. We laugh, we cry, we talk everything book-related, but most importantly, we support each other. You are all invaluable.

Much love

Kate xo

BOOKS BY KATE MCCARTHY

The End Game
Fighting Redemption

The *Give Me* Series
Give Me Love (Book 1)
Give Me Strength (Book 2)
Give Me Grace (Book 3)

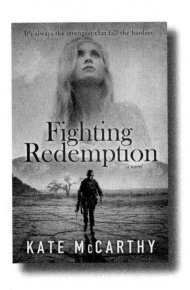

It's always the strongest that fall the hardest

Fighting
Redemption
a novel

KATE McCARTHY

Ryan Kendall is broken. He understands pain. He knows the hand of violence and the ache of loss. He knows what it means to fail those who need you. Being broken doesn't stop him wanting the one thing he can't have; Finlay Tanner. Her smile is sweet and her future bright. She's the girl he grew up with, the girl he loves, the girl he protects from the world, and from himself.

At nineteen, Ryan leaves to join the Australian Army. After years of training he becomes an elite SAS soldier and deploys to the Afghanistan war. His patrol undertakes the most dangerous missions a soldier can face. But no matter how far he runs, or how hard he fights, his need for Finlay won't let go.

Returning home after six years, one look is all it takes to know he can't live without her. But sometimes love isn't enough to heal what hurts. Sometimes people like him can't be fixed, and sometimes people like Finlay deserve more than what's left.

This is a story about war and the cost of sacrifice. Where bonds are formed, and friendships found. Where those who are strong, fall hard. Where love is let go, heartache is born, and heroes are made. Where one man learns that the hardest fight of all, is the fight to save himself.

Evie Jamieson, a former wild child, is not only a headstrong, smart-mouthed trouble magnet, she is also a lead singer with a plan. That plan involves relocating her band, including her two best friends guitarist Henry and band manager Mac, to Sydney to kick off their dreams of hitting the big time.

Jared Valentine is the older brother of Evie's best friend Mac and also the man determined to make Evie his. They strike up a long distance friendship which suits Evie because she's determined to avoid the distraction of love, not only because it doesn't fit in with her plan but because twice in the past it has left her for dead. Moving to Sydney however, has put her directly in Jared's path and he has decided it's the perfect opportunity to make his play.

Unfortunately Jared, co-owner in a business that 'consults' in dangerous hostage and kidnapping situations, makes an enemy who's determined to enact revenge. When this enemy puts Evie in his sights, Jared not only has a fight on his hands to make her his own, but also to keep her alive.

Is accepting the love he's so desperate to give worth the risk to both her heart...and her life?

Quinn Salisbury doesn't think she's cut out for this whole living thing. Even as a young girl she struggled. Just when she thinks she's found a way to leave her violent past behind her, the only thing that's kept her going is ripped away, leaving her damaged and heartbroken.

Four years later, she is slowly rebuilding her life and lands a job as an assistant band manager to Jamieson, the hot new Australian act climbing their way to the top of the charts. There she meets Travis Valentine, the charismatic older brother of her boss, Mac.

From his commanding charm to his confidence and passion, Travis is everything Quinn believes is too good for her, and despite her apprehension, she finds their attraction undeniable and intense.

When her past resurfaces, it complicates their relationship. Instead of reaching out for help, Quinn pushes Travis away, until a staggering secret is revealed that leaves her fighting for her very life.

Torn between running and opening her heart to the man determined to have her, can Quinn find the strength within herself to fight for her future?

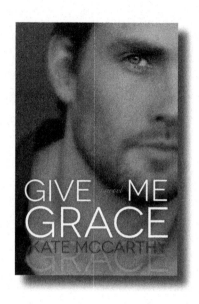

Casey Daniels has a past forged in Hell. Despite the friends, the endless supply of women, and the muscle car he spent years restoring, it still eats away at him.

Grace Paterson is in Sydney as a temporary bassist for Jamieson, the band Casey handles security for. She's also infuriating, off-limits, and complete irresistible.

A deal is struck, and despite their intense and powerful connection, both think it will be easy to walk away. But life can be more ruthless than either of them imagined. Not only does Grace have a secret she's desperate to keep, Casey has questions from his past that he's willing to do anything to get answers for.

It's not until someone wants one of them dead that Casey realises his love for Grace is the one thing he could never walk away from.

In a story of revenge, betrayal, secrets, and love, Casey will need to reconcile his past with his present, before the future he never knew he wanted is snatched away.

ABOUT THE AUTHOR

Kate McCarthy lives in Queensland, Australia.

Facebook:
https://www.facebook.com/KateMcCarthyAuthor

Check out Kate's blog:
http://www.katemccarthy.net/

Follow Kate on Twitter:
https://www.twitter.com/KMacinOz

Follow Kate on Instagram:
https://www.instagram.com/authorkatemccarthy/

Friend Kate on Goodreads:
http://www.goodreads.com/author/show/6876994.Kate_McCarthy

—

CPSIA information can be obtained
at www.ICGtesting.com
Printed in the USA
FSOW04n1335211015
12442FS